The Good Mistress

Born in Zambia, Anne Tiernan grew up in Navan, County Meath. She studied English Literature and Psychology at Trinity College Dublin and spent seven years working in banking. Anne left Ireland with her husband in 2004 to travel the world, arriving in New Zealand in 2005 where they still live – now with three children together.

Anne's debut novel, *The Last Days of Joy*, was shortlisted for the Kate O'Brien Award in 2023. *The Good Mistress* is her second novel.

The Good Mistress

Anne Tiernan

HACHETTE
BOOKS
IRELAND

Copyright © 2025 Anne Tiernan

The right of Anne Tiernan to be identified as the Author of
the Work has been asserted by her in accordance with the
Copyright, Designs and Patents Act 1988.

First published in Ireland in 2025 by
HACHETTE BOOKS IRELAND

1

All rights reserved. No part of this publication may be reproduced, stored in
a retrieval system, or transmitted, in any form or by any means without the
prior written permission of the publisher, nor be otherwise circulated in any
form of binding or cover other than that in which it is published and without
a similar condition being imposed on the subsequent purchaser.

Cataloguing in Publication Data is available from the British Library

ISBN 9781399714167

Typeset by Palimpsest Book Production Ltd, Falkirk, Stirlingshire

Printed and bound in Great Britain by
Clays Ltd, Elcograf S.p.A.

Hachette Books Ireland policy is to use papers that are natural, renewable and recyclable products
and made from wood grown in sustainable forests. The logging and manufacturing processes are
expected to conform to the environmental regulations of the country of origin.

Hachette Books Ireland
8 Castlecourt Centre
Castleknock
Dublin 15, Ireland

A division of Hachette UK Ltd
Carmelite House, 50 Victoria Embankment, London EC4Y 0DZ

The authorised representative in the EEA is Hachette Ireland, 8 Castlecourt Centre,
Castleknock Road, Castleknock, Dublin 15, D15 YF6A, Ireland

www.hachettebooksireland.ie

For Matt

MAY 2022

JULIET

Rory's body is in the wooden box on the altar so of course that's not him texting. He's not both dead *and* alive, a kind of Schrödinger's Rory. Still, she grips the phone in her pocket and, as its vibrations pulse hope through her, remembers the report in the news a few weeks ago about a woman who knocked on the coffin at her own wake. It's the type of story that would have amused him. Juliet had assigned a special tone to his message notifications, but since their last tryst in San Francisco in March, she'd changed it back again. (She prefers the word *tryst* – it suggests the old-fashioned brass bed of the hotel, their sweaty, entwined limbs. *Affair* evokes wills, solicitors.) The texts had been less frequent since then, but she needed to cling to that hopeful lurch between hearing the sound and checking the screen. Though lately, this had often been followed by a bellyflop of disappointment.

His way was to dazzle and disappear, a celestial body dipping away below the horizon. And now he's ghosted her in the most literal way possible. It's almost funny. Well, he'd think so anyway.

After a pause for a hymn, the woman beside her resumes sniffing. Earlier, during the eulogy, her weeping peaked, and Juliet had leaned in to ask how she knew him. 'I didn't,' she said. 'But the poor family, what a shock. God be good to them.' And she blessed herself in such a sorrowful manner that Juliet turned away in disgust. She'd forgotten how funerals are community events here, not just by invitation, like some drab wedding. *How dare you*, she thought, *snivelling like you loved him too*. At least, she hopes this was merely a thought; the sleeping pills she downed on the plane with a glass of wine failed to knock her out and have instead placed her into a sort of disassociated fugue. She also hopes this woman's tears aren't contagious because if she starts to cry now she'll never stop. Like when you go to the toilet for the first time on a night out. Breaking the seal, they used to call it.

She tries to remember the last time she was in a church, a proper one like this, with light struggling through stained glass, the heady perfume of incense and arse-numbing pews. Everywhere she looks, there are artefacts of pain: tortured sons, grieving mothers, treacherous friends. There'd be no mistaking this church for a community centre as you might do in Auckland; some Episcopalian place that teaches tolerance. (Tolerance! The nuns would be appalled.) From a distance, it's been easy to be repelled by Catholicism, but here, immersed again, the ritual pulls at her seductively. Death feels so ordinary that she finds a strange comfort in it. Maybe this has been the point all along. To make the suffering more bearable.

The priest at the pulpit in his ornate robes is ancient and gnarled, just as he should be. You need someone who looks only a generation away from the Famine. (Almost twenty years gone, and Juliet can still only see this capitalised. There it sits in her head alongside the Church and the Troubles, a sort of holy trinity of misery.) He has a face you could imagine side-eyeing you through the fly screen of the confessional box, demanding a decade of the rosary for your impure thoughts. *Impure*: it makes them sound murky when they couldn't be more explicit. Juliet could pray on skinned knees for a thousand years and still not do enough penance for the volume of filthy thoughts she's had about Rory.

Bless me, Father, for I have etc.

And adored every minute of it . . .

There are symbolic offerings on the table beside the coffin – a guitar and a golf club maybe? Something, anyway, that doesn't align with her knowledge of him and reinforces her sense of exclusion. She is meaningless amongst this crowd. (*You're my entire universe, Jules.* He'd said that. She'd heard him.) What gift would she bring in the offertory procession? A naked selfie? She imagines it, perched on the coffin, like a sassy Mary – Magdalene obviously, not Virgin – sinful but subservient. Actually, she could just prostrate herself naked on the coffin, offer up her whole being, as she had done, over and over.

The woman beside her joins in with the priest suddenly, whispering fiercely, *Blessed is the fruit of thy womb, Jesus.*

Why only this line? It was a lonely walk into the clinic in Liverpool all those years ago, Rory both present and absent then too. The old people with their gabardine coats and their placards, kneeling outside, chanted this, like a Satanic incantation, increasing the volume as she made her way, weak-legged, to the door. The cruel piousness of them.

She leans in and whispers back, 'But are we not blessed too? The bearers of the fruit?' The woman looks alarmed and turns away.

Juliet's own almost eighteen-year-old womb fruit (citrus maybe, definitely with an edge), Ruby, is at her mother's house, sleeping off the gruelling flight, while Juliet's mother, Denise, is sleeping off the effects of another gruelling round of chemo. Juliet was surprised that Ruby wanted to come with her back 'home' – funny how she uses this word still, she supposes she'll always feel cleaved in two, like a swallow's tail. Ruby's on her gap year, but instead of cutting loose (Juliet's interpretation of it) she's using the time to work and save for university. It's unnecessary given Tāne, her father, has always been generous with his maintenance. (He can afford to be magnanimous because he's loaded, but more importantly, he's now ecstatically married to someone whose most appealing quality is that she's not Juliet.) But that's Ruby, intent on doing the honourable thing at the expense of pleasure. A sort of reversed mirror image of Juliet's own life philosophy in fact. Juliet neglected to inform her own work she's here. Simply gave a spare key to her neighbour in the building in Takapuna where she and Ruby share an apartment (at her daughter's insistence, so he could water the plants) and here they are. She suspects she'll find missed calls and texts on her phone from Peter, the owner of the interiors shop she works in. She also suspects after three years he'll be relieved to finally have a bona fide excuse to fire her. She was hired as 'creative consultant' to help customers with decor, but it soon became apparent that while she may have the artistic aptitude, she doesn't have the appetite to advise North Shore housewives in their distressed Golden Goose trainers on how to achieve their Heritage Luxe design aspirations. So, she sits at the till now and simply takes their money. If they want to spend three hundred dollars on one noxious candle and a plastic bottle of hand soap, then fine. Juliet is resigned to the collusion.

If she leans, she can make out the back of Erica's chic blonde head in the front pew. The grieving widow. Why is it that widows get their own special title? Not bereaved children, or parents. Or lovers. And widower just a derivative, lacking the same pathos. Once upon a time, they used to say *relict*, like you were the leftovers. Juliet shudders. The woman beside her sighs and tries to nudge her back into her own space but she holds firm. It strikes her now that there is no male equivalent for a mistress. She supposes it's because women need to be put in some kind of box, categorised by their relationships to men. So, there's another thing she and Erica share.

She watches Erica intently, sees no revealing shake of her shoulders, no raising of a hand to dab away tears. Rory called Erica cold once and it thrilled Juliet. She was always trying to provoke a negative comment about her and then prove herself to be the opposite. Though it was rare this happened, he was so reticent about his marriage. ('But am I better than her?' she'd push when they were making love. He'd never answer of course.) If there was a suggestion that Erica was uptight, Juliet would be loose; moody and she'd be sunshine itself; frigid and she'd be insatiable – not that she had to try with that. With Rory inside her, it was the only time in her life she felt full. But she would give anything now to switch places with Erica. To *be* her. To wallow in the warm centre of the grief. Not out here in the cold, the pain pushed down, mutating like some cancerous tumour invisible to the human eye.

Someone in front shifts and blocks her view so Juliet swivels and scans the crowd for familiar faces. The woman beside her mutters.

'Oh, go and keen over the coffin like they used to do,' Juliet says.

'What the hell is wrong with you?'

'Where do I start?'

She looks for her old friend Maeve but is relieved in a way when she doesn't see her. They've not spoken since Maeve's low-key wedding to Cillian. Was it a wedding? A commitment ceremony maybe – very Maeve. Instead of a religious reading, that passage from *Captain Corelli's Mandolin* on the nature of love that was all the rage back then. Fourteen years ago now. Juliet flew home from Auckland to be Maeve's . . . what? Not bridesmaid. Maid of Dishonour maybe? The night before the wedding, Colum, Cillian's brother, propositioned Juliet while they were all in the pub, despite his heavily pregnant wife being nearby. Juliet declined, and not politely. During his speech the next day Colum congratulated Maeve for choosing a bridesmaid that wouldn't outshine her. When it came to her speech, Juliet stood and encouraged everyone present to raise a glass to Colum, the charitable best man, who despite not thinking her attractive nonetheless was willing to allow his cock in her mouth the night before. Much drama ensued. The owner of the restaurant in Dublin they were in – who turned out to be a devout Opus Dei member who considered even smear tests and yoga as evil – threatened to kick the entire wedding party out. Juliet, naturally, got all the blame. 'Why do you always have to create such a scene, Juliet?' Maeve, pregnant then with her younger son, and more sympathetic to her gestating sister-in-law than her walking nightmare of a friend, was livid.

Apart from the fact she's now a well-known writer, she has little insight into Maeve's life, which would have been unthinkable when they were young and so enmeshed in one another. Would spend the day together and still phone when they got home, Juliet lying on her belly on the thin, worn carpet of the hallway, running her fingers along the woodchipped walls, the coiled flex stretched as far as possible so that her parents in the sitting room couldn't hear. Things loosened between them once they left school, Maeve in Trinity and later working in publishing, Juliet in Dublin too but inhabiting a different world. She took a series of low-paid jobs in retail and hospitality for over ten years, a way of punishing herself after sabotaging her chance at getting a place in NCAD to study art. Not feeling any attachment to her career made life easier. Or so she told herself. And though they kept up a pretence of friendship, there was a gulf between their lives even before Juliet left for New Zealand with Tāne when she was thirty. Being plunged into motherhood brought them closer again for a time but of course Juliet, as is her way, had to go and ruin that too.

On the back wall of the altar is the Pietà, and this lifeless body of Jesus in his mother's arms makes her think of Dan, the other member of their little gang, and his funeral here too, over thirty years ago. She, Rory and Maeve, bewildered. Seventeen and stunned that death could happen – no, that it could happen to one of them. The grief was too big, too adult-shaped, for them. Grief or guilt, though, the lines were blurred.

At the end of the mass as people line up to offer condolences to the family, the choir sings 'Be Not Afraid'. She'd forgotten these lovely songs, the soundtrack to every Irish funeral. She pinches the skin between her thumb and forefinger now to stem the tears. She won't join the queue. She won't say *Sorry for your loss* because she can't imagine one greater than her own.

But then, she's always been accused of selfishness. Rory said it too, when they fought the last time she saw him in San Francisco airport. He was leaving early after a phone call from home, the details of which he refused to share. He always enjoyed that sort of opaqueness. Juliet followed him there, begging him to stay. She can still feel their final embrace, the musky smell off him, the ripe tang of their sex. He was in such a hurry to get home he hadn't showered. She clung to him tightly as though she might physically prevent him from leaving or, failing that, could imprint his body on her own.

She gets on her knees, puts her head in her hands, banishes that image and recalls instead the diner, Mason's, next to their hotel near Union Square where they ate breakfast. He was like a child ordering his eggs, changing his choice every day for the thrill of saying *over easy* or *sunny side up* like they did on American shows. They sat side by side in the booth, unable to keep their hands off each other.

That's it, it's all she gets. Fragments. Discarded scenes she rescues from the cutting-room floor that she replays, knows by heart. Erica has the rest. The slick Oscar-winning movie version.

The coffin is being wheeled down the aisle on a trolley. No pallbearers, detached now even in death. She's on the edge of the row and has an urge to reach out her hand and trail her fingers along the side as it goes past. He was ticklish; she would brush her hands along his torso, and he would convulse in a childlike agony. The woman beside her gasps and Juliet realises she's actually done it, she's touched the coffin. But Erica doesn't notice, or ignores it, all Death Becomes Her, walking erect and dry-eyed. The seventeen-year-old son, Charlie, looks so like Rory, something catches and flips in her heart.

―

Outside, Juliet stands apart against the shaded, damp wall of the church, watching as Erica and Charlie touch the coffin before it's slid into the hearse. People crowd around hugging them, and once age recedes from their features she recognises many of them as old neighbours or faces from businesses in the town. Like an inappropriate joke, the sun appears from behind a cloud and light bounces off the gilded details of the coffin. She pulls out her phone to see who texted earlier. Even now, with his casket only a few feet away, a tremor of hope runs through her. Like this is all a mistake.

It's from Shauna, the gallery owner who holds life-drawing classes that Juliet occasionally models for. She's been doing this modelling for a few years now. Posing naked in front of strangers feels like an authentic foil to the interiors shop, maybe a closer approximation to who she could have been if she hadn't fucked everything up. But still with that slight masochistic edge, being the muse rather than the artist. Apparently, Juliet was supposed to turn up for a class today. Three missed calls from her too. She knows Shauna is ringing out of concern rather than annoyance. Almost worse in a way. She puts the phone back in her pocket without replying.

'Grand day for it all the same,' says an old man in a flat cap, and Juliet winces. She moves away from him as though his indifference might contaminate her, and as she does she feels a familiar stickiness between her legs and the dull background cramp in her stomach makes sense now. Her period, how strange. How strange that the sun leers down and her employer thinks she should inform her of her plans and old men want to talk about the weather and her bodily functions carry on as normal.

As though He is not dead.

ERICA

There's crying but it seems as though it has nothing to do with her. All of this seems as though it has nothing to do with her. Like she's stumbled upon a service for a stranger and can't leave without appearing rude. If it wasn't for Charlie sitting to her left and looking to her for reassurance, she might try to run. She tries to gulp down some air because for days now, since it happened, she's felt like she can't pull enough breath into her lungs. And despite the yawning proportions of this old church, the perfumed air is so loaded, it's an extra strain.

It's crushing, having the crowd behind, like something pinning the back of her neck so that it's an effort to keep her head raised. Strangers, many of them, or business acquaintances. Or neighbours that she could ask to bring in her bins but none that would pop in for a cup of tea. The scrutiny makes her conscious of every movement. Her father used to hunt; she heard him once telling her mother about a deer he stalked, how it froze in front of him, one foreleg raised, eyes locked on his. He couldn't shoot it, he said, it felt unsporting. So she tries to stay as still as possible.

And somehow, she and Charlie are outside now, the service over, and people gather round and shake her hand. She's glad of the sunshine so that she can put on her shades. There's something too intimate about looking directly into their concerned, watery eyes when all she would like to do is be alone, crawl into the back of the hearse and bury herself under the wreaths. Peep out like the Cabbage Patch doll her mother hid in the flower bed for her to find on the morning of her ninth birthday.

Why is she thinking of this now? She's been fixating on the oddest things as though her attention is skewed and narrowed. Solving Wordle each morning as if her life depended on it. Maybe it did. She got her period this morning, her body as well as her mind subverting expectations. There had been times, with all those losses, when seeing this blood filled her with a kind of terror, because she understood then that the world was not the predictable place she'd known as a child, life was not the smooth journey her doting parents made her believe. But today when she saw the blood, on the day it was due, the punctuality filled her with a different kind of astonishment. That her body could behave this way, be so glib.

If only her parents were here now. But they'd both died – with the most thoughtful of timing – in the last few years, the inheritance digging Erica and Rory out of the Covid-ravaged pit in which their event promotions business was floundering. They'd be gracious, attentive, taking care of it all, like those parties they used to throw. Little Erica would sit on the stairs, hidden she hoped, content to watch from a distance, her childhood stammer making her shy, or maybe the shyness making her stammer. A few days ago (was it really?) when she reluctantly rang the undertaker – who sounded like he was expecting her, who called her Erica in an intimate way even though she introduced herself as Mrs O'Sullivan – to make arrangements, she said she'd prefer something private. Her mother died during lockdown and the restrictions on funeral size were the only blessing. That's the kind of wedding she'd wanted as well, would have happily eloped in fact, but Rory talked her out of that, persuaded her to wait until they could afford to throw the most lavish ceremony possible. Just as the undertaker talked her out of a small funeral. Not in any way that could be called bullying. It was more that he was so completely sure of himself, in that slick way only men can be. The more he spoke, the more she felt colonised by a terrible blankness. But actually, he was so deft she leaned into this void, let him have his way because it was a relief to have someone else make the decisions. Because that's something you don't think about. How suddenly, after more than thirty years, it's all down to you. She was so young when they'd got together, it was easy for her life to become absorbed into his. That happens with women sometimes, men not so much, she thinks. And Rory was that kind of person. Sort of all-consuming. Or maybe it's truer to say that it's because she was a particular kind of person – a weak one. She was happy to do it, though. It felt easy and natural to attach herself to his momentum because, unlike her, he held such ambition for himself, seemed so sure of where he was headed. Or at least, that he was headed somewhere. After college, she'd worked for a few years – without much conviction – in a bank on Ballyboyne's main square, a job her father had organised, while Rory managed a pub nearby. But since Charlie, she's stayed at home, a very silent partner in their business, a cheerleader for his dreams.

She notices a woman in a long black dress, leaning, with one leg bent behind, foot pressed against the church wall. Erica is struck by the languid pose, the easy possession of her own body. Her head is down and she's tapping at her phone in a bored way. The woman straightens, puts her phone in her pocket and looks around. Erica sees now she's older than her posture and figure suggested and she recognises her as Juliet, a childhood friend of Rory's. It's been a long time but she has the kind of striking features you never forget. When Erica first met Rory, both aged seventeen, at the tennis courts near his childhood home, where she had a summer job coaching younger kids, Juliet was part of the little gang he hung around with. He grew apart from them once Erica was on the scene. He liked to keep things in separate boxes. Juliet always struck her as kind of flippant, the type of person who didn't seem to take life too seriously. Maybe if you looked like that it was easy to be unconcerned. Erica is surprised to see her here; she lives abroad, Australia, she thinks. Juliet starts to walk away and Erica is seized by a desire to follow her, beg her to take her wherever she's going, let her ordinary preoccupations become her own. But she won't, of course, she'll do what's expected of her, as she's always done. As though he is not dead.

JULIET

In the carpark across the road from the church, Juliet panics because she can't remember what vehicle she hired at the airport. Or if she did hire anything. Maybe she's dreaming. Maybe she's still in New Zealand. Maybe, in fact, it's she who's dead, a thought that is not unattractive at this moment. As she's staring, bewildered, she feels a light touch on her arm from behind. She turns to see Maeve, but a kind of bad artist's impression of her. Like a composite of a suspect the police might issue. Maeve's once vibrant red hair has faded to a silvery strawberry blonde and her sharp features are slightly time blunted.

'Juliet! Jesus, *God*, it's been so long. I can't believe you came all the way over.'

There's a moment of hesitation before they hug. Maeve feels as twitchy as ever against her and pulls away first.

'I was coming anyway.' The lies roll off the tongue easily now. 'Denise isn't well. And I brought Ruby with me so we could all spend some time together.'

Maeve reaches out and pats her, then withdraws her hand. Her movements have always been nervy and quick. *That one's always up to high doh*, Denise used to say.

'I heard. Breast cancer, isn't it? Poor Denise.'

'Yeah. It's spread a fair bit. She says she always knew it'd be her boobs that would get her in the end.'

They share a sad, knowing smile that cuts through some of the estrangement of the last few years. When they were kids, Denise had a cleavage that rendered boys shifty-eyed. Not Rory, though, who could maintain a steady gaze but with a hint of a smile playing on his mouth as though he was in on the joke.

'How long are you here for?'

This is always one of the first questions she's asked. People seem to need to know she'll leave again. 'Almost four weeks.'

Maeve nods, as though reassured, then wraps her arms around herself and shivers. 'I can't believe Rory's gone. I only saw him a while ago. You'd never have known.' She gives a quick shake of her head as though annoyed at herself. 'That was a stupid thing to say. As if you can sense a heart attack lurking. What I mean is, he looked so healthy. You know, Erica told me his Apple watch kept indicating his heartbeat was irregular, but he decided that meant his watch was broken. Stubborn to the last. Cillian would have been straight on to the cardiologist. Sometimes I think he only believes things about his body if his Fitbit tells him.'

Maeve's words tumble out like she's been storing them up. She still sounds like she's arguing with herself.

'Why were you meeting him?' Juliet tries to keep her tone neutral. It's what she always imagines, that everyone back here is socialising, having a great time in her absence.

'What?' Maeve looks confused, as though away on some other thought tangent completely. 'Oh Rory, you mean. Um . . . just picking up Jamie from the house. Charlie had people over for his birthday. They're in the same year in school.' She frowns, then looks away, adds absently, 'Charlie has the same birthday as Dan, you know.'

'You moved back here from Dublin? I didn't realise.'

'Yeah, I know. Mad, isn't it? Four years ago. Cillian quit the bank so it was partly financial. And Mam's got dementia so we look after her. God, and I couldn't wait to get out of Ballyboyne when we were kids.'

Juliet makes a sympathetic face. 'What did you talk about?'

'Me and Rory?' Maeve waves her hand dismissively. 'God, nothing really. He was always awkward when Erica was around. Like he was ashamed of his old friends or life or something. We weren't close anymore anyway.'

'Maybe it's her he was ashamed of.'

Maeve raises her eyebrows in a sceptical way that irritates Juliet. 'Hardly.'

Juliet makes a non-committal sound. Of course not. She was the perfect elegant accessory for Rory, pretty and wholesome, an antidote to his own mother. Grew up in a big Georgian house a few miles away from the town in a parish near the Hill of Tara. Her father a judge or something equally mythical. Too good for the local convents, so sent to a posh school thirty miles away in Dublin instead. Only ventured near Ballyboyne to play tennis. She used to remind Juliet of the small, perfectly formed twirling figure in her childhood jewellery box. You half expected 'Greensleeves' to play whenever she appeared.

'When was the last time you saw him?'

Juliet pretends to think, as though the exact moment of it – his expression, words, clothes, the specific sandalwood and sex smell of him – is not etched on her memory. Despite not having picked up a brush in years she could paint it, reproduce the scene in detail. *Couple Fighting in Airport Terminal, March 2022. Artist – Juliet Quinn.*

'Years ago. Eh . . . 2018, I think. I came home to vote in the abortion referendum and bumped into him then.' This is both true and not. They did run into each other then – for the first time since she'd left Ireland fifteen years before – and rekindled their affair.

'Really? Amazing you did that. You know, when the marriage referendum was passed, I was so sad Dan wasn't here to see it. Imagine! He wouldn't have believed it. I hardly believe it sometimes. Thinking of back then. God, two men couldn't love one another but a man could rape his wife? It's no wonder we're all basket cases.' She sighs and turns her head back towards the church. 'Look, the hearse is moving off. Shall we drive together to the graveyard? We've years to catch up on.' She doesn't wait for an answer, just strides away.

Juliet hadn't intended on going to the burial. Rory had told her the night of Dan's funeral that he wanted to be cremated. He said he couldn't bear the thought of being underground, it was the dull thud of that first shovel of dirt on wood that did it. The sound would haunt him forever, though they both knew it was more than this that would haunt him. But she's hungry to hear more of him, maybe even find something of herself, so she follows Maeve to the car.

As they nudge through the town, Maeve tunes the radio in to some easy-listening station that deals in nostalgia.

'My music tastes have stayed firmly rooted in the twentieth century. When I got my Spotify summary for the year I was disappointed, though unsurprised, to see my listening type was *The Replayer*.' She makes air quotes around this. 'A euphemism I'm sure for ancient and boring. I don't know how or when it happens. Getting old. Being fearful of new stuff.'

'I don't know how it happens that we're burying old friends now.'

'Yes, burying old friends,' Maeve echoes, rubbing the side of her face. 'Is this it now? We've graduated from weddings and christenings to funerals? Surely there's a step in between that we've skipped.'

'Divorces,' Juliet says flatly.

Maeve gives a wry laugh. 'No-one can afford to divorce here.'

'Did you go to the viewing in the funeral home last night?'

'Yes, so sad. I had the most awful flashbacks to Dan.' She says softly then, 'We bring all our dead to funerals.'

'How . . . how did he look? Laid out, I mean.' The words feel nauseating in her mouth, she can hardly form them.

Maeve narrows her eyes. 'Odd. That's what I kept on thinking. They always look unlike themselves. I have this fear – and I mean obviously it's not the worst aspect of this scenario – that if I'm ever asked to identify a family member's body, I won't recognise them, and it'll all get super awkward. Like when our soul is gone, it alters us.'

'Soul? Are you religious now?'

'Huh. No. Maybe what I mean is essence. Yes, that's it I think.'

Rory's essence. What was that? Boyish charm? Insouciant cruelty? Whatever it was, it was addictive.

'You know, one of the things I miss about Ireland is all the ritual around death. Wakes, people laid out at home and all that. It's more hidden away in New Zealand. The white New Zealand anyway.'

They are static now in a long line of cars. 'That'll be the Anglo influence, I suppose. Or the Protestantism. Things all neat and tidy and sanitised. I mean, say what you like about Catholicism but at least it's got charisma.' Maeve makes jazz hands when she says the word *charisma*. She pulls at Juliet's voluminous layered black skirt then. 'Is this the kind of outfit they wear to funerals over there?'

'What's wrong with it?'

'Oh, nothing. Just very . . . Jackie O is all. The fingerless gloves are a nice touch too. I think I had the same pair circa 1984 during my Madonna phase.' Maeve's mouth is twitching.

'Bitch,' Juliet says, punching her playfully. She went shopping the day she flew out, bought the clothes especially. Why should only Erica get the widow's weeds? When Ruby saw her as she came down the stairs in Denise's house, she eyed her warily and said in a voice dripping with sarcasm. 'Oh look, it's Queen Victoria.'

'So, still modelling? You were doing that last we spoke.'

'No. It was a temporary gig anyway. Catalogues mostly, real budget stuff. Apparently, I've got a *divisive* look. I work in an interiors shop. Selling overpriced cushions to medicated housewives. Oh, and some life modelling too. That's where real models go to die.'

'Life modelling? Wow. Well, you always did love to get your kit off. You never went back to art?'

'Nah. I fucked that up, didn't I? Messing up getting into college.'

'It's never too late. Your choices don't all end at eighteen, you know. Look at me. I was nearing forty when my first book was published.'

'It's not the same.'

'But you were such a natural.' Maeve keeps pushing. 'I struggle with art. I never know what to think looking at it.'

'That's always been your problem, Maeve. You're not supposed to think. Just feel.'

'Well, all it makes me *feel* is stupid.'

Juliet is desperate for Maeve to stop talking about it. It's like poking at an abscessed tooth. She wants to distract her, herself too, so opens the glove box and starts rooting through it.

'What are you looking for?' Maeve asks.

'Tissues.'

Maeve pulls some out of her sleeve. 'Don't worry, they're clean. I didn't cry today, which is mad because since turning forty-five I've tended to leak from every orifice. Heavy periods, night sweats, sudden onslaughts of tears. Sometimes I feel like I'm liquifying. Like my family will find me one day, a mysterious puddle in the middle of the floor. And the worst part is they'd just step over me and carry on as normal. *God*. Anyway, is it that you're worried you'll break down at the burial?'

'Nope.' Juliet wads up the tissues and, lifting her skirt, shoves them in her knickers. 'On the rag.'

'My God, Juliet! There's a guy over there that can see.'

Juliet downs the window. 'Period poverty, mate. Go educate yourself on it,' she yells at the young man vaping and minding his own business outside a mobile phone shop. Juliet remembers when it was a video rental store. The man turns away, embarrassed.

Maeve puts her hand over her mouth and laughs. 'Jesus. You're still a liability.'

They move off again. Suddenly, Maeve reaches across and squeezes her hand. 'I remember what he meant to you back then.'

Juliet can't speak, just looks at her gratefully. She wants to climb over and curl up in her lap and rock and weep herself away into her friend. Maybe it was real. Maybe she's not crazy.

'Of course, you'd have been terrible together,' Maeve says, and Juliet turns from her again. 'So, are you in a relationship now?'

Her married friends in Auckland are obsessed with her love life. Is she having sex? With whom is she having sex? Is the sex any good? In what respect is it different to the (limited) sex they're having? They're especially fascinated by threesomes, as though all single people are gang-banging and throupling up at every opportunity. She invents things sometimes to entertain them, and herself. She sits in restaurants, or stands around barbecues with them, feeling like the comic relief. More than simple amusement for the men, though. As she narrates and embellishes, she senses a shift in their energy; dilated pupils here, a readjusted stance there. Fish-like wriggle as they're hooked. She gets off on it.

She says, 'Just casual stuff.'

'You mean like Tinder?' Her older married friends are also intrigued by The Apps, having dated in a more analogue era.

'Uh-huh. You wouldn't believe the amount of younger men who are into older women.'

'Seriously? I'm jealous. And a bit relieved. I always assumed fuckability and fertility were inextricably linked. What's the attraction, do you think?'

'I could kid myself that they find us really hot, but to be fair, a lot of young men will fuck anything with a heartbeat.'

Maeve sighs. 'Could be a fetish. Like being into feet.'

'Jesus, Maeve, thanks.' She'd forgotten the brutal candour of long friendships. Or maybe it's just Irish friendships.

'Seriously, it's a thing. Gerontophilia. Being aroused by the elderly. I had a plot line in my last book about it. This young lad who stalks nursing homes.'

'Sounds dark.'

'People love that kind of stuff. I can do all sorts of sick shit in my stories. But adultery and animal cruelty. Total no-nos.'

'Strange.'

They're silent for a few moments before Maeve sighs heavily and whispers something that Juliet doesn't catch.

'What?'

'Sorry, I didn't realise I said it out loud. It's that Sylvia Plath line about eating men like air that I've always associated with you.'

Juliet frowns. 'Not sure how to interpret that. Wasn't Sylvia Plath weak for your man, the poet who was awful to her?'

'Yes,' says Maeve. Then turns to look at her again. 'We contain multitudes.'

Juliet suspects this is another poem. Maeve was always dropping quotes in conversation. *Check out the big brain on Maeve*, Rory used to say. She changes the subject.

'And how's it all going with Cillian? You two happy?'

'God, who's happy? Sometimes it feels like mid-life is just muddling through.' She gives a wry laugh, then says, 'Middling through!'

'But Cillian?'

'Cillian.' Maeve sighs again. 'I don't know. When I looked at Rory last night in the coffin it occurred to me that in all likelihood the only other person who will ever see me naked is an undertaker. It made me panic.'

'But you two were great together. You laughed all the time.'

'A million years ago. Now he's driving me mental. He went to therapy to work on himself, had an epiphany, retrained as a psychotherapist. But he's only taken on a few clients so that he can *devote himself to them entirely*.' Maeve takes her hands off the wheel as she says this to make air quotes and the car drifts towards the centre line. She has to make a sharp correction but doesn't even acknowledge it. Juliet feels slightly unsafe. 'And he's become obsessed with CrossFit. It's like some kind of cult. He's on a journey to enlightenment. Meanwhile I'm having dark fantasies about murdering him.'

'Affair?'

'Is that a suggestion?'

'I meant him. The working out and that. Classic sign.'

'I don't think so. I mean, we're getting on each other's nerves at the moment. But he's so straight, Cillian. And he wouldn't want to upset the boys.'

'Well, marriage is a relic from the days when we all died young and didn't expect to have to stay with one person for so long.'

'Huh. Yes, I'm beginning to think a long marriage and a happy marriage are two mutually exclusive states. Like there isn't going to be any intersection in that Venn diagram.'

'Could have told you that years ago.' Then she says, 'I'm sorry, you know, about the wedding. Not my best work.'

Maeve waves her arm. 'No. I was too harsh. It was Colum's fault for being a lech, not yours for calling him out. I mean, I know he's my brother-in-law but he's a total melt. And, as it turns out, the wife left him a few years ago for her yoga teacher. A woman.'

'Whaaat?'

'Yep. Colum turned his wife gay.'

They look at each other and laugh.

'Oh, Juliet. I'm sorry I let you go. I miss you. I can't be like this with anyone else. It feels like I reached peak friendship at age sixteen.'

It's true. There was something so unique about those teenage relationships, the heightened hormonal states they were in adding an extra layer of meaning. Or maybe the lack of responsibility stripping away pretence. She sees it in Ruby's friendships now. The ability to just *be* with one another. Hearing Maeve's voice is like putting on an old beloved jumper.

'I know what you mean. I don't have close friends anymore.' The loneliness of this truth pierces her. She's on the periphery in both countries. A blow-in to New Zealand, unable to infiltrate the strong bonds formed in school or university or the formative twenties, where friends became family. She couldn't tolerate all those mother and baby groups when Ruby was little, was never one to strike up conversations at the school gates. And now, she's only an afterthought to her old Irish friends.

The narrow country road is light-dappled by the canopy of overhanging trees. She misses these quiet Irish scenes: the patchwork of fields, the tangle of hedges, the rusting iron gates. That distinctive loamy tang of silage. And crows, oddly. The beauty here subdued, but deeply affecting. It touches her in a way the showy New Zealand landscape can't. There's such a different quality to Auckland too; new, anonymous, bright. A city surrounded by water so that it feels washed clean each day. She swims every morning at their local beach. Juliet finds it impossible to feel sadness, or anything much, in the ocean, only an awareness of her body in the elements. It's so vast, she feels defenceless, and death lurks there, always only a hidden rip or rogue wave away. Emerging, she is a different person, reborn.

When they have parked, Juliet looks at the Gothic iron gates of the cemetery and her legs feel weak.

'I hate this part,' she says. 'It's so final.'

'There are no good parts,' Maeve says. 'Come on. I got you.'

They move with the crowd towards the freshly dug plot in the distance. Maeve stops abruptly in front of another grave. 'There he is.'

Daniel Anthony Flynn, beloved son, grandson, brother. Born 18th April 1973 – Died 1st September 1990.

Maeve bends and fingers the dash between the dates. 'The brevity of his life. So stark when you see it spelled out. It's odd, though, the summers seemed endless back then.'

She crouches, wraps her arms around her knees in a girlish pose and traces the words carved into the marble. 'Danny boy,' she whispers.

'Let's move,' Juliet says. 'I got *you*.'

Maeve stands and wipes her eyes. 'I still dream about him,' she says as they walk. 'Not about his death, he's just there in the most mundane of ways. Like out in his garden mowing the lawn. Remember that? Him and Rory, in their front gardens in the summertime pushing lawnmowers? I can't smell cut grass without thinking of them both. *God.* And the light. The light of those days . . . Was that real? Or is it some sepia tone nostalgia has cast over everything? Like those opening credits of *The Waltons*? I wake up after dreaming of Dan and remember, and it's like he's died all over again. He must have died thousands of times on me now.'

Juliet clamps her eyes shut and nods. She used to dream of Dan too. Now she dreams about Rory most nights. They used to be erotic; she would wake up breathless, her heart flinging itself against her sternum. Lately they've been full of frustration. Trying to find him in a maze of a building or sleeping in a room and hearing himself and Erica next door laughing and making love. She hasn't dreamed since she got the news. Then again, she's barely slept. Standing in her light-filled, open-plan apartment with its glimpses of the golden sand of Takapuna beach and the Hauraki Gulf, and beyond that the vast Pacific Ocean, a world away from the dark, cramped spaces in which she was raised, trying to grasp meaning in her mother's words. Denise relayed the news, and when Juliet – stunned into silence – failed to respond, proceeded to tell her about Tom O'Donnell's triple bypass and Shirley White running off with the arborist who sorted out the overgrown pines in her garden. How dare she. As though it was just another piece of the type of morbid gossip so prized by Irish mothers. 'No, no, no,' Juliet interrupted, insistent, when she finally found her voice. As though the word itself could change it. (Yes, yes, yes, she'd panted in his ear in that boutique hotel in Dublin, where they'd gone when she came back to be with him in 2019. 'For once in your life you're very compliant,' he'd laughed.)

And now? Now she dreads the dreams that are to come.

They stop near the back of the crowd, but Juliet can just about make out Erica. How she envies her. The soft-spoken words of condolence, the tender touch of comfort. Standing there by the grave, free to cry or fall to her knees or throw herself in after him if she takes the notion. She thinks of those mourners in ancient Egypt, the women who stood by the tombs and tore at their hair and clothes and smeared dirt on their breasts. Juliet imagines the blessed release of this. Yet Erica is calm, the picture of stoic widowhood, Jacqueline Kennedy at the graveside, not the Jackie Kennedy who crawled in confusion over the back seat of the car gathering pieces of her husband's shattered skull. This is the version Juliet relates to.

She closes her eyes and is transported to a late summer's day when they were all about sixteen, down at the river beside the old bridge. Lying next to Rory, as always, as they gazed upwards, trying to find shapes in the clouds. Rory talking about songs with clouds, Kate Bush's and Joni Mitchell's, the latter his favourite though it always made his mam cry. They couldn't understand the sentimentality of their mothers back then. They were sharing Silk Cuts Juliet had stolen from Denise and practising smoke rings. Rory formed his lips into a taut shape, tapped his cheek and a perfect circle would emerge. Juliet could never get the hang of it. 'It's because your mouth is too big,' he laughed, always teasing her. In her memory, the four of them lay there for hours, until night fell and slowed everything, even the traffic noise from the road overhead. In her memory, the winding call of the secretive corncrake rose up from nearby reeds. Was that real? Rory sighed and said, 'This is the life, hey, Jules?'

He said that, she heard him. That was real.

They talked then about how clouds are formed when vapour gets turned into water droplets and Dan said, 'You see, things just change form. Nothing really dies.'

Nothing dies yet the priest is talking now about bodies turning to ashes and dust and bodies being committed to the earth. How can that be Rory's body that was so alive and warm and responsive and touched every single part of her own? She starts to move forward, and Maeve looks at her in that old way as if to say, *What the hell, Juliet?* But she carries on, slithering through bodies, faces turning to look at her, and she is nearer the graveside now and people are staring. Erica seems to be looking towards her too, but she has sunglasses on so it's hard to tell. Maybe she's making a mistake, fucking up again, but it's too late and now it's as though a hand is reaching in and clutching at her stomach, urging bile to rise up her throat in a kind of maritime swell. She says, 'I remember he wanted to be cremated . . .' But before she can finish, she bends over and retches violently.

———

Later that evening, after the burial, Juliet and Maeve are sitting together at a low table in O'Malley's pub, which, along with a rugby club and tennis courts at the other end, bookends the semi-rural road, Ash Lane – two miles outside Ballyboyne – on which they all grew up and where Erica and Denise still live.

The place is packed with the funeral crowd; *House strictly private* was written on the death notice, as well as *Family flowers only, donations in lieu,* etc. People around here wouldn't have liked that. It must have been some proprietary move by Erica. Wanting to keep even this part all to herself.

'Tell me more about them,' Juliet says. 'Do you think they were happy?'

Maeve shrugs. 'Who's happy? And they were impenetrable. Like they'd this perfect smug and self-sufficient thing going on and that's all they needed. I used to drive past and imagine them having this fun and harmonious time at home. Like the Obamas . . . only less cerebral.'

'The Beckhams perhaps.'

Maeve grins. 'Ha, yes. She used to send out a family Christmas card every year. The three of them posing on the stairs under fairy lights. All that was missing was the golden retriever.'

'No way. Gross.'

Maeve sighs. 'I mean, I was envious, if I'm honest.'

'I bet she threw a gender reveal party too.'

'No. Charlie was premature actually. Anyway, they weren't ones for parties.'

'Do you think that was more her, though? Being all aloof and stuff.'

'Well yeah, she was always a bit stuck-up. But Rory was the same, distant. You remember what he was like as a kid. Difficult to get close to. And you know, he would have worked hard to create that serene family unit. I was surprised they only had the one. I always imagined Rory wanting a big happy family.'

'Maybe they couldn't have more.' She'd asked Rory. Of course he wouldn't divulge anything. Juliet thinks of the miscarriage she had when Ruby was a baby. How it seeded a little resentment and anger within her relationship to Tāne. She takes another large gulp of wine and then looks around. 'Jesus, is that Colum?'

Maeve glances over to the bar. 'Oh yeah. When he and his wife separated, he moved down here too.'

'Ugh. Oh no, he's spotted us.'

'Maeve.' Colum bends and kisses her cheek. 'And, Christ, would you look what the cat dragged in,' he says in his insufferable South Dublin croak that reminds Juliet of a malfunctioning lawnmower. 'You're looking well, Juliet.'

'It must be all the yoga.'

Maeve kicks her under the table.

Colum frowns. 'Interesting outfit choice there, though.'

'Thanks Colum,' Juliet says, reaching up and pulling at the contrast cuff of his blue-striped shirt. 'This is lovely too. Doesn't Gordon Gekko want it back, though?'

'Ha-ha. Very droll. How's about I get you ladies a beverage?'

Juliet holds up the bottle of wine. 'No thanks. We've got some. Remember, Colum, no matter what your hero Gordon says, greed is *not* good.'

Colum waves his hand and mutters something, then walks away. Maeve is laughing. 'Oh my God, Juliet. I almost feel sorry for him, despite him having the self-awareness of an amoeba.' She stands. 'I better get going. I need to get back to the utter shitshow that is my domestic situation. And I find my hangovers these days take on existential proportions. I mean, when we were young I would simply question the dubious choices I'd made the night before. Now, it's every single life choice I've ever made.'

'Ah, you're just out of practice.'

'Will you be okay by yourself?'

'Don't worry, I'll find something to amuse me.'

'That's exactly what does worry me.' Maeve kisses her cheek. 'I'll call you tomorrow. Be good.'

'Never.' Juliet winks at her.

When Maeve's gone, Juliet scans the room. There are plenty of familiar faces, but she can't bear the thought of speaking to any of them. Some irrational part of her still eyes the door every time it swings open, as though it might be him. He wasn't much of a drinker, though, a reaction to his chaotic childhood. Funny, you either go one way or the other in middle age, lean into it or fight against it. The country's full of hypervigilant adult survivors. It must be exhausting.

Colum is looking in her direction. And Liam, the owner, who said he would join her later for a drink, is out from behind the bar now and hovering at a nearby table chatting to a couple there. She sinks the dregs of her glass, picks up the bottle and puts it in her bag. She doesn't care about getting fucked up with a hangover but waking up with somebody she's fucked and wishing they were somebody else? There's nothing on this earth as lonely. She should know. She's been doing it her entire adult life.

ERICA

She's parked in the SuperValu carpark a few hours after the burial. She dreads the sympathetic looks and the rote conversations and, worse, the people who stop abruptly in their tracks in the bakery aisle when they see her, turn and scurry in the other direction. But there's no toilet paper at home. Life, with all its mundanity, is insistent.

She keeps her head down in the supermarket, turns in to the household aisle. And – *dear God no* – there a few feet in front of her is Maeve Griffin, one of Rory's childhood friends, whose son is in Charlie's year. Erica seizes momentarily, then pivots and flees back up the aisle and through the nearby barrier gate that leads into the wine section. Maeve had brought a shop-bought swiss roll over to the house when she'd heard about Rory. 'You really shouldn't have,' Erica had said, squeezing her arm. At least it wasn't another lasagne. Maeve terrifies her with her glamorous career, her tense neck and long undyed hair, but mostly her clever, distracted eyes that land briefly then flit away, like that's all she needs to get the measure of you. Erica finds her a touch . . . overwrought, if she's honest. A lot of the clients Rory worked with are like that too. Musicians and comedians that you expect to be light-hearted extroverts are, in reality, writhing masses of angst. Sometimes Rory said he felt more like their therapist than a promoter. He said they could never have them over for dinner. And definitely never go for a drink with them. That always ended in disaster, he said, because most of them were functioning alcoholics, or alcoholic adjacent, or recovering alcoholics, or alcoholics in denial. She's sure he was exaggerating because she would describe Rory himself as *alcoholic hypervigilant*. She sensed his judgement on her own drinking constantly.

'Can I help?' a young man with a fulsome beard behind the till asks, and she tells him she's fine. She is jealous of men's beards. Perhaps if she could grow one she wouldn't google *Will people be able to tell if I get a facelift?*

She walks straight to the New World section and chooses a bottle of Californian Chardonnay with a screw top, and after she pays goes to the car, where she removes the lid and takes several large gulps. A numbing warmth seals her insides. Just a pandemic spill-over, this sloppy wine habit. Everyone was doing it, a bit of a jokey cliché, all those memes. In fact, the validation that they were all doing it made her feel part of something, for once. One of these days she'll get round to breaking it. She could stop any time. But no point now. It's not like she ever has a *need* for a drink anyway. Just a *desire*. Mind you, desire is what undoes a person. In the vehicle next to her, a woman is unhappily swallowing a cigarette. They catch each other's eyes. Erica must look away.

She drives the short distance to their imposing house and sits in her car staring in at it. This place has always felt like solely Rory's, even if their joint names are on the deeds and her dresses are in the wardrobe. It embarrasses her, if she's honest, with its pseudo turrets, smallpox of skylights and random porthole windows, so different to the genteelly symmetrical ivy-covered home in which she grew up. She'd cried when they came to see it one evening, in its final stages of being built, the full horror of the place hitting her then as they sat in their car on the cobblelock driveway, Charlie asleep in the baby seat, the place lit up by the rash of wart-like exterior spotlights. It looked like the kind of house Bilbo Baggins – if he was a nouveau riche property developer – might dream up after a night on the mead. Rory mistook her tears for happy ones. 'Isn't it something?' he'd said, radiating pride. 'It is,' she'd replied. 'It really is *something*.'

And now it's a big ungainly house with a big ungainly to-do list. She is both grateful for and overwhelmed by all that needs doing. Affairs to be sorted, policies to be claimed, wishes to be executed, cards to be opened, acknowledgements to be written, clothes to be donated, lasagnes to be eaten, dishes to be washed and returned. And Erica will do it all and try to make it appear effortless because her effort should always be invisible to others. She has perfected the art, the no-make-up make-up, the capsule wardrobe, the strategically placed highlights that grow out seamlessly, the unfaltering speech, the orthodontically perfect smile that cost thousands and took years to mould but feels pulled and tight as though it's stretching her, as though she is the wrong shape entirely.

She gets out of the car and steps over the dish lying on the doorstep and through the large double entrance. *Hell*, she thinks, when she's standing in the grand hallway with its polished concrete floors. *The toilet paper.*

MAEVE

Maeve is spacing out in front of the wall of fridges in the SuperValu that she's stopped into on the way home from O'Malley's. She's momentarily paralysed by the array of yoghurt varieties. She closes her eyes and tries to recall the contents of the fridge at home, wishes she'd made a list like they advise. (Who exactly are *they*, she wonders, these people with their shit together.) Anyway, this feeling has become pervasive, the unsettling sensation that she's forgetting things: names, destinations when she's driving, reasons for entering rooms. Words hover just beyond her grasp so that when she writes now she has to have a thesaurus to hand at all times. But even that fails her. You must know a word to find one that's similar.

Focus. The yoghurts. Luke likes vanilla but not plain, Jamie fruit but not berries. Her mother refuses most solid food now apart from jelly so Maeve must make her special calorie-laden smoothies to keep her nourished. She's confused as to what food groups are acceptable to Cillian. Dairy bad but probiotics good? Who knows. He comments on her diet all the time, and sometimes she gets the impression he's suggesting her mother's dementia could have been avoided had she eaten differently. 'Listen to this,' he'll say meaningfully, as he reads aloud an article that claims a handful of walnuts a day is a defence against cognitive decline.

She shuffles sideways to the milk section. There was a story in the news this morning about the mummified corpse of a man being discovered in a derelict house down the country somewhere. The gardaí speculated that he had lain there for twenty years, judging by the date of the milk that was in his fridge. (Maeve got a sudden mortified urge to check the dates on bottles in her own fridge. She suspected she had jars of mustard almost that old.) When she'd read the article, as her boys scrummed around her in a chaos of missing PE kits and hastily thrown together lunches, her mother calling to her from her bedroom and her husband asking where his runners were, she'd envied that corpse's solitude.

Her phone buzzes with a message. It's from Cillian. Psycho out of food fyi x.

Psycho is Cillian's name for Simon, their mercurial cat. The *fyi* is a neat trick to absolve himself of responsibility. And the x at the end is the closest they get to sexting these days. She sighs and trudges towards the petfood aisle.

In the checkout queue, she stares at the gossip-magazine covers. *I'm actually here to kill you, confessed my mate! We do date night at hubby's grave!* The drinks fridge nearby discharges its droning chill. A strip light above her buzzes and flickers and she thinks of a fly, trapped and slowly dying. A bleakness that is both hollow and heavy settles inside her. At the self-checkout opposite her, there's a well-dressed man who she knows must smell expensive. His basket contains a bottle of Veuve, a jar of olives and a wedge of Camembert. Slung lightly on his shoulder is a cloth tote bag with the name of a cool independent Dublin bookstore. She imagines him going to visit a lover. She thinks of Dan, his warm eyes with their long, dark lashes. ('Wasted on a boy,' she'd say, thinking of her own stubby, translucent ones. 'Who says I waste them, darling?' he'd say, fluttering his at her.)

As the woman at the till scans her groceries, Maeve's throat constricts, making a sharp heat build behind her nose, and when she taps to pay, a fat tear slips out. No-one warns you about these sudden inappropriate assaults of emotion. Rage, despair. Or the lingering melancholy. She watched *The Bridges of Madison County* recently, a film that failed to affect her in any way when she was twenty-one – the idea of great passion in middle age seemed far-fetched – but this time she needed several days to recover. The checkout operator is unmoved by her tears, as though used to people breaking down as they're confronted with the bill. Maeve looks again at the stylish man and picks up a bunch of flowers from a nearby bucket. The operator sighs dramatically when she asks for this to be put through as well. Maeve imagines punching her.

On her way home she passes by O'Malley's. No doubt Juliet is still there, probably flirting with Liam, the owner, who was sweet on her when they were kids. Men have always been drawn to Juliet, the recklessness combined with the brokenness proving lethal. And her unusual beauty, of course, which is probably more salient. Men wanted to fix her *and* fuck her. Or fix her *by* fucking her. Or, who is she kidding, it's not an act of altruism – just fuck her. She loves her but also finds her exhausting. She brings back with her an ominous shift in energy, the mortifying graveside almost-puking earlier not atypical of her. But to be fair to Juliet, the destructive tendencies are generally solely directed against her own person.

She pulls into her driveway and sits for several minutes in the car staring at the house, trying to muster up the enthusiasm to go inside. She thinks longingly of their old red-brick Victorian terraced home in Harold's Cross and is suddenly sure her real life is being lived there, by someone else. This modern semi-d in a suburban housing estate on the outskirts of her childhood town thirty miles away has never felt as welcoming.

Every single light in the house appears to be on and she imagines the activity inside. Evenings are the most difficult time with her mother. 'Sundowning', the literature calls it, as though it's a convivial time spent imbibing gin and tonic overlooking the ocean. Perhaps it's the prospect of the nightmares that rip her sleep asunder that makes her mother agitated. The regime of drugs she's on helps, the lorazepam for the anxiety and insomnia, haloperidol for the delusions. Still, the downward spiral from those first vacant moments ('like a big nothing inside me, Maeve') to the almost complete annihilation of her personality has been both excruciating and rapid. Like that old truism about rearing children: endless days and all too brief years.

They considered a nursing home and even went to visit a place, a modern purpose-built facility furnished by IKEA, where instead of books, word art like HOME – a cruel taunt to the residents, Maeve thought – sat on the shelves. (Maeve imagined PURGATORY perched jauntily there instead.) Her mother repeated, 'I hate this,' in a tiny voice Maeve barely recognised, and Maeve wasn't sure if she meant the home or the dementia – possibly it was both – and felt so overwhelmed by guilt, she promised her she wouldn't have to come. Now, of course, the guilt comes from inflicting the illness on her husband and children. It seems to be an unavoidable part of womanhood.

———

Cillian's at the kitchen table with his laptop open. She catches a glimpse of the RIP.ie website. Another recent hobby. He may be addicted to this too – a whole new level of doomscrolling.

'Hey,' he says.

'Hey.' She dumps the groceries on the table in front of him and goes to pick up the kettle. She's annoyed to find it empty despite the Post-it Note attached saying *Please everyone ensure kettle full!* Her mother keeps boiling it dry. There are Post-its everywhere, some for her mother's benefit, some for the rest of the family to accommodate her mother, so that at times it feels to Maeve like they are characters in some dystopian novel. (Someone else – Jamie, she's sure of it – also feels this way and has stuck their own note to the television saying, *Remember, Big Brother is Watching You!!*)

On the bath – *Turn on cold tap first!*

On all computers – *No, we don't have family in Islamabad that need money!*

There used to be one on the toaster – *Only set dial to 3!* – but after one too many smoke-alarm incidents that made her mother hysterical, they gave up and hid the appliance altogether.

'You're late,' he says, his tone neutral. It's a statement but also, perhaps, could be interpreted as a criticism, were she in that frame of mind. Which she is. Lately, she's felt a sort of generalised irritability that needs no reason, has no shape. She suspects it's another perimenopausal gift. Her mother claimed that the menopause brought with it a host of benefits: better sex ('recreation not procreation, Maeve'), a yielding of fertility to real power, a reconnection to the creativity of childhood (though Lily's return to childhood has been far more literal). But Maeve feels none of these things yet, only a *low-key* (as her sons would say) anger swilling dangerously beneath the surface. 'Yeah, sorry,' she says in a deliberately unrepentant tone. 'I caught up with Juliet Quinn after.'

'Oh, she's home, is she?' Again, neutral, but the use of the word *she*, twice, chafes at Maeve. She knows he carries some resentment towards Juliet over the wedding debacle. Also, Maeve suspects, towards Maeve herself because Juliet is her friend. Even though it was his *own brother* who requested

Juliet put his cock in her mouth. She takes a deep breath in through her nose, tells herself to let it go.

'So how was it?' he asks.

'Oh, you know, horrific. I sat there with this heavy feeling of dread. That's two out of the four of our little childhood gang dead now. Half! God. Anyway, how are things here?'

'The boys are upstairs. On their phones or PlayStation, no doubt. Your mother is asleep in front of the TV.'

(She notes the *your mother*. Didn't he used to say *Lily*? Another way her identity is being stripped.)

'Okay.' She moves to the sink to fill the kettle. The boys' lunchboxes are sitting beside it, unemptied. She opens them and throws the squashed grapes, wizened carrot sticks and brown apple slices into the bin. 'You know, sometimes I think their lunchboxes are simply vehicles for transporting fruit and vegetables untouched.'

He doesn't respond, just taps at his laptop. So even the burden of their children's health rests on her shoulders. Another breath. She washes the boxes out, bangs them slightly harder than is necessary on the draining board. 'Cuppa?' she asks, even though she knows he won't drink anything caffeinated after midday. She's not sure why she still asks. Maybe it's an opportunity to be condescending towards his *rules for life*.

'No thanks.' Then, apropos of nothing, he sighs and says, 'I missed my CrossFit class this evening.' The mournful tone is infuriating.

'Sorry but it couldn't be helped, Cillian. I was at a funeral, you know, not a party.'

'That's not the issue. If your mother was in proper care, no-one would have to stay home to babysit.'

And so it begins. This old argument.

'But you can go to the gym anytime.' She reaches for the tea caddy and adds, pointedly, 'These days.'

'Again, not the issue. Come on, Maeve, this is not sustainable. What happens if you've to go abroad to do promotional work?'

She turns to him and leans back on the sink. 'You know I've told my publisher I can't travel this year.'

'But what about next year? Or the year after that? Your mother could live for years yet, Maeve. Meanwhile the boys will have left home and we'll never get this time back.' A switch flicks now inside her.

'Well, let's hope she dies a tad quicker than that then, so as not to inconvenience you, Cillian.' (They do this lately. Put each other's name at the end of their sentences. It manages to sound both condescending and accusatory.)

'To be completely honest, Maeve, the prospect of her slow death here in this house is not something that fills me with any hope.'

'I won't abandon her, Cillian. She was a single mother and kept me. God knows, it wasn't easy for her.'

He takes off his oversized black glasses and places them carefully beside the laptop. She hates those pretentious glasses. They scream of a mid-life ache for relevancy. That and his new uniform of all black. If he starts wearing polo necks, she'll have to leave him.

'That's not a rational comparison.' (The word *rational* makes her crazy.) 'It wouldn't be abandonment, quite the opposite in fact. She'd be going somewhere where she'd be taken care of by experts with greater skills than us.' (His tone is still measured. This is how it would feel to sit in his consulting room.)

'And by experts you mean strangers.'

'But she doesn't even know who you are half the time. Your sense of responsibility is skewed. How healthy is it for the boys living in this environment?'

She's raging now. Anger churning inside her like lava. Skewed sense of responsibility? She thinks of those lonely days at home full-time with the babies while he headed up a team in business banking. His evenings and weekends spent socialising with colleagues or schmoozing his property developer clients. Long boozy lunches in the latest trendy restaurant, eighteen holes on exclusive golf courses, all-expenses-paid trips to the grand prix in Monaco. The Celtic Tiger in its dying, debaucherous years and those Irish bankers acting like it was Wall Street. She might as well have been a single mother herself back then. She feels she might blow. Like one of those sulphurous geysers in New Zealand. Cillian would struggle with how to word the obituary for RIP.ie.

'Jesus, *God*, Cillian. She's got some cognitive decline, she's not a psychopath! I mean, are you going to cart me off as soon as I start forgetting the date or where my car keys are? Which is now, as it happens. And don't your manuals tell you that multi-generational living is the ideal? *Furthermore*, you're the one with the skewed sense of responsibility.' Her voice is a shrill, almost separate entity to her now. It is somewhere in the air around them, pinging against the walls and ceiling.

'What do you mean by that?'

'I'm shouldering most of the financial responsibility at the moment because you refuse to take on more clients.'

His face assumes a pointedly patient look. He does this on purpose, she's sure of it, in a typical *male manoeuvre*. He's generally a calm person but she's positive he makes his demeanour even more *serene* than normal to contrast with his illogical, screeching, harpy wife. She has a violent urge to slap him. Which now that she thinks of it, he's probably orchestrated all along.

'I'm not refusing to take on more clients, Maeve. I'm nurturing the ones I have and ensuring I'm doing it properly so that I can build a practice of integrity. Remember, at the start of your writing career I was the one working fifty-hour weeks and shouldering all the financial burden.'

That's it. Boom. It's finally happened. She's so angry she's now left her own body. Her consciousness has joined her voice as it ricochets around the room. 'That was completely different, Cillian, and you damn well know it. I was at home doing all the childcare and all the housework. I had to fit in my writing around that. The odd snatched half hour here and there if I was lucky. You have countless free hours a week that you choose to spend doing . . .' she searches for the most condescending word she can use, '*burpees*.'

'That's unfair, Maeve. You know it is.' He stands. 'I've an early class tomorrow. I need to go to bed.' He leaves the kitchen, shutting the door firmly – but not melodramatically – behind him.

'Great,' she shouts at the closed door. 'I'll just put away the groceries too, will I?'

She imagines throwing the cup of tea at the wall. Watching the liquid spatter in a spectacular fashion, leaving a large Picasso-esque stain there.

As though she's shot him.

She sits at the table and puts her head in her hands. She's so tired of this argument. A headache's forming, and she rubs her temples.

She thinks enviously of Juliet and her exploits on Tinder. Cillian was only the second person she ever had sex with. Why didn't she sleep around before she met him? Played the field and had some adventures of her own while her body was young and firm and looking at herself naked didn't require squinting, sucking in her tummy and forming her fingers into pincers to hitch up the loose skin at the top of her breasts. This is what she would tell a daughter. Have loads of carefree sex before the act becomes associated with pregnancy and labour and birth and breastfeeding and a sort of murderous exhaustion.

Their sex life has never recovered from those early baby days. They say it gets better again when the kids leave home, but honestly, that's a lot of scarce years. The Great Hunger lasted just seven. And she has a sneaking regret that hers never really got off the ground in the first place.

She and Cillian met in college. She had lost her virginity to a drunk politics student while in her first year. That experience was underwhelming. She slightly disassociated during the whole thing, lying there motionless while he rucked inelegantly, wondering why it was that people lost their minds over *this*. Why she and Juliet had spent so much time breathlessly speculating on what *this* would feel like. Still, she had butterflies going into college the following week, wondering if she would see him again in Front Square or the library. But it was as though he disappeared. And then about two weeks later, she passed him walking through the front arches and he pretended he didn't see her. His eyes landed briefly, flicked away, then he turned his head ninety degrees and became desperately invested in the society notices on the side walls. She put her own head down, mortified at this overt rejection, and went straight into the arts-block toilets where she sat in a stall for half an hour, shaking with humiliation and a deep loneliness and reading the graffiti in an attempt to connect with other disenfranchised souls. She took out a pen and scratched *What is wrong with me?* on the wall above the toilet-roll holder, beside where some joker had etched *Pull Here for Arts Degree!* And then, when she walked out, a girl from her American literature tutorial, a sardonic, popular girl with strong opinions on Hemingway, walked into the cubicle and Maeve worried that she would know it was her and consider her a freak. More of a freak.

She felt so out of place that first year in Trinity. Standing alone before lectures trying to look as though she was waiting for someone. Her year was full of tall English boys who wore long scarves and had names like Hugo and Alex and who had failed to get into Oxbridge and made her feel as though she was the foreigner. Or Irish boys from private rugby-playing schools who all seemed to know each other and referred to one another by surname only. And clever Dublin girls who travelled in by DART every day from their big houses by the sea and went on foreign holidays with their families and seemed certain of their place in the world. And none of these other students needed to rush off after lectures to a job in a kebab shop in Donnybrook. But worse almost than the loneliness was the bitter realisation that she was an average student at best. School suited her, with its regurgitation of knowledge. In college she came unstuck. The other students discussed the post-modernist literature they were reading – just for fun – while Maeve was still enjoying Maeve Binchy. She hadn't the faintest idea what the term *postmodernism* even meant (still doesn't). She felt incapable of having an original thought, and that would always separate her from the talented undergrads. In her first American literature tutorial, she described the imagery in T.S. Eliot's *Prufrock* as beautiful and was pulled up by the professor for using such 'inane and reductive' critical language. From then on, she sat mute in tutorials, while around her, her peers would confidently deconstruct and debate, full of exuberance and their own importance. The whole experience left her feeling defeated. Her dreams of being a writer seemed ridiculous. It was years before she regained the confidence to try.

But when she met Cillian, a thriving economics student,

and his friends she immediately felt comfortable amongst them. As with her old gang from home, they could converse without the self-consciousness of her English literature cohort, who all spoke in an arch, ironic tone that Maeve could never figure out. These new friends could be equally silly and serious. Suddenly she was someone who sat laughing with a crowd in the college bars. And some of the grief she felt since Dan's death was eased. Like Dan, Cillian had an ability to soothe her more neurotic urges, which helped her to not take herself too seriously. She felt lighter in his company.

But maybe she latched on too soon, settled down too quickly, was too frightened of spending her life alone like her mother, struggling to make ends meet. Cillian's calm level-headedness, which was attractive at first because it promised solidity, has started to become an irritant. Everything has. Maybe she's chosen predictability over passion. Serenity over sensuality. Listening to Juliet, she's more aware than ever that her own sexual narrative has been too threadbare. And her dissatisfaction feels self-indulgent and wrong too, because after all, it's a good life, a life she yearned for and chose. And one that she increasingly wants to crawl out of.

―

A small cry comes from the sitting room and Maeve rushes in. Her mother must have been calling out in her sleep because her eyes are closed, her head hinged to one side. There's a book fallen open on the floor beside her. Maeve picks it up, smooths out the rumpled pages. It's a collection of Heaney poetry. Reading novels has become too difficult for Lily. She tried short stories and essays for a while until they also proved too challenging, but poetry remains just about manageable. Maeve imagines she appreciates the fragmentary nature of it, which perhaps mirrors her own fragmented mind.

Growing up, Maeve felt her mother to be so robust as to be overwhelming, a person who moved in the world unapologetically. Yet here she is now, fragile and brittle. Maeve imagines the dementia like a dark, cavernous mouth, taking what it needs to feed itself, consuming her from the inside out. She's thinner, which hardly seems possible, her bones like toothpicks under the skin.

Instead of waking her to put her to bed, she fixes Lily's head to a more natural position then slinks back to the snug off the kitchen, where her writing desk is set up, feeling like she used to when she let the boys, against all the advice, carry on sleeping in their capsules after lifting them out of the car. She opens her laptop and retrieves the document with her working title of 'Sylvia – Ad Nauseam'. The deadline for submission to her publisher of her ninth *Sylvia Woolf* novel is looming and she's still thirty thousand words short. Sylvia is a character beloved by readers, a beautiful, spiky journalist who solves violent femicides with a mix of intellectual deduction and astute observation, bedding, without shame, a bevy of gorgeous, unsuitable men as she does.

But lately Maeve's come to detest her, finds herself procrastinating working on the manuscript. Like a long marriage, familiarity breeding contempt. She stares at the last paragraph –

who wrote this shite? – and tries and fails to muster up some enthusiasm.

Instead, she bangs out aggressively,

> *Sylvia, weary of the incessant noise and bullshit of her life, lays down on the cool tiles of her floor and sticks her fucking head in the oven.*
> THE END

She can hear sixteen-year-old Jamie in the kitchen – she knows it's him by the grating soundtrack of TikTok videos. Things have been difficult between them of late. Most of his time at home is spent in his room, but when he does speak to her, everything is delivered in the same tone – that precise tone being *Go Fuck Yourself*. And more worrying than the tone, the content. Comments that display a concerning lack of empathy when she and Cillian talk social issues at the dinner table. Dismissive of her then when she tries to engage with him, accusations that she's overreacting, just being a 'ragey feminist as usual'.

She puts her head down on the desk, wonders how it's possible that she's here, at almost forty-nine years old, in a near constant sweaty state, a low-level bewilderment and rage. She thinks of the dead boys, Rory and Dan. She thinks of Juliet. The way they were in those long-ago summers.

And she thinks of the mess it all came to in the end.

———

When Maeve was almost fourteen, her mother, over dinner one night, announced they were moving, which was generally the way Maeve felt things to happen within their autocratic little family unit. Her mother decreed and thus it came to pass. Lily had grown up in Galway but was estranged from her family who had tried and failed to ship her off to England when they found out she was pregnant. Even though this singular strength of her mother's was to be admired, it could be hard to live with.

And so, a couple of days later, they shifted from their rental in an estate in the centre of Ballyboyne town, to another rental on Ash Lane, a rural road of about thirty or so detached houses, a couple of miles outside of it. This place was more sedate, it felt like the kind of road that people left only in a coffin, whereas the estate had always been more of a rowdy holding pen. It had a pub at one end and a rugby club and tennis court at the other. The sports clubs gave the place a smug air, being the types of sports that rich people played, even if a few of the houses, their own small, boxy 1970s bungalow especially, let the side down a little. Still, the grander houses seemed to tolerate the shabbier ones, as you might tolerate a down-on-their-luck relative. Embarrassing, but, you know, family.

Maeve was miserable. She hated this new house and the way it compared unfavourably to its smarter neighbours. At least the uniformly ugly pebble dash and yellow brick exteriors of the estate had lent the place an egalitarian feel. Her first few days were spent crouched down behind the couch in the front room, spying out the window as groups of children, freed from school for the summer, walked past. Some of them carried rackets tucked under their arms. Maeve had never held a tennis racket, let alone owned one, and in the estate the only thing you might see tucked under someone's arm was a distressed football or maybe the distressed head of another child. There'd always been a grimy undercurrent to the place. Maeve missed even that. At least you knew where you stood with it.

Her mother, tired of the morose watchfulness, ordered her outside. Maeve decided the best approach was to go out prepared with some kind of prop, in case anyone walked past. You couldn't be caught alone and unoccupied – it would look completely desperate. Sadly, her only possessions were books, so after careful consideration she chose a Judy Blume – *Forever*, to signal her grasp on topics such as sex and boys – and went to sit on the stone wall that fronted the hayfield, opposite her house. After about ten minutes a blur approached from the left and she stuck her head in the book so as to appear engrossed. The blur got nearer, slowed down and stopped. Maeve turned the page as though oblivious, though her heart was clattering. The blur spoke in a girl's voice.

'Hey, Carrots. It's upside down.'

Maeve would have welcomed death in that moment. She was used to the Carrots moniker, occupational hazard of being, as Maeve herself described it, *Titian-hued*. But she wanted to throw that stupid book behind her into the long grass so that it would be degraded by the elements and chewed up and spat out by the hay baler that would come at the end of summer.

She looked up, her entire face and chest burning, *Titian-*

hued also, trying to feign surprise. There were three of them, two boys and a girl, and they looked around her own age.

'Oh hi,' she said, as nonchalantly as she could. Then, because, like everyone else in school, she'd just started watching *Neighbours*, and thought it would sound exotic, she attempted to add a breezy 'G'day'. Except it came out stiffly as *Good day*, so that she sounded less laid-back Australian surf dude, more Victorian-era spinster.

'And a good day to you too,' said the girl, taking a mock bow. She was like nothing Maeve had ever seen before, with pale skin and curly black hair, ten-hole oxblood Doc Martens on her feet that accentuated her thin colt-like legs. There was something strange about this girl's large wide-set eyes, but it was hard to figure out what it was. She had an intense gaze, looking at you like a dare so that it was difficult to maintain eye contact. Maeve wasn't sure if she was pretty or not. All she knew is she wanted to keep looking. 'Forsooth, from whence do you come, fair child?'

Maeve now wanted that hay baler to squash and mangle and spew her out along with the book.

'Don't be such a sneer, Juliet,' one of the boys said, jumping up on the wall beside Maeve. He was small and sandy-haired, and his legs were tanned in his white tennis shorts. In the estate it would have been rare to see boys' legs – not that you'd want to see those pasty things anyway. 'Pay no heed, she's just being a wagon because,' he leaned in and whispered, 'she's *on the rag*.' At this Juliet rolled her eyes and said, 'Sexist pig.' He stuck his hand out. 'I'm Dan. I live over there in *that* monstrosity.' He pointed in an exaggerated way in the direction of the two-storey red-brick beside the field that was visible from Maeve's front room. It was large, with lions' heads on the pillars, a central driveway lined by elms and white rose bushes, and Romanesque columns at the front porch. Maeve had considered it beautiful when she'd looked out at it wistfully from her own. 'More money than taste,' he drawled. Maeve decided now the house was ugly but that this Dan boy was adorable.

'I'm Maeve and I've just moved in over there.' She waved her hand as vaguely as possible in the direction of her own bungalow, wishing the high midday sun threw a kinder light on its exterior and that her mother's battered Ford jalopy was parked out of view in the garage.

Dan looked and nodded in a non-judgemental way. The other boy spoke then and Maeve looked at him properly for the first time but almost wished she hadn't. Unlike Juliet, he was unambiguously beautiful, with fair hair and green eyes, and the kind of teeth that wouldn't have looked out of place on *Dallas*, a show she could only enjoy if Lily wasn't around making condescending comments on it. Maeve found herself blushing again. It was like someone had peered into her subconscious and conjured up the perfect boy. Jon Bon Jovi combined with George Michael. She imagined dancing to 'Careless Whisper' with him in the slow set. She felt strange, quivery, had to avert her eyes from him because she was sure that everyone there knew.

'That's old Moany Maloney's place. Think Peig Sayers but with less teeth. We used to egg-bomb it all the time. She died in the kitchen, head down in her porridge, spoon gripped in her hand.' He held up a clenched fist, put his other hand around his throat and made an exaggerated corpse-like pose. Then he put his hand down, narrowed his eyes. 'Hey, which bedroom is yours? You haven't heard any strange banshee noises late at night, have you?' A smirk hitched up one side of his mouth. So, a dash of a cruel Byronic hero as well? Mesmerising.

'Don't mind Rory,' Dan said, nudging her. 'She died most prosaically of pneumonia in hospital.'

'So what other books do you like?' Juliet asked.

It felt like a test. Maeve blurted out the first thing that popped into her head. 'Oh, um, Sweet Valley High?' It wasn't true. She wasn't a fan. (Anyway, Lily had banned them from the house. 'Dross, Maeve. If you want hedonistic Americans, read this,' and she'd given her a copy of *The Great Gatsby*. It left Maeve cold.) The main problem with those Sweet Valley books was they made Maeve feel dissatisfied about living in a drab, inland, rainy town in Ireland where most people had bad teeth.

Juliet said, 'Never read them, they look shite. But *Flowers in the Attic* is good.'

Maeve kind of agreed. Virginia Andrews' books made her feel better about her own life. She may not be living in the Californian sunshine, surrounded by handsome jocks in convertibles, but at least she wasn't locked in an attic *riding her own brother.*

Juliet reached into the waistband of her leggings then and pulled out a ten-pack of Rothmans, which she shook. 'We're going down to the old bridge for a fag. You coming?' She pulled one out and put it in the corner of her mouth in a kind of James Dean pose. Maeve realised then what was so arresting about her eyes. One was blue, the other a deep hazel. Maeve wanted to get closer to her, really study them, but Juliet must have sensed this because she closed one eye and continued to stare at her out of the other one.

'Sure.' Maeve shrugged. 'I love fags.' Dan laughed, held out his hand and together they jumped off the wall.

As they walked down the road towards the river, Dan filled her in on the dynamics. Juliet went to one of the two local convent schools (Maeve went to the other, the 'less nunny one' according to Lily), Dan and Rory to the local boys' school. Maeve didn't mention that her mother was a teacher there; no doubt they'd figure out this mortifying information later. Dan had gone to boarding school in Kildare for his first year in secondary but kept running away. 'They were doing their best to turn me into an emotionally stunted excuse for a human being, just as they had done to my father. So I decided if I had to be reared by people who didn't love me then it might as well be in the comfort of my own home.'

The other two were a little in front, Juliet still with the unlit cigarette on her lip, Rory strumming his old wooden tennis racket, with its broken strings, like a guitar. Something about the way those two walked ahead, in their own world, gave Maeve a feeling she'd always lag behind. ('Siamese twins, those two,' Dan said. 'Joined at the hip.') Just as they were beside O'Malley's pub, near the junction of their lane and the new main Dublin Road, a silver Mercedes pulled up alongside them. Dan swore under his breath.

'Daniel!'

Dan sighed and came to a reluctant halt. The man inside the car had dark hair slicked back from a distinctive widow's peak, which gave him a sinister, vampirish appearance.

'What are you young bucks up to?'

'Just going to the river, Dr Flynn,' Rory said, straight-faced now and serious. Dan said nothing, just kicked sullenly at some stones.

'Oh, tremendous.' He pronounced it as *tremenjus*. 'For a swim, is it?'

'No, just to hang out and play some pooh sticks, Dr Flynn,' Juliet said, a picture now of innocence, the cigarette hidden in her hand.

'Just as well. Because you'd need your arm bands for that, wouldn't you, *Danielle*?' Dr Flynn said.

Dan continued looking down, swirling his toe in the gravel. 'I can swim.'

'That's not what I'd call that pansy-looking manoeuvre you do. What do they call it? Breaststroke, is it? Isn't that it, Rory? Breaststroke.' He gave a laugh that sounded like a bark and looked to Rory to acknowledge the joke as though he was an ally, but Rory's face was stony, refusing to be a part of it.

Juliet said, 'Well, we better get going. *Tremenjus* to see you, Dr Flynn.' She said it staring him straight in the eye and Maeve thought she'd never seen anyone as ballsy.

Dan gave the retreating car the finger and said, 'And that,

Maeve, is the *tremenjus* prick himself, my pater, the upstanding Dr Daniel Flynn.'

Maeve gave him a sympathetic grimace. 'You're nothing like him.'

'Thanks. I know.' And he gave a wink. 'I'm fucking fabulous.'

That boy may have been small, but he had a huge heart.

And so they crossed the new main road over to the bridge that lay opposite O'Malley's and formed part of the old Dublin Road. The apex of it curved gently above a wide stretch of the river Boyne and eight arches stood crumbling slightly in the water below. Juliet lit a cigarette, and they hunkered down out of view to smoke it, three drags each for fairness, taking turns to act as lookout. Juliet warned Maeve, under pain of death, not to put a 'duck's arse' on it. Afterwards they played pooh sticks, Dan commentating flawlessly as though it was the Grand National, giving the twigs bastardised thoroughbred names like *Red Bum* and *Yawn Run* so that Maeve ended up leaning against the wall of the bridge in hysterics. She went home that evening her heart full.

And that was it. She was hooked. She spent almost every day that first summer, and the years that followed, with them. During the long holidays, they would head off in the morning to the courts with their tennis rackets, though little tennis was ever played. In the afternoon they would head down to the river. Sometimes Rory would bring his ghetto blaster, and they would lie on the banks under the bridge listening to his tapes as he rhapsodised about some band or album that no-one else had heard of.

On warm days they'd swim, trying to avoid the lush reeds at the water's edge while Maeve would try harder still to avoid stealing glances at Rory's changing body, the way his shoulders were starting to broaden and the new hair under his arms that thrilled her in a way she couldn't yet make sense of.

But if Rory noticed Maeve's interest, he never showed it. It seemed to Maeve that he was aware of how good-looking he was but that it meant nothing to him. Or even was a kind of joke. He was a talented singer and guitar player but he was never one of those boys at parties who did it self-consciously, trying to make soulful eye contact as they serenaded you, as though you should melt in front of them with desire and gratitude.

He was different, though, with Juliet, like her opinion mattered more. There was always a palpable undercurrent between them. Even the teasing felt more intense, as if they were acutely sensitive to one another, or maybe more desperate to get under the other's skin. Juliet would call him *thick* – he failed every subject in school apart from music – and his jaw would tense up. Or Rory would talk about her mother, Denise, who everyone agreed was very pretty ('for a mam, like'), in an admiring way that made Juliet furious.

But on those swimming days, Maeve witnessed how he looked covertly at her as she stepped out of the river. Maybe noticing, as Maeve herself did in a way that confused her even more than her admiration of Rory, how the convex dimples just above her blue bikini bottoms were like dents in cream, how her hip snaked elegantly, how a drop of water would cling tantalisingly on her jutting clavicle. And Juliet would always find excuses to get physical with Rory, to touch him in some way, like play-fighting or trying to tickle him. Once, she hid his clothes while he was in the river, and when he got out she refused to give them back so he wrestled her to the ground, unzipped her fleece and put it on himself. Watching them, Rory in his swimming trunks, pinning Juliet down between his thighs while she breathed hard and writhed underneath him, felt too intimate, almost voyeuristic, and Maeve made herself look away, even though part of her was entranced by the scene.

Dan was aware of their chemistry too and it amused him. He'd nudge Maeve and waggle his eyebrows at their antics. 'Get a room already,' he'd say, or when they were a bit older, 'Check out Harry and Sally.' But Maeve never pictured them as those particular characters whose interactions were too light, too comic, too neurotic. To Maeve, obsessed then by Gothic melodrama, they were more Heathcliff and Cathy, compelling but self-destructive anti-heroes. As far as she was aware, nothing physical had ever happened between them, but that didn't stop Maeve imagining it. She suspected it wasn't entirely normal to fantasise about two of her best friends having sex, but she would never have the guts to ask anyone, so wasn't sure.

Sex became the major preoccupation in those years. If Maeve wasn't thinking about it, she was having long discussions with Juliet on the topic, on how they imagined the act itself would be. They'd share books, by authors like Shirley Conran and

Danielle Steele, the corners turned down on the titillating pages that seemed to suggest 'it' would be painful, but ultimately ecstatic. (Thrillingly, the men in these books all seemed to *explode* inside women.) Maeve's mother found a copy of *Lace* under Maeve's bed and was apoplectic, not because of the explicit content but because of her low opinion of the writing. 'For heaven's sake, if you're going to read something obscene at least choose someone literary, like Joyce.' Juliet and Maeve adored it, though, and the infamous line where the heroine demands to know which *bitch* is her mother became a favourite catchcry, both having mothers they considered less than ideal.

And so, they were a tight little gang for those few years. But the sexual frisson that existed felt like that first snag in a cut of cloth that was teetering on the brink of unravelling.

JULIET

It's two days since they buried him. Despite it being a mild night, the fire in the good room is lit and Juliet and her mother are sitting together gazing into it, Juliet in the same armchair her father preferred. She liked to curl up in it as a child too, if he was at work in the small furniture factory he owned, as though its synthetic fibres could transfer, by proxy, some paternal softness. She thinks of him, handsome, unknowable, with his Brylcreem and Old Spice scent, newspaper held up like a challenge to his children. Or folded severely on his lap, head bent, as he scowled in concentration trying to solve the cryptic crossword. He'd been in the army as a young man and it seemed to Juliet as though he believed his real life was still happening there. He'd look around sometimes and appear bewildered by the ill-disciplined people he shared a house with. He liked to say, proudly, that he was born on the day Pearl Harbor was bombed. As if it conferred some extra gravitas. Juliet's grandmother said that was true enough and she remembered 'the Japs' doing that but not her son being born, which Juliet thought maybe explained a lot about her father.

While the shadow flames lick the walls, a feeling descends on her of not needing to be anywhere except exactly where she is. There's something uniquely Irish about this – each time she comes home she's struck by it. Time and people appear to move more slowly, though perhaps that's only wishful thinking. She hates the idea of missing out when she's gone. And it's sad, too, the way some things remain unchanged. This morning she read the newspapers and noted the old stories in them. One moved her especially. Those photos of the disappeared young women in the nineties, their faces, frozen in time, pleading, as though prescient of their fates. Juliet knows their features like her own.

Auckland's energy is more vibrant. A city of early risers where everyone always seems to be doing something. And there, she's always hungering to be occupied herself. With Ruby so independent now, almost an adult with a busy social life and a job in a restaurant in the city centre, her own car, given to her by Tāne, there's so much more time to fill. Juliet takes as much work as she can get – in the shop or life modelling – which is a financial necessity but also a good way to distract herself from herself. Punishing early-morning runs around Takapuna, followed by a swim at her local beach. Intense sessions at the gym or drinks and dinner with friends to fill the hours after work. A constant need for busyness that has become the only way to escape obsessive thoughts about Rory. Though the modelling, she's found, is perhaps not the best for distraction. Holding a pose for thirty minutes necessitates her mind fleeing her body. Mostly straight to him.

Here, though, it feels easy to let the thoughts and the melancholy consume her. Like wrapping herself up in the old woollen blankets her mother has thrown over the armchairs and sofa. Scratchy but comforting, their grassy odour like a memory of childhood in her nostrils.

Denise throws another log onto the fire. It crackles and spits a spark onto the hearth that Juliet covers with her foot. The cream rug is freckled with little spots from previous emissions.

'Jesus, Denise, it's a miracle this house hasn't burned down by now.'

'And it's a miracle how we manage to stay alive at all when you're not around to boss us,' Denise says. 'I probably wouldn't have got cancer if you'd been here.'

Juliet rolls her eyes and slides her armchair back a little from the heat. 'Are you not roasted?'

'I'm freezing all the time with the chemo. I spent years not being able to sleep with the night sweats. Now I can't warm up to save myself.' She sighs.

'And where's Johnny tonight?'

Denise and Johnny have been together over twenty years. They met in O'Malley's, where Denise worked after Juliet's father died. It was the eve of Johnny's fiftieth birthday and his contentment with his bachelor status was swept away in an instant when he caught sight of the barmaid. Denise repudiated his advances at first, but he eventually wore her down with a devotion that aligned with her own opinion of herself. Denise, at that stage approaching fifty herself, said, without a hint of self-consciousness, 'I know I seem out of his league now, but he'll age better than me, the way men do, and in a few years the tables will have turned.' Juliet, sceptical at first, and dismissive back then of the possibility of passion in middle age, was swayed by the way Johnny looked at Denise, how the love he seemed to feel made his indistinct features appear more attractive. How gratifying it must be for her mother. To look at someone and easily know their heart. Denise only allowed Johnny to move in after her cancer diagnosis. 'Don't live with a man, Juliet. One minute you're sitting on his knee and he's telling you you're his girl. Next minute you're after sitting on the piss he's left all over the toilet seat.' Juliet recognises how good they are together, though. In their presence she gets the feeling that she's adrift outside of something grounded.

'He's off on some made-up errand or other. He's always doing errands these days. I think he does find it hard to be around me. I catch him looking at me sometimes, this tragic look on his face. Honest to God, it drives me mad, so it does. Then he'll go out and come back with some pamphlet or other. Like a pamphlet's going to cure me.'

Juliet understands Johnny's pamphlet compulsion. When her older brother Josh rang from London a year ago to say there was a shadow on a scan, probably a harmless cyst, nothing to be concerned about, Juliet's imagination bypassed any optimism and cleaved itself directly to terror. She felt useless living so far away, unable to leave New Zealand because of Covid, so spent her time googling information or joining online forums, as though any unchecked cell growth in her mother's body could be controlled that way. Looking at Denise now, the bald humanity of her, her head wrapped in a colourful scarf, her lips painted a defiant pink in a face that's starting to turn in on itself, the futility of it strikes her. At times she catches her mother with a faraway look in her eyes. She'll come back abruptly, reapply a swipe of lipstick, but Juliet wonders where she goes in those moments. When she was alone with Johnny on her first night home, he'd been pessimistic about her mother's prognosis, but his demeanour altered completely the following morning when Denise was around. He spoke then of gene therapy cures and experimental trials and the woman in the paper from Donegal whose tumours had disappeared after cutting out sugar from her diet. As he spoke, Juliet witnessed an unknowable shadow cross her mother and thought it a lonely place to be. Facing the possibility of death and everyone else averting their eyes.

'So you haven't filled me in yet on the funeral. How was it? I was sorry to miss it, so I was.'

A gash of words bleeds across Juliet's mind. *Devastating, surreal, torturous, like a corkscrew being driven through my guts.* She shrugs. 'What's to say? It was sad.'

Her mother shakes her head. 'What's to say? There's plenty to say. Poor Erica. I know how it is, so I do.' Denise, the pretty widow, barely forty then, at her father's funeral all those years ago. Juliet, seventeen, and with a teenage fury at her mother's practicality. Fussing over inane details like hymns and cars and flowers. Shaking her long shiny hair as she walked down the aisle after the coffin, basking, so it appeared to Juliet, in the sympathetic gaze of the church. And then, the strange keening noises at the graveside that sounded insincere, as hollow as the thuds of clay on the wood of the coffin. Juliet imagined her stoic father in there, hearing his wife's wailing, grateful for each shovelful that deadened the mortifying sound. As a teenager, she'd been suspicious that Denise, pretty and vain, had somehow tricked her more thoughtful father. Her mother was, unfairly she sees now with her own chastening experience of motherhood, the receptacle of much of her anger back then, but she'd swat it back too. God, the rows, the two of them hissing at each other like feral cats. Josh, unsettled, an introvert like his father, couldn't wait to move out of home and away from them both.

'You'll miss him now. You were thick as thieves, yourself and that boy, once upon a time. I remember you well as little kids. Inseparable.'

Miss him now? She's missed him her whole life.

'That's a lifetime ago.'

'Believe me, Juliet, a lifetime is no time at all. Anyway, I've a lasagne in the fridge that Johnny made. I'll drop it up to the house tomorrow, so I will.'

Rory's house. A 'supersize me' McMansion on a half-acre site, land once owned by the rugby club. Boxy Land Rover and sleek Audi in the driveway, sprinklers on the lawn. A far cry from the little cottage he grew up in – long since demolished –

that sat opposite the site and had a rotation of rusted, broken-down cars from his father's garage, some on concrete blocks, on the grass. He would have derived so much pleasure from being able to build a house like that in view of where that old cottage with all its ghosts stood. Trying to buy his way out of his shame.

A notion seizes her, and she stands abruptly.

'I'll drop it up now. She might be glad of it for dinner tonight.'

'It's far too late! They'll surely have had the dinner by now.'

'You'd never know. She'll be all over the place.'

'Erica O'Sullivan does not seem the type you just drop—'

Denise is interrupted by Ruby walking in. Her face lights up at the sight of her granddaughter and Juliet can't remember it being the same for her. Ruby sits on the arm of Denise's chair, takes her hand on her lap and strokes it. Juliet senses a purity in their relationship, love as strong as the mother–child bond but without the fraught tensions around responsibility or rebellion.

Denise sniffs the air. 'You smell gorgeous, Ruby.'

It's true, Juliet thinks. Her daughter is always so fragrant, like cherries and marshmallows. She thinks of herself and Maeve, doused in White Musk or Impulse, scents that would assault rather than caress.

'And that gorgeous sallow skin of yours.'

Denise's need to comment on appearance at every opportunity irritates Juliet. She says, 'Ireland is the only country in the world where sallow is used as a compliment. Everywhere else it implies you're dying of liver disease.'

Denise rolls her eyes at her daughter. 'Pity about them, though,' she says, pointing at Ruby's Birkenstock clogs. 'Why do all you girls these days wear such ugly shoes?' Then she pulls at her granddaughter's oversized sweatshirt. 'And hide your lovely figures in these yokes.'

Ruby laughs good-naturedly. 'It's so we can do stuff, Nana. Now, can I get you a cup of tea?' She lifts Denise's hand to her mouth and kisses it.

'No, love. A cigarette would be nice though.'

'Nana, you're a hard case.'

'A what now, Ruby? I don't understand all your New Zealandisms.'

'It just means you're very naughty, but I love you.'

This otherworldly daughter of hers, with her strange accent, dark eyes and olive skin, and those broad, high Polynesian planes of her face that are a replica of Tāne, as though she was created solely from his genetic blueprint, with Juliet merely her Celtic surrogate, carrying a child that bore no relation to her. Christ, though, the brutal pain of the birth was all hers, both buried deep inside Juliet and surrounding her, bearing down (how, *how* was that even possible?), so that she felt reduced to nothing but a squeezed, contracting cervix. As it was happening, she wondered if maybe she was hallucinating, that natural childbirth was in fact some kind of lie, because no other woman could have possibly gone through *this* and lived to tell the tale. Afterwards, she stared at the baby, trying to make sense of the alien, red-faced being, with her vernix-covered skin and cone head shaped by the forceps and ventouse needed to extract her, probably reluctant to meet a mother she sensed, even suspended in her dim, watery cradle, might not be entirely up to the job. Juliet didn't feel as she expected to feel. It wasn't as the books said, it was not love at first sight. Maybe Ruby's ambivalence towards her now is some kind of consequence of those first moments. She lay there, on a humid night, in a room on the ninth floor of Auckland City Hospital, Tāne gone home, longing, in a way that took her by surprise, for her own mother, who would surely know what to do. Wondering how to console this creature, worried that maybe some notion would just take her to hurl her out the window instead. 'Please, *please* check on us every few minutes,' she begged the tired midwife on night duty who must have thought she was mad.

'Ruby, I'm heading out now, have my seat.'

'I'm good beside Nana.'

Does her daughter need anything from her anymore? Juliet is the needy one now.

In the kitchen, she lifts the hearty-looking lasagne from the fridge then lays it down on the table in order to put on her shoes. As she does she thinks how Denise was on a perpetual diet when she was young: The Grapefruit, The Liquid, The Ryvita, The SlimFast, and the worst, The Cabbage Soup, when the putrid smell from the boiling pot on the element lingered for weeks afterwards. Her mother spent her entire life at war with her body. Juliet wonders if the cancer is its way of retaliating.

Once outside, she strides up the road with purpose. She could walk it blindfold, knows every curve and tree and pothole, the number of steps between pillars. It's both familiar and unsettlingly strange that she is here again. It's dusk. She misses these long Irish twilights. Night falls abruptly in Auckland, like the city doesn't give itself a chance to brood.

She passes Dan's old house and turns her head reluctantly. She can't go by it without experiencing a deep ache. All these dead boys. Dr Flynn lives there alone now, the older brother a surgeon over in the States, Mrs Flynn dead years ago, 'from a broken heart' according to Denise. Juliet was unmoved at the idea of that at the time, but now, from this distance, she finds she's more empathetic, being better acquainted herself with the failures and regrets of motherhood. The once-imposing house looks done in, the white rose bushes, Mrs Flynn's pride and joy ('She loves those flowers more than me,' Dan used to say), running wild, the long stems trailing the ground, heavy with dead blooms. There are mosses pushing through the tarmacadam on the driveway, curtain rails hanging askew. A solitary light is on downstairs, and Juliet imagines Dr Flynn moving like a shadow between rooms.

Just past the Flynns', where the hayfield used to be, is a new estate of red-brick houses. They played Irish bulldog, tip the can and catch there as young children and then, when they were a bit older, hid in the crumbling stone shed that used to stand at the edge of it and smoked stolen cigarettes. The first time she had sex with Rory was in that shed. The two of them so young, and trembling from more than just the cold. 'I always knew this would happen,' she whispered, guiding him into her and lying there, smiling up at him in the dark. 'Did you, now?' he said, and she could hear the slight curve on his lovely mouth. He was a virgin; she pretended she was too in some ingrained, barely conscious deference to his masculinity. But it felt like the first time for her anyway. Every time with him did. That was the same night Dan drowned, though they weren't to know that yet. It happened the next night too, when his body was found – those couple of weeks in the aftermath they'd been insatiable, looking for comfort from each other – and afterwards he cried, thinking about what they'd been doing as their friend was dying. 'We weren't to know,' she soothed, trying to convince herself as much as him. But she often wondered if the two events became joined in his head anyhow. Some bind of self-loathing trussing them together.

The moon is visible, hanging low and heavy behind a row of ash trees that borders the new estate. Juliet is glad they kept them. Maeve's old home sits opposite these new houses. The owners have extended and landscaped it extensively, but Juliet misses the previous façade. It's like an old friend with an ill-fitting facelift.

This whole road feels haunted, and she shivers.

As she nears Rory's house, her pace quickens along with her pulse, excitement coursing through her at the prospect of maybe getting inside. As a kid he was always reluctant to let anyone in. If you called, he never invited you. Instead, he'd shout behind him into the darkness, though you'd never hear a reply. Then he'd slam the door and march away with you purposefully, as though he'd been waiting all day to leave.

Poor Rory, his whole life an escape from that little house he grew up in, his drunk for a mother and weak father who at best ignored what was happening, at worst facilitated it. Such a toxic force, shame. It set him on an endless cycle of selfishness and self-sabotage. God, though, how he romanticised pain, believing himself unlovable yet, confusingly, so damaged and unhappy that he deserved *more* love. No wonder she was addicted. He was dopamine and cortisol, pleasure and pain, the drug and the withdrawal symptoms. He was love and hate.

She is slightly winded with anticipation walking up his driveway, so stops and looks in the window of the Audi. It's spotless. There's a pair of Ray-Bans in the well between the front seats. She can see him now wearing them, staring out to Alcatraz on the boat that took them for a cruise around San Francisco Bay. 'Imagine it,' she said, 'being locked up in there.' And she shivered in the strong breeze that whipped about them. He wrapped his arms around her then from behind and said into her ear, 'I'm in prison when I'm not with you.' She turned and they kissed and a little boy near them giggled and pointed, and Rory stuck his tongue out at him and winked.

His emails and messages were full of these hyperbolic declarations. Sometimes she suspected he loved the idea of them, the idea of her, rather than the reality. Her own messages were more tangible, corporeal, full of graphic descriptions of their lust and lovemaking. She sent him naked pictures of herself and asked him to reciprocate but he would ignore her request, quoting instead some Leonard Cohen line on longing that frustrated Juliet but also increased her desire. He knew how to play her. So she'd respond with another Cohen lyric, but something deliberately and exquisitely filthy. Cohen was perfect for that.

A feeling of righteousness settles inside her and calms her heart. He loved her. Maybe he couldn't marry her, but he loved her. And she could have forced his hand. Told him about the baby all those years ago. Really, when you analyse it, she allowed Erica to keep him. He only stayed for the boy, his own unhappy childhood making him acutely sensitive. She and Rory had known each other all their lives. They were a part of each other. She thinks of those books Maeve loved when they were teenagers, where true love could only be torturous, depraved. '"I *am* Heathcliff,"' Maeve used to sigh melodramatically. Well, she *is* Rory.

On the porch she doesn't hesitate and presses the doorbell. She waits a minute, then presses again. Through the thick veins of glass, he comes towards her. She closes her eyes. She is sixteen again.

'Hey,' a boy's voice says.

It's Rory. It's Rory standing there. He's come back to her. She always knew it would happen.

ERICA

She's standing in Rory's study for the first time since he died, drinking wine. This room, with its walls hung with framed business awards and publicity posters and newspaper cuttings, its air of professionalism and success, has always intimidated her. If she tries to pin it down, maybe it's a feeling of inadequacy. It's the same reason she's uncomfortable sitting in waiting rooms, filling out those forms that ask for her occupation. It always feels like a test she's failing. She mostly leaves that part blank.

There's a photo on Rory's desk of them on their wedding day, standing with Erica's mother and father. It's always made her sad that he has none displayed here of his own. She's felt so unmoored since her parents died. And also inadequate; surely, as the adult in the room, she should have achieved more by now? She thinks of that neat theory in pop psychology about how we all end up marrying our parents. Something to do with a basic compulsion to repeat, or an attempt to resolve some childhood issue. Freud, of course, the old pervert, would have said it was all about desiring the opposite-sex parent. Erica is sure these theories are suspect. She studied psychology in college – a worthy enough degree but also suitably vague for an averagely intelligent girl like herself who lacked any great ambition – and even as she was learning about them was told they'd been debunked. (Sometimes Erica thought the course should have been entitled *History of Psychology* or *Some Theories on How the Mind Works Now Considered Obsolete*.) But more than that, she feels them to be wrong, because her husband was as diametrically opposed to her solid avuncular father as it was possible to be.

Erica wasn't sure if her parents ever had romantic feelings towards one another, but it worked despite, or perhaps because of, that. The first time Rory visited her childhood home, he laughed and whistled the theme tune from *I Love Lucy* when he saw the twin beds in their room. It never occurred to Erica that her parents' sleeping arrangement was something to be mocked. Politely – always so polite – she did not point out that his parents' cohabitation of a bed in their smoke-yellowed bedroom was hardly indicative of a healthy marriage. You never went there with Rory. It was like squirting lemon juice into a paper cut. She learned from early on that his sense of humour was not robust enough to encompass his parents, or more specifically, his mother. But then, Erica thought his humour in general was an avoidance, a substitute for intimacy. When Rory made you laugh it felt like warmth.

Of course, none of this occurred to her back then. Why would it? Sitting down at the tennis courts as a teenager, pretending she wasn't looking at him as he played with his friends. Later, when she accompanied him to his gigs in local pubs, no pretence then, greedily watching him and basking in the heat as he sang, the promise of it. This boy whose looks were enough to make you forget your own upbringing, forget yourself. His beauty and voice like a trap, like staring down into a deep well that you might fall into if you weren't careful. Which is of course exactly what she did. Fall? She dived. If someone who looks like that loves you, you can't help but be grateful.

There's an eye-wateringly expensive bottle of whiskey Rory got as a present from his very first client, a musician, that has sat unopened for years on a shelf behind his desk. She remembers him researching it and his pride when he saw the price. Rory didn't like whiskey much, so Erica suggested giving it to her father who did, but Rory said it was too precious. And so, it has remained perched here like a useless trophy instead. She knocks back the last mouthful of wine, takes down the whiskey bottle, pours some into the glass, then sits at the large oak desk. She sips and grimaces; she doesn't like the taste, but she is grateful for the dulling warmth. She's not sure when it happened – when drinking changed from something that she appreciated because it made her feel giddy to something she appreciates because it makes her *not* feel. It's seeping out a bit since he died, maybe even a little before then, the drinking hours, from just around dinner to other times of the day. (But who's counting? He would be. *Well, that's what you get for dying on me, Rory.*)

She loosens the belt on her robe, rubs the back of her neck, her skin clammy after the bath. She opens his laptop, runs her fingers slowly over the keys. He loved typing. Said it was elegant, like muscle memory, like playing the guitar, a series of patterns and then a word formed correctly.

The laptop wallpaper is a baby photo of Charlie. Erica doesn't know how he could stand to look at it every day. She finds these photos too accusing now that he's almost an adult. Like she hasn't paid enough attention to time passing. The computer doesn't recognise her, of course it doesn't, and is asking for a four-digit PIN. She types in Charlie's birthday, one, eight, zero, four, and hey presto! It's both surprising and not that he used this date. She can hear her mother's voice, *Men must be allowed their secrets, Erica.* But surely it only counts if they're still alive? Anyway, she's not looking to find evidence of any infidelity, which is why most women snoop. She just wants to feel him again. She hasn't in so long.

She looks at his search history. The last thing he googled was the name of a comedian whose Irish gigs their events company organised. Before that, *Amateur MILF Porn.* She can't imagine looking up a porn site with your baby son smiling in the background, but he was good at compartmentalising.

Erica finishes the whiskey and pours some more. She leans back, swivels on the plush leather chair. She wonders if he ever masturbated here. She clicks on a website.

The woman in the thumbnail video that pops up has large breasts. In fact, as she scrolls through, she sees all the women on this particular site do. Enormous boobs and Rubenesque arses that seem to devour the lower half of the men they're straddling. (They all seem to confidently *straddle* away. Erica never went on top, not because of worrying how she looked, she simply wasn't sure how to *move* when she was mounted there. Was it a rising trot or a seated grinding gallop? She never much liked horses either, much to her mother's disappointment. They were so big and unpredictable.) When she first met Rory he claimed to be a *legs man*. She thinks he only said that for her benefit because she has small breasts, but also maybe to appear sophisticated, more your haute-couture-model sort of guy than a page-three-girl kind.

She watches one of the videos and finds it unarousing, like she's watching a nature documentary. The woman is vocal, she makes annoying gasping noises with each thrust, so Erica turns down the volume in case Charlie hears. She wonders what Rory made of that. He used to get annoyed at women's tennis matches on the television because of all the grunting and would have to watch them muted. Maybe he watched the porn muted too. Erica was never vocal during sex. It made her feel self-conscious. Even when she faked her orgasms, she did it by giving a sort of silent faux shudder and rolling her eyes back a little, as though she'd been electrocuted.

All that holding in, though. It came out in her dreams. When Charlie was a tiny baby and still in the NICU, she had a recurring dream that she'd given birth to him consciously and vaginally (as per her birth plan) and in this dream she alternated between bellowing like a cow and baying like a wolf. It felt primal and cathartic. She also dreamed that she was able to breastfeed him and would wake up, her gown drenched with milk. But whenever she deliberately tried to express for him her ducts would immediately dam up and refuse to surrender even the tiniest drop. 'They're not very large, are they?' one of the nurses said, as she attached the pump with one hand, cupping her other one under Erica's breast and bouncing it as though it was a market stall orange (satsuma, actually) that she was testing for juiciness. 'Didn't they grow much during your pregnancy?' Erica looked down at them and said, 'They were caught a little on the hop, to be honest.' *Poor wee things*, she thought.

She closes the video; it feels like another failed test. Sex, what to say about it? She and Rory hadn't slept together since her last miscarriage. She's never told anyone about this. That she was a substandard mother and wife. Who would she tell anyway? And they had their pragmatic ways of dealing with Erica's missing libido. Other people wouldn't have understood. But it worked fine for them.

Really, the only time in her life when she felt strong sexual desire was during her pregnancies, and more specifically while she slept during her pregnancies. Her dreams then were charged and sensual. Animalistic almost. This had been a strange, dislocating experience. One afternoon when she was pregnant with Charlie she was drifting off to sleep on their bed when Rory lay beside her and put his mouth to her bump. 'Hello in there, peanut,' he said. She ran her fingers through his hair and then, to his astonishment and her own, pushed his head down further. He looked up at her, a hint of a smile on his lips. 'I think I like you pregnant,' he said. And as his tongue explored, she blanked out almost, feeling as though her entire body was both reduced and magnified to that one tiny nub of her. A wave started in the pit of her stomach, and as the swell grew she became afraid of the intensity suddenly, as though she was about to be consumed by something vast and uncontrollable. It was like when she was a little girl, before her stutter was cured, and a stranger would ask a question and as she opened her mouth to reply, felt as though she was on the edge of some precipice, about to fall off. Didn't the French, who know a thing or two about sex after all, refer to orgasm as *la petit mort*? So she moved away from him. She'd read that during pregnancy a woman's body carries an extra forty per cent above the normal volume of blood and she wondered if it was all that increased liquid merging, like a confluence of rivers, in a very specific part of her anatomy as she lay down. It made her uncomfortable to think of it, because sexual longing seemed incongruous with motherhood, despite the two events being inextricably linked. Mothers are not supposed to be horny.

Sometimes in Erica's darkest moments she even worried that the rushing of blood to that part of her played some hand in her miscarriages. Blood that was meant to nourish the babies, instead feeding her selfish groin. Another theory to add to the list. There were so many – that felt more like accusations – that she'd been presented with over the years.

She had an incompetent cervix . . .

Or her womb was irritable, as though it had its own personality, like a grumpy old man . . .

Or worse, it was actively hostile, like an incalcitrant teenager . . .

Or her hormones were imbalanced . . .

Or it was her genes . . .

Or she'd eaten something poisonous . . .

Or she'd touched cat's pee leaving out the bins . . .

Or she was too stressed . . . or too thin . . . or too fat . . .

Or on and on and on . . .

The language always of failure. A very feminine failure. And then suddenly she was too old and her fertility, or more accurately *subfertility*, had fallen off a cliff (the only context in which she ever heard that phrase being used.) Men's fertility, it seems, declines subtly, gracefully, women's catastrophically. (And also, no-one ever suggested it was Rory's defective sperm that created a faulty foetus that couldn't go the distance.) But it was a relief in a way to be too old to get pregnant anymore. Hoping became such a prison, harder than the losing, in a way.

Anyway, Erica has a theory, her own empirically tested one.

How about you're thirty-two weeks pregnant with your first child and you come home from a happy outing spent nursery-furniture shopping with your mother and you go into your husband's study to excitedly show him what you bought and instead of finding him there you find a long note telling you how he can't do this, he simply can't carry on and he can't be any sort of a father and this baby and you and the whole world in fact would be better off without him. How about after reading those first few lines you frantically search the house and the garage half mad with fear and as you do all you can see is his mother's body in the nicotine-stained bedroom of her little cottage. How about you get in your car and drive to your parents' house to get help but you're so crazed, out of your mind, you forget to give way at a roundabout and the next thing you know you've woken up in hospital, to be told by a doctor that your little baby boy that you and your husband had agreed to call Charles after your own father was delivered by emergency caesarean and is in the neo-natal unit. And your husband? The one who left the note? This husband is sitting on the other side of you, sobbing into your hand, telling you he's sorry, things just got a bit too much for him, that's all. He didn't mean it, he didn't mean for you to find that note.

How about you're not sure, you're no expert and you've never put it to any of the gynaecologists or obstetricians or acupuncturists or herbalists or homeopaths or naturopaths or charlatans or influencers or online quacks you've looked to for answers because you want to protect this fragile husband of yours, but how about you think maybe your body, your womb in fact, holds the unbearable weight of this memory and is simply unable to get past it. That six or seven or ten or twelve weeks in, it suddenly remembers and, traumatised, flushes out its little occupant. That no amount of progesterone or needles or meditation or money or supplements or quack juice is going to remedy that.

She goes to his emails. His inbox looks very clean. He was always so ruthlessly organised. 'Tidy house, messy mind,' her mother would say but it was probably easy to be blasé when you had a housekeeper. They had abrasive old Maggie, who also doubled as Erica's nanny when required. (Her mother, for all her practical kindness, had a rich person's entitlement to other people's time.) There are a handful of unopened work-related ones. Business contacts who haven't heard the news or sent emails prior to hearing. She scrolls through, finds an unopened one from a contact she doesn't recognise, themightyquinn255@gmail.com, the subject line blank. She recognises the Bob Dylan reference; she's absorbed these song titles over the years, even though her taste in music diverges wildly from his. (Her 'sad girl' music Rory used to call it.) She pictures a middle-aged man with a goatee and band T-shirt, nicotine-stained fingers. He sits, stoned, in his studio flat that he had to move into after a divorce. She feels sympathy for this man, being slightly useless but without any malice.

She clicks on the email, feels a twinge of guilt at reading correspondence not intended for her. But something about the text and technology makes it seem less personal. Or maybe it's just this chair, the porn, the whiskey corrupting her.

There's only a couple of lines. Melodramatic nonsense about longing and despair. Like bad teenage poetry.

The image of a middle-aged man recedes, and she sees the vague outline of a young woman instead. The deal was that she must never be confronted with it. She searches through his past emails and folders but finds nothing else from this address. Even checks his trash folder but there's nothing there either. She sits with the words for a few moments, drains her glass, refills it. This quote is so fevered, intimate. Adolescent actually. And it crosses a line. The deal was there should be no emotional involvement. She googles it. A Dylan lyric, of course, how predictable. She almost pities this girl. Women don't naturally idolise Bob Dylan the way some men do. All those songs where a female's done him wrong. That man has a problem. 'Just Like a Woman' indeed. That song pisses her off more than most.

She types:

Oh, haven't you heard, darling? He's dead. Sorry if that scuppers any plans you had to fuck him.

So tell me, what was the arrangement between you two? Were you aware that he was married? Or does that make it more enticing for you? I'm genuinely curious, so be honest. I think you owe me at least that, don't you?

Mrs Rory O'Sullivan

The doorbell rings and she startles, hitting send as she does. She slams the laptop shut, feels a twinge of exhilaration, or at least a feeling of not being quite so deadened.

JULIET

Juliet opens her eyes slowly, just to cling to a few more seconds of this dream. The boy, Charlie, is standing in the doorway. His hair is sticking out at odd angles as though he's been lying down. His feet are bare and this, along with the dishevelled hair, makes her heart yearn for him. The likeness to Rory is both a kick and a balm. She finds herself mute.

His eyebrows are raised in expectation as he waits for her to speak. 'Will I get my mother?' he says eventually.

'Yes. Please. I brought . . .' She looks down at her empty hands, turns them over as though this could conjure the dish up. She's left it on her mother's kitchen table. 'Oh shit. I forgot the bastard thing.'

His face breaks into a smile and it's wide and open-hearted, and unlike Rory's which never looked entirely convinced of itself. Her heart swoops at the sight of it. 'That's pretty funny.'

She curtsies. 'I aim to amuse.'

'It's literally the first laugh I've had in a few days.'

'I can imagine.'

Looking at him is like a hypnotist's trick and she could just fall back into the past. She digs her nails into her palm to rouse herself.

'Well . . .' He scratches his head as though unsure of what to do with her. Rory called her a puzzle but it wasn't true. He only said that to let himself off the hook. She was straightforward in her desires for him. Charlie says, 'I'll get Mum for you. I think she's in Dad's study. Hang on.'

He disappears back into the hallway, leaving the door half-open.

Juliet pushes the door a fraction to get a better look inside. There's a table at the base of the grand staircase with a lamp and a bunch of white lilies lying on their side, still in their cellophane wrapping. Also on the table is a framed photo of Rory and Erica, who's adorably pregnant. Juliet did not do pregnancy adorably. She hated it, felt almost *violated*. Erica's wearing a bikini and a pair of unbuttoned jeans and Rory is standing behind her, his arms wrapped protectively under her cute protrusion of a belly, his chin on her shoulder. He's shirtless. She's jealous at first of the intimacy but the portrait, which she's sure was his idea, is tacky, reminds her of those Athena posters they all had in the eighties, and she experiences then a thrill of condescension. She tries to summon this sense of superiority over him when she's feeling abandoned. Focus on the corny aspects of his communication, the sentimental lyrics he'd quote, the hackneyed metaphors in his messages. Then she'd remember his struggles in school with reading and writing and feel tenderness towards him again.

Erica appears and is wearing a thick white bathrobe with a white towel wrapped around her head. Her skin is scrubbed-looking. She always had expensive-looking skin. Her cheeks are flushed which gives her a childlike quality, but Juliet is gratified to see the crow's feet around her eyes and the hint of crepiness at her neck. Your neck always gets you.

She has an almost blank gaze, her face an inscrutable mask. Juliet finds it mildly sedating, as though she's swallowed half a Xanax.

'Hello, Erica.'

'Hello there.'

Juliet wonders why she hasn't said her name. Her look is so cool and unsettling that Juliet then experiences a rush. Maybe she knows. Maybe Rory said her name out of context, and it raised suspicion. He'd called her Erica once. It was when they were fighting, so Juliet didn't mind. Maybe he called out Juliet's name when he had sex with Erica. After he left her in San Francisco and she had returned to Auckland, she sent him a message: When I'm fucking other people I close my eyes and pretend it's you.

She hadn't been with anyone else but had wanted to make him jealous.

He'd responded: Me too.

And she was devastated, knowing he still slept with Erica. Logically, she knew they must. But to have so emphatically replied? He did it deliberately, she knew.

I can't do this anymore.

She'd written it impulsively, then went out and hooked up with a guy despite his profile picture being a shirtless gym selfie. What she hadn't said to Rory was that lying under a body and fantasising it's someone else's is the loneliest thing in the world.

'It's Juliet.'

Erica seems to soften. 'Yes, I know. Sorry, Juliet. I'm just . . . I've been . . . I don't know which end is up.'

'Anyway, I had a lasagne. And then I forgot to bring it.'

'Thank goodness for that. I've about twenty of them in the freezer.'

Juliet is surprised at the candour. She's always imagined Erica as polite but humourless.

'Do you know what the funny thing is, Juliet? Rory hated lasagne. Have you ever heard of anyone who hated lasagne? It's like hating David Attenborough.'

It's such a strange thing to say and Juliet wonders if Erica *is* drugged. And no, Juliet did not know this about Rory. How could she not know this about him? She says, 'Well, I guess he did hate Christmas.' He'd said it was the one day of the year when he knew his mother – unpredictable in her binges – was guaranteed to be drunk.

Erica frowns. 'Rory? No. He loved Christmas. Goodness, he'd dress up as soon as Hallowe'en was over in that stupid Santa suit if you let him. Such a big kid.'

Juliet feels herself losing this edition of *Mastermind*, specialist subject Rory O'Sullivan. 'So . . . I just—'

Erica holds up her hands. 'I know, I know. You're very sorry for my loss. Please let you know if you can do anything, et cetera. Here's the thing, Juliet. What I'd really appreciate instead of the sympathy is someone who'll sit with me and share a bottle of wine.'

Juliet is astonished. She is being invited into the inner sanctum. 'Sure.'

Erica turns and walks down the hall like she expects Juliet to fall in line. As Erica passes the table with the unwrapped lilies, she stops and says, 'Lasagne and lilies. I despise the smell of lilies, it's exhausting.' She walks through into the kitchen.

Juliet hovers awkwardly in the doorway. 'It's a bit like coriander. You either love it or hate it.'

Erica turns around, looks confused, as though she's forgotten that Juliet was behind her. 'Oh, I see.'

The kitchen is huge, Juliet could fit her entire apartment in here. There's a right angle of couches at one end, a large rectangular island lined with stools in the middle and a dining table that could seat twenty comfortably standing next to a wall of glass bifold doors that look out over the lawn. Juliet tries to drink in the evidence of him here but there is too much to process, she feels blinded. She looks beyond the kitchen instead, out through the glass, and sees a garden shed. The idea of Rory as a man with a corrugated iron shed in which he might store a leaf blower or a step ladder seems absurd to her. In fact, the whole house and his role in it seems absurd. Did he make beds? Separate out the laundry? Put Erica's bloodstained underwear in the washing machine? Did he leave out bins, make Bolognese, pull out strands of hair from the drain?

Erica gestures to the stools and Juliet, giddy, takes a seat at the marble-topped island directly opposite the fridge that is covered in photos of Charlie.

'How's he doing?' Juliet asks, pointing at the pictures.

'So-so. This of course is the easy part, when everyone is rallying around him. There's a kind of morbid drama surrounding everything. Pretty soon everyone will go back to their own lives and I suspect that's when it will all begin in earnest. His sadness, I mean.'

Juliet thinks they are lucky to get this part, which is a main one. What is Juliet's role? A member of the Greek chorus? The audience?

'Yes, I'm sure it's unspeakably difficult for you.'

Erica looks at her and narrows her gaze. 'Thank you for saying that. Instead of being optimistically glib, I mean.' She moves over to the fridge, opens it and seems to space out for a few moments. 'I went to the supermarket today and bought salami. He was the only one who liked salami.' She makes a strange sound in the back of her throat then pulls out a bottle of white wine. 'Is this okay or shall I open some red?'

'That's grand.' Juliet finds she falls back quickly into the vernacular. The island is littered with debris. Erica makes no attempt to clear a space. She places a glass in front of Juliet and pours generously, then fills her own.

'Rory didn't like us drinking at home. He thought we should be setting a good example for Charlie. I thought he took it too far. Kids aren't going to become alcoholics because they see their mother enjoying a glass with dinner. He was so melodramatic.' She tips her glass against Juliet's. 'Sláinte,' she says, then gives a bitter laugh. She guzzles a mouthful and leans across the bench. Juliet realises she is, in fact, tipsy. 'Maybe if he chilled out a little, he wouldn't have had a heart attack.'

'I suppose it was his childhood that made him so vigilant,' says Juliet, glad at last to be able to state something irrefutable. She was there from the start, witnessed it first-hand. Erica only came in on the tail end of it.

Erica takes the towel off her head and drops it on the counter. Her blonde hair is thick and poker straight, even when wet. 'Oh yes. His childhood. At what point, though, Juliet, do you stop using it as an excuse?'

'An excuse for what?' *To fuck me?* she longs to say.

'Being sad. It becomes toxic after a while. They talk about terminal uniqueness in addiction.'

'I've never heard that term.'

'Rationalising your behaviour because you think your circumstances are particularly grim. It can kill you if you're an addict.'

'But it was his mother who was the alcoholic. Rory wasn't addicted to anything.'

'To his own pain he was.'

She is so sure of herself, of him. Erica reaches for the wine bottle then, and as she does knocks over a mug. The murky remnants splash onto the marble, but Erica makes no effort to clean up. The liquid starts to creep towards an unopened card nearby. Juliet has an urge to rescue it. She must have that ambivalence towards mess that comes from being wealthy. 'Too posh to clean,' Denise would say. The family were old-money horsey types, with their big property out the country. Back then, Juliet imagined them like the royals. Wankers in wellies and wax jackets.

Erica frowns then as though remembering something. 'Why did you say that thing at the funeral? About Rory wanting to be cremated.'

'I'm so sorry about that. I'd taken sleeping pills but hadn't slept. I was a bit out of it. It was just a remark he made when we were kids. After our friend Dan died.'

'Oh yes, Dan. Another one of Rory's sad stories.'

Juliet feels uncomfortable. Angry too, at the tone. 'Well, it was traumatic for a bunch of kids.'

'Of course. It was a horrible thing. But you'd swear he murdered the boy himself.'

Juliet thinks of Rory, distraught, the night of Dan's funeral, when she again offered herself up as consolation. *I'm a bad person, Jules. You need to stay away from me. Please stay away from me.* Which of course made her want him more.

'Well, we all blamed ourselves. It's what kids do.'

'Anyway,' Erica continues, as though they haven't just been talking about Dan, 'my father always said the way to carry on living is to nourish the soil you're buried in. Rory would have wanted that.'

Her sense of entitlement over him makes Juliet's stomach hurt. She takes a large gulp of wine and has difficulty swallowing it.

Erica yawns suddenly. 'Goodness, I'm sorry. I'm so tired. I wish I could go to bed for a year. Wake up and everything has been taken care of. That's what they don't warn you about. All the bureaucracy when your spouse dies. It's like extricating yourself from a cult.'

'Poor you.' Juliet hopes this came out as sympathetic, not with a sarcastic edge, as it sounded in her head.

'So, Australia, isn't it? How did you end up there?'

'New Zealand. Actually.' This will be her epitaph. (Or perhaps, 'Ireland isn't a part of the UK. Actually.' Both countries mere footnotes.) 'And you know, a guy. The same old story.'

She gives Erica the official accidental-emigrant version. Nearing thirty, meeting Tāne, the laid-back, good-looking, rugby-playing Kiwi, when he and a crowd of his rowdy mates were eating in the Temple Bar restaurant where she waitressed. Leaving Ireland to do some travelling with him for a bit of fun, falling pregnant accidentally and deciding to stay in New Zealand as a matter of convenience. In this official version, Juliet is an almost passive figure, tagging along with a man and fitting in with his life. The truth – that after Rory and Erica's wedding earlier that same year she had come to the end of hope, so she targeted Tāne, saw him as a way out of Ireland, a way out of loving Rory, and got herself deliberately knocked up over there because there could be no coming back from that – is a version she's never disclosed to anyone.

'So did you come all the way over for the funeral? I didn't think you and Rory were in touch anymore.'

'No, no. I was here anyway,' she lies. 'Visiting my mother.'

'And are you still together? With the guy?'

'Hell, no. We split when our daughter was three. I think Tāne enjoyed me at first. The impulsive, party-mad Irish girl. But the novelty wore off quickly. I thought another baby might fix things. But that didn't work out and things got worse between us.' Juliet pauses. Then, 'He's a good man, but he tired of my, quote unquote, "messy head-wrecking bullshit". What's appealing in a girlfriend is not so appealing in the mother of your child, I suppose.'

'Ah yes. It's always the way. What attracts them at first later repulses them.'

Juliet had been about to take another sip, but she lowers the glass from her lips in surprise. 'What do you mean by—?'

'More wine?' Erica interrupts, and without waiting for an answer empties the last of the bottle into their glasses. She appears composed of some sort of deflective material, fending off questions. She taps her finger against the side of the bottle so that her engagement ring makes a clinking sound on it.

It's a large, rectangular, platinum-set solitaire. Juliet sees Rory, at the cosy hotel bar on Drury Street when she'd travelled over to be with him three years ago, leaning towards her and looking into her eyes, as his finger made slow circles on the rim of her glass of whiskey in a gesture that almost made her lose her mind with desire. In San Francisco he'd taken off his wedding ring at her insistence even though he'd claimed not to understand why it was necessary. 'It's just a token,' he'd said. 'It's meaningless.' Juliet hid it the morning he was getting ready to fly home, so hurt that he was leaving early. 'Have you seen it?' he asked her, suspicious, as he lifted cushions and checked under the bed. 'Fuck, *fuck*,' he kept muttering, then kicked the leg of the armchair. 'What does it matter? It's just a token. Meaningless,' she taunted from the bed and he punched a cushion, furious. She walked down to Pier 39 later that night and was about to fling it into the water when she saw a blind man begging outside a restaurant, so dropped it into his cup instead. (Or maybe not so blind. 'Fuck you, lady,' he'd shouted after her. 'Fuck you too,' she'd yelled back.) It was petty, she knew, but then, the power she wielded over him was petty too.

'Were you two happy, though?' she blurts out.

'Goodness. What a question.'

Juliet shakes her head. 'I'm sorry. Maybe it's the wine.'

Erica looks at her as though weighing something up. 'Well, it's been hard, the last couple of years. Covid hurt the business.'

Yeah, Covid hurt us too. We couldn't see each other for two years.

'But . . . things were picking up,' Erica continues. 'Till now. Now he's gone.'

Gone. What a hopelessly benign word. If only he was just gone, then he could just return. He isn't gone. Or passed, a term that makes her feel murderous. And he isn't a soul reposing somewhere, a puzzling expression that makes her think of a corpse lounging on a La-Z-Boy. He's dead. Juliet swallows furiously to hold back the tears.

Erica waves the empty bottle. 'I'm going out to the garage to get another one.'

Juliet wonders if she had to hide them out there. When she's gone she notices a drawer beside the hob that's half open as though something is jammed in it. She walks over and yanks it free. It's full of bank statements, bills, invoices, insurance policy forms. Rory and Erica O'Sullivan printed at the top of everything, fully, officially entwined together. She pushes the drawer shut just as Erica walks back in. She looks quizzically at Juliet, who experiences a throb of exhilaration.

'Can I use your bathroom?' Juliet says, her heart beating rapidly.

'Of course. The flush is busted on the downstairs guest but there's another one at the top of the stairs.' She seems to remember something then. 'Rory said he'd sort it.'

The type of guy who fixed toilets? Ludicrous.

Juliet picks up her handbag from a stool. 'Period,' she explains and Erica grimaces sympathetically.

The wall leading up the stairs is covered in black and white framed photos of the family. They're arranged in chronological order, most recent at the bottom, so walking up is like time-travelling into the past. After Charlie's newborn photos she half expects a close-up of Erica's perfect vulva, with its delicately scalloped lips, effortlessly expelling a baby's head as if by peristalsis alone, no need for any vulgar pushing. She remembers then Maeve saying that Charlie was premature. So probably just lifted politely out of her belly, no need to sully the whole event by involving her genitals at all. Her vagina still pristinely intact. Her own is grievously war wounded from Ruby's traumatic birth, a scarred veteran back from a punishing tour of duty.

She stops at one near the top, a wedding portrait, Rory and Erica sitting at a table, the registry book opened in front of them. Rory's face looks unusually serious, his hand is hovering in mid-air gripping a pen and he is looking off to the side slightly. Waiting to be rescued maybe.

God, twenty years ago now. A couple of months before, she'd been in her flat on the South Circular Road getting ready to go to work in a pub on George's Street when she saw a call coming through from an unrecognised number. He left a long message. He'd run into Denise and got her number and he knew they hadn't seen each other in over ten years but, well, he still thought about her all the time, still dreamt of her actually, and he just happened to be in Dublin, and he just happened to have a spare VIP ticket to The Cranberries who were playing at the Point Depot that night and Dolores O'Riordan reminded him of her, kind of gobby, and, well, he wondered if she'd like to come. No worries if not . . .

And she definitely wasn't going to call him back after the first time she listened to the message but after the sixth time, she crumbled. And when Dolores sang a plaintive 'Linger', Juliet looked at him and decided she definitely wouldn't be a fool for him. And as they walked up Grafton Street, linking arms, to The Westbury, she decided she definitely wouldn't sleep with him. And in the bar and all the way upstairs, and then . . . And then the touch of his hand behind the closed bedroom door that destroyed her. He never once mentioned the wedding. She'd asked about Erica, but he'd been vague, dismissive, they'd been together so long by then it was as though their relationship didn't need clarification or discussion. Juliet woke up in the bed the next morning, alone. A note written on the hotel stationery. *Early meeting, Jules . . . Last night was amazing. I'd say you worked up an appetite. I certainly did! Breakfast on me so fill your boots, Rx.*

And then a message on her phone from her boss in the pub telling her he'd had enough of her bullshit and to come in and collect her P45.

She'd texted Rory over the next few days. He never replied. And in the post a month later a wedding invitation, *Juliet plus one* written in Erica's elegant cursive. The *plus one* enraged her but even as she held the invite in her hand she was sure he wouldn't go through with it. She didn't bother RSVP-ing.

Maeve told her later that it was opulent, a peak Celtic Tiger affair: a castle in Kildare rented for the weekend, helicopters and Dom Pérignon, three hundred guests, even a few of Rory's celebrity acquaintances. Juliet didn't turn up for her shift in the clothes shop on Henry Street that day, went drinking in The Bleeding Horse on Upper Camden Street instead and woke up the next morning, with no memory, in a bed with grubby sheets in some student flat in Rathmines, a saucepan beside the bed filled with black vomit that smelled like sambuca. 'No offence, missus,' a foetus in a beanie, sitting on a deckchair and toking on a spliff, said to her as she walked through the tiny sitting room to leave, 'but you should probably sort yourself out.' Juliet stopped. 'No offence either, little boy, but your own life choices don't look all that sound right now.' The boy looked her up and down. 'Ain't that the truth.'

———

The bathroom door is open; it looks as messy as the kitchen, globs of toothpaste like paint chips on the sink, splatters on the mirror, towels on the floor. An empty toilet roll sits forlornly on the holder. She walks in and shuts the door, opens the cabinet above the sink and sees a bottle of Armani cologne, with its distinctive black and gold lid. It's the same aftershave he wore in San Francisco. 'Mmm,' she'd said, fingering the collar of his shirt and burying her nose in his neck when they'd first arrived at the hotel, 'you smell like you'd be excellent at giving me financial advice,' and he'd laughed and wrestled her onto the bed. When she'd got home she went in to Smith and Caughey's department store on Queen Street to buy it but they told her it had been discontinued. She sprays some now on her throat and wrists, closes her eyes and inhales deeply. Just as she's about to replace it she thinks of Erica's knowing possessiveness and slips the bottle in her bag instead.

Back out on the landing, as her foot hovers over the first step, she hears a strumming of a guitar from further down the hallway. She turns and follows the sound and stops outside a closed door. 'The One I Love', one of Rory's standards. He discovered REM the summer of '88, played *Document* on repeat, then later *Green*. Rhapsodised on their genius. He was so articulate about music. His passion was attractive but also made her jealous because it seemed like nothing else could come close to touching him that way. Charlie's voice is just like his, sweet and sad. He's singing the line about the prop that occupies him. Funny, she used to think this was a love song. She places her hands on the door, leans her forehead against it and closes her eyes. When the song ends, she knocks.

'I'm busy.'

She opens the door anyway. Charlie is cross-legged on the bed, the guitar beside him. He looks embarrassed.

'Sorry, I thought you were Mum.'

'That was beautiful,' she says. 'You sound just like him.'

'Michael Stipe?'

'Yes, but also your dad.'

He nods, gives a shy, proud smile that makes her heart catch. 'Did you know him?'

'Yes, we were friends as kids.' Then, 'My dad died too, when I was about your age. It sucks.'

'Yeah.' He sounds choked, looks down, as though embarrassed by his emotion.

The guitar seems old, she wonders if it was Rory's. 'May I?' she says, gesturing to it.

He hands it over. 'Do you play?'

She sits on the edge of his bed, holds the guitar against her stomach and strokes one hand along the smooth upper curve of the body. 'I think my favourite part of you is this right hip,' Rory had said, running his fingers over the swell and kissing her there as she lay propped up on one arm on the bed in The Westbury.

'A little. Badly. Your dad tried to teach me when we were kids. About the only song I ever mastered well was a Tracy Chapman one.'

'Let me guess. "Baby Can I Hold You"?'

'How did you know?'

'It's the easiest one.'

She can hear Rory in the teasing edge to his voice, throws back her head and laughs, and he smiles, pleased with himself.

'Give it a go.'

'Shit, it's been years.'

He tilts his head to one side, a mannerism inherited directly from his dad. 'Please?'

'Oh, okay.'

She closes her eyes, thinks for a few moments, then takes a deep breath and starts to strum. Her fingers are clumsy and stiff to begin with but soon the muscle memory returns and they are somehow stumbling on the right chords, the lyrics bypassing her brain and forming in her mouth. She can feel him watching her. When she finishes she smiles to herself and opens her eyes. She starts when she sees Erica standing leaning against the doorframe, her arms folded, that impassive expression again. Erica claps, unsmiling.

'That was great,' Charlie says. 'Your voice has a Stevie Nicks vibe. Kinda sultry.' Juliet isn't looking at Erica but she senses her wince at this. 'You should learn "Landslide". I could teach you.'

'I think Juliet probably has to leave now, Charlie,' Erica says in a cold way. 'It's getting late.'

'Yes, I should go.' She hands Charlie back the guitar. 'Thanks, though. I enjoyed that.'

As she walks past Erica she catches a glimpse of confusion cross her face.

'You smell nice,' Erica says, frowning.

'Thanks, it's new.'

Erica walks behind her down the stairs as though shepherding her out. On the front porch Juliet turns. 'Thanks for the wine. I'm around for three more weeks so if you wanted to do it again?'

'Sure, I'll text you.'

As she walks away, she remembers she hasn't given Erica her number. She turns but the door is already closed.

There are no lights on in her mother's house apart from a flickering blue glow from behind the curtains in the front room. There's a deckchair on the lawn and she turns it towards the house and sits down. Looking in, she thinks of her father who, unable to sleep, would stay up late into the night watching old films. He loved Alfred Hitchcock. Juliet would watch them with him occasionally. She always felt that with her father, the only way to have his attention, to have him notice her, was to be directly under his nose. He tolerated her being there while he watched those films; it was probably easier that way, not having to engage with her. She would sit quietly, afraid to speak in case he suddenly objected. As she got a bit older she started to wonder what he saw in the films because she noticed an unsettling pattern. The women were weak or, worse, treacherous, the men innocents, victims of things they didn't do. Still, she sat through them, careful not to show her scepticism, grateful enough to be near him. She still misses him.

She takes out her phone, sees an email from Rory's address and is winded with the shock. Even his ghost is toying with her. She clicks on it with trembling hands and reads the reply to the Dylan lyric she sent him before she'd heard the news, when she'd been angry at his silence. And then the release and, despite herself, she laughs at the profane bluntness of it. Some heat beneath Erica's cool. She wonders who she thinks she's writing to. The idea of her suspecting an affair thrills her a little. He liked to keep her a secret. It feels good to know she exists, that she lives for someone else. Erica wants honesty. She'll give her honesty.

Then . . . she thinks of Charlie, standing barefoot on the doorstep. Thinks of herself after her father's death. She glances up towards the house again, the television off now and a desolate, lifeless look to the place. She recalls that summer, the unnatural energy of it. The summer of death bookended by those two devastating funerals. She puts her phone away without replying and quietly lets herself in.

―

1990. It was a year that sounded and felt futuristic and space-agey to Juliet. But more than that it felt kind of . . . hopeful.

Finally, they were leaving the tired old eighties behind, a decade that appeared neon and debaucherous and well, *sexy*, in proper places like London or New York but in a dreary inland town in Ireland seemed as monochromatic as ever, the pre-tornado *Wizard of Oz*. (A film they still showed on prehistoric RTÉ at every opportunity.) It might as well have been the fifties. Just another decade of recession and repression and emigration and unemployment. A decade of dead girls in grottos, dead babies on beaches, a failed divorce referendum, the insertion of the eighth amendment into the constitution. Juliet wasn't at all interested in current affairs, truth be told, but sometimes being in Maeve's house meant bearing witness to a monologue on these topics, amongst others, from her friend's mother, so you'd absorb things, whether you wanted to or not.

'Sorry about this,' Maeve would whisper, mortified, while Mrs Griffin pontificated on the overreach of the Catholic Church or how women had no autonomy over their own bodies or what a pathetic little country we were that people celebrated like maniacs over a *drawn* football match. But even Maeve's mother appeared more optimistic that summer. A woman was running for president and according to Mrs Griffin was even tipped to win. And one of Mrs Griffin's heroes, Nelson Mandela, had been released from prison and when he visited Dublin she'd stood with a crowd outside the Mansion House to greet him and his wife with a raised fist. Maybe things were looking up.

They had all turned or were soon to turn seventeen, something that moved them all much more than politics. Maeve and Juliet had always decreed seventeen the perfect number at which to lose their virginities. Not too young, not too old. The Goldilocks of ages. Rory claimed the age held a special place in music, an age so imbued with romance and symbolism that it was immortalised by artists such as Stevie Nicks and Bruce Springsteen and The Beatles and Janis Ian and ABBA. Dan argued with him and said it was simply a fitting number with the optimal amount of syllables that handily rhymed with other words. 'Try substituting the word *twenty* instead,' he said, 'see how inappropriate that sounds.' Rory sighed and called him a philistine with no vision in his soul. Juliet would say nothing during these debates, she was just happy to listen to Rory. There was something intoxicating about hearing him speak so passionately on a subject. She'd close her eyes and imagine him talking about her in the same reverential tones he reserved for music.

The romance of their age aside, there was still all the drab mundanity of school and parents to contend with. Breaking up for the holidays that summer felt particularly special because come September they would be heading back for the dreaded final year, full of college applications and exam pressure. They all planned to go to college apart from Rory, who just wanted to become wealthy in some vague, unspecified way. Maeve planned to study English in Trinity, Dan wanted to do something that would annoy his father, like drama or philosophy, perhaps both combined, to doubly enrage him.

Juliet knew that to have any chance of getting into NCAD to study fine art she would have to be on her best behaviour, not having had the most auspicious of penultimate years. As far as talent went, she was easily the best art student in school but staying out of trouble was always more difficult. She'd been suspended twice, first for writing 'But Where the Fuck is The Clit?' in coloured chalk over a very basic and inoffensive outline of the female reproductive system – which resembled in fact a hollowed-out ram's head – that her biology teacher Miss Dolan had drawn on the blackboard. (The lesson? Basically, as women, they and their bodies were mere empty receptacles, just waiting to be filled – by penises, sperm, babies . . . hell, maybe even sheep brains.) When Miss Dolan asked who'd written it, though probably already knowing, Juliet raised her hand and said, 'But Miss, God Himself must be proud of the clitoris, the only organ in the human body devoted purely to pleasure.' Miss Dolan had reached the limit of her patience with Juliet, who only a few weeks before had raised her hand and asked if the rhythm method of contraception, the only one sanctioned by the church and thus their science curriculum, meant screwing in time to the Ave Maria. The second suspension was for getting caught behind the bicycle sheds with a cigarette in one hand and the other down the trousers of a boy from Saint Brendan's. 'I was only trying to find his Zippo,' she protested to Sister Michael. Honestly, for a group of people totally obsessed with sex, or at least sexual sinning, the nuns had zero sense of humour about it.

With regard to parents, they were all mortified by their own to a greater or lesser degree. Denise was a constant source of irritation for Juliet. Young and pretty, she'd won a 'Sally O'Brien' lookalike competition in O'Malley's in the early eighties and never shut up about it. Sally O'Brien was a fictional character in a popular television ad for Harp Lager, whose provocative glance apparently – according to Denise anyway – drove men around the country wild with desire. As for her father, he was a mystery to Juliet and yet she adored him, in a way that felt theoretical, slightly removed, how she imagined the nuns at her school might adore Jesus. (Although sometimes, to be honest, Juliet thought they harboured more than just platonic feelings for the Son of God. There was something almost *fetishistic* about their devotion.) There were rare lapses in his aloofness, if he'd had a whiskey or two, and then she'd bask in the brief warmth, like some sun-deprived Irish tourist in Spain. 'My old segotia,' he'd say, messing her hair. But while he was often austere and formal with his children, he was strangely indulgent around Denise, and there seemed no way for Juliet to compete with her for their father's affection because she could think of only one reason for the spell he seemed under in her presence. Sex. When Juliet was eight she'd walked into her parents' bedroom one Sunday morning to be confronted by a baffling, twisted configuration of limbs and hair. From somewhere within this bestial form Denise's damp and flushed face had emerged and mouthed at Juliet to get out. The other half of the muddled mass on the bed didn't alter its rhythm, seemed totally blind to the interruption, or at least too in thrall to its own momentum – like one of those swinging pendulum desk toys – to be able to stop itself. In that moment Juliet, though not understanding what it was she was witnessing, nonetheless believed in her mother's superior agency in it.

Maeve didn't know her father. Everyone called her mother Mrs Griffin (except in school where she was known as '*The Griffin*' after the legendary Greek beast with an eagle's head and talons and the muscular rear legs of a lion) even though Maeve told Juliet that she'd never been married but that when she applied for her teaching jobs she had to pretend she was a widow. That's how backward Ireland was. Maeve said that her mother told her she was the product of a one-night stand in Paris with a stranger. No-one bought that, least of all Maeve. 'I bet he was some muck farmer from Portumna,' Maeve would say glumly. 'I mean, look at my hair, for fuck's sake.'

But it was the boys who fared worst when it came to parents. While Juliet and Maeve might have found theirs, or specifically their mothers, embarrassing, it was nothing like the distress Rory and Dan carried. No-one saw much of Rory's mother; she was like a ghost in a dressing gown hovering in the background of their run-down little house. He never spoke about her but it was common knowledge that she was an alcoholic. Denise said she was once a pretty and promising young textiles student but had to leave Saint Martin's college in London when she became pregnant to a good-looking young Irish mechanic who had gone over there to try his luck. 'He came back to Ireland with more than he bargained for,' Denise would say, meaningfully. Juliet could see that Rory wore his shame about her like a brittle armour. So she always forgave him his occasional cruelty because she understood it to be a defence tactic. Throwing barbs before anyone could inflict their own. The stories about Mrs O'Sullivan were legendary. Inebriated early-morning car crashes into the rugby club walls, late-night wanderings to neighbours to beg for wine on the pretence that she was throwing a dinner party, extra money paid to the delivery guy from the local Chinese takeaway to bring a bottle of gin along with her beef in black bean sauce. Even rumours that she had stolen painkillers from another neighbour who was dying of lung cancer. Rory carried a lot of resentment too towards his father, who seemed like an ineffectual figure in their family's life. From what Juliet could see, he enabled his wife's addiction or maybe just turned a blind eye. Probably the poor man was simply beaten down by it.

Dan's parents were even worse. Dr Flynn was domineering and cruel, the sort of man who'd spend the day in his surgery, behind his oak and leather desk, smug in the knowledge of his superiority over his patients. Passing down prognoses and prescriptions like a judge. Lecturing the peasants on their lifestyles, reserving a special contempt for 'fat, lazy housewives'. Mrs Flynn meanwhile appeared zombie-like for much of the time, a strange, shutdown look on her face. 'The lights are on but nobody's home,' Rory would say. According to Dan, this was courtesy of a special cocktail of Prozac and Valium. ('My mummy has two little helpers.') He told Juliet that he walked in one time on his mother writing her own prescription out on Dr Flynn's pad that she must have stolen from his surgery. Juliet thought that if she was married to Dr Flynn, she'd be doubling down on the tranquillisers too.

—

One muggy evening that summer the four of them were gathered in Dan's sitting room, discussing some gossip passed on gleefully by Denise about a particular neighbour, an MEP with a wife and six children, who, it was discovered, had a whole other family living in Brussels.

Dan said, 'You know, I don't understand them. I mean, it's not rocket science. Meet someone, get married, be nice to them, have children maybe, be reasonably nice to them too. Where's the difficulty?' They didn't usually hang out in the Flynns' house, as the tension between Dan and his father was excruciating to be around, but this particular night Dr and Mrs Flynn were out for dinner and not expected back till late. *Top of the Pops* was on the television, and they were semi-engaged with it. Juliet had brought bags of Skips crisps and Penguin bars from her house and the evidence of empty wrappers was littered all around the floor.

The rest of them nodded sadly. Adults were total fuckups, incapable of running their own families, never mind the EEC.

'At least it gives us something to strive against,' said Rory. He was lying on the floor, his head propped up against the base of the couch. He never seemed to be able to sit normally on furniture, was always too restless. Juliet was beside him, cross-legged, her thigh resting against his shin. She was in her usual state of agitated happiness that possessed her when she was in his presence. She had a constant need to be touching him in some way. Maeve made fun of her over it, called her Rory's limpet, but honestly it was a barely conscious decision. Sometimes she would startle suddenly when she'd find her hand had made its way on to his arm. It was like waking abruptly after being hypnotised. Maeve had asked her once when she'd stopped seeing him as a platonic friend. Juliet couldn't explain. She'd known him since she was five years old and in the same class in their local little primary school, and the truth was there was no revelation, she'd simply always loved him. Maeve might as well ask when she became aware of her own selfhood. And now she longed to be with him in every way imaginable.

'Write something on my back, Rory, and I'll try and guess what it is.'

Rory sighed. 'Seriously? Are we seven?' But he traced a word anyway, his fingers deliberate and unhurried on her back. It seemed to Juliet as though a direct line ran from them to her groin. A pleasant ache tugged at her. She closed her eyes, imagined his fingers moving in slow circles between her legs.

'Blow job,' she said.

Rory sighed. 'No, Jules. *Bon Jovi*.'

'Go again.'

'Big dicks!'

'No, *Bob Dylan*. I'm not playing this anymore. You're a total pervert.'

'It must be your terrible spelling. Thicko.'

Rory pushed her from him and sat up on the couch.

'Sorry,' she said. 'I was only messing.' She tugged on his shirt sleeve, but he pulled his arm away.

'I think I'll go home,' he said, his jaw set. 'This is boring.'

Juliet had a sick feeling, like she'd ruined things. He could turn his coldness on you in an instant. Make you feel as immaterial as a ghost. As absent as his own mother.

Boy George came on the television then, singing in a white flowing robe, and Dan, who'd been sitting with Maeve sharing a cigarette and blowing smoke up the chimney, stubbed out the butt, jumped up on the couch beside Rory and started to gyrate suggestively along to the song. He loved to dance. When they went to discos he spent the entire night on the floor, not like Rory who only got up for 'The Whole of the Moon' where he and the other boys swayed with their arms around each other as though they were in a sporting huddle.

'You can't possibly leave now, Rory,' Dan said, his dancing becoming more outrageous. 'I'm just getting going.' Rory started laughing and hitting his ankles with a cushion trying to make him stop. That was the thing about Dan, he'd always pull you out of your mood somehow.

Just then the door to the sitting room opened and Dr Flynn walked in. Dan hopped off the couch, breathless, and sat down beside Rory. Dr Flynn turned the big light on and Juliet thought she'd never seen anyone cast such a shadow. Whenever he appeared, Dan's star dimmed. Immediately the atmosphere became tense and brooding. Juliet got off the floor. Maeve waved her hand in front of her to dispel any lingering smoke. Rory bent down and started picking up the empty wrappers around his feet.

'Why are you home so early?' Dan asked, making no effort to keep the resentment out of his voice.

Dr Flynn eyed Dan coldly and then sat down in his armchair. It was a deep red leather monstrosity with a mahogany side table by one arm that had a Waterford crystal decanter and glass permanently perched on it. 'Welcome to this extension of my father's no doubt tiny, flaccid penis,' Dan had said, doing a pirouette, when they walked into the room, which was opulent but ugly in a masculine way. Framed medical degrees adorned the walls, a collection of antique hunting knives hung over the fireplace, rugby and golf trophies stood on display in a glass cabinet. There was a trophy in front of the others that Dr Flynn had won for getting a hole-in-one at his local golf club. Dan said he'd told the family, without any self-consciousness, that it was the best day of his life. 'Stupid prick.'

'Your mother wasn't feeling well,' said Dr Flynn. 'Tremenjus waste of a perfectly cooked steak.'

He poured himself a large one. 'Who's that gobshite?' he said, gesturing at the television. He appeared almost jovial. He did that sometimes, attempted to inveigle himself into the conversation, as though they would think him funny. But the humour was always cruel and usually at the expense of his son.

Dan said nothing, probably sensing how the conversation would go. There was no way Dr Flynn wasn't aware of Boy George's existence.

'Boy George, Dr Flynn,' said Maeve a little too brightly.

Dr Flynn made a disparaging sound. '*Boy?*' No wonder he has to clarify that. Otherwise, we'd have no clue what it was, eh, Rory?' He gave a short mean bleat of a laugh. 'Dirty shirtlifter.' Rory looked away, refusing to engage.

It was such an ugly expression, Juliet felt it viscerally. She looked at Dan, who was staring at his hands. Earlier that day, bored, Juliet and Maeve had taken a hand each in Juliet's bedroom and using Denise's varnish painted his nails a fluorescent pink. Juliet was suddenly sick at the thought that his father might notice, and she tried to catch Dan's eye, but he wouldn't look up. She silently willed him to stop drawing attention to his hands, but he carried on staring at them and turning them over. Juliet realised then that he was doing it deliberately. Maeve must have been conscious of it too because she jumped in and said, 'So . . . how was work today, Dr Flynn?'

He sighed and leaned back in his chair, delighted with the opportunity, and proceeded to rant at length about time-wasting patients suffering with nothing more than a dose of women's troubles.

As he spoke, Juliet could see Dan shift uncomfortably. When he finished, Dan said, 'We're leaving now.' They all stood up to go, relieved, and then the phone, which was sitting on the side table next to Dr Flynn's decanter, started to ring.

'Get that, Daniel, will you?' said Dr Flynn, despite the phone being within his own easy reach.

Dan sighed but walked over anyway, his shoulders rounded, and put his hand on the receiver. Juliet saw something flash across Dr Flynn's face then as he looked at his son's nails. He lifted his own hand and swiped Dan's away, as though it was a diseased fly. His jaw squared, and maintaining steely eye contact with his son he picked up the receiver himself.

'Yes,' he barked into the mouthpiece. He shifted forward while he listened, and as the one-sided conversation continued he moved his eyes away from Dan and fixed them on Juliet instead. It was disconcerting. Juliet felt a coldness run over her, as though she'd made some terrible transgression. It occurred to her that she was in trouble in some way. Which was not unusual. But the nuns, even Sister Michael, were pussycats compared to this man. His gaze was so brutal, for that moment she understood how it might feel to live in Dan's body. She shivered involuntarily.

Eventually, Dr Flynn spoke. 'Calm down, Denise. Now, I want you to hang up and call an ambulance. Do you understand me? I'll be down to you shortly.' He replaced the receiver.

Juliet could feel something loosen in her stomach. Her mind went blank except for a single word. *No.*

She pointed at the phone.

Dr Flynn stood up and cleared his throat. 'Now, Juliet. Try not to get hysterical but it appears your father has just collapsed. Heart attack, I suspect. Fatal too, by the sounds of it.'

That's the way he said it. No hesitation. No gentle cushioning. It was pitiless. Rory touched her arm, but she flung it off. Her entire body was shaking uncontrollably. It was the most bizarre sensation, as though her nervous system had been suddenly overloaded by some drug. Despite her profound distress, there was a part of her that looked on, disconnected, intrigued by this phenomenon.

'I'm going down to your house now. You stay here. You'll only be in the way.' When he saw she wasn't paying any attention to him he looked at his son. 'Daniel, don't let her go.'

But Juliet was already out the door and none of her friends made any attempt to restrain her. They knew better than that.

MAEVE

She pulls up outside a yellow bungalow that's situated a few miles from Ballyboyne, out the Dublin Road. Were it not for the Alzheimer's Society Day Centre sign on the wall it could pass for a large, well-maintained family home. There's a water feature on the gravelled area to the front and a wooden bench where a man and woman – in their nineties maybe – are sitting, laughing, their hands clasped. What could make you so happy when you're that old and the past isn't available to you anymore? Surely not the future. Only the present left.

It's been three days since Rory's funeral and Maeve can't shake the sticky nihilistic angst that's clung to her since then.

Maybe her mother feels the same. She has been happily coming here once a week for the past year but now she eyes the place with disdain, or fear. 'Did I do something wrong?'

'You like this place, Mam.'

'I do not. I have never been here. And don't tell me what I like.'

'Fair enough.'

Maeve looks at her and wonders what it would be like to be missing pieces of yourself. If we are made up of our memories, our past versions of ourselves, then who are we if we forget? Maybe it's freeing, leaving regret behind.

Walking her to the door, Maeve thinks of herself in early motherhood, leaving the boys to creche. Luke would happily be handed over to anyone, but Jamie would throw himself dramatically on the floor and cling to her ankles as she tried to walk away. 'Just leave,' the kind staff would reassure her, 'he'll be grand once you're gone. And don't turn around.' She always would, of course, and be punished like Lot's wife to see him being held back, his face wet and puce, his little arms reaching in distress. Maeve used to pretend to the staff that she had an office job to get to because she felt such guilt that she was only heading straight home to work on a book that nobody was expecting or asked her to write in the first place.

On the doorstep she says, 'Are you okay, Mam?'

'No, I'm not,' she replies matter-of-factly.

Maeve can only nod in empathy.

'Lily! So nice to see you again.' One of the volunteers, Ted, walks out and links her arm.

'I've never met you before in my life.'

Ted winks at Maeve and says, 'Ah now, Lily, don't be like that. Didn't we dance together last week, you old tease.'

Maeve enjoys Ted's refusal to humour his charges despite all the literature that tells you never to contradict. ('Let the patient save face.') Maeve thinks her mother appreciates Ted too. She'd rather be dead than condescended to.

When she reaches the gate of the centre she turns around to wave but her mother has already disappeared from view.

In the car, as she indicates left at the end of the small side road the centre sits on, she sees a discarded bin bag caught on a hedge, its entrails seeping out through a gash in the plastic. She thinks of the mess from the morning left in the kitchen: the cereal cementing on breakfast bowls, the crumbs on the countertop, the dregs of browning banana smoothie in the Nutribullet. She thinks of the dirty PE kits and soiled underwear and basket of orphaned socks in the utility room. She thinks of the unmade beds, the clutter on bedside tables, the smeared mirrors. She thinks of the hardening globs of toothpaste on the bathroom sink and the collection of jumbled shoes inside the front door. She thinks of her laptop with its incomplete *Sylvia* manuscript.

And she thinks of Rory, laid out in his coffin, his face changed utterly as though it was his personality that gave it structure, not the physical bones and muscles.

She takes her phone from her bag and messages Cillian, who left the house early for a CrossFit session. Mam at Day Care. They'll drop her home in the minivan at 4. Have meeting with agent in Dublin I forgot about. Will be back at dinner time x.

Then she flicks the indicator to signal right. Away from Ballyboyne and towards Dublin.

The meeting's a lie. She was woken at 5.30 a.m. by the sound of Cillian's alarm, set to a high volume because of the ear plugs he wears at night to block out Lily. She'd been up till midnight trying to work, was woken at two by the sound of her mother's cries through the baby monitor, so was annoyed at this unnecessary intrusion into her sleep. He could go and star jump pointlessly around the gym anytime. She pretended to be asleep as he dressed and performed his ablutions, which reverberated noisily around the ensuite. She imagined him and the other males grunting around the class, like a troop of gorillas. Men get obnoxiously loud as they age, she thought, take up more air.

Lying in bed, she shrank into the sheets, seethed silently.

She'd dropped the boys to school before bringing her mother to the centre. Jamie was beside her in the front passenger seat. Someone came on the radio complaining about the one-parent family payment which, they asserted, was both encouraging promiscuity *and* bankrupting the taxpayer at the same time. This small payment, apparently, was ruining the country, both fiscally and morally.

Maeve turned it off in disgust. 'Oh *sure*. Eight men have more money than four billion people in the world and the single mum with a couple of kids is the problem? Give me a break.'

Jamie sighed. 'What do you want those guys to do? Give away the money they worked so hard for? They made it. That's just the way the world works.'

Maeve looked at him in disbelief, wondered if it was abnormal to sometimes dislike your own child. His attachment to the idea of the natural and intrinsically just hierarchical character of life is so at odds with her own.

'Yes, Jamie, that's exactly what they need to do. They didn't get rich in a vacuum. The accumulation of extreme wealth depends on exploitation of workers and tax breaks and loopholes and lobbying and access to power that's beyond the reach of everyone else. They don't, as you say, *make* money. They just take it. It's an immoral system.'

'What's immoral is those women. Everyone knows they get pregnant on purpose to trap men and exploit the system.'

It was like he'd kicked her. 'What? That's bullshit, Jamie. I can't believe you would say something like that. Can you hear yourself? You know I was raised by a single mother and let me tell you—'

He interrupted her. 'Oh. My. God. Can you hear *your*self? You're literally screeching.' Then he stuck in his AirPods. Maeve wondered if he was receiving subliminal right-wing messages through them.

'I love you,' she called after them both when they got out of the car, feeling bad about the disliking thing. Neither of them heard her but a group of boys walking in behind did and pointed and laughed. 'I'll be sure to pass it on,' one of them said. Maeve turned puce but was slightly consoled by the fact that it wasn't only her own teenagers who were assholes.

—

After forty minutes or so of driving she sees the sign for the airport and takes the off-ramp. It's busy and she experiences a buzz of anticipation joining the queue of traffic. The airport inspires her. Every single suitcase-laden car on this route contains so much story, holds so much humanity. Holidays and homecomings, reunions and separations, emigration and immigration, bereavements and births and business and pleasure. All of life.

She parks in the multi-storey and walks the short distance to Terminal 2. In the café in the arrivals hall she takes a suspiciously shiny muffin from the display cabinet and orders a coffee, then sits at a small table at the edge of the semi-circle of seating, observing. Two young women with smooth, tanned skin and hefty rucksacks stand looking confused under a display screen. *Run*, she would like to say to them. *Escape!* A middle-aged woman is berating her husband for something while he stares up at the ceiling. A child in pyjamas is having a tantrum on the floor while his parents pretend not to notice. A recently reunited couple standing nearby kiss passionately. The man's large hands cup the woman's face, his thumbs rest on her cheekbones, his fingers laced through her black hair. They can't be married she thinks. Marriage kills kissing.

When she's finished eating, she exits the terminal, validates her ticket and heads back to the carpark.

An old woman is looking across the sea of vehicles, scratching her head. 'Can I help?' Maeve asks. Worries then she is being patronising, so adds, 'Sorry, you're probably fine.'

'I can't remember where I left it,' she says. 'I was just dropping my son and grandchildren off. They're back to Australia, you see.' Her eyes are pale and wet. Together they track the car down eventually, and as Maeve turns to leave, the woman tries to give her ten euro. Maeve is mortified and pushes her hand away, so the woman hugs her.

'Thank you now,' she says into Maeve's shoulder. 'Thank you.' And Maeve sees herself then in thirty years' time, wandering lonely and bewildered around cavernous carparks while her children get on with their own lives. Trying to pay strangers for a tiny kindness.

She's still thinking about the woman when she gets to the roundabout and instead of taking the right turn towards the motorway turns left towards the nearest airport hotel.

'You're in luck. We have a room available,' the pretty young woman with a strong eastern European accent at reception tells her, checking the screen.

As Maeve hands over her credit card she says in a way that she hopes sounds businesslike, 'Can I get a wake-up call for five a.m.?'

The woman types on her screen. 'Of course. Do you require help with luggage?'

'No,' says Maeve. 'I'm travelling light.'

The room is soulless but smells of other people's routines. She takes the cushions and throw off the bed, tries not to think of what bodily fluids may be present on them and stuffs them away in the wardrobe. She removes her shoes, switches off her phone and lies down. She's so tired.

When she wakes, the light coming through the net curtains has changed. The clock radio beside her bed reads 4 p.m. She's been asleep for hours. She takes a shower and uses the hotel toiletries that are all fixed in a mean-spirited way to the wall in large pump dispensers. Afterwards, as she dresses, she regrets not bringing a change of clothes. It feels seedy putting on dirty underwear from the bathroom floor, like she's made questionable choices. She will leave them off. This also feels seedy, but with a redemptive edge of wantonness.

Downstairs, the cocktail list is quite retro and she takes a seat at the bar and orders a Cosmopolitan. They thought themselves so sophisticated drinking them around the turn of the century. (This phrase still conjures up images of the Victorian era for her. How is it possible she is this old?) She also orders a Caesar salad without chicken because chicken that other people have cooked always unnerves her. She finds she needs to forensically examine it for pink bits. The salad arrives with the chicken, but she doesn't like to complain.

She likes airport hotel bars. Everyone appears more interesting and she finds herself more interesting in them. She wonders if other people look at her, as she does them, and speculate on her story. Or is she just as invisible here? The bar has two wall clocks and a television screen in the corner that lists the departures and arrivals. A man sitting beneath the screen is reading a newspaper and eating what looks like a fried breakfast. It's like some broken portal here; time moves differently, is both important and meaningless.

She hears a jangle of jewellery and turns to see a woman, perhaps in her mid-thirties, claim a spot a couple of stools away. She's tall with black, chin-length hair and a straight short fringe – the kind only certain people could wear without looking deranged – which draws attention to her angular face with its expertly applied graphic eyeliner and red lips. She's wearing gold hoop earrings that bounce and catch the light when she turns her head. She isn't beautiful exactly, arresting maybe. It's a quality that reminds her of Juliet, and arouses a desire in her to keep looking.

The woman smiles at her. The contrast between her glistening white teeth with their attractively pointed canines and the matte red of her lipstick is so stark that Maeve is momentarily dazzled. She is still disproportionately impressed by good teeth. Maybe it's an Irish thing. (Juliet told her that bad teeth are referred to as 'British' in New Zealand. 'At least not Irish then,' said Maeve. 'Same diff to Kiwis, to be honest,' said Juliet.)

An image comes to her then that shocks her, of this woman's mouth on her navel.

'Hi.'

'Hiya.' Maeve blushes at how unsophisticated this sounds.

'Flight cancelled too?'

'Yes,' Maeve says, rolling her eyes. Which maybe is a bit much.

'Utter shitshow in that airport. Where were you going?'

'London.'

'Snap. You live there?'

'No, just some business. You?'

'Live there. Here for work.'

'What's work?'

'Advertising copywriter. You?'

'Writer. Novels. Ugh. I still can't say that without feeling silly. Admitting I sit in a room and make things up.'

The woman gives a throaty laugh. 'What kind of novels do you write?'

Maeve waves her hand. 'Just your by-the-numbers thrillers. Not exactly Nobel Prize-winning stuff. Perfect airport books, I suppose. Even though, as a genre, I'm not entirely sure what that means.' Oh God, she's babbling, words erupting vomitously from her mouth.

'Listen to you. Putting yourself down,' the woman says. She looks coolly at the young barman who's standing in front of her drying a glass. 'You guys would never do that, would you?'

The barman shrugs. 'Leave me out of it. I'm just here to get the drinks.'

'Ah, so young, but so wise.' She grins at him. 'Okay, a glass of Syrah for me. And . . .' she looks at Maeve, 'is that a Cosmo?'

'Oh Jesus, busted. It's a bit 2001, isn't it?'

The woman laughs again. It's such a gratifying sound; you could spend your life trying to hear it. 'So retro it's actually on trend. Let me buy you another. I've an underused expenses account and a twat of a boss that both need exploiting.'

'That sounds lovely. The drink, I mean. Not the twatty boss bit. Thank you . . . eh?'

'Nisha.' The woman pats the stool beside her. 'Join me, I can pick your brains. I've a manuscript languishing in the proverbial bottom drawer that I'm unsure what to do with.'

Maeve can't imagine anything to do with this woman languishing, but she says, 'Okay,' then moves along and holds out her hand. 'Maeve.'

Nisha takes her hand. 'Maeve. Beautiful. It really suits you.' Hearing it on Nisha's lips, for the first time in her life Maeve loves her own name.

'Thank you,' she says, blushing again, as she settles into her seat.

'So, what is it that attracts you to crime writing?'

Maeve puffs out her cheeks. 'God, there's a question. Eh . . . I'm going to say my father?'

'Oh, it's always the father's fault. If we can't blame the mother, obviously. How did yours fuck you up?'

'Well, honestly, I don't know a thing about him. My mother has kept it to herself. So my husband – who's a psychotherapist and likes to explain me to myself – informs me my writing comes from some impulse to explore secrets and lies. That space between what is known and unknown.'

Nisha widens her eyes. 'Wow, that's all so delicious.' She leans in closer, chin on hand. 'Tell me more, Maeve.'

The next morning she's jolted awake by the shrill intrusion of the hotel phone. She fumbles it to her ear. 'Hello?'

An automated voice tells her it's 5 a.m. Has she woken up in some dystopian hell? 'Thank you,' she replies, in a stranger's voice. She lets the receiver fall to the ground.

She sits up, rips her Velcro tongue from the roof of her

mouth. Her head throbs and is too heavy. Her skin feels shrivelled around her muscles and bones and organs, her whole body sucked airless, like one of those compression packing cubes. She tries to piece the night together, but it's disjointed from the third Cosmopolitan on. A bottle or two of red wine? Clear liquid in a shot glass. Tequila? Jesus, *God*, her alcohol nemesis. They'd moved to a corner table of the bar at some stage, and she has a grainy recollection of the irritated barman cleaning around them in a pointed way as they giggled.

As she drinks water straight from the bathroom tap her brain seems to absorb it too, some capillary action that defies gravity and expands her memory. More scenes flash in her head. Nisha's room. Plundering the mini bar. The two of them wearing bathrobes over their clothes and those clownish slides over their shoes. Maeve crying, her head on Nisha's lap. 'My flight wasn't cancelled. There was no flight. I was just so *tired* of it all.' Telling her about Rory, Jamie, Dan. Telling her how her life felt like a knotty, uneven braid, all the different strands plaited around each other haphazardly, the end result a styleless mess. Nisha stroking her hair. A vape that tasted like menthol. Cigarettes. Passing smoke between their mouths.

She straightens and looks at herself in the mirror. The gloomy light casts unattractive shadows on her face. She breathes on the glass to shroud her reflection, but the fog recedes quickly and there she is still. Older than Methuselah. Too old now to even start Botox. ('That horse might have bolted, Maeve,' the beauty therapist said.) She understands why people kill themselves in hotels. They probably hadn't intended to. They'd just woken up with a hangover, limped across the ugly nylon carpet and been filled with an existential despair when they caught sight of themselves.

'Loser,' she says. 'What were you thinking? You're married.' She taps her reflected forehead then with each word. 'To. A. Man.'

In the shower more liquid is transferred, like osmosis, and memories are rehydrated and resurrected.

Doing everything she could to amuse Nisha, who professed herself 'terminally single', with her *petty scenes from a marriage* routine. Nisha was especially tickled by the *upside down vs right side up* long-running battle. Cillian storing drinking glasses, mugs, bottles of honey, shower gel and ketchup on their heads, Maeve forever turning them the correct way up.

'Sounds exhausting,' Nisha said.

'It is,' Maeve sighed, 'it really is. Almost as exhausting as the *which one of us is more exhausted* debates. Actually though, what's most exhausting is being perpetually resentful towards another person.'

Nisha at her bedroom door, her lipstick smudged.

Numbers exchanged. A promise to keep in touch.

A kiss.

Jesus. A kiss?

As she dresses, she panics about her family and checks her phone. She sent a message at 8 p.m. So soz. Meeting dragging on and on u ok if I stay night soz.

A thumbs-up in reply.

Oh God, she can sense the passive aggression reverberating off it.

She makes it home by seven-thirty. When she opens the front door, a disorientating ginger projectile in the form of Simon the cat whizzes past. 'Fuck me,' she says, clutching her heart, which is feeling skittery enough with all the alcohol. The kitchen is a flurry of activity.

'Who are you?' her mother says, startling.

'Where's my PE kit?' Luke asks. 'Did you not wash it?'

'There's nothing in this stupid house for lunch,' Jamie says, looking into a fridge jammed with food.

'You look terrible,' says Cillian, frowning over the top of his glasses.

Get bifocals, she screams on the inside. 'Gee thanks,' she says and picks up the kettle. It's empty again. The Post-it Note – hanging valiantly by a corner – gives up and floats down to the puddle of water beneath.

ERICA

She's in their walk-in wardrobe. His shirts hang, colour coded, from bright white through to a deep grey, on the top rail, all facing the same way, the trousers, pressed and folded with a military precision, on the rail below. She hugs one of the shirts, buries her nose into the armpit and inhales, but it smells of sickly lavender detergent so she moves to the next one, and the next, all the way down to the last. Of course he'd never hang an unwashed shirt back up.

When Juliet was here a few days ago she wore an androgynous perfume that for the briefest of moments made her think Rory was in the room. Or maybe it was the music, listening to her sing, the hurting edge to her voice, that reminded Erica of him. She was intrigued by her, had been when they were teenagers too. When she'd first met Rory he was dismissive when she asked if anything had ever happened between them. But it seemed to Erica that two people who looked as they did must surely be drawn to one another. It was like some fundamental law of physics. Rory laughed that off, said they had been friends forever, he didn't see her that way, and anyway, Juliet was not his type. 'Too messy. A living, breathing nightmare, that one,' he'd said, rolling his eyes. And he'd drifted away from that little gang anyway after that first summer together, after Dan's death. But when Juliet was sitting in her kitchen Erica had felt a spark, a shared understanding, that maybe could have blossomed into something approaching friendship. She knows that in school she herself was considered prim, didn't fit in with the cool girls. (Or the not so cool girls, come to think of it.) She was a day pupil at a Church of Ireland boarding school in South Dublin that her parents sent her to because they thought it was better than the local convents in Ballyboyne. They thought they were doing the best thing for her but really it was a horrible idea, which maybe sums up parenting. That school was full of strange, wild girls. Girls who were sent there because they were a handful. Girls who felt abandoned. Girls who felt trapped. Girls sent there because their parents were overly involved and pushy. Girls sent there because their parents didn't give a damn. She didn't fit in with the boarders and had to travel a long distance home by bus every afternoon so didn't make friends with the other day girls either. She always felt inept around people her own age anyway, being an only child and living rurally. She was one of those odd teenagers who adored their parents. It's why she wanted siblings so badly for Charlie.

But Erica is embarrassed now about how she acted in front of Juliet. It's the way she used to act around the alpha girls in her school too, kind of catty and bored, when really her entire body felt clenched in a pathetic desire for them to like her. She'd had a bit too much to drink, to be honest. And also the way Juliet was bursting out of herself with a kind of bruised sensuality, like overripe fruit. Her blouse gaping open and slipping down her shoulder, the slit in her skirt revealing her thighs as she sat. It made Erica's skin prickle. But mostly, it was the way Charlie was around her, his eyes too dark and wide, that turned her off. She seemed aware of her magnetism, encouraging of his admiration. It was twisted, and she felt a flush of protectiveness, understood then what Rory meant about her being a nightmare.

Underneath Rory's trousers sits a pair of shiny black dress shoes, positioned as though waiting patiently for his feet to step back in and take them out dancing. They only ever danced together at their wedding, a choreographed and rehearsed number to Mama Cass singing 'Dream a Little Dream of Me', Rory's choice, of course. But she still hasn't dreamt of him. Her doctor prescribed sleeping pills that knock her unconscious for six hours and make her wonder if that's what death is like. A void. It's a relief, in a way, nothingness she can handle. 'Are you scared, Daddy?' she asked her father when he was in the hospice, near the end. He patted her hand and said he was looking forward to dying, was imagining it as one eternal holiday, without the nuisance of packing. 'The way I think of it, darling, is like the time before I was born. A blissful ignorance.' He took everything, even death, in his stride. No dramatic exits for him.

There are the clothes Rory died in, of course, which surely must smell of him, but Erica doesn't know where they are and was too embarrassed to ask anyone at the hospital or mortuary. They were judging her, she knew that. She'd had a bit too much to drink that night too. A little before dinner, then you might as well finish the bottle. Rory making a performance out of jamming the cork back in once she'd poured that first glass, Erica yanking it out again, a routine they performed silently, like a mime, both conscious of not upsetting Charlie. Pretending she couldn't see Rory watching her, his face clouded with concern, or contempt maybe. But whose anger was greater, more justified?

The next morning, she'd woken up to see that his side of the bed was empty. He often got up before her, so this wasn't strange, but then she noticed that the bedclothes on his side were undisturbed and still tucked severely. A guilty creep started in her stomach. She'd always feel it there first before it made its way to her brain and informed her memory. She got up, walked down the hallway, checking the guest bedrooms. It wasn't unusual for him to sleep in one of them, especially if she'd gone to bed before him. She gently pushed open Charlie's door too – he was still sleeping soundly. It was Sunday and he probably wouldn't get up till lunchtime. She watched him for a few moments, feeling shame at what he may have witnessed. She always sensed Charlie to know everything even when he was a small child. Like he could feel their unhappiness, purely and exquisitely, but without any of the data or language to name it. Downstairs she checked both living rooms, his office, the rarely used dining room. In the kitchen there was no evidence of the previous night's dinner – he always cleaned up before bed – no remnants of breakfast either. She sat at the kitchen island drinking a glass of water and staring out into the back garden. It was a squally morning, the sky was a bucket of grey, the kind that made her long to live in another country.

There was only a small thing she was missing, she was sure of it. He must have told her why he wouldn't be here, and she just couldn't remember. She felt a surge of pulsing headachy heat then, and her heart started palpitating strangely in her throat, which maybe was the wine, and she stood up to concertina back the glass doors to let in some air. Her handbag was hanging on the back of a dining chair, and she reached in and pulled out her phone. She thought for a moment as to how to word the text. Nothing incriminating. Something vague. Just checking in x.

She pressed send and immediately a beep from somewhere in the kitchen. She looked around and saw his phone on the arm of the couch. He never let it out of his sight, even bringing it with him into the bathroom. She'd barely begun to process the meaning of this when there was another sound, a rhythmic tapping, hollow and desolate, and a sandy rattle like glass rolling on concrete, coming from outside. She poked her head out the doors. An empty white wine bottle lay rocking on the patio near the side of the house where the bins were kept. Another one lay smashed on the ground beside it. The sight of them made her want to run back upstairs, hide under her bedclothes. But she forced herself to walk towards them and when she turned the corner, that's when she saw him, half-kneeling, face down on the recycling bin that was leaning now at an acute angle against the wall, his arms trapped between his chest and the bin in a bizarre way, as though he'd been praying before toppling forward. The bin was open, and the lid was being lifted and banged against the wall by the wind. Rory was getting rid of the evidence, as he always did. Shielding Charlie. He wasn't wearing shoes. She thought about that a lot. He was unprepared, imagined he'd only be a few seconds. When she gave his burial clothes to the undertaker she'd included a pair even though he said it wasn't necessary, started saying something horrific about it being too difficult to place on . . . but Erica had cut him off, pushed them into his hands.

Eight hours but no more than twelve, they told her, that his shoeless body had lain there in its semi-penitent pose. A long time to be alone, to have no-one come look for you. They didn't say that to her, of course, but she knew that's what they were thinking. It would have been quick, they said, nothing you could have done anyway. She thinks they can't know that for sure, that they were just being kind.

When she'd got home later that night she'd gone outside to check but somebody had cleaned up the broken glass and put the other bottle into the bin. She'd no memory of doing this but prayed it was herself as she waited for the ambulance. Or one of the paramedics or guards. Please God, though, let it have not been her son. Taking over where his father left off.

—

She starts to take the shirts off individually and fold and place them carefully in a black sack but gets impatient then and pulls them all down roughly. She does the same with the trousers. She quickly fills up three bags. Tucked in at the back of the wardrobe is a shoe box that had been hidden by the clothes. She carries it to the bed and sits down. The box is full of photos. Lots of his mother, in London, young and beautiful, smiling shyly in floral minidresses or flared jeans, surrounded by arty-looking students. Poor Rory, he had to live in that disappointing gap between his mother's ambitions for her life and the way it all turned out. She supposes that's the way of many of their generation, though. All the thwarted women. Sarah O'Sullivan hanged herself in 1997, the day after Princess Diana died. Erica always felt those two events were not unrelated. At the time, she and Rory were living in a one-bedroom flat in a newly built apartment block just off the main square in the centre of Ballyboyne. He was managing a pub and involved in organising local music gigs. She was three years out of college and still working as a teller in the bank, a job that was only ever meant to be a stopgap while she figured out what she really wanted to do, an epiphany that never happened. Rory told her the night before his mother's funeral how relieved he was that she was dead. No, *glad* in fact. 'You don't mean that,' she said, stupidly, cruelly, so certain of herself. She was too young, her recent closeted childhood too happy to understand that mothers were complicated, grief could be ambivalent. What did she know then about anything? 'It's just the shock talking,' she insisted. His face took on a shutdown look then, and he turned away. She knew she'd made him feel ashamed and tried to backtrack. But it was too late. He never said it again.

There are a few photos of him as a teenager with his friends. Juliet is in many of them. In one of them, dated 1990, she's facing away, her arms wide, her back arched, the top of a tattoo peeping over her low-slung jeans. Erica always wanted to get a tattoo, Rory persuaded her not to. He had his own, but he told her he didn't like them on women. Looking at this photo, she thinks maybe what he meant is he didn't like them on his wife, because she has a sudden, strong sense he very much liked this image. She thinks she would get one somewhere hidden, a secret place that she could touch to remember the heat and vibration of the artist's needle. Maeve is in the photos too and another boy, small and sandy-haired, open-faced. Dan. No relief for Rory with his death, just guilt. It grew around him, choking him, like the bindweed in her mother's garden she was always waging a war against. She'd tried to talk him out of that also. She was impatient. 'You were teenagers,' she said, 'you need to forgive yourself.' From what he'd told her, it all seemed harmless enough, an accident, kids being kids. But again, what did she know? And again, the checked-out look on his face.

Nestled in amongst the photos is a folded strip of shiny paper. She holds it up and it unravels to reveal a series of black and white stills that seem to fall into a moving image, like those figures they'd draw on consecutive pages of a notebook as children and then flick through to animate. She's confused. An ultrasound memento. Why would he keep this? Maybe the same reason she's kept all those pregnancy sticks and remembers and marks in a calendar all the due dates that never came.

They'd had few scans, her body rarely able to cling on long enough. She was so hopeful. He was young, the sonographer, she was disarmed by it. He started digging into her stomach with the probe, as though that might be enough to revive the lifeless bud on the screen. Poke harder, she wanted to scream, ram it in there, will you? Angry at the still, black sac that was swallowed then by more blackness as the screen was turned off. And the suffocating silence filling the room like it had seeped out of the blank screen. Out of her dead, dark womb. Rory, not comprehending at first, looking at the sonographer's solemn face, a face too childlike to be imparting bad news. 'What is it?' he said. But Erica and the sonographer stared at each other, no words necessary. Then he looked down at her stomach that had known the outcome all along and held firm, wiped off the gel tenderly with the paper towel, pulled down Erica's blouse as though it was made of fragile tissue. The softness felt wrong though. She closed her eyes and imagined a violent punch to her gut, enough to dislodge her useless shell of a womb. She longed for it. 'What will I do?' she said aloud, to herself really, and the poor young man misinterpreted this. 'Go home and wait to bleed.' His voice was shaking with the intimacy of what he had to say. Erica never forgot this, the honesty of him. 'I'm very sorry,' he whispered then. And Erica said, 'I know. I know that you are.'

Rory tried to cheer her up in the car. Not to worry, they'd try again, blessing in disguise really with the amount of work they had on. How angry she was that he was dismissing her reaction. Just as she had done years before to him when his mother died. And anyway, he said, when she didn't respond, sat staring stonily out the window, they had Charlie. Which was always the ace to be played. Which you couldn't argue with because how ungrateful would that be? They arrived home and Rory started talking about dinner and Erica went upstairs and curled up in this bed, made herself into a hard, tight ball, waited for the bleeding as the sonographer said. She wished she could haemorrhage herself away into the mattress.

She notices the date now at the top: 2005. Charlie's ultrasound images, of course. Charlie, her living, breathing son. What is wrong with her? Seeing death in everything.

There's a couple of old yellowing sheets with typed text folded on the bottom of the pile. She lifts them out and is about to unfold them when it strikes her with absolute certainty what they are: the letter he left the day Charlie was born. The fact that it was typed preyed on her mind afterwards. The deliberateness of it. An anguished scrawl of handwriting she could have forgiven more easily. Because here's the thing. She loved Rory less after this letter. She made herself love him less after this letter. How true that belief in Buddhism about attachment being the root of all suffering. She had deliberately detached herself. His mother hadn't left anything. 'Didn't need to,' Rory's father said, bitterly, the night of her funeral. 'Her entire life was a suicide note.' Erica was shocked. *Why didn't you do something about it then?* she'd thought. God, the judgemental naivety of her. She came to understand Rory's father though, even to like him. He died of a brain aneurism aged only sixty-two. Rory believed it was the shock of seeing some blood that he coughed up on a tissue, his own father and three of his uncles having died of TB. And Erica understood this all too well. The fear and shame a spot of blood could bring.

She'd looked for Rory's letter when she got out of hospital after Charlie was born, wanted to read it properly, understand. She'd only managed a few lines before dropping it and running to search for him. In the intervening years she'd presumed it was gone, destroyed. But seeing it again now, she's not that surprised that he's kept it. That masochistic instinct of his. Though isn't masochism meant to bring some pleasure? Maybe it was that he planned to use it again someday.

'Mum?'

She jumps. Charlie's at the bedroom door. 'Oh, hi there, sweetheart.'

'What's that?'

'Nothing, just some boring old documents for the accountant.' She puts the letter back – she's no strength to read it now anyway – replaces the lid and slides the box under the bed.

'Can I take your car? I want to go to Sam's house.'

'I could drive you?'

'That's probably not a great idea.' He's looking at her the same way Rory looked at her sometimes, a barely perceptible disgusted flare of the nostrils. She feels a knot of something – defensive, shameful – deep in her ribs.

'I've only had a little glass, you know. With dinner.'

'I'd rather drive myself.' He makes to go.

'Charlie?'

He turns back. 'Yeah?'

'How would you feel about us selling this house?'

He frowns, then looks at the ground. 'But Dad loved it.'

'Yes, but . . .'

She breaks off. His face is pained, he's biting his bottom lip. She forgets sometimes how young seventeen is.

'I don't know why you'd even say that. It's full of him. I don't know how you could say that.'

'I know. I'm sorry, Charlie.' She walks over and hugs him. 'I'm so sorry, sweetheart. I don't know what I was thinking. My head's a muddle.'

'He loved this house,' he says into her shoulder. His body feels unyielding against her, but his breath is warm and she can feel a dampness through her shirt. She thinks of his hot, sweet baby breath.

She rubs the back of his head. 'I know. I'm sorry, it was a stupid thing to say. It's a great house. It really is.'

He lifts his head off her shoulder. 'What are they?'

He is pointing accusingly at the black bin bags.

'I was just going to donate some of his clothes.'

He pulls away completely from her. 'He's only been buried a few days. How come it's so easy for you to move on?'

'Charlie! That's not how it is at all.'
But he's already walking out the door.

Later, when the paralysis wanes, she forces herself to stand and goes downstairs to Rory's study. She tugs open the wooden blinds and specks of dust dance in the slatted light that bursts through. She read somewhere that dust is made up partly of dead skin cells and she wonders if particles of Rory are swirling around her now, landing on her. Maybe even bits of that woman whose cells were clinging to Rory. She sits at his desk, pulls one of the drawers and takes out the bottle of whiskey and the wine glass she's left there. She knocks back one, then pours another. When she's finished this one she opens his laptop and checks his emails. No reply from that woman. This annoys her. Wine softens her, loosens everything, but this whiskey subverts her, like some ancient and powerful Celtic spirit has taken hold.

> Hello there,
>
> I'm wondering why you can't even do me the courtesy to answer. It's quite rude.
>
> I'm not angry with you if that's the reason you're hiding. I'm simply curious. I have some questions.
>
> What was the arrangement between you two?
>
> Did he ever mention me? Were there rules? We had rules. He liked rules.
>
> Had you slept together yet? Or just building up to it?
>
> If you had, what was it like? Where did you do it? What

did *he* like, from you? Was there anything off-limits? Did he have any kinks?

What do you look like? What is your body like? What do *you* like?

Please don't ignore this again. It's important that you're honest. Your existence is not surprising. And trust me when I say there is nothing you can describe that will shock me. There are no scenes more vivid than the ones in my imagination.

Erica O'Sullivan

She presses send quickly before she has a chance to change her mind.

MAEVE

The boys have left for school, and she's in Jamie's bedroom, which smells like a foreign country to her now. She's wondering how it happened. How her baby who once smelled like baking has turned into a malodorous creature she barely recognises. There's a musty funk of feet and vinegary sweat overlaid with the sickly spiciness of the Lynx he douses himself in every morning. It's redolent of school-hall discos and awkward boys with acne-blighted faces trying to probe her mouth with tongues while the slow set played. She places a neat pile of folded washing on his unmade bed that she knows will eventually get swallowed by the jumble of clothes on the floor, then pulls the curtains and pushes the window open wide.

There's a single Nike runner by her foot and she picks it up to try to reunite it with its partner. The size of it shocks her and she gets an urge to hold it against her stomach. When she was eight months pregnant with Jamie she picked up a Baby-gro in a shop and draped it over her bump to show

Cillian. He laughed, thought it adorable. 'So tiny!' he said, in awe and delight. But Maeve experienced a bizarre feeling of dislocation, almost a sense of denial, that something that size could be forming inside her. And have to come out. She nearly threw up then and there, in the middle of Mothercare. Now the size of this giant shoe makes her feel similarly unhinged.

She sifts through the items on Jamie's desk: ragged-edged foolscap pages with bewildering-looking equations written on them (how could there have been a time she understood this?), coins, two crusty forks, a tangle of chargers, a broken hairbrush, a mangled packet of gum that looks like it's been through the washing machine. She's not sure what it is she's looking for. Clues, maybe. Some insight into this almost-stranger, with his alien pronouncements, who spends most of his time holed up in this bedroom. When she passes by his closed door in the evening she lingers for a moment outside, hand hovering, thinking of some excuse to knock. Mostly she changes her mind and walks away. Sometimes she will venture in and then she skirts around the periphery, making conversation with his back as he sits hunched over the laptop, one ear of his headphones pushed back the only concession to her presence. He prowls the house at night. She's alert to his noises, wondering if she should get up and order him back to his room but at sixteen he's a little old to be put to bed. Before they started giving her sedatives at night-time her mother used to prowl too but she knew the difference between their nocturnal outings. Her mother was an indecisive shuffle, dry feet barely lifting off the carpet, stopping and starting, as though making wrong turns. Jamie sounds purposeful; he scurries and creaks between rooms with some sort of intent that at a certain time of night manages to sound malign.

'What are you up to?'

She jumps. It's Cillian.

'Oh. Just the washing.'

'Okay.' He turns to go again, and she feels suddenly lonely, standing here in this room with its oppressive, masculine smell.

'Cillian?'

'Yeah?'

'Jamie feels so closed-off to me. I was wondering if you think we should ask to look at his phone or laptop?'

'I'm not sure what that will achieve apart from you getting freaked out about him accessing porn.'

'I wasn't even thinking about porn, to be honest. But, Jesus, now I am. And do we just accept that? Isn't it harming his brain in some way? I find it all so confusing – like, which is better, to be open and permissive or, you know, repressed and warped like our parents' generation?'

'I think there are ways to navigate it without extremes. Teenage boys will always find a way to access it, Maeve. I did it myself.'

'Yeah, but I think passing around sticky copies of *Penthouse* in the school playground was slightly different. It seems almost quaint. God, the stuff they're looking at now. Like, choking someone is just the norm. How did that happen? So vile and dehumanising.'

'Porn has always been dehumanising.'

'Like that, though? Has it? And what's going to happen the first time they have real-life sex with someone? Will they expect their partners to be up for anything? Are they going to feel inadequate because they don't have a huge artificially enhanced erection? Will they be turned off by natural breasts or labia that haven't been surgically altered?'

'Look, I can talk to him again about it but we don't even know if it's a problem. It's pretty common for teenagers to withdraw from their parents. It's not necessarily indicative of some kind of pathology.'

He turns to go again and Maeve says, 'But that's not even what's been worrying me. What about the remarks about single mothers and stuff? Where is that coming from? It's disturbing.'

'You know, I think a lot of that is him trying to be provocative. And you always take the bait.'

'Oh. So it's my fault?'

'No, of course not. Just the two of you are kind of . . . highly strung. That's all I'm saying. It's exactly how you used to be around your mother. Remember?'

She's feeling strung-up now, but she won't give him the satisfaction of showing it. 'Well, I feel like there's something deeper going on with him beyond just being provocative.'

'Maybe you're projecting?'

She knows he's referencing Dan. He's run out of sympathy for that sad old confession. How different his attitude is now to when they first met. She told him all about the guilt she carried when they had that first precious all-night conversation. When they spilled their souls. Said *here you go, you can have my heart now, because I trust you with it.* When they listened to each other's stories with wonder and empathy and engaged expressions. Now they just roll their eyes at all the old anecdotes, could recite them themselves. And not in the cute, finishing for each other kind of way, with the perfectly timed interjections so that their origin story or shared experiences are almost a performance for their audience. Now it's a case of *yes, yes, we've all heard this one before.*

'Aren't you concerned, though? I mean, he spends so much time alone. Shouldn't he be sneaking out? Drinking in fields?'

'Well, Covid hasn't helped them socially. And just because we did that doesn't mean it was healthy. Kids are different these days. They're more into wellness and mindfulness than getting shitfaced.'

'Or maybe they're too addicted to their phones to have real fun. And didn't you just say that you used to access porn as a kid and there was no harm done? Aren't you contradicting yourself?'

'Jesus, Maeve. I was trying to reassure you. But you're always looking to pick holes. It's like living with a lawyer.' He walks away and she feels so completely alone suddenly.

She needs to check on her mother. Lily is sitting on the old Jacquard armchair – brought from her own house – looking out her bedroom window.

'Hi, Mam.'

'Hello, *you.*'

She says this by way of greeting to everyone now. It's a trick Maeve taught her back at the beginning to prevent her becoming frustrated when names wouldn't come straight away. (And it sounds so warm. Not Lily's natural disposition.) She's clung to it and it surprises Maeve because so much else has vanished. But then, the whole trajectory of her illness has been surprising. There's no order, no neat descent into oblivion. A bit like grief in fact, peaks and troughs, but perhaps, unlike grief, with the troughs getting a little deeper each time. She has good days and bad days, but sometimes the good days aren't a blessing. The good days can bring an unwelcome lucidity. An awareness of exactly what's being lost.

'Are you okay? Are you warm enough?'

'Oh yes. I'm fine. You're very kind, aren't you?' She looks at her daughter then as if only just seeing her. 'Maeve!' she exclaims as though delighted with herself. Despite everything, there are brief moments when Maeve finds herself guiltily preferring the demented version of her mother.

'That's right, Mam. Maeve.' Her mother told her that she was named after the legendary Irish warrior queen. 'It means intoxicating,' she said, looking at Maeve with a resigned air, as though nothing could be further from the sober reality of the child who stood in front of her. That's the thing about children's names, Maeve supposes, they reveal more about the parent than the offspring. She used to often leave her mother's company with her disappointment clinging to her. Could feel it, physically, a cloying viscous layer on her skin, like the vernix babies are born with, except with a malign function rather than a protective one.

Maeve stands above her now and looks down on her mother's scalp, a rosy sunset peeking through wispy white clouds. She thinks of her babies with their sweet-smelling crowns and soft downy hair. A wave of tenderness engulfs her and she bends and kisses the top of her head. Lily looks up, surprised.

'I've been thinking about your boy,' she says.

'Which one?'

'Ach, the little one. I can't think of his name.'

'Luke?'

Her mother frowns. 'No, not him. Oh, it's like a dream that I've lost.' Maeve understands the frustration of that, how a barely remembered dream dances maddeningly on the edge of consciousness.

Lily scrunches up her face then, as though excavating the name is painful. Like her remaining hair, the memories and details that are intact are being stretched to cover the ever-increasing gaps. And sometimes they won't reach far enough so she invents her own facts to fill the spaces.

'Oh yes, I know who you mean, Jamie.' Maeve says it in a reassuring way. She must be careful not to push the unsteady scaffolding of her brain too hard.

Her mother sighs. 'I suppose I do. I was just trying to help. His parents are no good.'

Maeve chooses not to take offence. Pathological, not personal, as the doctor said.

She sits down on the bed opposite her. 'Help with what, Mam?'

'There was bullying, you see.'

'Did Jamie tell you something? Is he being bullied?'

'Who are you talking about?'

'You said it was something to do with Jamie.'

'No, I didn't. Who's Jamie?'

'Your grandson. My son.'

'Oh no, I don't have any grandsons. Only a daughter.'

'Yes, that's me.'

She claps her hands and laughs. 'You're not my daughter. Look at you, you're far too old.'

Maeve starts to laugh too. 'I know, I am. I really am.' And they both laugh till their eyes water. Maeve feels as though she might tip over into hysteria at any moment, but her mother stops abruptly and slumps back then as though exhausted. Her eyes, which had been engaged, change, like a camera shifting focus. 'I'm not sure what you're going on about half the time.' And away she slips.

'Shall we get you something to eat?'

'I ate already, I told you. You never listen to me, do you?' She sounds as though this has just dawned on her, not as though it's an accusation she's thrown at Maeve her whole life. Maybe dementia is like that, being disappointed all over again by your family.

'Okay, I'll be downstairs if you need me.'

'I'll call my daughter if I need anything.'

'Right.'

―

Later, in the kitchen, Maeve opens her laptop and stares at her unfinished manuscript. Then she shuts it again and googles *When does the nadir of happiness occur?* Forty-eight seems to be the consensus, her exact age. Figures. She falls down a rabbit hole of studies into contentment and is only pulled out of it when Cillian comes in.

'Did you know that happiness has a shape?'

'What?' He's bending down, putting on his runners.

'Apparently over the course of a life it's a U-shaped curve. We're swilling in the troughs now.'

'Ah yes. Turds on the bottom of the U-bend, about to get flushed away.' He laughs, pleased with his own joke.

'Wow. I didn't think I could feel any worse there, Cillian.'

'Look, I'm aware of those studies and it's good news, though, isn't it? The only way is up and all that.'

'Or maybe all the stressed unhappy people drop dead in middle age. Only the deluded optimists left at the end.'

'That's the spirit, Maeve. Turn a positive into a negative. I think we do become more content in old age.'

'Like Mam, you mean? Huh.'

'Well, maybe in her case oblivion *is* happiness.'

'I can't decide if that's encouraging or discouraging.'

'How we perceive things is key.'

'Well, the more I think about it, the more I think the bible got it right with the whole three score and ten thing. Seventy seems like the perfect age to shuffle off. Not too old, not too young.'

'Hmm. Maybe, but you might have a hard time convincing a sixty-nine-year-old of that.'

She studies the top of his head as he ties his laces. His height means she hasn't seen it in a long time. His hair has thinned. She's irritated by this and tries to figure out why. Maybe it's because it's normally out of view for her. Maybe it's because he's never mentioned it or shown any insecurity over it. Possibly, he isn't even aware of it. Which strikes her as unfair. Her own ageing is always cruelly obvious to her. Her bodily hair is doing crazy and very visible things. Like her eyebrows falling out and growing instead on her toes. For a moment she experiences an urge to comment on Cillian's scalp but stops herself.

Instead, she says, 'And did you also know that women are unhappier than men but that we smile a lot more?'

'I'm off to the gym,' he says, as though this is the answer to her question. He rummages around in the drawer full of plastic and eventually pieces together a matching bottle and lid. 'Someone really needs to sort that drawer out,' he mutters, which enrages her. Then he kisses the top of her head and leaves.

'Yes,' she says to the closed door. 'And more prone to autoimmune diseases because of all the repressed anger.'

And what shape does happiness assume over the course of a marriage? she wonders. A sharply declining line graph, a dangerous downhill ski run, the steep slope of a forehead away from a receding hairline . . .?

She checks her emails. She and Nisha have exchanged several since the night at the hotel. They have become infused with a thrilling undercurrent of flirtatiousness and are the highlight of her day. She's disappointed to see there are no new ones, so she rereads the latest exchange. She knows she should delete them in case Cillian was to come across them but reading them makes her feel something of that lost teenage excitement again. Anyway, Cillian would never snoop – he's far too well adjusted. And enjoys occupying the moral high ground.

Hi Maeve,
Thanks for all that advice on what to do with my book. And thanks for the offer to look over it too. I'll spend a bit of time polishing and then send it on to you although I'm slightly embarrassed. Sometimes I read over what I've written and I feel so disheartened when I realise how far away I am from the writers I admire.

By the way, I bought your latest book yesterday and stayed up all night reading. Loved it!! It's so twisty and suspenseful. How on earth do you do that?

I also really enjoyed the sex scenes. Mmm. They must be difficult to write though? Please send tips. I've one in my manuscript that flops (pun intended).

N x

•

Hi Nisha,
You're so welcome. And I can't wait to read the manuscript.

I understand completely that feeling of being disheartened by your own work. It's totally normal. At the beginning I felt like giving up so many times when I read books by my favourite authors. What was the point? Why would anyone read my crap when there are thousands of better books out there? But I try to use it now as a motivator. I know I'll never come close to their brilliance, but I can keep trying to make my own work better. In that way I can attempt to close the gap. It's all we can do.

As for sex scenes, yes, they can be difficult. So exposing! And every writer is terrified of being nominated for that Bad Sex Writing award too. Initially I used to feel as though it was like having sex in front of an audience and then asking the audience to rate my performance. A wiser and much better writer than me told me that you've just got to get over yourself, don't try too hard to make it beautiful, and most importantly, write as though all your family are dead. (In fact, that's a good way to approach all writing!) As time goes on, I find it easier. And the vulnerability you feel with those scenes is a good thing, in a way. Because making love with someone is surely the most vulnerable you can be?

Maeve x

P.S. To be honest though, I'm getting bored of Sylvia and her male conquests. I thought I might try something new. Perhaps Sylvia sleeps with a woman instead? Unfortunately, I don't have any experience to draw on there. I suppose I'll just have to let my imagination wander . . .

She added that postscript after much agonised internal debate. There was a part of her that was fearful, this same denied part that had been confused about her teenage admiration for Juliet's beauty. But Nisha is so self-assured, so lacking in any sort of shame, that Maeve feels more embarrassed about her own predictable and unsophisticated Gen X Irish convent girl inhibition than about making any suggestive comments. 'God, everyone in London under thirty is *at least* bi now,' Nisha said lightly when they'd been talking in the hotel. (Maeve wondered about the *at least* but felt too ignorant to ask.)

She checks Instagram then, responds to the positive comments on her latest post, deletes one comment that calls her character a whore and a 'cum-dumpster'. The spark of lightness from reading Nisha's words is quashed again. She blocks the person whose profile picture looks like a video game character.

Erica has uploaded a rare post and in it is thanking everyone for their kindness. Maeve is surprised; the post is so intimate and revealing, so unlike Erica in every respect. It's a recent photo of Rory on a beach, somewhere in Ireland judging by his warm clothes and the mournful demeanour of the sea and sky, both the colour of lead. The photo is taken from behind. He's barefoot, his trousers turned up and his head is down, looking at the sand. The beach is eerily deserted so that he appears completely alone, with nothing but his shadow and a trail of footprints following him. She thinks of T.S. Eliot's ageing Prufrock paddling in the sea with his trousers rolled and it adds to her feeling of bleakness. Rory won't grow old now. Just like Dan. Maeve stares at the post for a long time, trying to find the right comment to make. Eventually she shuts her computer. Nothing feels adequate.

———

In 2005, nearly fifteen years after Dan died, on what would have been his thirty-second birthday, Maeve – on her day off from the publishing house she worked for as a sales administrator – took the bus down from Dublin to visit his grave. As she entered the cemetery, she could see another figure standing at his headstone, a man, and at first she was afraid it was Dr Flynn so held back and pretended to read the monument in front of her. After a few covert glances she realised the person was too young to be Dr Flynn. There was a familiarity in his movements and, more than that, something in these movements that stirred a long-discarded desire in her. She approached, nervous, trying to come up with something witty or profound to say.

'Great minds think alike,' she said to his back, and hated herself. It was so feeble.

Rory turned and smiled at her, which, as always, felt like a gift being bestowed. She hadn't seen him since his lavish wedding three years before, and even then he'd been constantly surrounded by people so that she barely got a chance to speak to him. Not that it mattered; she got the impression he was more concerned about showing off how far he'd come rather than connecting with any old friends. He was as lovely as ever, more so, his face angular, all the roundness of youth gone. His fair hair was longer, and he had a reddish stubble. The slight dishevelment suited him, highlighted the contours of his bone structure and intense eyes. The sadness in his face seemed more acute too.

'And fools seldom differ.'

They hugged. He smelled of Lynx, and it made her tearful that he still wore it. She pulled away first.

'Are you okay?' he asked.

'Yeah, it's just, you know.' She gestured at the grave.

He sighed. 'Thirty-two. My God. Remember how we'd talk about thirty? It seemed an almost mythical age. One we'd never reach. Or if we did, we'd be completely sorted.'

'I know, it's crazy to be so old.'

'Mad.'

'And I hear you're soon to be a dad. Congratulations.'

'That doesn't even feel real, to be honest.'

Maeve frowned. She could sense no excitement in him. He seemed disconnected. Instinctively she put her hand to her own as yet flat belly, felt a flutter of protectiveness, as though Rory's detachment could affect what lay in there. She decided not to tell him about her own pregnancy.

'I've been standing here wondering what he'd be doing with his life now,' Rory said.

'A big star on Broadway is what I'd like to think.'

'Or dealing drugs to a big star on Broadway.'

Maeve laughed, felt some of that old warmth towards Rory. 'And I'm trying to imagine him older. He always seemed ageless. Like he could be seventeen or seventy. Very young and very old at the same time.'

'I know what you mean. He was always himself.' He sighed, looked up from the gravestone, fixed his eyes to a point beyond it. 'The thing is, though, he was different in school.'

'How do you mean?'

'Rigid, uneasy. Everything about him was . . . cautious. The way he held his body, moved, spoke. Afraid of attracting bullies. You remember how he was around his father?'

'Yeah. Scared of giving himself away.'

'That's it exactly.'

'At least he could be true to himself around us, I suppose.'

'Well, he must have believed he could anyway,' Rory said.

He held her eyes then, as though he was looking for something, acknowledgement, or understanding, or forgiveness, but Maeve, overwhelmed, ashamed, had to look away to get a grip on herself. When she looked back, it was the strangest thing. He was completely still, with fat, silent tears falling down his cheeks. Maeve felt like she was witnessing some miracle, one of those weeping statues they lost all sense over in the eighties.

'Oh,' she said uselessly. 'Oh.'

'I'm a bad person, Maeve. Everything and everyone I touch turns to shit.'

She searched for something to say. She thought about the devastation on Dan's face when he'd left her house the last time she saw him but she thought also about how protective Rory had been of Dan. How whenever Dr Flynn made a joke at Dan's expense, Rory refused to engage, would look away, his closed expression making it clear he didn't approve, though Dr Flynn with all his self-righteousness would never pick up on it. And she thought too about her own culpability and considered reminding him of this, but suddenly it was too late to say anything because Rory seemed to gather himself. He brushed his hands across his eyes, then squeezed them shut, pinched the top of his nose and took a deep breath. When he opened his eyes his face looked composed again, the dampness dried, the usual almost amused expression.

They stood not speaking for a few moments, Maeve fighting with herself all the while. It was a fine, still day in spring. Lambs were bleating in the distance and the sound, carried a long way over the tranquil air, was transformed into something yearning and melancholy. She thought of the pop of tennis balls being lifted up the lane from the courts and long, idle summer days spent on the benches there. She thought of afternoons on the old bridge or under it by the riverbank and missed them with a sudden, fierce intensity. Almost two years in and she still didn't feel ready for her thirties, everything felt much more serious. The stakes too high.

'Do you see much of Juliet these days?' he asked suddenly.

'Haven't you heard? She's in New Zealand. She went there a couple of years ago, left not long after you got married.'

'Yeah? Good for her. Getting as far away from here as possible. She never did things by halves. How long is she gone for?'

'For good maybe. She's got a baby daughter there too, Ruby. She'd be nearly a year old now.'

Maeve tried to read his look, searched for some regret or jealousy or disappointment but could find nothing. He seemed blank.

'Wow. I can't picture her being a mother. Tell her congratulations from me.' His tone was flat.

'No. I don't think I will tell her that actually, Rory.'

'Huh. Yeah. I suppose not. But I am glad for her. If ever she was to wonder, like.'

'She doesn't.'

He gave a wry smile. 'It's nice to see you still have her back anyway.'

Maeve shrugged.

'Look, I need to go,' he said. 'Can I give you a lift anywhere? Back to your mam's house?'

Maeve imagined being with him a bit longer, the windows of his car rolled down, the breeze in her hair, his hand resting close to her thigh on the gear stick, stealing glances at his lovely profile as he drove. And a bit of a shiver ran through her that felt initially like anticipation but she realised then was foreboding, and she didn't know if it was being there, in the graveyard, or the deep dark pit that was Rory.

'Thanks,' she said, 'but I think I'll spend a little more time with himself.'

He nodded. 'It's been nice to see you, Maeve. I've got great memories too, you know. We had some good times all the same, didn't we?'

'I suppose.' It was as generous as she could be in that moment, towards him and herself.

She watched him as he walked away, his head down, his hands jammed deep into his pockets as though he might squash his whole body into them. She again thought of Dan leaving her house that night and was reminded too what an awful lonely thing shame was.

JULIET

She's in O'Malley's. It's a week since they put him in the ground. Her eyes drink Liam in as he pulls a pint of Guinness. There's a sensual contrast between his tanned, sinewy forearms with their coarse, dark hairs and the soft, white satin of his rolled-up shirt sleeves. She can see the edge of a tattoo peeking out, just a couple of letters. It's tantalising but also self-assured in a way that he isn't, and she's curious to know what it says. Rory had got a new tattoo on his upper back in San Francisco the day before she arrived. She'd rubbed Vaseline tentatively over it, the edges red and raw. 'It's a Dylan quote. For you, Juliet,' he'd said, turning her then and kissing the angel wings tattoo on her own lower back. 'I remember you getting this after your dad died. That summer.' Then he'd pinned her wrists and prised apart her thighs with his knee. And there was a different, greedy quality to him that night and she'd wondered what demons he was exorcising.

Liam has the lean, fit build of a man who does physical work – hauling kegs, lifting crates – for a living rather than a hobby.

Lanky and hawk-nosed as a teenager, he has grown well into himself. She doesn't find the short-necked, steroid-shaped bodies of many of the young men in the gym she goes to as attractive, though she has been tempted. She wishes she could touch his upper arm. She's always found a man's biceps to be singularly arousing, the way they might swell and strain against a sleeve.

Liam places the pint in front of her and she watches, mesmerised, maybe a little drunk, as the caramel clouds swirl and settle and her head spins a little in sympathy. She's already shared two bottles of wine at home with Johnny. She touches the glass in anticipation. Her father used to drink it. One afternoon she studied him intently in the pub beside the shopping centre in town where he brought herself and Josh, while they waited for Denise to do the big Christmas shop. He had three in a short space of time, as though keeping himself busy to distract from the cloying presence of his children. He drank each pint the same, bringing it to his mouth only four times, his lips pursed at the rim as though sucking it down, so that at the end there were three creamy rings left clinging to the glass. Josh drinks it the same way now, so he must have been studying him too. This causes a sudden tenderness towards her older brother.

She hears a chuckle to her right and swivels her head, too quickly perhaps, because her vision bounces a little. When it resolves she takes in the three elderly men also sitting at the bar. They're seated in a row, facing forward, towards the optics, rather than each other, carrying on a half conversation that seems to involve long stretches of silence. Women would never interact like that. Juliet likes it. She likes old men, they move her. There's a gentleness there, she can never assign any malign intent to them. She would be useless on a jury to try old Nazi war criminals. She wonders how age would have softened her father. If it would have.

Liam leans down on the counter in front of her. 'Well.' He says it in that unique way of the people around here, elongating the *eh* sound. It's shorthand for a lot of things, can be friendly or wary, depending on the relationship that exists. She enjoys hearing it again.

She reaches over, wraps one hand around his wrist and with the other folds back his shirt cuff. She can feel him tense to her touch. He has always been easy to interpret. 'What does it say?' she asks.

He pulls his sleeve up further, but her eyes are a bit unfocused and she can't make out the words. He folds it down again and says, 'Beckett, as I'm sure you're aware. I got it at a particularly low point after my divorce.'

'I wasn't aware actually. Maeve's the bookish one. Not me. But I do love the idea of a romantic, literary soul trapped in the ripped body of a barman.'

He smiles. 'You like tattoos?'

'Love them. Although they're ubiquitous now. Hard to find a man under fifty in New Zealand without one. It was a novelty when I went there first. A bit like all the circumcised men.'

He raises an eyebrow. 'And you're into those too?'

'Hmm. It's funny. Lately I've found myself drawn to the Catholic guys. They're intact. That's how you can tell someone's religion over there, you know. You're still Catholic, right?'

He shakes his head. 'Catastrophically lapsed, actually.' He laughs then. 'I can see you've not changed one bit, Juliet Quinn.'

'Aren't you glad of that, though?' She thinks of the two of them, twenty maybe, when she'd come home one weekend from Dublin, out the back of the pub, the pebbledash of the wall scraping her back as he thrust into her. His father, Liam Senior, walked out and caught them. He barred Juliet for a month. 'What are you doing with that little tramp?' she heard him say to his son, as she bent to pick up her underwear from the cold concrete. 'She's had more sausage in her than the butcher's.' She slept that night with her arms wrapped around herself as her fingers rested in the stinging grooves on her back. Liam Senior died in a car accident a few years later. Juliet remembers not feeling sad about that.

Liam grins at her and she hopes it's because he's remembering too. She wonders if he feels the same pleasant drag between his legs as she does right now. She has a perverse need for every man who is not related to her to desire her. Or maybe it's not perverse. She suspects it's not entirely normal, though, that maybe it's even a sickness, but she's never asked anyone else if they feel the same so doesn't know for sure.

She lifts the pint to her mouth and, maintaining eye contact with him, takes a deep drink. She remembers her father, closing his eyes, as though taking communion.

'Jesus, you even make drinking a big, dirty pint look sexy.'

She rests one finger on the rim of her glass.

'Tell me, Liam, why did we never get together? Properly I mean.'

'Ah here. How much have you had to drink? Are we really going to go there now?'

'I'm serious. Why?'

'Where do I start? Okay. Let's skip to the heart of it. Back then you weren't interested in me.'

'But how could you know? You never asked.'

'I'd have been too afraid of the answer to ask. Anyway, it seemed to me you were the one who did the choosing.'

Not where Rory was concerned. 'Well, you should have asked.'

'Maybe. Or maybe you had a lucky escape. Suzy would probably tell you that you had.'

'Where did it go wrong for you two?'

'Ah, I don't know. Marriage is hard. But maybe we gave up on it too easily. The grass being greener and all that. Which it most definitely isn't. Now I'm forty-eight years old and on my own and it's a whole different level of being alone than in your twenties. Then it was kind of hopeful, now . . . not so much. Meanwhile, Suzy's gone back down to Cork, married to some SEO analyst. Whatever the fuck that is. Living her best life, so it seems.'

'You realise that's also you believing the grass to be greener.'

He grins. 'True.'

She reaches out, slips her finger between his shirt sleeve and forearm. 'You know, we could make each other feel less alone right now.'

Gently, he removes her hand, places it down on the counter. 'Trust me, I'd like nothing better. But you're a bit drunk and I think I should walk you home.'

'Come on, I'm fully aware of what I'm doing. I won't MeToo you or anything.'

He shakes his head. 'I feel like I'm the one being harassed here. Get your coat on.'

'Is that *get your coat on* you've scored?'

'No, that's get your coat on, it's cold out.'

'Well, I don't have a coat. And is *walk you home* a code for something else, then? As I recall, you, quote unquote, *walked me home* once before and we ended up fucking in Denny's field.'

'Mother of God.' Liam looks around as though to check no-one else has heard. The other barman is out collecting glasses. The three old men appear oblivious. 'No, it's not code.' He leans on the bar and looks very directly into her eyes. 'Also, Denny's field is now filled with houses and, more importantly, Juliet, I'm way too old for al fresco sex. I'd be getting chilblains.'

She sits back petulantly. 'Way to kill the mood, Liam. I've completely lost my boner now.'

He laughs. 'You're a headcase. I'm going to go upstairs to grab my jacket. Please wait and I'll be back in a sec.'

'Tell me, where else am I gonna go, Liam?' She takes another long gulp of her Guinness. Her head tips back as she does and for a moment she feels as though her body might follow. 'No, really, tell me,' she says aloud to herself after he's walked away.

He disappears through to the back where she knows the staircase lies that leads to the large flat above. She's been up there with him too, although she doesn't remember the specifics. One drunken screw bleeds into the other. He has always lived there, even when he was married. She wonders what it requires to spend your entire life in one place. Does it imply integrity or simply a lack of imagination? Rory was dissatisfied with everything. That didn't go so well.

She takes out her phone and goes to her emails, which she hasn't checked in a few days. There's one from her boss in the interiors shop. She doesn't bother opening it. With any luck it's a dismissal. Another one from Tony, her neighbour in the apartment building, some inane bullshit about a body corporate meeting. She doesn't bother with this either. It'll be someone banging on about the recycling in the basement not being sorted properly or some such. She goes to the folder where she's kept all of Rory's. Reading them makes her feel that she and Rory weren't just a figment of her imagination. But he would have had to delete all of hers, which makes her feel the one-sidedness again. She opens the last one he sent her before they met in San Francisco. The words blur and collapse on the screen, but she knows it by heart anyway.

Jules,

So . . . I've booked a hotel off Union Square called The King George. It's a boutique place, kinda eccentric, faded glamour, all of that. I was thinking of the Chelsea in New York. (Let's stay there next . . . commune with the ghosts of Hendrix, Cohen, Joplin!) I think you'll like it. I can't picture us in some modern soulless place. Believe me I've pictured us in lots of places. The rooms are dark and old-fashioned, with brass beds and velvet blankets, and I can see you now . . .

Well, I'll leave the rest of that up to you and your

imagination, Jules. Because you know how bad I am at writing. And because pleasuring you is all that matters anyway.

R x

P.S. Do you think you could still play? We could jam together. Dylan and Baez!

Of course Bob Dylan had broken Joan Baez's heart too. Been so careless with her, married someone else. She wrote that raw song about him, 'Diamonds and Rust'. Beautiful but corrosive.

God, they'd been frenetic for years, those emails and messages after she met him in 2018. She had come back especially to vote in the abortion referendum, had to go to considerable lengths to pretend she was still a resident. She'd worn a light cotton Repeal T-shirt through the arrivals hall, was cheered by young people holding banners. She was so proud of her country. How different to her lonely journey back from Liverpool, through this airport, almost thirty years before, where she'd shuffled, sore and bleeding, a sodden pad between her legs that impeded her gait. And more than the loneliness: anger – that she was then too young and close to, to fully define – at the hypocritical little country that turned away and exported its problems. But in May 2018 Ireland suddenly appeared a place where she could belong again. And Rory, who had never stopped inhabiting her, a person to embrace her home. She was euphoric that night after learning the result, went into town to celebrate and bumped into him in a pub. They were tipsy and loose, poring over the past, dangerously, indulgently nostalgic. The taxi dropped her off first and he got out as well, hugged her a little too long and then that kiss which was saturated with the past and regret but also seemed a prelude to the future. 'I've never stopped wanting you, Jules,' he said. 'You're the only thing from my past I've wanted to hold on to.'

And when she came home again the following year he picked her up from the airport and they drove straight to the hotel on Drury Street. Standing at reception, riding the lift to the room, the porter fussing over her suitcase, it was all pure agony. When the porter went, all speech left her; some strange throaty moan came from her and they fell on each other, and she felt something inside her unspool, all those years of longing. And that whole first night, like some fever dream. No sleep, couldn't sleep, just wanting him inside her, the whole night, nothing left inside her except him, wanting to squeeze every last drop from it, from him.

And those two long Covid years when they couldn't see each other but, God, that lustful correspondence sustained her. San Francisco was supposed to be the light at the end of that dark pandemic tunnel. She was so hopeful.

How stupid, though, how naïve. Hope. Was there any emotion more futile? As worthless as regret. Things were different after San Francisco, the messages much less frequent, the heat taken out of them. His way of punishing her. But nothing you could put your finger on. Not in any way that he could be accused of anything. Subtle, innocuous-seeming differences to the untrained heart, but to Juliet's, like a knife being inserted, because she understood the deliberateness. *Jules* changed to *Juliet*, signed off as *Rory* rather than *Rx*, he stopped mentioning the Chelsea Hotel, Bob Dylan, stopped quoting lyrics. He always claimed to be bad at words, but what it was, really, is that he was very good at being vague. That had always been the way of him. Engage and then withdraw. Become like his pale, flaxen-haired mother hovering in the background of the house. There but not really. Of course, he'd have emerged again eventually when he'd stopped sulking, to dazzle her, she's sure of that. Make her more grateful for it.

But then to die!

She closes the folder and is about to close the app when she notices one from Erica. She struggles to read it but Erica is saying something about the truth and she feels a strange sense of gratitude. They were real. People need to understand how real they were.

Hi Erica,
Yes we fucked many times.

She erases this line, types,

Yes we made love many times.

She deletes this too.

It wasn't an 'arrangement' but it was pre-ordained. It was fate. I loved him. I loved him. I loved him.

He loved me.

She thinks then of Charlie and deletes again. Anyway, she can't do it justice. God, she's angry now, thinks of Erica complaining that it was like extricating herself from a cult. Juliet could have made him hers too, over thirty years ago, instead of taking that trip to Liverpool. That's how you ground someone so elusive. Instead of doing the right thing. She knocks back the rest of her drink, gets off her stool and bends to pick up her bag which has fallen to the floor. As she straightens, she stumbles and bangs against one of the old men at the bar.

'Shit, sorry,' she says, and rebalances herself by leaning her hand on the stool beside him.

'No bother,' the man says, without looking at her.

'Listen, could you tell Liam that Juliet couldn't wait. She got so tired of waiting.'

The man turns stiffly and with great effort. He is shrunken inside a long wax jacket. His eyes are cloudy and there are stunted whiskers poking out of his chin, patches of flaky skin on his forehead and nose. He smells mouldy and sour, like a person who's decayed right there on the bar stool. She's glad of her blurred vision. 'I know you,' he says. 'You're the Quinn girl.'

'Yes.' She tries to focus on his features, dissolve the years, but still doesn't recognise him. 'How are you?' she says, bluffing.

He waves his arm as though it's a stupid question. 'Ah, still alive, more's the pity. It's a disappointment to wake up every morning.' He lets out a heavy sigh. 'Don't let anyone tell you different, growing old is a tremendous curse.'

As soon as he says it, *tremenjus*, she recognises him as Dr Flynn. She experiences a wave of revulsion. 'Well, it's better than the alternative, as they say.'

'Only young people say that.' He turns back to face the bar as though he's had enough of the conversation.

She looks at the back of his head. She could convict this old man. Hand down the death penalty in fact, though it seems he'd welcome that. She thinks of Dan. Charming, funny, liquid-eyed Dan, sitting on the low wall of the bridge, smoking with exaggerated relish, or waving his spliff around, expounding a theory on why rock stars die at twenty-seven or ruminating on the idea that we are standing on a planet spinning on its axis at a thousand miles per hour and orbiting a huge fireball in infinite space and time. 'The insane thing is, Juliet, that we don't even *know* what we don't know,' as he shook his head in disbelief. 'Just give us a drag, Dan, you're making my head spin.' God, maybe he was better off dying then with some modicum of wonder left in his soul.

Outside, to quell the rising nausea, she gulps in the cool night air. The lack of humidity here is a gift; Auckland in summer can feel like a hot breath. She starts to make her way up the road. The moon is casting malevolent shadows on the ground. Behind her, she hears the door to the bar open and a clamour of conversation escape.

'Juliet!'

She turns to see Liam jogging towards her.

'Sorry. I needed to let the dog out for a piss.'

'I'm grand, Liam. To be honest, I want to be by myself and I'm only around the corner.'

'You're a bit wobbly. I'm worried you'll end up in a ditch.'

She pulls at his jacket. 'That's a good idea. We could do it there. For old times' sake.'

He shakes his head but has a wry smile on his face. 'You're unreal, do you know that? Unreal.' He takes a strand of her hair, says softly, 'But you don't need to be like that with me, Juliet.'

'Ah spoilsport.' She steps back, throws her arms out. 'Look, I'm fine. I'll text you when I'm home.'

'Okay, I'll give you my card so you have my number.'

'Ah fuck off, Liam. Since when do you carry a card?'

He laughs. 'Here, give me your phone then.' She hands it to him and he keys in his number.

He touches her bare arm after he hands back her phone. 'You've got goosebumps. New Zealand must be making you soft.' He takes off his jacket and puts it around her shoulders.

'I'll drop it back to you tomorrow.'

He winks. 'All part of my cunning plan. Now go on. I'll wait here. If anyone jumps you between here and your house just scream, and I'll be there in a flash.'

'My hero.' She reaches up and kisses his cheek. She can feel him flinch, and for a moment she's sad for him. She knows what it's like to be so vulnerable for someone.

As she walks away, she's aware of him watching so tries to keep a straight line but the effort makes her weave more. Just before the bend, she looks back and he's still there. He gives a corny, exaggerated wave followed by a thumbs-up. It makes her smile. Why can't she love a man like him?

There's a light on downstairs when she reaches her mother's house and she lets herself in as quietly as she can. As she turns to gently close the door she sees a shadow outside the gate and knows that Liam must have followed her home after all. She does not deserve his care.

As she tiptoes up the stairs her foot slips on a smooth, worn piece of carpet and she crashes forward, banging her face. She lies unmoving, stunned for a moment, then repositions her head to the side so that her cheek is resting on the step. She looks through the banisters and there is an ethereal glow of light seeping out from under the sitting-room door. Her nose throbs in a way that might mean it's painful tomorrow but for now it's almost pleasant. The fuzzy edges of light roll towards her like waves and she thinks of the ocean.

Her eyes close; it would be nice to let sleep take her now. Maybe she'll dream a good dream of Rory. He spooned her in all their hotel beds, the only person she allowed do that, and the weight of Liam's jacket on her back now is a comfort. 'I feel like we had the same dreams last night,' he'd say when he woke. 'Well, I dreamed of you all night,' she'd say. And she wasn't sure if she really had or if she simply spent the entire night alert, barely believing her luck that he was right there beside her. Barely believing it was real. She thinks of Erica's email then, feels grateful. Someone else understands it was real.

She hears a door creak.

'Juliet! Sweet mother of divine Jesus.'

ERICA

It's Saturday morning, eight days after the funeral, and she's in Rory's office looking for some documents that their accountant has requested. She opens a drawer in his desk and as she rifles through some papers sees a miraculous medal in the shape of a cross. She pulls it out. It's gold and chunky and she remembers his grand-aunt bringing it home for him from Lourdes many years ago. She'd fretted about his soul, having a heathen Englishwoman for a mother. Erica feels tender suddenly at his sentimentality. She holds the cross for a while in her hands, a reassuring weight to it. And she remembers that crazy woman in Dublin. When Erica was studying psychology in college in the nineties – she commuted up and down because by then she and Rory were living together in Ballyboyne – this woman, always dressed in a beret and a trench coat with a large crucifix around her neck, used to march the length of Grafton Street carrying a placard with photos of aborted foetuses with alien features; black dots for eyes, stunted fingers, an extraterrestrial glow of amniotic fluid surrounding their misshapen heads. The pictures were so graphic, grotesque, you'd have to look away, nauseated, which, Erica supposed, was the whole point. The young Erica would look at the woman with pity, wonder why she bothered. Why she would be so moved to do this same thankless thing every day, walk in every kind of weather, bemusing or disgusting passers-by in a country where abortion was illegal anyway and looked like it would stay that way for some time. Erica dismissed her as a joke, a curiosity, a person who belonged in the conservative Ireland of the past, with photos of the Sacred Heart and the pope and JFK on the walls.

But years later, after her fifth and final miscarriage when she bled a clot out onto their bed, that crazy woman and her placards came back to her. Afterwards, Rory, believing he was being helpful, tried to console her by talking about how it was nothing more than a bunch of cells, with no awareness of anything, even of itself, not understanding that for Erica, every part of her, every organ, every single atom in her own body in fact, was adapting and accommodating and aware of that baby's presence. This baby was fully formed, was both utterly present and in her future, had grown up and gone to college, had children of their own. And she'd thought of that strange, singular woman again and wondered if maybe the madness was literally that; she was simply furious. That maybe a person – her husband, or a doctor, or a friend, or maybe all of them – had dismissed some grief and so she woke up one morning in a rage and there was nothing to be done except take to the streets to vent it. Erica still didn't agree with this woman's politics but she thought then that she understood her a little. Understood how denied pain like that could seethe and wriggle around inside you and eventually make you go insane.

Maybe she also thought of this woman again with this final miscarriage because it was May 2018 in the intense run-up to the abortion referendum. Rory remained upbeat about their chances of having another baby. It'd be okay, he said. They'd try again, he said. But Erica knew she was done. Her body was telling her something, yelling at her in fact, and it was time to listen. She was almost forty-five years old and it seemed the correct number at which to call it quits. Even with a womb that didn't malfunction as hers did, the rate of miscarriage after this age increased exponentially. The following morning, when she was home from the hospital, she walked into the utility room to find Rory sorting the bloodied sheets from their bed to put them in the washing machine. 'We could adopt, or foster,' she said to his back. 'I've looked into it. We could give an unwanted child a lovely home. We have so much to give.' He turned around. 'Another man's child?' he said, and visibly shuddered.

And it was then, that precise moment, that the dull cramping sensation in Erica's stomach became a tight band of fury. 'Just get rid of them,' she said, gesturing at the sheets, and when he looked unsure, she walked over, ripped them from his hands, carried them outside and stuffed them in the bin. She came back in and told him that she was going to stay with her parents to get some rest and she packed Charlie into the car and drove the short distance to her childhood home. She stayed there for a week. Eventually her mother told her that, much as she loved having them, Erica needed to go home and attend to her marriage. 'It's not that hard to be married to a man, Erica. They're simple creatures at the end of the day. Just feed him and fuck him, darling. And if either of those things is a problem for you, well, you can always outsource.' She paused, then added, 'Maggie used to feed your father.' With this odd declaration she left the room. In the car on the way home later that day, thinking about her mother's words, it dawned on Erica that despite Maggie doing their housework and nannying for years, she had never, in all that time, made a meal for them. Once back, Erica told Rory that if he needed sex, she was fine with him getting it elsewhere because she would no longer provide that service. There would be no questions asked, no recriminations. Erica felt confident he wouldn't leave her. Rory loved the idea of their marriage. Erica wasn't stupid, she knew how much respectability he believed that she conferred on him. It doesn't get much more respectable than having a judge for a father-in-law. There was too much at stake with their business anyway. Divorce would have been messy, expensive. And as long as she didn't have to know about what he got up to, Erica felt she didn't care.

She buries the medal, pulls another drawer, sees the whiskey bottle and is immediately assaulted by a memory of sending those drunk emails. She opens the laptop, feels scared, and so closes it. She takes a swig of whiskey straight from the bottle, then opens the laptop again. There's a reply sent at six this morning. She takes a breath and clicks on it.

Hello Erica,

It was real. I'm sorry but you asked for the truth. We had a very strong connection. The type that I think only comes once in your life so you have to seize on it otherwise you die wondering. I'm not saying this to hurt you by the way, just the opposite in fact. I want you to understand that he didn't do it flippantly. Honestly, I believe he could not help himself. *We* could not help ourselves.

We got together in 2018. We were in hotels mostly. We were never in your house, if that's a concern. He didn't talk much about you but don't be offended by that. He needed to separate us. I tried my best to get him to talk about you actually. He never would. He was so stubborn. Of course you know this.

He was a very generous lover. But you must already know this too. While he liked blow jobs – of course he did, what man doesn't – he preferred to give oral pleasure. He was sensuous but wasn't kinky in any way. He was pretty vanilla as these things go actually. I always felt with him that the emotional connection in sex was more important than the physical one.

I'm not sure what you mean by rules, though? Is that something you had with him in bed? A safe word? There was nothing like that between us. No rough stuff. That kind of thing has its place but I wouldn't have liked that with him. I think it would have tainted it.

What do I look like? I've been called both ugly and beautiful. Neither of these descriptions moves me greatly. And my body? My relationship with it is uncomplicated. I know I'm lucky in that respect. My mother has waged a war against her own for as long as I can remember so I think I decided at a very young age to accept mine. That's not to say it's a perfect body, but it does everything I want perfectly.

What did he like when he was with me?

Oh boy . . . Are you sure?

He liked when I undressed slowly in front of him. He liked me in white cotton underwear. He liked when I described what I was about to do to him, how I was going to pleasure him. He liked to watch me pleasure myself. He liked the lights to be on. He liked the dents on my lower back. He liked when I took his fingers in my mouth before he put them inside me. He liked that I liked to kiss him deeply after he went down on me. He liked having his neck kissed, especially the tender hollow just above his collarbone. I liked to kiss that spot too because it seemed to me a defenceless place where I might just be able to reach inside him. He liked my collarbone. And my right hip. He said it reminded him of the curve of a guitar. He liked all my scars. I had an emergency operation a few years ago because I had a ruptured cyst on my ovary. I was pregnant and I bled so much during this operation that I lost the baby and the scar runs flattened and silver and severe across the top of my pubic bone now and means I have an overhang of skin above it. He liked it, played with it, called it my little kangaroo pouch, but the scar under it also made him very tender and sad, for some reason. He never explained why. He liked when I went on top because he liked to look at me. But he also liked when I leaned forward and my hair fell around his face. He liked the coconut shampoo I used. He said I smelled like a holiday. He liked me to say his name when I came. He liked the way I laughed after I came.

I always laughed after I came. I always came.

What did I like? Well, all of the above, of course.

But mostly . . .

There's a moment, raw, fleeting, when you make love to someone, and you can see on their faces that they've forgotten themselves. That's what I was always searching for with him. That's what I liked. I wanted him to forget everything except that precise moment with me.

MAEVE

Maeve and Cillian are on the sideline watching Luke's rugby team, having left Cillian's sister at home with Lily. Maeve suggested they come together this morning, usually it's one or the other. They're better outdoors, away from the oppression of her mother's decline, Jamie's moods, the resentment and micro-aggressions around household responsibility.

The usual alliances are on display. The parents of the gifted players stand together, near the beleaguered coach and the subs bench, giving their unsolicited advice, advocating for their own sons, remonstrating with the volunteer referee, yelling at the kids on the field – despite most of them never having played a game in their lives – to make a *counter ruck* or a *clearout* or something else Maeve doesn't understand. They are the same parents who in the team WhatsApp start posting possible tactics for the upcoming game straight after training on a Tuesday evening and then post-match analysis as soon as the game finishes on a Saturday. Cillian, wisely, refuses to be part of the group. (He has a healthy relationship towards social media and messaging platforms in general. That is, he doesn't partake at all.)

The parents of the less talented players stand further along in smaller groups or separately. Cillian and Maeve are standing alone. Cillian knows nothing about the game, Maeve even less, so neither can offer any intelligent contribution to the sideline banter. Even after three years of watching Luke play, Maeve finds the lingo and rules impenetrable. 'Why is that a penalty?' she'll ask Cillian, who'll shrug and say, 'You're the one who grew up beside the rugby club.' And she'll reply, 'Well, you grew up in South Dublin.' But they both tell Luke after every game that he was great, no matter how he played. In fairness, neither has any clue whether he played well or not. 'But I missed all my tackles,' he'll protest and Cillian will pat him on the back and say, 'Oh well, what I'm hearing, Luke mate, is that you missed them so that shows you attempted them, which is the most important thing.' And that would be the end of any post-match analysis in their family. Maeve feels conflicted about this. Obviously, it's healthy not to pressure him but maybe he'll grow up with an inflated sense of his own ability. Like those deluded kids you see on television talent shows whose parents have never been honest with them. Cillian tells her she's overthinking it and that this is the problem with modern parenting. Maeve suspects it's less to do with modern parenting and more to do with the enduring doubt that has been inherent in motherhood since the dawn of time. You can bet your life Mary wasn't too convinced that sacrificing her only son for the good of mankind was such a hot idea. God, meanwhile, seemed confident of his plan from day one.

She texts Jamie.

Are you up?

Um yeah?

Could you empty the dishwasher please?

I literally did it last week.

Literally is redundant in that sentence. Also, just do it!!

Jeez woman you have ZERO chill.

She's about to text an angry reply when she sees Jamie is typing again.

Aunty Caitlin says she will do it.

Maeve puts the phone away. 'Whoever has the misfortune to marry that boy is going to curse me. I know it.'

'If it's any consolation, I doubt anyone will marry him.'

'Funnily enough, that's not. He's going to live at home forever.'

'That was probably on the cards anyway given housing unaffordability. They'll just be waiting for us to croak it so they can inherit the place.'

Maeve sighs. 'Have we fucked the world for them, Cillian? I mean, was it ethical to even have children?' She feels guilty then for saying this because she suspects her doubt is a result of her elder son's disposition rather than any virtuous impulse.

'Most people don't ponder the ethics of it. It's much more personal.'

'Young people these days do. They're much more cognisant of these issues than we ever were.'

'Well, it's true they are more anxious. They don't suffer

from post-traumatic stress these days, it's all pre-traumatic stress now.' He peers over the top of his glasses, his forehead ridged. 'Where's all this coming from?'

'I don't know. Maybe it's with Rory dying I've been thinking about my youth a lot lately and feeling very far away from who I was then.' A cheer goes up from the opposition supporters and Maeve can't figure out why. 'I wonder if my seventeen-year-old self saw me now what she would think.'

'Firstly, she'd think, *Wow, there I am in thirty years' time still over-analysing everything to death.* Then she'd think, *But woah! Look at the total stud I've bagged myself. Go me!*'

Maeve doesn't feel generous enough to laugh at this. She's annoyed by her own mean-spiritedness now too. She shakes her head in exasperation and looks down the pitch towards the goalposts. Luke has just been subbed on and is being run at by a boy twice his size. She scrunches up her eyes in fear. When she opens them again, he's sprawled on the ground. Her heart catches but he gets up and immediately launches into a mass of writhing, jostling bodies. 'I fucking loathe this game. I can't look anymore. I'm going to get a coffee from the van. Do you want one?'

Cillian looks at his watch as though for permission. 'No, thanks, too late for me.'

'Apple says no?'

'Eh?'

'Never mind.'

This was a stupid idea. She's as irritated by him as ever.

As she walks to the van in the carpark on the far side of the pitch she passes a group of teenage girls watching the game from the sideline. They're all about fourteen, in that glorious leggy stage of adolescence where growth spurts come in fits and starts and their bodies haven't quite kept pace with their limbs. They stand huddled together, entwined almost, with near identical outfits of grey sweatshirts and black leggings, so that it's hard to see where one starts and the other ends, and Maeve feels a pang, remembering the ease with physical closeness they had as children.

As she passes the girls she hears a snippet of conversation.

. . . anyway Grace likes Luke Halpin . . . he's so hot . . .

She smiles when she hears her younger son's name, stops, bends down pretending to tie her shoelace to hear some more. They tell you so little about themselves, teenage boys. He is a good-looking lad, she thinks proudly.

. . . his brother is such a loser, though . . . No way, that incel Jamie Halpin is his brother? . . . Total small dick energy . . .

Instantly, Maeve's pride is crushed by fear. Why this push–pull of motherhood all the time? She knows he's not popular the way Luke is, but *incel*?

She thinks back to the discussion over dinner last night when Cillian had bemoaned the seemingly sudden explosion in anti-immigrant sentiment in the country.

'These *Ireland is full* yobbos depress the hell out of me,' he'd said. 'Previously our anger has been directed against the ruling parties. Now we're picking on the already dispossessed.'

'I know,' Maeve replied, picking up the salad bowl. 'And us seeking refuge all over the world. What short memories these people have. It makes me so sad.'

Jamie, often mute at mealtimes, sitting at the table with his hood over his head, had looked up from his plate and said, 'Well, what do you expect? They're taking our houses and our jobs. Clogging up the health system. Stealing and raping our women. And you know those Irish people seeking refuge in other countries? Well, check out what they did to Black people in New York or Aboriginals in Australia.'

'Excuse me?' Maeve said, slamming down the salad bowl. '*Stealing and raping our women?* What kind of bullshit is that, Jamie?'

Cillian reached over and placed his hand on hers. 'Maeve, now, don't get upset. He has a right to express himself. And he's not wrong about the Irish in New York.'

'A right to express himself, sure. A right to spout hatred and lies, no.'

Jamie sighed. 'No point carrying on this conversation. It's impossible to reason with you. You'll just get all irrational as usual. I'm done.' And with that he left the table.

Maeve was furious and wanted to go after him and interrogate it but Cillian convinced her to leave it alone. He reassured her it was merely some ill-informed view he'd read online somewhere and regurgitated. Pushing it with him risked pushing him to hide what he was really thinking. The most important thing is they should remain calm and open and approachable. Maeve had brought up the topic again with Jamie this morning and he'd shrugged it off and said she was making a big deal out of nothing. It was 'just the same stuff everyone was saying'. Cillian said, 'There you go, I don't think it's a worry. Just a kid parroting something without truly understanding.'

But this? He's known for this beyond the confines of home? It's not just him trying to wind her up?

She continues to the coffee van, her mind twinned with her stomach in a conjoined knot of worry. Reading the menu, the thought of coffee makes her queasy so she heads back to Cillian a different way to how she came to avoid walking past those girls again.

In the car on the way home, she turns to Luke in the back seat and gestures for him to take off his headphones.

'Yeah?'

'What's Jamie like in school?'

'Huh?'

'I mean, what does he do at lunchtime? Does he have friends?' She can sense Cillian's eyes on her.

Luke shrugs. 'I don't see him at lunchtime. He doesn't play football or basketball or anything.'

'So what does he do?'

'On his phone, I suppose.'

'Do people like him? Has he ever had a girlfriend? Do people say anything to you about him?'

Cillian says, 'What's all this about, Maeve?'

'Just wondering.' She turns to face Luke again. 'Well, do they?'

'I mean, he's kind of weird. A bit emo.'

'What does that mean?'

'Like, sad.'

'Sad as in unhappy? Or sad as in pathetic?'

'I dunno. You're being weird now.' Then he puts his headphones back on. Maeve gestures at him to take them off again but Cillian takes his hand off the gear stick and puts it on hers.

'Leave him, Maeve. Where are these questions coming from anyway?'

This new habit of his, placing his hand on hers as though placating her, is driving her mad. She wonders if it's some therapy strategy. She pulls her hand away and tells him about the overheard conversation.

'Well, maybe we could ask his teachers how he's getting on in school. But I think you're worrying too much. Those girls wouldn't have meant the word *incel* literally. Probably he's just a bit awkward around them, you know how he is. And when Luke says he's weird I would take that with a pinch of salt too. Teenagers think everything is weird and, I mean, I was a bit of a goth myself back in the day. I enjoyed being misunderstood. Not everyone feels the need to fit in with the popular jocks, you know.' He turns on the radio. 'Friday I'm in Love' by The Cure is playing. 'See!' he says. 'Robert Smith, the ultimate emo. He did alright for himself. And made this cheesy, happy song.'

Then he sings along, off-key, and Maeve experiences an acidic gurgle of irritation. Like she's curdling on the inside.

At home, she knocks on Jamie's door and when he doesn't answer walks in anyway. He's lying on his bed, scrolling on his phone. His black hair is falling over his eyes and he doesn't look up to acknowledge her. Not for the first time, Maeve feels a wave of animosity towards Steve Jobs. Apparently, he wouldn't let his own kids have iPhones. *Well, fuck you, Steve Jobs*, she thinks. *Where will it end? When our children merge completely with these devices, become some weird, hybrid cyborg?* It depresses the shit out of her. To add insult to injury, her phone sends her almost daily memories now, photo montages set to sentimental music, of the boys when they were little, just to remind her of what they were like before they were lost to technology.

'Hey,' she says. 'I was going to go for a walk. Do you want to come?'

'Nah.'

'It'll be healthy to get some fresh air.'

'I'm good.'

She sits on the edge of the bed, tries Cillian's trick of placing her hand on his. 'Is everything okay? Like in school and stuff?'

He looks up at her and scowls, as though she's deranged. Takes his hand away. 'Yeah, why wouldn't it be?'

'Just checking in. You know, you can talk to me or your dad about anything that's bothering you.'

He sighs. 'Yeah, okay.'

'Yeah, okay you'll talk to us? Or yeah, you're okay and don't need to?'

'Ugh. Jeez. I know. I know I can talk to you.'

Maeve thinks about the word *incel* and tries to work out how she can broach the topic without enraging him.

'Good . . . and so . . . I was wondering. Do you like girls?'

'What the hell? Are you on drugs, Mam? Do you think I'm gay or something?'

'No. That's not what I'm asking. Even though it would be wonderful, obviously, if you were. I was just, I suppose . . . em . . . checking your thoughts on females.'

'My *thoughts on females*? Oh my God, you're such a freak. I'm not gay. Even though I think you'd prefer if I was. Now, can you please get out?'

'No, Jamie. I'm not asking about your sexuality. That's not the issue. I'm just trying to ascertain—'

'And shut the door.' He picks up his AirPods and shoves them in his ears.

'Splendid,' Maeve says aloud. 'This has gone well.'

Cillian sticks his head round the door then. 'Maeve? Your mother wants you. She won't let me or Caitlin make her anything to eat. She says we're trying to poison her.'

'Je*sus*,' she mutters under her breath and, taking one last look at Jamie, whose eyes are fixed on his phone, shuts the door and goes downstairs.

Later, at her desk, she opens her laptop to do some work to try to distract herself and she sees a new email from Nisha. She can feel the coiled tightness in her chest unravel as she reads it. Like she can take a proper breath again.

Hi Maeve,

I've been working on drafting some agent query letters. Thanks for your help. I've attached one at the end of this for you to have a look at.

I'm so excited to finally (with your encouragement!) be doing this. I turn thirty-seven next week and it feels like an important age. An age for getting one's shit together. Maybe it's just because *seven* ages always feel that way to me . . . more symbolic than those zero milestone ones, for some reason.

N x

P.S. And hmmm . . . I've been thinking about your lack of experience with women. If your imagination fails you I've also attached links below to some sites that might help . . .

Maeve smiles, then stands and checks there is no-one in the kitchen before closing the door to the snug and sitting back down at her desk.

———

They made a pact, she and Dan, that summer. They were lounging one evening on the benches down at the deserted tennis courts, not long after Juliet's father had died, smoking cigarettes and swatting away the midges with their rackets, after a half-hearted game where Dan had gone deliberately easy on her. She'd never really caught up with the others' skill level. Maeve felt things to be disintegrating in their little gang and it seemed to her that sex was the problem. The constant tension between Juliet and Rory was getting in the way. They were either arguing or finding excuses to touch each other, sometimes both things at once. You always felt as though you'd interrupted something, like walking in on your parents having sex. Maybe the nuns had the right idea after all, never mind Juliet's theory that they were all banging each other with strap-ons. ('That's why half of them take men's names, Maeve.') Maeve thought it might be nice to get back to the innocent days of pooh sticks and tip the can and annoying the neighbours by knick-knacking on their doors. Sex and fancying each other made everything complicated and ugly. She said as much to Dan, who told her she'd feel differently if she ever fell in love. Maeve thought to herself how wrong he was; her own confused feelings around sex, around finding both Rory and Juliet attractive at times, heightened everything. But she said, 'Have you ever been in love, Dan?'

She heard him sigh. 'There is someone. In the musical society. I'm not entirely sure yet if he feels the same. I'm not sure where he's at with himself. Nonetheless, I remain optimistic.'

Maeve's eyes welled and she was glad they were lying side by side, their faces upturned so that he couldn't see. He'd never explicitly told her he was gay, it was just kind of understood. Maeve also knew what it would cost him to ever come out to his father. The thought of that scenario filled her with terror, so she held a deep gratitude that he was trusting her now. She put her cigarette in her mouth and held it there, then reached across and squeezed his arm.

'It'll happen for you too one day, Maeve.'

'Yeah, maybe.' Love, you could keep it, as far as Maeve was concerned. She took a deep breath. Dan was able to be open about these things and he had a bigot for a father. Lily would probably throw a party if Maeve told her she was a lesbian. Maybe it wasn't such a big deal. 'But you know, I get . . . distracted. I'm not certain how I feel about different things.'

'What do you mean? Get distracted?'

'I mean, I can't figure out who I like or what . . .' But she still couldn't say it, the words were wedged in her throat. 'Ugh,' she dropped her tennis racket to the ground in frustration, 'I just wish it was all straightforward.'

'Don't stress, Maeve.' He said it so kindly. 'It's normal to feel confused about this stuff. And you know, when it comes to what we like, or who we like, well, it's not rigid. Personally, I believe there's a continuum.'

'Juliet's not confused.'

'True. Even in grief that girl is firmly tethered to the *loves dick* end of the continuum.'

Maeve laughed then too. A sort of relief flooded her body. 'Is she ever.' She took a drag of her cigarette. 'You know, whatever about all that stuff, I would like to have kids one day.'

'Me too. I'd love kids. I think I'd make a good father.' She heard him exhale. 'Or at the very least I'd know exactly what kind not to be.'

'You'd make a great parent, Dan.'

'Thanks. You too.' He sat up then and looked at her. 'Hey, given what terrific individuals we are, and the superior genes we possess, let's make a pact. In twenty years, when we're thirty-seven, if we haven't met *the one*, let's have a child together.'

Thirty-seven. It seemed impossible that they could ever be that old. Thirty-seven was the age that poor Lucy Jordan, in the Marianne Faithfull song, had decided enough was enough – rides through Paris in convertibles with the wind in her hair were never going to happen – and climbed up on that roof. If Maeve was still confused and single and a virgin at thirty-seven, which felt likely, to be honest, she would jump off that roof for sure.

'Okay. On one condition.'

'Anything, my dear.'

She grinned at him. 'It's by artificial insemination.'

He laughed, lobbed a tennis ball gently at her. 'Oh, I'd insist on it, don't you worry. Have it inserted into the contract.' He held his cigarette like a pen then and wrote words in the air as he spoke. 'Section five, subsection twenty-one, paragraph three, article seven, otherwise known as The Turkey Baster clause.'

And Maeve laughed again. You kind of felt you could put up with anything when you had Dan as your friend. Even involuntary celibacy.

JULIET

When she comes downstairs, Denise is at the kitchen table in her pink dressing gown with a cup and a glossy magazine in front of her. RTÉ 1 is booming from the ancient radio on the windowsill. 'Morning,' she says.

There's something missing from the scene and Juliet realises it's a cigarette. She'll never get used to seeing her mother without one. She turns down the volume on the radio and opens the press over the kettle where the mugs are kept. There's one that has *World's Best Dad* written on it. Josh bought it for him for Christmas many years ago. Wishful thinking maybe, poor Josh. There's another *Smarties* one that came with an Easter egg sometime last century. Its continued presence in this cupboard irritates her, but she knows when she's back in Auckland, thinking about her mother and Ireland, that things like this will make her tender and homesick. So, she chooses this one, then sees the muddy interior which reminds her of a grotty public toilet and sighs heavily.

'Good afternoon,' Denise says eventually, looking up from her magazine.

'Don't be hassling me. I'm on holiday.'

'How are you?'

'I won't lie. I'm hanging out my arse.'

'Yeah, you're horrid pale, so you are.' This is the fourth time this visit that Denise has accused her of this. Juliet deliberately passes no remarks on Ruby's appearance though she wonders if maybe she's taken this too far. Ruby asked her once why she never compliments her the way other mums do.

'Thanks,' says Juliet cheerfully.

'I thought you'd get some colour on you over in New Zealand.'

Juliet doesn't reply, picks up the teapot and pours the treacly liquid into her mug. She takes a gulp. 'Far out, Denise, it's like tar.' She opens the lid and pokes around with a spoon. 'How many teabags?'

'Five, as per.'

'My mouth feels like something's died in there now.'

'That'll be the drought from the booze. Not my tea.'

'I'm making coffee instead.'

She rummages in the cupboard and takes out the jar of Nescafé. It always feels like 1986 in this place. She digs a spoon in to excavate some granules which have fossilised together. 'I need a pickaxe,' she says, but eventually mines enough to fill a teaspoon. She flicks on the kettle and sits down to wait. Despite it being nearly summer, the light is gloomy in the low-ceilinged room and she thinks of her bright, open-plan apartment in Auckland with longing. She tells herself it's only the jetlag. Only the hangover.

Denise holds up the magazine. A model looks vacantly out of the page. Her mouth is slightly agape. Juliet wonders if it's to avoid tasting the wet slick of glutinous pink gloss that has coagulated on her bottom lip and looks as though it's about to drip. It makes her queasy.

'When my hair grows a bit I was going to get a do like this. What do you think?'

Juliet shrugs. 'Yeah, it's grand.'

Denise sighs. 'You're a great help. And your nose is in some state, so it is. It's not broken again, is it?'

'If you'd sort out that carpet on the stairs. Anyway, it was never broken. Just a slight fracture.'

'You had black eyes for your father's funeral. I was mortified. Drink-related then too, I'd say.' Denise squints at her. 'I think it's a little bit crooked still so it is.'

'Can we not talk about it?' Juliet brings her hand to her face and touches the grazed skin. It stings and she winces. Denise stands and opens the press under the sink. She takes out a large tub of Sudocrem and puts it in front of her daughter.

Juliet picks it up to look for the expiry date, but it's been rubbed off. 'This is probably the same tub you had when I lived at home. I might as well rub mayonnaise on myself. You know I found a bottle of sauce in the fridge yesterday that was five years old.'

'It's grand. Your generation are so wasteful and yet we get all the blame for screwing the world up. Here.' Denise takes the lid off, dips in a finger and dots it on Juliet's nose. 'Rub it in there yourself.'

Juliet massages it gingerly. The antiseptic and faint lavender scent is like a hit of childhood in her nostrils. There was no ailment the magic ointment couldn't cure. Sudocrem for the outside, Lucozade for the insides. She feels her eyes well and blinks furiously. She always feels more loaded in this place, like she's a rubber band that's being stretched and might ping away at any moment.

'Where's Ruby and Johnny?'

'Gone to get the messages and then into his shop to get a few bits for tomorrow. He's up to Dublin again. Ruby says she'd like to go with him.'

Johnny owns a barber shop in town and business is booming owing to the current fashion for well-maintained facial hirsuteness. Once a month he drives up to Dublin and offers free haircuts and shaves to homeless men. Away he goes, his tools on his belt and a collapsible stool under his arm, and he finds clients – he always refers to them that way – in the train stations or in the doorways of O'Connell Street and he comes back full of the stories of the men he meets. 'They just want to talk and be heard, that's more important than the trim.'

'I'll text Ruby to buy some decent stuff.' Juliet picks up her phone.

Grab some plunger coffee while you're there, darl?

Some Panadol too for your sore head?

Hahaha.

Juliet sighs and puts down the phone.

'So, what are you going to do about her?' Denise says.

'What do you mean?'

'Ruby says she'd like to stay here till Christmas. Then head back over in time for the start of college.'

'She's mentioned it already but I'm not so sure. What would she even do?' But she's thinking of herself really, trying to imagine herself back in Auckland, more exposed and heartbroken without her daughter there. The apartment so much quieter, lifeless, no Billie Eilish from her bedroom. No peals of laughter as she FaceTimes her friends.

'Get a job, like most people. There's a few shifts going down the pub. She could do that for a while. I've asked Liam already, so she could start next week if she liked. Some time here would be good for her. Experience a bit of life.'

'Experience a bit of life? Here on this road? In Ballyboyne? In O'Malley's pub? Don't make me laugh.'

'What's wrong with here?'

'Where do I start? And what about your treatment? You can't be having added stress on top of everything else.'

'Sure that dear child could never cause one day of stress. She's a delight so she is. And I'm not dead yet. Everyone treating me like I am. Honest to God, you're as bad as Johnny so you are. He looks at me sometimes like I'm already a corpse. I'm surprised he's not trying to thread rosary beads around my fingers while I'm asleep. The worst thing about chemo is the boredom of it. If Ruby was here I'd feel a lot better.'

The kettle clicks off. Juliet stands and fills the mug with water. The brown liquid reminds her of the Bisto gravy Denise used to make for their roast dinner every Sunday. The whole house would stink of fatty beef till Tuesday. The little antique clock on the shelf ticks along as someone on the radio complains about having to put a euro into shopping trollies. It's bucketing down outside now. Rory absent and rain and RTÉ 1 and stewed tea and roast beef and Sudocrem and instant coffee and ancient mugs and ticking clocks and her mother's disapproval. She thinks of the stale, weary months after her father died. The heaviness of it. It's as though she's right back there, she's seventeen years old and she's never left. She wants to scream suddenly.

'I'm going out for a walk.'

'Are you demented? The rain is slanty out there. You'll be drowned.'

'With any luck.'

Denise shakes her head. 'You've the heart scalded off me, Juliet. I don't suppose you packed a raincoat either.'

'Correct.'

'Mine's in the hall closet. Put it on so you don't catch your death.'

If only it were that easy.

—

Outside, the sky is a solid bank of grey in every direction. She takes a deep breath, tries to shake off the irritation. The problem has always been that when she's in Auckland, she's homesick for a version of home that doesn't exist, but she knows that back there again she'll think of her mother and feel guilty about her impatience. She stands by the gate trying to decide which way to walk. It's a bit early for the pub so she turns left and heads towards the rugby club and tennis courts. She pulls the hood of Denise's raincoat tight under her chin and puts her head down just as a large SUV sloshes past, hits a pothole and sends a wave of dirty water over the bottom half of her jeans. 'Thanks a million, asshole,' she says aloud and raises her middle finger in salute. The car pulls in abruptly and starts to reverse. Juliet stands aside and wonders if she's about to be involved in a road rage incident. Bring it on, she thinks. She notes then the N-plates on the rear window and a heavy bass pulsating from the interior, which worries her. She'd imagined a middle-aged woman driving a car like this. When the car is alongside her the tinted window lowers and for the briefest of moments a ghost is revealed.

'Sorry for splashing you.' It's Charlie, leaning across the passenger seat, his eyebrows raised apologetically.

'No worries. You're allowed do stuff like that when your father dies. Sorry for giving you the finger.'

Charlie laughs and it sounds exactly like Rory. 'I probably deserved it.'

'Well, you were going a little fast for this road, in fairness.'

'Yeah. Mum would kill me. Can I make it up to you and give you a lift?'

'Yes, actually, you can.' She opens the door and hops up on the seat.

'Nice,' she says, trailing her finger along the leather trims. 'Not too many teenagers get to drive something like this.' Rory drove from the age of thirteen. He used to take his dad's collection of bangers out for joyrides. She can see them now, not a seatbelt on any of them, cruising back roads, all ducking, including Rory, whenever another car passed, so the occupants must have thought they were hallucinating.

'I prefer Dad's car. I just haven't been able to get into it since . . . you know. It smells like him.'

Juliet brings her wrist to her nose where she has sprayed his aftershave and inhales.

'I know.'

He cocks his head to one side and says hesitantly, 'Em, I hope you don't mind me saying something to you?'

'No. What? Go ahead.'

'You appear to have something on your nose.'

She remembers the Sudocrem and laughs, brings her sleeve across it. 'Better?'

He grins. 'Better. So, where to?'

'I could quite do with a decent coffee. Can you bring me up to the café at SuperValu?'

'Sure.'

As he drives, she watches him from the corner of her eye. His left hand rests on the gearstick the entire time, and the skin is plump and hairless. His seat is pushed back to its furthest position so that his arms are fully outstretched. It's how Rory used to drive too.

'So, what stuff did you do when your father died?' he asks.

'God, basic enough stuff. Drank a lot, got high. Snuck off to Dublin, got myself a tattoo.' Got myself accidentally knocked up too, she thinks. Sometimes, though, she wonders how accidental that was. There was a new recklessness certainly but maybe also some unconscious desire to grasp at life, to create one, even. ('Just don't come inside me, it'll be grand,' she'd said. Those optimistic words the undoing of many a girl.) 'Now, shall we change the music?' She nods to the sound system that's throbbing out a rap song.

'You're not into this? I thought you were cool.'

'I mean, ordinarily I am. Totally cool. It's just all the n-words make me feel anxious. I'm not sure what to do when they come on. Old white awkwardness, I guess.' Juliet prefers to call herself *old* which she hopes sounds self-deprecating and funny to him rather than *middle-aged* which is too on the nose.

He smiles. 'I think as long as you don't sing along, you're grand. But you choose something.'

She searches through the Spotify app. There's a playlist called *Drivetime* and she selects it. The opening bars of 'Thunder Road' start, and her heart seizes. She thinks of the taxi ride in Liverpool, on the way to the abortion clinic, hearing it, and how it reminded her then of Rory too. He used to call it the ultimate driving accompaniment. He'd put his *Born to Run* tape into the deck, rewind it back to the start to play it. And Juliet would close her eyes, let the lyrics and music envelop her, and as it built to its climax, she'd imagine it was just the two of them in the car, like the kids in the song, busting out of their shithole, full-of-losers town. 'You look like the cat who got the cream,' Rory would say, grinning, and she'd think she didn't need another thing in the world at that moment.

Sometimes if they were racing down small country lanes Maeve would start fretting but Juliet would think, with that foolish romanticism of youth, that to crash and burn with him, there and then, would be the way she'd want to die.

When she can manage to speak again, she says, 'Your dad's playlist, am I right?'

There's no reply, so she turns to look at him and sees his face is flushed. 'I'm sorry, Charlie, I'll change it.'

She touches the screen but he raises his hand and gently brushes hers away.

They don't speak and that small space is filled with the frenetic piano and saxophone and their intense, silent remembering. As they pull into the supermarket carpark, it reaches its defiant crescendo. Charlie cuts the engine and they sit there, stunned, for a few moments.

'Wow,' says Juliet. Her heart is racing.

'What was he like? As a kid, I mean.'

Juliet must search for words that are appropriate to say to a son.

'Funny, stubborn, complex,' she says eventually. 'What was he like as a dad?'

She's imagined it often. He never knew about her pregnancy. He and Erica together a few months by the time she finally admitted it to herself, or rather was forced to, by Maeve, and her own pride – often absent when it came to Rory and maybe having had enough of being suppressed – rose up and stopped her from telling him. Maeve gave her the pregnancy test before school one day. 'Time to get real, Juliet,' she said, pulling out the brown paper bag from her school satchel. 'You haven't had a period in months and, no offence, girl, but you've actually grown boobs.' During maths class, Juliet pushed the test up her sleeve, wished it was a tampon; how many dozens of times had she pulled down her knickers over the last few weeks praying for blood? She excused herself, went into the bathroom, peed on the stick hovering over the seat, reading the graffiti etched onto the walls, a girl's ugly black school shoes visible under the gap on one side of her, smoke coiling over the top. The sense of unreality then as her eyes moved between the stark blue line of the test and the scrawl of words on the door in front of her: *Kelly Flanagan Is a Slag. Mr Collins Is a Ride. CD has VD.* She had a sudden sense of being outside all those childish preoccupations then.

'Funny, stubborn, complex,' Charlie echoes. 'The best.'

And she thinks of her by then eighteen-year-old self, her arms wrapped around her knees that were pulled up to her face, lying on that narrow bed in the B&B, the room illuminated by the amber glow of a streetlamp. On the side of the locker near her face was scratched *Deirdre 19/08/85* and beneath it *Louise 7/12/87*. She grabbed a pencil and wrote, *Juliet 22/11/90*. Then she closed her eyes and felt bound by a tough sinuous cord to Deirdre and Louise and all the frightened girls that had been there before her. From outside, she could hear Liverpool breathing: the music pulsing from nearby bars, the hum of conversation pleasantly dulled, the swoosh of cars along the city's veins. She thought of Rory, who always talked of making a musical pilgrimage here, visiting the Cavern Club,

Penny Lane. She'd imagined herself coming with him. She cried then, full of self-pity at the godawful loneliness of it, of being in a strange town, alone and cramping and bleeding, and when she finished crying she swore she never would again.

She realises with shock then that her hand is resting on the side of Charlie's face and he has covered it with his own. She withdraws it quickly. 'I'll get the coffee. Want one?'

'Sure.'

They are quiet on the return journey. When they pull up again outside Denise's house he says, 'I found a photo. Of you and Dad.'

'Oh?' She has none. She'd brought no photos of him with her when she'd left Ireland after his wedding. She really believed she was done with him then. After their row in San Francisco she drunkenly deleted all the ones she'd taken there. She stamped on her phone the next morning when she realised what she'd done. Had they even existed, she and Rory?

'It's nice, you look great in it.'

'Do you think I could have it?'

'Sure, call down and get it.'

'When?'

He thinks for a moment. Then, 'I'll text you when it's a good time.'

'Brilliant, thanks.' And once she's given him her number, she steps out of the car and closes the door.

As she walks away he downs the window.

'Juliet?'

'Yeah?'

'I'll text some night when Mum's out.'

She nods once and stays looking at the car as it retreats down the road, tries to pin down the liquid feeling inside her.

———

The night before her father's funeral the four of them were gathered in Juliet's sitting room. She'd kept her friends close for the last few days as a buffer; Maeve had even slept over every night. And it anaesthetised her somewhat, although beneath the numbness, a sensation that she had been changed in some indefinable but fundamental way, as though the cells and neurons and organs and whatever else her body was composed of had been rearranged by the shock. Palpitations in her middle like her heart had displaced her stomach, which now cramped nauseatingly in her head instead. And at times, an anger began to spasm through the numbness, like nerves tingling and coming to life. Flashes of rage at her father for leaving so suddenly. Or no, for never having been there in the first place.

The kitchen and dining room were filled with adults there to comfort Denise. Juliet had swiped a bottle of whiskey that someone had brought as an offering, and they were passing it round taking swigs. Occasionally an adult would stick their head in to check they were okay, and they would hide the bottle, but no-one really cared. They were all drunk themselves anyway – at wakes it was almost an expectation.

From the kitchen they heard one of the women start a song. Another old lament buckling with loss and woe and separation. The unforgiving sea and unsuitable boats and desolate people leaving, and even more desolate people left behind. The woman's voice was thin and reedy, which added to the mournful quality.

'Fuck me,' said Juliet, placing two fingers to her temple and pulling an imaginary trigger. 'Somebody shoot me now. I am so sick of that depressing shite. Honest to God, it's more painful than Daddy dying.' She stood up and walked over to the stacked stereo system in the corner and switched on the radio. It was tuned to some pop station and an over-excited DJ was introducing a new song by the band Heart.

Juliet was about to change it when Maeve said, 'No, leave it, I like this one.'

Rory groaned. 'You've got shite taste in music, Maeve, it has to be said.'

'Sorry, Mr Pretentious Prick who pretends to like Sonic Youth but actually prefers Musical Youth,' Maeve said, giving him the finger. Then she started to sing 'Pass the Dutchie'.

'Piss off.' Rory laughed and threw a cushion at her.

'And this song has a great story, if you paid attention to the lyrics. The woman's husband is shooting blanks, so she goes out and sleeps with another man just to get pregnant. Then the next morning she writes him a note, sneaks out of the hotel and goes back to her husband. And she's a little heartbroken. They both are. But she got her baby, so you know, the end justifying the means and all that.'

Juliet snorted. 'Oh my God, Maeve, you've got it all wrong. The story is the husband is absolutely crap in bed and can't make her come to save his life so she goes out and rides a fella who can. And I don't blame her. If I was married to a fella that couldn't give me an orgasm I'd be straight to the nearest hotel with someone who could.' She started to sing along then, her eyes closed, rubbing her hands over her breasts, her face contorted in mock ecstasy. She hoped Rory was watching and hammed it up for his benefit.

She opened her eyes and Dan was laughing but Rory was looking away with what she knew to be a studied indifference. Sometimes she thought she was going to lose her mind. Maeve was shaking her head and rolling her eyes.

'Whatever, Juliet, you total nympho,' she said. 'You read sex into everything. You're obsessed.'

'Yeah,' said Juliet. She glanced at Rory, who still refused to look in her direction. 'Probably. No-one's ever complained about it, though.'

'You even found *Peig* a turn-on.'

'Well, Peig Sayers had about a hundred kids so I'd say she was a horny little bitch, actually.'

'I'd say the poor woman had no choice in the matter. Actually,' said Maeve.

'I must admit, Maeve,' said Dan, 'I'm partial to Juliet's interpretation of the song. It's far more titillating. It makes middle-of-the-road soft rock suddenly much more interesting.'

Juliet could see that Maeve was annoyed. She never liked to be told she was wrong or have people disagree with her, and would argue a point to the death. She was probably a lot more like her mother than any of them would ever dare to point out.

'Well, yours and Juliet's *interpretation* of the song is irrelevant, Dan, because it's incorrect. God, why does everything have to be about sex anyway? It's driving me mental. Can't we talk about anything else? Aren't we more than that?' Maeve put her head down. There seemed to Juliet to be some sort of prickly static around her.

Rory stood up suddenly then. 'Okay, losers, I'm going.'

'No, you can't go, Rory.' Juliet hoisted herself off the ground. She was drunker than she realised, and her eyes felt a bit unfocused. She tugged on the sleeve of his jacket and made a pouting face. 'Please stay?' She sounded childish and petulant and it annoyed her then. Her voice seemed to do this around him, as though of its own accord.

'Sorry, Jules, I really have to go.' He squeezed her arm. 'But I'll be there tomorrow.' He was never one to be talked out of anything. There was a stubborn propulsion to him that Juliet found infuriating but also deeply sexy.

'Okay, I'll walk with you for a bit. I need some air anyway,' Juliet said, stumbling behind him. At the sitting-room door she turned around to the others. 'Don't wait up.' Dan grinned and Maeve rolled her eyes.

Outside, she linked his arm and leaned into him to steady herself. The night was dry and clear, with a low, heavy moon, but there was a swirling, foreboding wind. They were silent, Juliet afraid to speak and draw attention to herself, as though this spell might get broken, that he might remember she was there, remember who she was, and send her away. She couldn't be alone. And how could she be sure that if she said goodnight to him now, she'd ever see him again? Everything was too precarious. She held her breath, then closed her eyes, felt the breeze and the reassuring heat from his body, the solidity of it next to her. It let her know that he was alive. That she was too. At her gate he stopped, turned to her and put his hands on her upper arms as though holding her up. 'You should go back in now. I'll stand here till you get in the door.'

'So, you do care about me.'

'Of course I care about you, you dope. You're my friend.' She could hear the smile on his lips.

She looked up at him. His face in the moonlight was ethereal, paler, eyes darker, the bone structure finer, the shadows under his cheekbones starker. The texture of his skin, like polished marble. She thought of her cold, dead father, waxy and stiff, laid out for eternity in a suit that he disliked – the one he rarely wore because he said it was scratchy – never to feel the warmth of human touch again. But Rory, he was a living sculpture. She thought of the works of Rodin that they'd been studying in art. He was the perfect height for her, their bodies would fit together in the right way, as though they'd been made for each other. Her eyes were level with his lovely mouth, and she looked at his soft, pink lips – blushed with blood and life – greedily. They were so close. He smelled musky and warm, almost sweet. She could lean in now, tilt her head, reach her arms around his neck so that her back arched in a seductive way. His hand would find her hip, rest there gently, then pull her towards him. They could become Rodin's sensual couple in *The Kiss*, locked in an infinite, erotic embrace. She closed her eyes, ran her tongue over her lips, let them fall open suggestively, then pressed her mouth to his.

He shifted away. She opened her eyes.

'What are you doing?' he said, his mouth curved, eyebrows raised.

'It's called kissing. It's delicious. It makes you feel alive.' She started to giggle.

'Go on, go back in now.' He said it kindly, gesturing towards the house.

'I know you fancy me, Rory. I know it. I can feel it. And I'm crazy about you. You must know that too. There's a mad heat between us. I'm not imagining it.'

He shook his head. 'Listen, your dad's just died. It'd feel wrong.'

'No! Don't you see? That's the whole point. It would feel like the most right thing ever. We're all going to die. And we don't know when. So let's not die wondering.'

'It would change things. I don't want to lose you. We've known each other since we were little kids. You're my best friend. Do you know that? Do you?'

'Good! I want to change things. I think it's obvious I don't want just a friendship with you, Rory.'

Her hand found the waistband of his jeans. She pulled out his T-shirt and then slid her fingers beneath the button. She kept her eyes on his and could see his expression turn groggy as he grew hard. She edged her hand down further, gripped it around him and smiled. 'Friends don't do this, do they?'

He opened his mouth, as though to say something, but he shut it again and then his face became serious suddenly, pained almost. But it seemed to her like acting. Some leading-man posturing he'd seen in a film. She didn't believe it. He lifted her hand away. 'Stop it, Jules. I can't do this.'

She laughed at the melodrama of it. 'Yes, you can. Don't take everything so seriously, Rory. Look, it's easy. I'll show you.' She placed her hands on the side of his face then and lifted her chin. Their lips brushed but he jerked his face away.

'The thing is, Jules ... It's, it's not just that. There's someone else. That I like.'

'What?'

'I think you heard.'

'Who?'

'Erica Fitzpatrick. We've been hanging around a bit. I'm going to ask her to go out with me.'

Juliet laughed again. She knew Erica to see from the tennis courts. She was blonde and pretty and always wore an Alice band and immaculate tennis whites that showed off her legs, that tanned like honey, to perfection. She never swore when she hit a bad shot, or ever in fact, and in summer she helped to coach the younger kids, which she did with abundant patience and rewards of bags of sweets that she kept in her expensive leather gear bag. Naturally, Juliet couldn't stand her. 'Erica? Miss Frigid Prissy Knickers? Yeah, right.'

'Please don't talk about her like that.'

Juliet snorted and it was an ugly sound. 'No offence, Rory, but she's way out of your league. I mean, get real. Daddy probably has her promised to some rugby wanker from D4. You don't stand a chance.'

His face changed, mouth in a straight line now, jaw squared. Like she'd dared him. She knew she'd said the wrong thing.

'I'm going. Please go back in the house, Juliet.'

'No.'

'Okay, suit yourself.'

He untangled himself from her and strode away. She followed him. A few steps down the road he turned. 'Jesus Christ, will you just go back in? I know you're upset about your dad but you're starting to piss me off now.'

'I don't care about Erica Fitzpatrick, Rory. Whatever. It doesn't matter. Ask her out. But you can still have me too.' And immediately she understood, again, that was the wrong thing to say.

'Have some self-respect, Juliet.' She knew he was thinking of his mother.

He turned again but she continued to shadow him. He reached the first bend, a stretch of road where it was darker, a dearth of houses there, so he was only a vague outline before her. She heard his footsteps grow heavier and quicken as though he was jogging and then they turned into a sprint and soon he was completely out of sight. She tried to accelerate too but her legs were wobbly from the whiskey and wouldn't lift properly so her foot skimmed a rock, and she toppled – no, it was more a sensation of being catapulted. It happened in slow motion, and her thoughts, muddled till then, suddenly became very, horribly, lucid. But also slightly funny, as though she was watching someone else. *This is not good*, she thought, *this is going to hurt*. She cried out and it sounded like a kitten mewling. This was funny to her too. Her reflexes were slowed, and her arms failed to brace in time to break the fall so her face slammed the tarmacadam, followed by her hands slapping down. She lay there stunned, warm liquid gushing from her nose, as though in two different directions, so that the iron taste of it was both on her lips and down the back of her throat. River bifurcation, they learned about it in geography. These were the kinds of facts that would never come to her in an exam. Perhaps they needed violence to shake them loose. Her knees and palms stung already, an ominous sign. 'Rory?' she called. 'Rory?' There was that pathetic voice again. But he didn't hear her. Or at least, if he did, he didn't answer.

ERICA

She's in bed listening to the rain on the roof. She's lying directly on the mattress; the effort of a clean fitted sheet proved too great last night, and she'd given up and then wept so much it felt like vomiting. It's their wedding anniversary, twenty years. She'd forgotten until she picked up her phone and the date registered. The time since he died has been so elastic, could have been many months or a matter of hours. In reality it's been just over two weeks. This shapelessness is terrifying. Like there can be no possibility of an end to the sadness. They went last month to Greece to celebrate the anniversary early, as there was a gap then in his schedule. Summer and its lead-up would be too busy with gigs and festivals. (There'd have been no allowance in his schedule for death.) She spent most of the time trying to entertain herself while he sorted out some crisis or another. There was always a crisis, he thrived on it, was energised by the drama. She didn't make a fuss, though. Instead, every morning, she left him in the hotel room talking urgently into the phone and took long walks alone, down through the village, where she would pass by an old woman sitting under a pomegranate tree tying bundles of dried herbs together, while above her the ripe, ruby fruit cracked and split, revealing their innards of decaying arils. 'But why does no-one pick them?' Erica asked one day, pointing upwards, and the woman grinned toothlessly and nodded, and carried on with what she was doing. When they arrived home, Rory headed straight out, citing some emergency, and she sat in the kitchen, staring at the suitcases with the aeroplane tags hanging sadly off them, the rain beating sideways against the window, the sky beyond a solid shelf of grey. She would like to go back with Charlie and reclaim that holiday. Rescue the weeping fruit herself.

A sense of foreboding descends now at the thought of all the firsts lurking ahead of her. Not just the significant things like birthdays or Christmas, but things that she hasn't even begun to think of yet, lying in wait, ready to trip her up. And everything tied to him. Or motherhood. And now with Charlie almost an adult she's got nothing but this formless time stretching ahead. Days bleeding into nights, into weeks, into years.

She hears a car and for a moment, despite herself, pictures Rory in his Audi. It keeps happening. At times, she's been convinced that he's about to walk in the door. Or when her phone rings she's sure that it's going to be the funeral home saying they got it all wrong and the person they buried was someone else entirely. She even starts to feel pity for that other family, about to go through the same heartbreak. She had this same illogical pattern of thought after her miscarriages too. After each loss she would enter a brief, surreal phase of magical thinking where she believed she was still pregnant. The phone would ring and she would think, *Oh, there's the hospital calling to say they've made a mistake.* Or Rory would tell her he had some good news and she would think that he was about to say he met the doctor on the street earlier who told him that actually the baby is fine.

She hears the click of the front door then, looks at her phone again and realises suddenly that it's also a school morning. That must have been Charlie leaving. A tight knot of guilt forms at the self-sufficiency. Rory was usually the one to make his breakfast and lunch or give him a lift. Often, she was awake, could hear them moving around downstairs, but she hated the way if she walked into the kitchen she could feel the atmosphere change, Charlie going quiet, Rory more jocular to make up for it.

She forces herself to the window so that she can at least wave him off but when she looks out she sees a silver Golf parked in the drive and the feeling of dread intensifies. Liz, the cleaner. She'd turned up last week too, all red-eyed and twitchy, catching Erica off-guard. 'Oh, you're here. I really wasn't expecting you to clean today,' Erica had said, hoping she'd take the hint, but Liz headed straight to the shelves where Rory kept his vinyl and wept as she dusted. Erica insisted she go home, and Liz kept thanking her, told her she was very kind, but in fact Erica was relieved to have an excuse to get her to leave. Rory hired Liz as a surprise for Erica when they moved here, and Erica has always hated being in the house when she's around. Often, she would retreat to the garden, or on a wet day to the shops on some made-up errand. Something about Liz's confident industriousness makes Erica feel unnecessary, like a guest in her own home. For the first few months Liz tried to engage, would lean on the handle of the mop and reel off anecdotes about her friends and family. After a while she gave up. Their relationship now is polite but perfunctory. Liz adored Rory, though, would spend extra time in his study, especially if he was in there, gently and meticulously wiping the framed posters and business awards with a special microfibre cloth. She reminds Erica of their old housekeeper Maggie, who seemed to become doughier and more pliable around her father. She's pretty sure Rory wasn't sleeping with Liz, who's in her late sixties. Honestly, though, you'd never know.

She puts on her dressing gown and goes downstairs in the hope of catching Charlie. The door to Rory's study is open and she pokes her head in. Liz is standing at the desk, her back to Erica, head bowed, as though she's praying.

'Good morning, Liz.'

Liz startles and turns, and Erica sees she's holding the bottle of whiskey. Her breath catches a little when she sees the contents are gone. She has no memory of finishing it.

'Erica, you frightened the life out of me! How are you doing today?'

Has she raised the bottle a little, drawing attention to its emptiness?

'Oh, you know.'

'Ah, I do.' Liz nods sympathetically, her eyes are moist and Erica worries she might start crying again. 'I was a mess after Gary. Rory was so kind, though.'

Erica has no idea who Gary is or what happened to him. She feels a deep twinge of discomfort. 'Well, I'll let you get on. I need to catch Charlie before he goes.'

'What will I do with this?' Liz holds the bottle up higher, like an exhibit. 'Now that it's all gone.'

'Did you find that in the drawer?'

Liz looks offended. 'Of course not. I'd never open his drawers. It was on his desk, next to his laptop. Which was still on, by the way.' She sniffs. 'That wasn't me either.'

Erica looks at the desk, sees the open laptop, remembers then sitting here last night reading that woman's email. She's been reading it repeatedly since she received it three days ago.

'You can just put the bottle in the recycling, thanks.'

'Are you sure? God, he loved it. He had it for years. I remember it was here when I first started. I was always so nervous when I dusted that shelf. I was terrified I'd smash it!'

Erica feels herself stiffen. 'It's fine, Liz. It's only glass.'

Liz looks down at it. 'Well, it is now. He was so proud of it, though. God be good to him.'

'*I'll* get rid of it then, will I?' She can't keep the impatience from her voice.

Liz seems not to hear, the bottle cradled in the crook of her arm now as if it's a baby. 'You know, I'd leave it up on the shelf as a memento. It's a lovely, expensive-looking thing. Even if it is empty.'

Erica moves forward and holds out her hand. 'Thank you,' she says, tersely.

Liz takes one last forlorn look at the bottle, sighs, then hands it over.

As Erica leaves, Liz says, 'Oh, by the way. Charlie. I meant to say he's already gone. Breakfast and lunch all sorted for himself. Such independence!'

It's like a blow between her shoulder blades. She stops abruptly at the door, turns back around. Liz is looking down at the desk, trailing her hand tenderly along its edge. The gesture looks so intimate. Erica feels a sudden flutter of hatred in her stomach, and it surprises her. Like those first ripples of movement in pregnancy, she's unsure if what she feels is real.

'Actually, Liz, I've been meaning to have a chat with you. Unfortunately, with Rory gone now, our circumstances have changed. I'm very sorry but I'll have to let you go.'

Liz looks up, surprised. Her face reddens. Her mouth makes a shape as if to say something, but nothing emerges.

'I'll pay you, of course, for the next eight weeks. But really, there's no need to come back after today.'

Liz's chin pitches upwards. 'No. If you're paying for it, I'll work for it. Never let it be said.'

'It would be better if you didn't, to be honest. We need to start learning how to stand on our own two feet. Thank you for everything, though.'

Erica makes to go again and then thinks of something. 'By the way, how *do* we pay you? Cash?'

Liz's face turns redder, so that even the tips of her ears are burning. Her chin tilts higher. 'Your husband pays me by standing order, all above board. It's a legitimate business I run,' she says coldly.

'Right. Of course.'

Erica reaches for the door handle.

'Oh, and Erica?'

Erica looks over her shoulder. 'Yes?'

'I think you'll find the bottle bin is a bit full out there. It mightn't fit.'

They hold each other's eyes for a moment before Erica looks away. She slams the door behind her. In the kitchen she pushes back the bifolds, crosses the wet patio and flings the bottle towards the hawthorn hedge at the bottom of the garden.

A couple of hours later, Erica, in her bedroom, hears the click of the front door. She goes to the window. Liz, packing her car, glances up in her direction and Erica steps back quickly. Once she hears the car leave, she goes to Rory's study and opens his emails. When she was eleven, she found a book belonging to her mother that opened with a sex scene between two women in a department store changing room. Something about that scene intrigued a young Erica in a way that she couldn't quite make sense of and she would sneak the book from her mother's bedroom at every opportunity. There's something of the same unsettling quality in this woman's words. Erica starts to type,

Hello you,

Goodness, I asked you to be honest and you certainly were. I admit I wasn't expecting it, thought you'd run for cover, so thank you for that, at least.

I imagine you to be much younger than me. The younger generations of women seem much more sexually forthright and aware than we ever were. And you seem to have a much more positive relationship with your own body than we ever did. You seem also to have a strong belief in your own exceptionality, your importance to him. Knowing him, knowing us, our situation, I'm not sure how warranted this is. But I admire the conviction, however misplaced it might be.

For all this confidence, though, you sound as though you may be unfortunate enough to have fallen a little in love with him. I feel pity for you over this. Obviously, he was a good-looking man, could be charming and funny too, but maybe you hadn't known him long enough to realise that there was also something damaged at the heart of him. Or maybe you did know this. Over the years I've come to understand, and it makes me uncomfortable, ashamed even, that actually I loved him *because* of his darkness, his selfishness, his pain, not in spite of it. So that makes me . . . what? Foolish? Weak? Culpable? It's so clichéd, isn't it? The irresistible bad boy. Did I think I could heal him? Did you? Because for all your seeming strength and knowing you have fallen for it too.

I'm sorry too that you lost your baby. I know you speak of this scar in the context of his reaction to it but the fact that you single this one out, mention it at all, gives me a sense that the loss affects you deeply. Trust me, I understand this kind of pain.

Tell me, though, was it his baby? Please, again, be honest with me.

But all this aside, I'm also envious of you. You have a chance to build another life for yourself. It's too late for me. Mine was so tied to his, I can't see a way to forge my own. And I'm hurtling towards fifty and with this age comes the grim knowledge that I've almost certainly lived more than half my life. Maybe much more. But there's hope for you. Don't squander it.

Erica

She closes the laptop and goes to the kitchen. When she opens the door she's immediately mugged by the lemon and eucalyptus cleaners Liz uses. The smell is like a provocation and scrapes at her throat. She closes the door again and heads back up to her unmade bed.

MAEVE

She's walking out the school gate back to her car after dropping in Luke's forgotten PE gear, when she hears her name. She turns to see the deputy principal, Mr Archer, jogging towards her. Maeve sighs. This won't be good. He's one of those people you can't imagine existing beyond the confines of their work. She tries to imagine him as a child. It's impossible. There's a vibe of immutability off him, like he arrived fully formed into the world as a middle-aged greyhound-faced teacher. Maeve imagines he writes his name in permanent marker on his lunch container that he leaves in the staff-room fridge: Mr Archer's – Do Not Touch!

'Maeve, how are you?'

'Great, thanks, Clive. You?'

'Good, yes, great. Lovely. Look, I'm glad I spotted you. I was going to contact you anyway.'

Maeve holds up her hands in mock surrender. 'Oh God. Busted! I know we're not supposed to drop stuff off for the boys if they forget something, let them take the consequences and all that, but Luke has training and I was thinking of myself and trying to get the grass stains out of his uniform.'

Clive clears his throat. 'Eh no, that wasn't it. Look, it's a bit delicate. It's about Jamie. Are you free to chat?'

'Absolutely.' In fact, what she would really like to do now is put her hands over her ears and sing *la-la-la*.

'So, it's not a big deal, no panic.'

Of course, if someone pre-empts with an instruction not to panic, then it's time to panic.

'Okay.'

'It's just something me and a couple of the other teachers have picked up on.'

'Okay.' It's not okay.

Clive looks supremely awkward. So awkward that Maeve herself starts to blush.

'So, he's been a little . . . unfriendly . . . in his attitude towards certain people in the school.'

'Unfriendly?' The word seems out of place, clumsy.

'Yes, towards a couple of the kids who identify as gay or trans. Now, I want to emphasise that we have never heard him using any specific homophobic or transphobic slurs but I'm wondering if their sexuality or gender identity is at the root of it.'

'Wow, okay. I don't know what to say. I'm mortified, obviously, Clive. I mean, it's not something he'd ever hear at home.'

'I'm aware of that, Maeve. And, you know, it's not overt bullying or anything. Like I said, just an . . . attitude. But I think it's best to nip these things in the bud. Maybe you could have a word with him to try to get to the bottom of it. As I said, no panic.'

Maeve, of course, is in full-blown panic.

They'd held a naming ceremony when Jamie was a baby. Neither she nor Cillian wanted a religious christening, so they chose instead to have an informal get-together with close friends in their back garden in Harold's Cross. It had been a stunning early-autumn afternoon, and they drank champagne and ate from a large charcuterie board and congratulated themselves on their unorthodoxy. Even her mother approved. 'Thank heavens there'll be none of that melodramatic renunciation of Satan as though you've stumbled into an exorcism,' she said. Instead, as the light started to fade, Maeve read Kahlil Gibran's poem 'On Children', standing beneath the craggy old apple tree, the garden alive with birdsong, truly believing that this poem was a signifier of her values. This sleeping baby she held in her arms did not belong to her, he was only his own person. She would not try to mould him in her image. She and Cillian were purely the vessels from which this child emerged and the steady non-judgemental place from where he would be sent forth to find his own way in the world.

A fruit fell from the tree then and landed beside her, and Cillian, with perfect timing (they were a perfect couple that day too, as well as being perfect parents, so in synch!), made the inevitable quip and everyone laughed. Maeve was filled with a smug optimism.

What horseshit. She knows now she was lying to herself, or at least had not yet been tested. It's less complex to parent a baby – your main priority is to keep them alive. With teenagers you feel like you could kill them yourself sometimes. And it turns out she is happy to let her children be their own people but only if they are people whose attitudes align with her own. Part of her is terrified that maybe Jamie's attitude does in fact align with her own, that he is giving voice to some homophobia in her subconscious, has inherited a bigoted gene just as he has inherited her green eyes. She remembers Dan's wounded eyes. How she used his vulnerability to hurt him. How she did that to deflect from something confusing and unspeakable she felt within herself.

And you blame them. You can't help it. The bewildered-looking parents sitting in courtrooms or being harassed on doorsteps, whose children have committed heinous crimes. You say that they can't have loved enough, or they loved too much, or they must be psychopaths themselves. You say, smugly, *Thank God we raised our child to be better than that.* You don't say, *There but for the grace of God*, because you are certain it took more than simply the grace of God to not make them into monsters.

Later, at home, she relays the conversation with Clive to Cillian. He tells her Jamie is a good kid, not to blow it out of proportion. He says, 'Don't panic, Maeve.' He suggests they broach the topic the next time the three of them are in the car together so that Jamie is a captive audience, which makes Maeve feel as though they're planning to kidnap their own son. Cillian says the lack of eye contact will make it easier for them all to speak openly, be less confronting for him, as though he is a rabid dog. Maeve thinks all their communication with him now is impeded. By phones, earbuds, lack of eye contact.

She agrees, though, because Cillian has always been possessed of a greater equilibrium than her, capable of talking her down. And he has an ability to soothe her more neurotic urges, mostly by not taking them too seriously.

But lately, she's begun to feel less soothed, more managed. This defensiveness may be another perimenopausal gift. So that's why – once Luke has left the dinner table, with Cillian having steered the conversation onto inoffensive topics such as the Premiership and his latest personal-best tally of unassisted pull-ups at the gym – Maeve, looking at her first-born sitting at the table with his hood up, his face lowered towards his dessert bowl, is overcome by a spiky surge that won't be quelled.

'How was school today, Jamie?'

'Fine,' he says, without looking up.

They couldn't shut him up as a young child. Question after impossible question. 'Mammy, who do you think would win in a fight between a giant RoboBaby and a baby Godzilla?' he'd ask, and she'd have to come up with a fully justified answer that satisfied his exacting, logical nature. He asked her once, aged five, if he would ever die and her heart almost collapsed in terror at the thought of it. 'No, of course not,' she'd lied, looking at his sweet, perfect face, his large eyes flecked with yellow just like her own, while Cillian looked on reproachfully. Maeve knew he'd pull her up about it later.

'I ran into Mr Archer.'

Cillian puts down his cutlery and clears his throat. 'Maeve.' It is said quietly.

'That's nice,' says Jamie, his eyes still on the bowl.

'Not really, to be honest. He says you're being unfriendly towards some people in school.'

Jamie drops his spoon theatrically and looks up. 'What? Who?'

'Maeve.' This time Cillian says it more forcefully and touches her arm. She shakes it off.

'Certain gay and trans students.'

'That's bullshit.'

'Is he lying about it?'

'If it's the guys I'm thinking about, it's nothing to do with them being gay. They're just dicks in general. And they get away with it because they're gay.'

Cillian says, 'There you go, Maeve, maybe it's—'

Maeve cuts him off. 'So, it's just a massive coincidence then, is it? That all the people you're being unfriendly towards happen to be queer?'

'You sound so stupid using that word. And yes, it is a coincidence. It's just his warped perception.' He stands up.

'Please stay at the table, Jamie.'

'No, not when I'm being attacked for no reason.'

'I'm hardly attacking you.'

'You are. You're always accusing me of something.'

'Even if it's true that the reason you're being unfriendly has nothing to do with their sexuality, you know you shouldn't be unkind to anyone. It's important to be inclusive.'

'Tell that to them, then. Oh no, I forgot, no-one is allowed to say anything to them, are they?' He picks his bowl up from the table and leaves it on the island, then walks towards the door.

'Jamie!'

But he's gone.

Cillian sighs. 'Told you.'

'Oh, shut up, Cillian,' she says, and pushes her chair back aggressively from the table.

Her mother, who was quiet during the exchange, pushing food around her plate, puts her hands over her ears then. 'Stop it,' she says. 'Stop it, stop it, stop it . . .'

Maeve stands over her and rubs her back. 'Sorry, Mam,' she says. 'I didn't mean to frighten you. It's okay. You can take your hands down now.' She prises them away, a little roughly perhaps, thinking of the lectures she's had to endure over the years.

Her mother says, 'He's a good boy, you know. I told him that. Nothing to be ashamed of.'

'I know, Mam.'

'You don't give in to bullies. You stand up to them.'

Maeve rubs her temples in frustration, doesn't want to get into some strange circular conversation.

'Did Jamie say something to you, Mam?'

'Who's Jamie?'

'Never mind, Mam. It's okay.'

Maeve starts collecting dishes from the table and Cillian does the same. They move around each other wordlessly, the only sound coming from plates being scraped with a little too much force, cutlery being thrown into the dishwasher basket, drawers being slammed.

When the kitchen is clean Maeve goes to her snug and shuts the door. To distract herself she opens her laptop and checks her social media pages. She reposted a favourable review of her latest book this morning. In this novel, her fictional journalist Sylvia is on the case of a serial rapist, a plotline that is mentioned in this particular review. Underneath, the same account has posted four separate comments.

Who Cares?

No-one likes a showoff.

This book sucks ass.

You don't have to worry about getting raped. Ur too ugly to rape.

She is so sick of this shit. What is wrong with the world? She puts her head in her hands, then forces herself to sit up again, deletes the comments and blocks the account.

She opens the current *Sylvia* document, reads a random paragraph, decides it's weak. Never before in the history of literature have words been put together so ineptly, in fact. It's like a toddler has thrown magnetic words at a fridge. This is the problem. She swings between thinking what she has written is genius (rare) to believing it's all beneath contempt (less rare). She knows the truth must lie somewhere in between those two extremes, yet she can never find that objectivity either. She closes the document and opens her emails, and a feeling of gratitude washes over her when she sees a new one from Nisha. Her heart recovers a little.

Hi Maeve,

Thanks for the advice. It's true, sex can be so vulnerable, of course writing about it would be the same. I've tried to pretend my mother is dead, to rewrite the scenes. Also, my entire family. Especially my creepy 'Uncle' Stuart who corners me at every family function to ask me why I don't have a boyfriend. When I explain to him, yet again, that it's because I'm queer, he tells me that is only because I haven't met the right man yet. He says this while making a gesture towards his genitals. *Sighs*

I'm glad you enjoyed the websites I suggested. I've attached links to some more authentically 'woman-friendly' porn for Sylvia's 'awakening'. You can subscribe to these for a small fee . . . it's less exploitative. If you simply google 'woman-friendly porn' you'll just be directed to the same old websites made *by* men *for* men which will mainly feature two women with huge breast implants and Barbie genitalia taking it in turns to ecstatically give one terrifyingly endowed bloke a blow job.

sighs again

N x

A couple of weeks after Mr Quinn's funeral, Dan took a bottle of gin from home and the four of them made their way down to the river in the early evening to drink it. Maeve was happy to hang out with Dan again. She'd been avoiding him a little, if she was honest, self-conscious that she had come close to revealing herself to him. That he understood anyway without her saying anything. Not that he'd judge, of course not, and maybe it would have been kind to speak openly with him, but it felt so raw within herself that she needed to protect it. He'd been spending more of his time away from them anyway, rehearsing with the musical society crew, who were putting on a performance of *Joseph and His Amazing Technicolour Dreamcoat* in the community centre in town. And though she was happy to see him, maddeningly, he kept humming 'Any Dream Will Do' as they walked down the road.

The old bridge looked perfect that evening, with its gently crumbling arches, the surrounding foliage lush with summer, and the sunlight glittering on the water below. They tripped down the well-worn path that led to the riverbank, avoiding the sheep shit and nettles as they did, and settled themselves in a flat, grassy area upstream from the bridge. They had no tonic so instead mixed the gin in an empty lemonade bottle with some orange juice. It was warm, a rare balmy night, and they lay on the banks in the fading light, listening to The Sundays' new album on Rory's ghetto blaster, waving their glowing cigarettes to swat away the clouds of malign midges that congregated there.

Maeve lay on her back, loosened with alcohol, smoking, her other hand reaching beside her to pull up daisies, and she remembered making necklaces out of long chains of them as a small child. Finding dandelion clocks to make wishes, holding buttercups under a friend's chin, making petal soup from the cornflowers that grew in ditches and laneways that bordered the old estate. Something of that simple childhood contentment came over her then, being with her best friends, all of them warmed with gin, listening to the fresh and bittersweet music, weeks of summer holidays still to go. Everyone was in a good mood, tensions forgotten. There was a hypnotic hum of cars from the road above and she watched the smoke spiralling skywards from her cigarette that appeared to merge with the wispy clouds above.

The Browning line about God being in his heaven popped into her head and Rory, who lay beside her, turned his head to look at her and she realised then that she'd spoken it aloud. She was sure he was going to mock her but instead he said, 'This is class, hey, Maeve?' and moved his hand so that their little fingers were touching.

Maeve blew a stream of smoke upwards and it mingled with Rory's and she imagined herself as one of those alluring girls, French mostly, you saw in films, like Béatrice Dalle in *Betty Blue*, who smoked their post-coital Gauloise naked, and with a cool detachment. Pleasured and confident – though still with a Gallic indifference – that they'd given pleasure.

Juliet distracted her from her fantasy then with her restlessness. She was being especially provocative that night and Maeve was trying her best to be patient with her. Though that was the thing about Juliet, she always pushed your limits. While the others were content to lie on the grassy bank and smoke and chat, she kept moving, pacing in front of them, swigging greedily out of the bottle or dancing suggestively to the music. Maeve could see she was performing for Rory. She had tried to find out what had happened between them the night before her father's funeral, but she had become so infuriatingly reticent that Maeve was convinced they must have slept together. She had disappeared for so long with Rory that herself and Dan ended up going home. At the funeral mass the next day she was sporting two black eyes, which she claimed was a result of opening a door in her own face. If they had slept together, though, Rory was not treating her any differently, in fact he was being dismissive of her, which made her play up to him even more. Rory had been elusive the last couple of weeks too. He'd started coaching some of the younger kids down at the tennis courts, along with a preppy, pretty girl called Erica, who seemed too good to be true. She looked like she came from the Long Island enclaves of some F. Scott Fitzgerald novel with her blonde bob and immaculate whites.

'Who wants to swim?' Juliet said.

'We've no togs. Or towels,' Maeve replied.

'Who needs them?' Juliet said, and started to strip off.

'Cop on, Juliet. You're locked. You'll drown.'

But she was already standing in her underwear.

'You're a goddess, Juliet Quinn!' Dan, who was pretty buzzed at that stage, cried.

Juliet opened her arms out wide and said, 'Takes one to know one, Dan Flynn!'

Maeve sat up and the blood that had pulsed between her legs as she imagined herself as some kind of femme fatale scuttled to her face in embarrassment. The idea of anyone wanting to have sex with her with Juliet around, looking the way she did, was ridiculous. She was wearing ordinary white cotton underwear, Dunnes Stores finest, but it somehow made her look even more alluring. As though anything overtly sexy would lessen the effect of her effortlessness.

Juliet reached behind her then, unclasped her bra and slid it down her arms. Dan whooped. And then, she hooked her thumbs into her knickers and sidestepped out of them. She held them over her head like a trophy. Dan started laughing hysterically. 'You're also completely insane!' he shouted. Juliet threw her underwear in Rory's direction. He didn't react.

She stood unmoving in front of them, her hands on her hips, the reddish pre-sunset light from behind making her appear like some kind of ethereal nymph, albeit one with small erect pink nipples and a dark wedge of pubic hair. She looked beautiful but Maeve felt guilty for thinking it, as though she was somehow violating their friendship, so she looked instead at Rory, who was still gazing skywards, toking thoughtfully on his cigarette, as though none of it was happening. He sat up, glanced at Juliet, yawned ostentatiously, before turning away.

All the bravado seemed to drain from Juliet in that moment and she clasped her hands in front of her crotch.

'Come swim with me, Rory.' Her voice was pleading.

Rory stood up and pulled his T-shirt off. Juliet gave a small, hopeful smile, but it faded when he walked to her, placed his T-shirt on her head and pulled it over her, binding her arms to her sides as he did. Then he came back, sat down in the same spot and fiddled with the controls of his stereo.

Maeve studied him then, the calm, composed look on his face. She thought about his poor, broken mother and it all seemed so clear to her, the whole trajectory of his relationship with Juliet, the whole story of them, that she wanted to shake Juliet and yell at her that it was never going to work out, he would never choose her. He might pick her up occasionally, play with her and then discard her. And always, always, with rationality and clarity he would select the self-possessed girls with glossy hair who went to schools like Mount Anville and could negotiate a room full of Daddy's work colleagues and Mummy's golf set with polite and charming conversation and a plate of hors d'oeuvres.

Maeve felt such a swell of love and tenderness for Juliet then, trussed up in Rory's T-shirt. She was angry with him for humiliating her. How dare he? For a moment it looked like Juliet was fighting tears. Maeve had never seen her cry, not even at her father's funeral. But Juliet pushed her arms through the sleeves, pitched her chin upwards and said, 'God, you're all such dry shites. I remember when you used to be fun.'

She turned then and splashed into the water, not crying out as they all usually did when the shock of the cold hit them.

'Come back, Juliet, you've had way too much to drink,' Maeve yelled after her, but Juliet ignored her and instead dived under.

They sat, peering over the riverbank reeds at the rippling place where she had gone down. After a few moments Dan said, 'She's taking her time coming up.'

'She'll be fine,' said Rory. 'Juliet can take care of herself.'

The ripples were gone now, the spot where she'd dived smooth and flat again.

'No-one can hold their breath for that long. She's not a fish,' Maeve said.

Rory stood up, ground out his cigarette with his runner and swore under his breath. 'She's always pulling shit like this. I'm so sick of it. Constantly looking for attention.'

Dan turned and looked at him. His face was red. 'Why did you do that to her, Rory?'

He looked confused. 'Do what to her?'

'Put the fucking T-shirt on her like that.'

'She was making a show of herself.'

'No. You made a show of her.'

Rory shook his head. 'She doesn't need my help for that.'

'You fucking love seeing her humiliated.'

Maeve had never seen Dan argue like that with him. Dan was such a pacifist, always the one to de-escalate tension, try to smooth things over, make everyone laugh and feel better with some outrageous comment. He was fuming now.

'No, I don't. I actually feel humiliated for her.'

'Fucking prick. Think you're such a man, treating her like that. She's too fucking good for you anyway.'

They squared up and for one ludicrous moment it looked like they might fight. Maeve almost laughed.

'Cop on, you two,' she said. 'I'm worried. It must be a couple of minutes now.'

'She's a good swimmer,' said Rory, turning from Dan and looking towards the water again.

Dan said, 'I'm going to go in after her.'

'No,' said Rory, holding him back with his arm. 'I will. I'm a stronger swimmer.' He kicked the ground. 'Fuck!' he yelled. He pulled off his runners and jeans and went in. Maeve kept looking at the spot where Juliet had dived, waiting for some sign of movement, but nothing came. Rory put his face down in the water, swam around, then lifted his head. 'I can't see a thing down there,' he shouted. He put his face in again, swimming in a wider circle this time. He did this several times as Maeve became more and more frantic on the bank. She paced uselessly, trying to peer into the water but the light was greying now and the water looked murky and opaque. Every time Rory raised his head he looked a bit paler. It was clear he was tiring because the time in between his surfacing for gulps of air was shortening.

Maeve called to him. 'Stop it now, Rory. You need to stop now. We'll get help.'

He swam to the bank and crawled up. His breathing was ragged, and he sat down, facing the water. He was shivering and Maeve put her fleece top around him.

'I don't get it,' he said. 'How can she have just disappeared?'

'Do you think . . .' She wasn't sure how to say it. 'Do you think she's caught on the bottom?'

'I couldn't see anything. It was too cloudy.'

'We need to get help.' Maeve looked around. 'Where's Dan?'

'Huh?' Rory said.

'Dan. Where the hell is Dan gone?'

'Ah Jesus. Don't tell me . . .'

'He was here a second ago. Christ, do you think he went in too?'

'Stupid prick. I hope not. He's a terrible swimmer.'

'It's your fault if he has, you know. Acting like a dick to Juliet earlier.'

'What? How the fuck is any of this my fucking fault?'

Maeve stared at him, disbelieving. He appeared absolutely convinced of his own innocence. She thought then how oblivious we are to ourselves.

It was then that they saw her, Juliet, more a bedraggled water nymph now, coming towards them rounding the bend just beyond the bridge. Her dark hair was plastered to her face and Rory's white T-shirt, turned translucent, was catching between her legs as she walked, so she had to keep picking it out of her thighs.

Maeve stood still as she got nearer, not knowing whether to run to her and hug her or slap her face. Her expression was triumphant, she didn't appear to be traumatised. It struck Maeve that maybe she'd played some kind of trick on them. Rory must have decided the same thing because he shouted, 'What the fuck, Juliet? What was all that about?'

'That was wild,' she said when she got to them. 'Wild!'

Rory glared at her, his breathing hard and laboured as though he was trying to control it. Out of the corner of Maeve's eye then she saw three figures clambering down the bank near the bridge. Dan was leading, his father behind and Liam O'Malley, the publican's son, bringing up the rear.

Dan started to run so that he ended up slipping at the end of the path and landing on his backside. He got up and bounded over.

'Juliet. Jesus, girl.' He embraced her and she laughed.

'Good to know I was missed. What about you, Rory, did you miss me too?'

Rory had a closed look on his face, and he didn't answer. Dr Flynn and Liam had reached them too by that point.

'So what on earth was the tremendous drama about, then? Danielle here arrived into the pub screaming like a little girl that you'd drowned.'

Juliet spoke rapidly, her expression becoming almost rapturous. 'Oh my God, lads, it was so trippy. I dove under the water and started to swim towards the far bank because I thought I'd get out on that side as you were all being so annoying but it was like when I got to the middle of the river I was pinned by a really strong current that swept me along. When I resurfaced it was just before the bridge and I remembered watching this old film with Daddy and this guy was caught in a current and he knew not to struggle, just floated along with his toes pointed downstream. So I flipped on my back and it was kind of intense. It was like Daddy was helping me. And I remembered when we used to play pooh sticks and how sometimes the sticks would fly really fast like they were being squeezed in the current under the bridge and then they'd slow down. And I was kind of laughing to myself looking at the underside of the bridge covered in slimy moss and graffiti. And I was thinking, I am a pooh stick. And also I was thinking, who are all these IRA supporters and how do they manage to spray paint in these places?' She gave a manic sort of laugh before continuing. 'And it was like I just surrendered to the power of the water and I had this strong feeling that I was going to be fine. And on the other side of the bridge the current slowed and I remembered in the film the man swimming diagonally towards the shore. So that's what I did.' She shrugged, like it was the most normal thing in the world.

'A pooh stick?' Rory said it in a low, dangerous voice.

Juliet laughed. 'I know. It was mad.'

'Perhaps the poor child is concussed,' said Dan, putting his hand up to her head.

'A fucking pooh stick.' Rory spat the words out this time. He banged his open palm to his forehead, then went to where his jeans and runners lay and started to pull them on.

Dr Flynn sighed then and looked at Juliet, his eyes moving over her in a way that made Maeve, fully clothed, feel exposed. The T-shirt appeared as a flimsy gauze, and Juliet's beautiful body under it almost offensive. 'I would advise you to cover up, then get home and warm yourself, young lady.'

Then he looked at Dan. 'I'll deal with you later.' He turned to Liam. 'Sorry, Liam, about all this nonsense.'

'No bother,' Liam said. He touched Juliet's arm and smiled shyly at her. 'Come into the pub if you like and I'll make you a hot drink.'

Juliet waved him away. 'Ah no need. I'm grand.' Maeve watched as Liam's pimpled cheeks burned redder and felt a wave of compassion for him.

Dr Flynn and Liam left then, and Dan watched after them, his face tight and anxious.

Juliet turned around to Rory, her face eager, as though something had just occurred to her. 'Why were you in your boxers, Rory? Why are you all wet?'

He didn't reply, didn't even look at her. Instead, he picked up the empty bottle of gin and cast it angrily into the river. It disappeared for a moment before bobbing up optimistically and he stood and watched it till it was swept away under the arch of the bridge. Then he grabbed his ghetto blaster and stalked off in the direction of the path.

'Your T-shirt!' Juliet yelled after him, but he ignored this also. 'I'll drop it in to you tomorrow!'

On the way home, deflated versions of the boisterous crew who had walked down there a few hours before, Juliet asked Maeve and Dan if Rory had gone into the river to look for her. 'Did he say anything? Was he upset? Was he worried about me, do you think?'

Neither of them answered her. But she smiled and hugged herself with pleasure anyway and, looking at her, Maeve had a brief, spiteful thought that she wished maybe she had drowned.

JULIET

It's Saturday, a little over two weeks since they put him in the ground. She's sitting beside Ruby in the back of Johnny's car as he drives them to the Hill of Tara for a walk. It's cleansing to be away from the house. Denise has been tired and much of the time has been spent sitting in the sunless kitchen drinking tea, trying to remain calm while her mother gossips inanely about people she barely knows.

Denise is in the passenger seat now providing a running commentary on the places they pass. She points out the O'Briens' house a few doors down with a For Sale sign outside it because 'poor old Joe passed away on Christmas Day although luckily they'd already had the dinner'. And the seminary a couple of miles out the road where they used to train missionary priests but not any longer 'because we have to get our priests over from Africa now. Imagine!' Juliet sighs, wonders why she reverts to feeling like an intolerant teenager back here around her mother.

Ruby had asked to go to Tara because she has a favourite photo taken there when she was little that still occupies pride of place on her dressing table. In it she's sitting smiling in a meadow, the sun-yellowed grass grazing her chin, a wizened hawthorn tree behind her laden with colourful ribbons and, beyond that, fields gently undulating to the horizon. Her daughter's sense of connection to Ireland has always been a puzzle, involving some deep-rooted genetic inheritance rather than any overt effort on Juliet's part. Not for her the expat Facebook groups or the St Patrick's morning fry-ups in the local Irish club. 'Tell me about the wishing tree, Mumma,' she'd say when Juliet was tucking her into bed, and they'd look at the photo together while Juliet spun a tale about Irish fairies and their portal between worlds. Juliet finds that photo hard to look at now because she understands that the magic wasn't in the tree at all but in the gift of an eight-year-old daughter.

Denise isn't up to walking so she and Johnny wait in the café by the carpark and Juliet and Ruby go together through the creaking gate, Ruby stopping to read all the information signage. They ascend the gravel road and cross the church grounds and cemetery, pausing at the headstones, some so old their inscriptions have been weathered away completely. Ruby is touched by these older, unknown graves. 'No-one to remember them,' she says. She's always been fascinated by history, that's what she plans to study in university. It's deeper than any intellectual curiosity; the accounts of boy soldiers in the First World War or the mistreatment of Chinese miners in the goldfields of Otago ignite a deep compassion within her.

Ruby picks some daisies from a patch of grass and places them on one of the anonymous plots, and Juliet, not for the first time, wonders at the strange alchemy of procreation. How, somehow, two imperfect people can indulge in a grasping self-serving impulse to produce something better than them both.

They hop over the squat wall and out onto the hill. It's a blustery day and the normally expansive view is smothered by low-hanging clouds. They pick their way along a muddy path worn into the hillside and as they approach the spot where the photo was taken, Juliet can see the hawthorn tree is bent on its side almost to the ground. 'What the hell?' Ruby says, and a man passing stops and tells her that the tree became so laden with the objects visitors tied to it when they made their wishes – rags, underwear, coins, even handcuffs – that it suffocated.

'You could say it buckled under the weight of people's expectations,' he says with a grim smile.

'I hate people sometimes. Such selfishness.'

'I suppose what they hoped for felt so important it obliterated everything else,' the man says. Juliet thinks of San Francisco and Rory leaving her at the airport. She stood there, stranded at the base of the escalator, watching him being lifted away, and she willed the plane to crash, sure that the pain of his rejection in that moment was worse than any grief she would feel. If she couldn't have him, she didn't want Erica to have him either. It frightens Juliet to think what she is capable of wishing. Or what wishing might bring. Sometimes being around her daughter, with her idealism and hopefulness, makes Juliet feel as twisted as the tortured old hawthorn itself.

Ruby shakes her head and Juliet squeezes her arm. 'Let's go back to the café and get a hot chocolate.'

On the drive home Ruby is still downcast and Johnny commiserates with her. He says that trees are always a powerful reminder to him of the divine. 'Whenever I look at an old oak I understand how small and insignificant I am.'

'Did you know,' says Ruby, 'that some trees can hold their breath in wet soil so that they don't drown? And others can grow hairs on their leaves to keep them cool in a drought.'

'Is that right?' says Johnny. 'Aren't we lucky to live in a world with all this wonder?' He turns to Denise then and winks at her. 'And beauty.'

Catching this look, Juliet is punctured by it. She thinks about Auckland, going back soon with winter looming to their uncluttered, modern apartment. Jobless, probably. Maybe even daughterless. Her life uncluttered by the past there too. No-one knowing anything about her family, her childhood, Rory. Like she was born into the world as a thirty-year-old woman. She thought it would be freeing, she could be anyone she wanted. But as Denise would say, *Wherever you go, there you are.* She turns away to stare out the window.

Denise suggests stopping into O'Malley's for a drink. It's busy for an afternoon. There's a football match on and small groups of people are congregated near the two televisions. They claim a low table near the door and Johnny goes to the bar. Liam appears and waves over to them. He helps Johnny carry the drinks back.

'Hello, my favourite family,' Liam says as he arranges the glasses on the table.

'You seem to have the punters in today, Liam,' says Denise.

'Yeah.' Liam looks around. 'Half of them here though to watch television. It's not like the old days. Dad would turn in his grave.'

I hope so, Juliet thinks. *Old bastard.*

Liam continues, 'But ye should stick around. We've got Rory O'Sullivan's young lad in doing a session soon. He's great.'

Denise nudges Ruby. 'And he's a real looker too, Ruby. About your age, I'd say. More reason to stay in Ireland with me.' She waggles her drawn-on eyebrows comically.

'Jesus, Denise, he's only just lost his father.' Juliet takes a swig of her drink and places the glass down forcefully on the table.

'Mother of God, calm down. I don't remember you taking a vow of chastity when Martin died. Quite the opposite, in fact.'

'I suppose I could say the same for you, Denise. And I wasn't the one who was married to him, was I?'

The table goes quiet. Denise flushes and Johnny pats her hand. Juliet looks at Ruby, her kind, open-hearted face, and Liam with his warm, affable eyes and feels immediately ashamed.

'I think I'll go,' Juliet says, standing up.

No-one tries to stop her.

'Right, I'll see you all at home then.'

Outside the pub, she stands looking up the back road towards the house. It's windy and drizzling softly now and she starts to walk up the slight incline but then changes her mind and heads across the main road to the old bridge. She leans over, her forearms resting on the wall. It's eerily quiet, as though the misty swirls of rain have scooped all the noise out of the air.

It rained heavily for much of that August before Dan died. The river became swollen and fast-moving. Everyone said it was typical. No doubt the sun would appear once the kids were back in school. Juliet can't remember if it did or not but it certainly didn't feel that way. That awful drudgy September, the rest of that year in fact felt miserable and never-ending, regardless of what the weather did.

But in August, before Dan died, it was cosy and dry on the banks of the river, as they sheltered under the low side arch of the bridge. And private too, the unseasonal weather keeping walkers and swimmers away. Herself and Dan would meet there every day at three, digging up the ziplock bag hidden under a boulder. It was filled with green Rizla papers, a lighter and small chunks of hash. Dan seemed to have a never-ending supply from some friend in the musical society. It was the only bearable part of those days. At home, the initial searing jolt of loss was dulling into something stagnant and jaded. Her mother, normally so vain, was shuffling around in her dressing gown all day, make-up-free, her hair unwashed and lank around her face. Josh, on holidays from college and living at home – no longer able to afford the rent on his flat in Dublin, money tighter now with the factory being sold under duress and the amount they would get for it barely enough to cover all the debts – was a combination of hungover and bitter most of the time. There were tensions within the gang since the episode down at the river when she'd got caught in a current. Maeve angry with her. Dan and Maeve angry with Rory. Rory angry with everyone.

But those drugged afternoons with Dan felt like escape. From her house, from her pain, from Rory's indifference. She loved the whole ritual. The set time, the retrieving of the bag, the two of them taking it in turns to hold it to their face and inhale. Dan saying, 'Ah, sweet Mary Jane,' every time, making them giggle before they smoked anything. Burning off the hash and crumbling it evenly into the tobacco. Competing with him to roll the tightest, tidiest joint possible. 'Look at this one, Dan. Perfection!' she'd say. And he'd reply, 'Perhaps. If tampon was what you were aiming for. Super plus at that.' Dan was the only boy she knew who could say the word *tampon* without being mortified. Sometimes after smoking he'd become so relaxed he'd fall asleep. She knew he'd been raiding his mother's medicine cabinet, had taken tranquillisers of some description. She'd check that he was breathing, he became so still. But Juliet felt both at peace and alert. While Dan dozed, she would sit with her legs crossed, lulled by the traffic noise from the road above which seemed to meld with the sound of her blood rushing in her veins and fixated on the water pulsing under the arches or the rain that ran down the side of the bridge before pooling and dropping rhythmically onto the ground below. By the time they were both in a fit state to leave it was often late in the evening, but it didn't matter because no-one at home had missed them. There were no dinners being kept warm in ovens. They'd go into Juliet's house, ravenous, and scavenge for food – careful to avoid Josh who would sniff the air around them suspiciously – although pickings were often slim as Denise had lost all interest in shopping then too.

A siren passing intrudes. She's not sure how long she's been standing here but she's wet through and shivery. She's reminded how even the most insipid-seeming Irish rain can make you feel you'll never know warmth again. She looks up from the water, straightens, gets a head rush as she does. She makes her way back across the main road. As she passes the pub, the door swings open behind her, a snatch of Green Day over the clamour of voices escapes, and she smiles. She checks the carpark, making sure Johnny's Hyundai is gone, and heads in.

Charlie is sitting on a high stool, eyes closed as he sings. There's an empty table directly in front of him and she slips into it. He opens his eyes and she sees him startle when they land on her. She nods in acknowledgement. When he finishes the song he covers the microphone with his hand and leans past it.

'Hey.'

'Hey.'

'Wanna join me up here? Do "Baby Can I Hold You" again?'

She laughs. 'I'll pass. Liam might ask you for a refund.'

'Okay,' he smiles. 'Any requests, then?'

'Surprise me, Charlie.'

He flushes, thinks for a moment. 'Right. I've got it. Another Tracy Chapman for you.'

And he starts to play 'The Promise'. And how can he possibly know? She'd sent Rory a message, told him to listen to the lyrics. *It's like I wrote this song for you, lover. Every word rings true.* She shuts her eyes so Charlie can't see how moved she is.

ERICA

She sits waiting at a table for her takeaway coffee at the café in the small shopping centre near home. She rarely goes to cafés. There's something so intimate and forced about them. Her mother used to bring her to Bewley's on Grafton Street when she was a little girl after doing some Christmas shopping and meeting Santa in Switzers. And Erica loved that, sitting in a high-backed booth, just the two of them, the place felt big and bustling enough to be private. She has a fancy Nespresso machine that Rory bought for her if she wants a coffee, but she dislikes those mean-looking capsules, the way they are compacted exactly into their little compartment, punctured and squeezed before falling away, all used up, into the tray below. Often, she'll just make herself a cup of instant even though Rory used to tease her about that. Said it was trashy. She says tease but there was an edge. Really, she knew he needed to leave everything about that little cottage and his mother behind. Even her jars of Maxwell House.

'Hello, Erica.'

She turns to see Juliet standing behind her shoulder and she feels her entire body tense. Juliet with her cigarette voice and those wild, rare eyes. She thinks again of the way Charlie acted around her, a besotted little puppy, his face flushed, pupils enlarged. Some women had that effect on men, narcotic-like. She had looked at him, this boy – who only last week it seemed was sitting beside her in his nappy on the lawn, transfixed by a butterfly – and felt a gouging ache.

'Hello.' Erica notices with dismay that there are no other free tables in the café. 'How are you?'

'Okay, I suppose. I was just grabbing a coffee to go, and I saw you here. Can I join?' She doesn't wait for an answer, just slides into the opposite seat, which is jammed tight between the wall and the table, as though her entire body is lubricated. She's wearing that androgynous perfume again. The smell claws at Erica.

'I'm not staying. I'm waiting for a takeaway. Just out for a walk.'

'Me too. We could head back together if you like?'

Erica holds up her earbuds. 'I like to listen to podcasts actually.'

'No worries.' Juliet doesn't appear offended. She leans forward, her chin on her hand, insinuating herself into Erica's space. 'So, how've you been?'

Erica leans away. 'Oh, you know, good days and bad.'

'Yes, exactly.'

She's so odd, this woman.

The waitress puts a cup down in front of Erica. 'Skinny cappuccino?'

'Thank you.' She looks up and smiles. When she turns back Juliet is studying her in an unnerving way.

'I hate that way of describing a drink. *Skinny*. Like it venerates thinness.' She gives a small laugh then. 'God, I've been home too long. I sound like Maeve.'

'I haven't thought about it, to be honest.'

'Haven't you?'

The way she says it, surprised, irritates Erica. 'No. It's not foremost in my mind at the moment. Anyway, I better go, Charlie will be home from school soon. I like to be there when he gets in. Nice seeing you though, Juliet.'

She stands, takes the cup from the table.

'Look, I head back next week but I was wondering if you'd like to do something together before I go? Get a manicure or something.'

Erica frowns. 'A manicure?'

'Yes, it's what women do together, isn't it?'

'Is it?'

Juliet shrugs. 'Seems to be. In New Zealand every second shop is a nail salon. Maybe it's a younger-generation thing. They're much more high-maintenance than we ever were, aren't they, with their long nails and their Bambi eyelashes? Well, me anyway. I don't get them myself.' She holds out her hands, which do look kind of neglected. 'You know, when we were kids Rory used to give me a hard time for being sloppy. My hands were always a mess from pencils or paint.'

Erica is unsettled by the intimate anecdote, the sound of her dead husband's name on Juliet's lips. 'Thank you but I don't think I'm up to it yet. Things like that.'

Juliet nods. 'The manicure was a stupid idea. Too frivolous. I don't know why I said that. Maybe a film, though? Drinks? Dinner? We could ask Maeve too.'

It occurs to Erica then that Juliet is on some kind of spectrum, has trouble picking up on cues. Rory never mentioned it. But then, often these things weren't picked up back then. Like his dyslexia.

'Truly, Juliet, I appreciate the intention. But I'm not there yet. It's not even three weeks since we buried him. Now, if you'll excuse me.'

Juliet leans suddenly over the table, grasps her hand, looks up at her plaintively. 'The thing is. I just wanted to let you know, I've been on my own for a long time. And it's not so bad. It's good in many ways.'

Erica snatches her hand away. There's something greedy about this woman. The way she's looking at her, like she thinks she knows her. 'I happen to think having the love of your life die unexpectedly is pretty bad, actually. It's not the same as choosing to be single. It's not the same thing at all.'

Juliet sits up straight again. 'Of course. I didn't mean to offend you, Erica. To trivialise it. It's possible, is all I'm trying to say. To carry on living. Without them. It's hard, but it's possible, I think.' She sighs. 'I hope.'

Erica gives a stiff nod, leaves. Outside she takes a deep, cleansing breath. It's a relief to be away from that woman.

Later that evening, there's a reply to her email.

Hello Erica,

You're right. I did love him. So, I think I understand a little of your grief. I'm aware it's not the same as living together, raising a child, being a family. That's all yours, I don't want to take from that. Though I longed for that with him. I even long for your justified grief.

Yes, I did know his darkness too. And yes, it's shameful to admit, but it was part of the attraction. I'm as culpable as you on that.

No, the baby I miscarried wasn't his. (That *I miscarried*? God, it sounds like I did it deliberately. Didn't carry my own child right.) It was my ex's. And yes, it was painful though at the time I had to pretend it wasn't. I never talk about it. I lost so much blood during that operation that I almost died on the table. I was told the surgeon performed some kind of miracle by saving me, so it seemed as though mourning the loss of a foetus was supremely ungrateful.

I feel I have spent a lot of my life pretending and being grateful. Maybe we all do.

x

MAEVE

They're out for dinner. Maeve suggested the seafood restaurant in town, fish being the one food group they can agree on, and they're sitting at a coveted table by the window. The place is new, it was hard to get a booking, and there's a self-satisfied buzz in the air. The way everyone is scanning around, checking the room and each other out, puts Maeve in mind of hungry, long-necked cormorants scoping for prey at the water's edge.

They're sharing a dozen oysters as a starter. When she read the menu, the price of them made Maeve feel a bit queasy but she adores their briny, plump decadence. She spoons vinaigrette on one, loosens it with a spoon, harvests it from its shell by sucking it out and bites down. It explodes in her mouth and it's as though she's holding the ocean there. The taste is transformative, it's like finding a pearl, except the treasure is the memory of where it came from and she thinks of the little cottage, near Curracloe, that a friend of her mother's rented to them the summer she was fifteen. It was the only holiday they ever took together. Money was always too tight. The cottage was crowded with mismatched furniture and chipped crockery and scratchy woollen throws, and the shelves heaved with tattered paperbacks and eclectic, dusty ornaments. Every morning for that week in June her mother got her up at seven because she insisted that there was to be no breakfast, not even a cup of tea, until they had a swim. Maeve resented every second of that trembling walk to the water's edge, feet glancing over the sharp stones that separated the beach from the lane on which the cottage stood, a thin rag of a towel clasped around her shoulders. As her mother strode in front of her, she would take in her legs, with their knotty veins, and her broad freckled back topped off with a ridiculous swim cap invaded by rubber flowers so that she reminded Maeve of some alien creature from *Doctor Who*, a programme that creeped her out. Then she'd look down at her own mottled limbs and, with that disappointing image, yearn for a mother like Denise, who, she imagined, would lie in bed till midday on holiday, reading *Cosmo* and smoking and letting her daughter do the same if she so pleased. But eating her hot porridge and jam afterwards, wrapped in a blanket that had a kind of unwashed lanolin odour, she was always glad she'd done it. Later they would take the two ancient High Nellies that lived on the back porch and cycle to a pub in the village for lunch where they would eat deep bowls of creamy seafood chowder with shell-on mussels bobbing like shiny black canoes, and chunks of buttered brown soda bread. She wonders if eating oysters would evoke the same memories for her mother. Or if not a memory, at least some visceral sense of contentment.

'You look nice tonight,' Cillian says.

She smiles at him. 'Thank you.' She has made an effort. She's wearing a black dress, even put on red lipstick, because she knows he likes that look, the effortless French ingenue vibe. The opposite of how she feels really, which is more your neurotic Irish crone. She's regretting the lipstick. She finds it difficult, as though her mouth is being petulant, demanding attention like a self-absorbed toddler. She was thinking of Nisha's mouth when she applied it, smiled at her reflection wantonly, even winked, but when she came downstairs her mother eyed her, fearful, almost, and Jamie asked her if she'd had an accident.

They'd already rowed this morning about the fairness or otherwise of trans athletes competing in sport. Maeve argued that there have always been slight natural advantages for certain people owing to their differing physiques, and Jamie said, 'Oh sure, well I think a cock and balls that produces a shit ton of testosterone might be more than a slight advantage,' then left the room. 'What the hell, Jamie?' she yelled after him, once more reduced to a baffled anger. Turned to Cillian then, 'Did you hear that?' He just shrugged, said it was a fraught topic for a lot of people, in fairness, and went back to lovingly tending to his shakshuka in the cast-iron skillet. An image skimmed through her mind of picking it up and hitting him over the head with it. Like some cartoonish caricature of a housewife.

'Sexy, in fact.'

'Maybe these oysters are doing the trick.'

He raises his eyebrows. 'Well, here's hoping.'

She bristles. It's been nearly six months since they had sex. She knows the exact date because it was when she received her last half-yearly royalty statement, which was more than she was expecting and suddenly their mortgage repayments didn't appear as ominous. The problem for Maeve is that money has always been a worry, even when it isn't a worry. On a whim, she bought a bottle of champagne, as opposed to the usual prosecco, to celebrate. After they drank it, they crept upstairs and had sex, that was rushed as opposed to urgent, (more prosecco than champagne, quality-wise) while the boys and her mother sat downstairs watching television, unclear as to exactly who was babysitting who. The pleasure she'd experienced was short-lived, however. She had drunk most of the bottle herself and already felt a premonition of a hangover. This was further magnified by the regret over leaving the boys and their mother unsupervised. They'd watched *Stranger Things* and Lily had nightmares for a week.

When a teenage Maeve thought about marriage, and possibly inspired by the glorious, pulpy novels she'd smuggled from the library like contraband and hid from her mother, she'd imagined one of the many upsides was having daily sex. She honestly believed this. How could you share a bed with someone every night – a man, no less, with all his rapacious, corruptible body parts – and not take advantage of that? Sometimes she'd like to go back and give herself a good talking to.

'Is that a dig?'

'No, it's not a dig,' says Cillian. He fiddles with his glass. 'You know, I've been thinking. We could try role-play.'

'What are you on about?'

'In bed. It might . . . revive things a little.'

Maeve frowns. 'Where has this idea come from?'

'A sex therapist friend of mine sometimes recommends it to clients who are a little . . . blocked.'

'You've a friend who's a sex therapist?'

'Yes, well, colleague really. Someone I studied with.'

'Male or female?'

'What? Female. Why does that matter?'

'And have you talked about us? You and your sex therapist friend?' For some reason she makes air quotes around the words *sex therapist friend*. She's not sure why.

'Jesus, Maeve. Why do you do this?'

'Do what?'

'Choose to fixate on an irrelevant detail rather than the substance of the thing. What do you think of the role-play suggestion?'

She leans back, toys with the idea. An image pops into her head of Cillian dressed as a mafia boss smoking a fat Cuban. Her as a mobster's *gumar*. No, stripper. The idea is not repellent. She always found Tony Soprano strangely hot. The sleepy eyes, his appetites, the shamelessness of them. Does that make her a bad feminist? But something strikes her then and she leans forward.

'So, let me get this straight. What you're saying is that you want me to pretend to be someone else.'

'Well—'

She cuts him off. 'Huh. Figures.'

'No! That's not the—'

He is silenced by the waiter refilling their water glasses. She remembers that this is one of the reasons she avoids fancy restaurants in general. It's infantilising, and also the idea of someone being servile to her makes her feel uncomfortable, as does the particular way they are servile, which has an undercurrent of contempt. Another waiter comes and clears their plates. As he fusses, in a way that also manages to feel condescending, the door to the restaurant opens and a woman about their own age in confident white knee-high boots walks in. She smiles and waves at Cillian, who waves back, and is ushered then to a table near the kitchen.

'Who's that?' Maeve asks.

'Just someone.'

'Just someone? What does that mean?'

'Just someone I met through work. You wouldn't know her.'

'Well, obviously. That's why I'm asking who she is.'

'You know I can't really talk about it.'

'Is she your *sex therapist*?' There she goes, making those air quotes again.

Cillian sighs. 'Fuck's sake. I'm sorry I said anything now.'

The swearing lets her know he's reached the limit of his patience. 'Whatever,' she says, and folds her arms.

The waiter brings their mains too quickly and Maeve knows they're being rushed. She's all hot and prickly under her skin. She picks up her fork and takes a few lacklustre bites. The brown butter sauce that her fish swims in reminds her of bodily excretions. She thinks of her mother's incontinence pads. She pushes the plate away. When the waiter comes to clear the dishes, they both wave their hands automatically at the suggestion of dessert. They always refuse dessert now.

Tony Soprano would order the fucking dessert.

They finish their wine in silence. The waiter brings the bill without being asked. 'How was everything?' he says.

'Lovely,' she replies.

Cillian doesn't say anything.

—

In the car, Maeve turns on the radio to fill the silence. She looks at Cillian's hand on the gear stick. He's not wearing his wedding ring.

'Where's it gone?'

'What?'

She taps his naked finger.

'I haven't worn it in months. Ring rash. I'm sure I told you. It would hurt when I'd deadlift at the gym.' He says it like she has any idea what that means.

'But you'd been wearing it for years and it never bothered you before.'

'Apparently it can become an irritant at any time.'

'Huh.'

'You don't mind, do you?'

'I suppose not.'

She checks her phone. There's a new email from Nisha. She'd

prefer to read it alone but she's too excited. She angles the phone towards herself.

> Hi Maeve,
>
> Thanks so much for your critique of the first three chapters. Though I suspect critique is not the right word as you are being gentle with me. You're right about the first paragraph being shit . . . of course you used the word superfluous! No-one needs a weather update. Will cut. I'll make adjustments and resend, if that's okay? I don't mean to overwhelm you though so please let me know if I'm being a bit *extra*. I have been accused of this before . . . by lovers mostly and not just the male ones. My mother says it too. My mother is Indian, conservative . . . and quite the martyr! *Nishaaaaa, why this always trying to stick knife in my heart and kill me dead when I carried you in my tummy for nine months?!*
>
> Are Irish mothers like that too? Of course . . . I forgot, you are an Irish mother yourself and I'm sure you're nothing like this!
>
> It's a beautiful sunny evening here in London (whoops!! Redundant weather chat, hahaha). How is it there? I'm sitting on my little rooftop terrace. That's somewhat misleading. In reality it's a damp square of wooden decking with plantings that look to have been killed by acid rain (is that still a thing?) and a brief glimpse of the east London skyline. If you close one eye you can block out the chimney pots, dead flowers and television aerials and it becomes almost pretty.

I've been thinking about you a lot today as I did some revisions as per your brilliant suggestions. (And also, when reading your books which feels so intimate to me. A little like looking inside your head. I suppose that's the frightening thing about writing: all one's preoccupations and neuroses are laid bare. I wonder if I'm ready for that. Were you?)

I'm glad you found those websites . . . um . . . educational? And sorry they've been distracting you from getting work done. Although that's probably a little disingenuous. The thought of you discovering them distracts me too. And drives me a little crazy, if I'm honest.

Anyway, I should go. I'm working on a new ad and I need to come up with a scintillating line of dialogue between two frozen green beans. I kid you not. Tarantino will be quaking in his boots!!

N x

'What are you smiling at?' Cillian asks, eyeing her warily. 'You're actually blushing.'

'Just *something*,' she says, those pesky air quotes reappearing again.

Her mother is sitting in the armchair in her bedroom when they arrive home. Simon the cat is sitting on her lap purring loudly as she strokes him rhythmically. She's noticed they both seem calmer in each other's company as though accepting of the other's whims and eccentricities.

Maeve takes the cardboard carton from the restaurant out of her bag. 'I've got a surprise,' she says.

'I don't like surprises.' Lily's expression brightens, as though pleased to have remembered an essential truth about herself.

Maeve thinks of those first disquieting moments when she couldn't put her finger on what was different about her mother, but there was a blankness to her, like she was absent from herself momentarily. Maybe this feels like finding herself again.

'Sorry, it's not a surprise. Just an oyster. I thought you might like to eat it.'

Maeve digs it from the shell and then holds it in front of her mother, who opens her mouth. Her tongue is pale and spotted with white. Maeve places it inside, remembers her boys as toddlers: *Here comes the choo-choo train!* As her mother bites down, her face twists in disgust and she spits the oyster onto the floor. Simon hops off her lap and grabs it before running out the door. Maeve hopes he chokes on it.

'It's like snot. Why is everyone trying to poison me?'

Her mother is not a developing toddler, she is an atrophying old woman. Maeve's face stings with the effort of not crying. 'Do you remember Curracloe, Mam? We swam every morning. Do you remember that? Do you?' Her voice sounds pleading, childlike. They tell you not to ask so directly. Let them lead with their own reminiscences. Be gentle. Don't cause distress. Do no harm.

'Curracloe,' her mother says. Softer now. And Maeve is hopeful something might have dislodged.

'Yes.' She is encouraging.

'Curracloe,' she says again, as though she enjoys the feel of the word in her mouth. She's always loved words. She used to challenge Maeve's vocabulary: *Can't you find a better word than 'cool', Maeve? Sublime? Stupefying? Staggering?* Even her malapropisms now seem by design rather than accident: Fakebook instead of Facebook, monotonous for monogamous, fraud for Freud. But maybe that's just Maeve, hoping.

'Is that a place?'

'Yes, it's in Wexford.'

She frowns like that's made things too complicated.

'Did I like it there?'

'I think so, Mam. I think you did. Remember?'

Because Maeve remembers her clearly. Striding out the iron gate of the cottage to swim again in the evening as the sun set, a towel rolled tight and rifle-like under her arm. She never asked Maeve to join her for those night excursions. Maeve would sit on the armchair underneath the sash window, the net curtain pushed aside, waiting for her to return. Anxious, because she always suspected her mother had sacrificed too much, and with little to entice her back, maybe this would be the day when the lure of the wide-open sea, the freedom, the lunar pull of it, would prove too great and she would just keep swimming towards the horizon.

But her mother shakes her head, her eyes shift and dull. She is a receding tide. She is gone.

JULIET

He offered her a glass of wine when she first arrived and she refused, so now he's making her a cup of tea. It's done in such a careful way that she knows he can't do it too often. He places the large mug on a tiny saucer and puts it in front of her, some of it sloshing and pooling at the rim as he does. He goes to the fridge and takes out a bottle of Budweiser for himself and the bravado of it makes her smile. He starts to root in a drawer.

'Here, give it to me,' she says.

He hands her the bottle, and she twists the top off. 'You don't need a bottle opener. American, you see. They're all about instant gratification.'

'Right.' He seems embarrassed, and she feels bad.

'Does your mum let you drink?'

'Yeah. Dad was mad strict about it, though. They used to fight about it.'

'Oh?' She raises her eyebrows hopefully.

He shrugs. 'Ah, you know yourself. Parents.'

He looks uncomfortable now, pulling at the hem of his jumper, so she changes the subject. 'And how are you holding up?'

'Okay, I suppose. Mum thinks I should go to therapy.' He takes a swig of beer. 'Did you go? When your dad died.'

Juliet gives a wry laugh. 'Jesus, no. Therapy wasn't invented back then.'

He looks confused and she's reminded how young he is. She needs to be more tender with him.

'Only kidding. No, we all did the Irish thing and swallowed the pain down with the booze.'

'Oh, right. Some things don't change. Well, cheers.' He holds up the bottle, then takes another gulp.

'And anyway, here's the thing, Charlie. People die and obviously you're sad about it because you miss them and you know you'll never see them again. That's crazy hard. And it's natural that it's hard. Not some pathology.' She nods at his bottle. 'Another American invention.'

'How long does the sadness last for?'

'Honestly? I don't think it ever goes away. And you can't outrun it. Believe me, I've tried. I suppose you can only learn to live with it. And grief is not some straight line or a series of five neat stages like some would have you believe.'

'Probably Americans again.'

She laughs and she can see that he is pleased with himself. 'Definitely Americans.'

'So, what's it like, then?'

'Grief?'

'Yeah. Like, in the long run.'

What can she say? *I'll get back to you in a few years, it's too massive now to be articulated in any meaningful way*? Or maybe, *Life's a bitch, Charlie, then you die*? She's forty fucking nine years old and she hasn't a drop of wisdom to offer this boy. But he's so gentle and open. There's a kind of unsullied lustre to him. It'd be like stomping on an emerging shoot. She tries to reach back, summon that time when her father died. But it was such a weird, shapeless space where the overriding sensation was one of numbness.

'Do you surf at all?' she asks.

'No, I'd like to, though. Do you?'

'Yeah. My ex, Tāne – Ruby's dad – was into it. I don't do it as much anymore, but I love it. The feeling of freedom from yourself and connection to the ocean when you catch a wave is mad and beautiful. Anyway, when you first start you spend more time under the water than you do above it. But the balance changes after a while. Same with grief.'

He nods. 'Okay, I like that idea.' He stares into space, starts picking at the label on his bottle. A shred falls on the floor but he doesn't notice.

'And you know, Charlie, the only acceptance is to accept that you'll probably be fundamentally changed by it.'

He nods again. 'Yeah, I think I'm starting to see that.'

She takes a sip of tea. 'So, what are your plans? Once you finish school.'

He pushes out his bottom lip, shrugs. 'I don't know. Dad really wanted me to go to college. Mum too. But I don't want to. So I don't see the point of doing my Leaving. I think I'd prefer to travel, play my music.'

'Well, if that's what you decide, come see me in Auckland. You can teach me how to play more than one song on the guitar. I'll teach you how to surf. We live right beside a beautiful beach.'

His face lights up. 'Can I really?'

'Absolutely. It'll be fun.'

He takes a swig of beer and says, 'I can see why my dad liked you. You're different. You're not all uptight about stuff the way Mum is.'

'It's a mother's job to be uptight. And trust me, you don't want to be that kid with cool parents. There was a girl in my school who did. Last I heard she's married to her cousin, living in a squat in Camden and wears a tinfoil hat when she goes outside.' He looks unsure as to whether she's joking so she smiles and he smiles back. 'But how do you know he liked me anyway?'

'I just do. There's something about you. How could he not?'

'Thank you,' she says, feeling what she knows is a disproportionate gratitude.

'Hey, do you want to listen to some records? Dad has a big collection.'

'Love to.'

She picks up her mug and he leads her into the large sitting room at the front of the house. It's much tidier than the kitchen, and with a different vibe: cool, pared back, Scandinavian, everything in shades of beige and white, one original abstract painting on the wall. It feels like Rory's space. She thinks of Denise's sitting room, the eclectic colours, the reproduction prints. The decor like someone's vomited up soft furnishings. *Oh and here by the fifty-inch plasma screen we have van Gogh's* Sunflowers! There's a whole wall here of blond wood shelving and two rows are crammed with vinyl. Charlie walks over to the record player perched next to them.

'Any requests?'

'Surprise me.'

He grins at this, blushes, like it's their little code word. He spends a long time looking through the records, as though it's important to get it just right. He's so careful in a way Rory never was.

Juliet sits on the couch and takes the room in. What did Rory feel sitting here? Through the window she can see out over the front lawn where his little childhood home once stood. The place his mother killed herself, though she was embalmed with alcohol and entombed there for years before that happened. It must be like living with her grave. She never understood that impulse of his – control or stubbornness, she can't decide.

The last time they had sex as kids was in a car from his father's garage that was parked on bricks on that small patchy lawn. A fittingly ignominious ending. It was a couple of weeks after Dan's funeral. 'It's my fault,' he'd said. 'I did it.' So broken. She really thought she could fix him. For that brief time as she straddled him on the passenger seat of the rusty Capri her tenderness gave way to a sense of power over him. Over him and Erica, they were official by then. That power ended though when she pretended to come – loudly – and Rory shushed her and put his hand over her mouth. 'Am I better than her, though?' Juliet asked, her hands holding the side of his face, looking down. 'I told you already, we decided we won't sleep together yet. We're taking it slow,' he said. 'What you mean is, she won't put out, Rory.' He took her hands away. 'No, we both want to wait. Make it special.' She knew the words were chosen deliberately. She moved back over to the passenger seat of that clapped-out old car, chastened and ordinary. He was full of remorse then over what they'd done. Cheating on Erica again. More self-loathing. It was his way of punishing her, she understood.

She hears the gorgeous crackle and pop of the record Charlie has chosen and the unmistakeable opening bars of Dylan's *Blood on the Tracks*. It upends her, and for a moment she's under water again, struggling to breathe. Rory's favourite song from his favourite album. He wrote to her about it, just before she came back to Ireland in 2019. That first precious night in that hotel on Drury Street. Always on beds and in locked rooms that belonged to other people.

She knows that email by heart too.

> Jules, I'm listening to 'Tangled Up in Blue' and I know this song is about us. More star-crossed lovers. Also how insane is it that your name is Juliet? The narrator of the song lives on Montague Street! It's a sign, I'm certain. This song is timeless love. Or no. Maybe it's more that time is irrelevant . . . yesterday and today and tomorrow all intertwined.

Dylan says the song took him many years to live and a few more to write. It's an epic love story. As are we.

R x

Charlie sits down beside her on the couch and she is aware then of how truly large the room is when he is so close. She looks at his lovely profile which, when you think about it, is in fact Rory's too. Yesterday and Today and Tomorrow. Time is irrelevant. She is seventeen. She is forty-nine. And all the ages in between. All versions of herself, all our layers superimposed, carried inside us forever. The girl that loved Rory, the one that was loved by him. The layers since then: losing her father, losing Dan, leaving Ireland, becoming a mother. It will be the same one day for Charlie. Their hands are resting close together on the couch. She can hear him breathing and feels the music pulsing, though maybe it's her heart.

'Jules?'

And did he just say that?

She keeps her eyes closed. His song and his hand next to hers and the scent of him on her wrist. That trembling boy in a shed in a field, in a broken-down car, a locked hotel room. A grave. Resurrected now beside her.

The front door slams. Her eyes fly open. There's a pause before the door to the room opens and Erica is there, in tight active wear, a modest glister of exercise on her skin, not anything as vulgar as sweat, just as though she's been buffed. She looks at them in her impassive, possessing way.

Of course, Bob Dylan wrote that song about his wife. At the end of the day it was always about the wives.

Erica's eyes fall on the bottle of beer on the coffee table. 'Oh. It's you. You're everywhere.'

It's said so coolly, without any discernible tone, that it might even be a compliment. Juliet stands. 'Hello, Erica.'

'What's going on?'

'I popped in to get a photograph that Charlie said he found. One of me and Rory. I don't have any myself.'

Pause. 'Can I see it?'

Charlie stands then too. 'It's upstairs. I'll go and get it.'

When he's gone, Erica walks over to the record player and jerks the needle away with a jarring zip.

'So, did you enjoy your podcast and walk the other day?'

Erica turns to the shelf so that she is facing away. 'Yes. Thank you.'

Juliet looks at her straight, erect back, her sinewy arms, her hair pinned back into a severe bun. She thinks of her tiny twirling dancer locked within her childhood jewellery box and suddenly she is destroyed by her restraint, wants to prostrate herself in front of her and say she is sorry. Rory feels so dark and heavy inside her right now and this woman's sadness so vast.

Erica puts the record back in its sleeve and slots it into the shelf. 'I never got his taste in music.'

'Didn't you? That must have been irritating.'

'Not really. It wasn't a big deal.'

'But music was a big deal to Rory.'

Erica shrugs. 'More of an amusing diversion really. Like a lot of things in his life. Distractions from himself.'

'What do you mean? It was the very core of him.'

'The very core of him?' She turns suddenly and looks at Juliet in a surprised way. Something shifts, a wrinkle in the air.

Juliet starts to explain, stumbles a little over her words. 'Yes, well, as a kid I mean, he—'

But she is interrupted by Charlie walking back in. 'Here it is.' He's just about to hand it to Juliet when Erica takes it from him. 'Oh goodness. Charlie, are there no better ones? It's not the most flattering.' She hands it to Juliet without meeting her eye.

'I think it's great,' says Charlie. 'It's a bit rock 'n' roll. Candid.'

Juliet studies it. It's of herself, Rory and Maeve sitting in a pub in town in front of a Happy New Year banner. She turns it over, *New Year's Eve 1990* written in neat cursive on the back. For a second, she thinks that Dan must have been the one to take it and then it strikes her that Dan would have been dead for four months. The table in front of them is strewn with pint and shot glasses and cigarette packets and there are two huge overflowing ashtrays. Maeve has got a coloured party hat on her head and is making a peace sign. Rory is beaming at the camera. Juliet is turned towards Rory, a smudge of black make-up under her eye, her face slack, collapsed looking.

And she has a sudden and visceral reaction to it.

'I should go,' she says, placing the photograph back on the coffee table. 'But thanks for showing me this, Charlie.'

Erica picks it up again and presses it into her hand. 'You keep this. I insist. I have so much of Rory.'

Outside, she looks at the photo again. Bleached and faded, peppered with ghostly white patches. So long ago. So long since she was young, yet here she is still making the same mistakes, nothing learned. She has a sense of herself now, a pathetic, middle-aged woman, bleached and faded too, desperate for a boy, a grieving child, to . . . what . . . admire her? She'd put on lipstick before she called down. Did she want him to desire her? She wipes her hand roughly across her mouth in disgust, leaving a bloody smear on her wrist.

She tries to rip the photo up but it's that tough, shiny paper so she scrunches it instead and pushes it into the hedge that borders Erica's house. On the walk up the road, she thinks of it, burrowed in there, an unhappy little time capsule.

Ruby is watching a film with Denise and Johnny when she comes in. The three of them are sitting cuddled together on the couch. She sits on the arm. Ruby side-eyes her.

'What's wrong?' Juliet asks.

'Nothing. What's wrong with you?'

Ruby turns back to the film. Juliet stands and hovers at the door. She has a sense of herself, as she does when she's in New Zealand, of being apart from everyone. A flimsy, inconsequential thing, unnecessary. A fading image in a photo. They don't notice her leave.

—

New Year's Eve. She and Maeve were in a pub in town, in a seat near the door. One of those lax places that didn't ask for ID. Juliet had turned eighteen in October but Maeve was still underage. Neither of them felt much like celebrating but what were they going to do? Sit at home with their mothers watching the countdown on RTÉ and singing 'Auld Lang Syne'? If they weren't feeling suicidal before, that would push them over the edge. Anyway, maybe they needed to say goodbye to this year. No, more a *good riddance.* Juliet had gotten her period that morning as a final way of that poxy annus horribilis punishing her. It was the first since Liverpool and so heavy; the squeezing in her stomach and the light-headedness from the hash and the beer evoked the clinic and the drugs they administered to 'soften her up', as the nurse had put it. It felt nothing like softening to Juliet, more her cervix forming a hard kernel. The term petrification that they'd been learning about in geography kept popping into her head as she lay on that narrow iron bed. Again, another word that would never occur to her in an exam. Before the operation the kind anaesthetist had patted her hand and told her not to be frightened. *But I am petrified*, she thought to herself, high as a kite. *I am petrifying.* Those drugs they gave her were the only good part of that whole experience. They made her feel as though her consciousness was separate to her body, so that even as she was aware of the sensations, they felt as though they were happening to someone else. Someone broken and deserving of them. She'd been chasing that feeling, trying to recreate that sense of dislocation ever since, but that night Maeve was on a total downer and kept talking about Dan and, to be honest, Juliet just wanted her to *shut the fuck up*. He'd been dead for four months and raking over it at every available opportunity wasn't doing anyone any good. No wonder Rory was keeping his distance from them. He had more to feel guilty about than anyone.

Juliet went to the bar and brought back a couple of tequila shots. 'Here, drink this,' she said to Maeve. 'And then lighten up, will you?'

It was then that she saw them coming through the door. Rory and Erica, holding hands. A cold wind swept in behind them and they looked as though they were being carried in by it, vital and lustrous. Erica's face under her beanie was flushed and healthful. She was the kind of girl who could wear a hat cutely, Juliet was not. She looked as though she'd spent the day skiing. She was probably the kind of girl who went skiing. Looking at her, Juliet felt like one of the soiled, greying rags her mother kept under the sink for polishing the silver. They were about to walk past, though Juliet was sure Rory had seen them by the way he angled his body. She wasn't going to let him get away with it. He'd gotten away with so much already. She leaned forward and made a lunge for his arm and pulled him down between herself and Maeve.

'Well, stranger,' she said. 'I haven't seen you in ages.'

'Well, Juliet,' he said, keeping his eyes fixed on Erica, as though waiting to be saved by her.

The *Juliet* was articulated with intent.

'Where've you been lately? Aren't we good enough for you anymore?' Her voice sounded wheedling. This is what she had come to. She was a person who wheedled around him.

He made a non-committal noise.

Maeve was looking at Rory in a way that Juliet couldn't quite interpret. 'Jesus, is that really you, Rory? I'd forgotten what you looked like. I wish we had a camera.' Her tone was combative.

'I do!' said Erica. Of course she fucking did. She reached into her bag and took out one of those yellow disposable Kodak ones. 'I'll get a photo of you guys. For posterity. Say cheese, everyone!' God, could she be any more perfect?

She held it to her eye and then Rory said from the corner of his mouth, so low you could hardly make it out, 'You better not make a scene, Juliet. Make any trouble, I swear . . .' Then he turned and gave Erica his most devastating Hollywood smile.

Juliet wondered if she'd misheard him. She turned to him. 'What did you say?' It was then that the flash of the camera went off.

He stood up abruptly. 'Happy New Year!' he said to no-one in particular, and just like that, they were gone, disappeared into the throng at the bar. They must have left through another door because that was the last she saw of them.

She lurched around the pub for the rest of the night, bolshie but fragile. Maeve tried to get her home at closing time, but she was having none of it. She'd been flirting with Donie, the guy who owned the place, and he asked her to stay behind for a drink. She ended up having sex with him in his flat upstairs. 'Jesus, you bled all over me good sheets,' he said to her the next morning as she dressed to leave.

'Yeah,' she said, in a voice heavy with sarcasm. 'I forgot to mention I was actually a virgin. And you're *so* enormous, Donie.'

Then she slammed his bedroom door on the way out.

'Cunt,' she heard him say as she walked down the hall. Downstairs, she searched the shelves behind the bar till she found what looked like an expensive bottle of Midleton whiskey, shoved it in her coat pocket and stumbled out the door into the bitter, watery light of January.

ERICA

It's after midnight, Charlie is in bed. In the kitchen, she takes a bottle of wine from the fridge and pours herself a large one. *The very core of him.* Juliet's phrase taunts, feels almost carnal. She takes the glass into the sitting room and sits down on the couch. The smell of her perfume lingers still and burns the back of Erica's throat. She swallows some wine to soothe it, then stands, walks over to the window and opens it. It's a mostly clear night, just a few clouds congregating like angry thoughts over the moon. She sits down again but can't relax. The mug Juliet was drinking from earlier sits on the coffee table, a smudge of lipstick at the rim. She picks it up, smears her thumb across it, then looks at the red stain it's left on her skin. It could almost be blood.

She downs the rest of the wine, then goes to his study, opens his laptop and pounds her fingers against the keys.

Hello,

It seems unfair that you have my name and I don't have yours. Another woman who knows about me and I don't know the truth about her. You keep crawling out of the woodwork these days. It's a rather unsporting advantage, don't you think? Could you tell me your name at least?

All you women who claim him. Do you realise how deeply your description of him sexually has affected me? I keep picturing it, feeling a mix of anger and sadness but mostly shame. You see, there wasn't a huge sexual connection between us ever. Not even at the beginning. We didn't sleep together for a long time. That was down to me. I was *romantically* attracted to him, besotted even, thought he was beautiful, but I've just never been a highly sexual person. I suppose a woman like you finds that difficult to understand. Laughable in fact. I even discovered he was still having sex with someone else back then and didn't care all that much. After we'd been together for a few months he asked me to lend him some money. He'd gotten some girl in trouble. In trouble! What a stupid euphemism. In Ireland we use it to cover a multitude, don't we, from pregnancy to war. I think I was so in love that I justified it. I thought if I wasn't going to sleep with him then it was only fair he got it from somewhere else. As though men are somehow entitled to sex, can't survive without it. Pathetic, I know. I was pathetic even back then.

Anyway, there was a woman here earlier. An old friend of Rory's. I say friend but from the way she spoke about him tonight, so possessively, I think maybe it was more than that. She could even have been that girl. You know, when I had my miscarriages I used to think about that girl and the money I gave her, and even though I'm not religious and believe absolutely in bodily autonomy, I thought I was being punished in some way by God. A God I didn't even believe in. My final miscarriage happened just before the abortion referendum and my thinking was so distorted, I believed it to be some kind of karmic retribution.

Maybe this is more of it. You writing to me. It seems I'm destined to be haunted by Rory's lovers. Or maybe my own weak, pitiable nature. I won't write again.

Erica

MAEVE

She sits at her kitchen table, staring at the space between the utility-room door and the pantry which is covered in blackboard wallpaper put there when they renovated. She was inspired by one of those property-porn shows that she was fond of at the time. She came to realise later, after their own renovation, that, much like actual porn, the process, proportions and ecstatic denouements portrayed were completely unrealistic. The shows she was fond of were American and involved the homeowners going away for, oh, an afternoon, and then returning to discover that, hey presto!, for a pittance, their entire house had been remodelled beautifully and, uncannily, to the exact taste of the homeowners, but crucially for Maeve, without any need for their input into the project. This was not Maeve's experience. Not only was their renovation anti-climactic, it left her with slight PTSD. The only 'learning' she took from it – to quote the annoying corporate speak of the project manager who oversaw the ordeal – was the 'learning' that she was not the type of person who cared one iota about the width or design of the skirting board or the orientation of the door handles yet these were the types of trivial yet head-imploding decisions she was being asked to make on a daily basis.

Aspirational design features, such as open shelving, that made sense in other people's houses – the kind of people with matching, unchipped crockery, the kind of people who didn't have drawers filled with lidless Tupperware and Nerf bullets and spent batteries – were considered and, mercifully, thanks to Cillian, discarded. When Maeve showed the designer the pictures she had ripped from magazines, Cillian looked at her over the top of his glasses and said, 'Bear in mind, Maeve, we'll have to keep the shelves neat. All the time.' Maeve said, 'Oh, right, hadn't thought of that.'

This blackboard wallpaper, however, with a chalk holder and eraser attached, was the one design feature that Maeve was genuinely excited about. She imagined manageable shopping lists: *Milk, Bread, Bananas!*; witty literary quotes about food that she would update weekly: *After a good dinner, one can forgive anybody, even one's relatives (Wilde)*; cute reminders to each other: *Please defrost chicken casserole for dinner tonight!* This small strip of kitchen wall would be a testament to their well-run, harmonious home, a microcosm of their ordered lives.

It lasted a week. She came to realise that the sheer volume of needs and wants and logistics involved in running the house and the people in it would require an entire gallery to cope. Now, the wall is blank, except for a few ghostly smears of erased chalk, and the to-do list spins in Maeve's head instead like some noisy out-of-control carousel. Her focus flits between each item like a child unable to decide which horse to mount so the ride keeps swirling and not much ever feels pinned down.

Clean windows – renew Mam's prescriptions – FINISH NOVEL – book NCT car – plant herb garden – google how plant things – engage glutes when walking – research reminiscence therapy Mam – research Profhilo – hoover car – enquire Pilates getting 'thick waisted' – try intermittent fasting – have date night Cillian – HAVE SEX Cillian – dental appointment Jamie – remember Kegels at traffic lights – invest in capsule wardrobe – worming tablets Simon – mammogram – clean fridge – practise mindfulness – new rugby boots Luke – grouting in shower – FINISH NOVEL FINISH NOVEL FINISH NOVEL . . . Sometimes this very unmerry-go-round rotates so fast and tight it turns into a maelstrom that Maeve might just get sucked into one of these days.

—

She did manage a gynaecologist's check-up for a strange rash she's had, followed by a coffee with Juliet yesterday morning, two things crossed off the list. At coffee, she'd been telling Juliet all about the appointment and also trying to engage her on the topic of oestrogen replacement.

'I don't think I need it. I'm still juicy,' Juliet said. Smugly, perhaps, Maeve thought.

'The whole thing was mortifying. She had to do a biopsy. *On. My. Vulva.*' Maeve shuddered with the memory. 'Apparently the rash I have could possibly be something called lichen sclerosus. If left untreated, it means your bits can fuse together.'

'What? So no more sex?'

'I'd say that would be the least of your worries, to be honest. Mine doesn't get much use anyway. You know she had a look up there with some kind of probing torch. It was like being fingered by E.T.'

Juliet grimaced. 'You realise you've completely ruined that film for me now.'

Maeve carried on. 'Then she started providing a running commentary to the nurse chaperone. Merrily throwing around terms like *increased genital hiatus, vaginal laxity, vulval atrophy*. My legs nearly slammed together with the shame. I mean, I know after pushing out a couple of kids it was never going to win a beauty contest, but still. *God*, I've just realised I'll never be able to let anyone else besides Cillian see it now. Do you know we're supposed to be moisturising up there? I told her those Koreans better not invent a ten-step routine for it. I can't even cope with basic skincare for my face.'

'Do you remember when we were kids and christened our vaginas after reading *Forever*?'

'I do! You still rocking a Kate Bush?'

'Sure am. How's Virginia Woolf?'

'Bit depressed if I'm honest.'

They laughed.

Maeve sighed then. 'Are you dreading what's going to come in our fifties? I mean, on the basis of what our forties are like?

More stress and money worries and work pressure and ungrateful teenagers and insomnia and hot flushes and no sex and sick parents and weird aches and pains everywhere that you google and are convinced it's cancer or MND?'

Juliet shrugged. 'There are worse things.'

Maeve was incredulous. 'What could possibly be worse than all that?'

'Jesus, Maeve. What about dying of a heart attack at forty-nine, for fuck's sake?' And Juliet looked so stricken that Maeve felt chastened.

Her phone pings now with a message from Nisha. Was googling you and saw some pretty publicity pics.

Maeve flushes with pleasure. Hmm . . . next thing you'll say Wow I didn't recognise you because you look older in real life. Actual comment I get from people at events btw.

Maeve watches the dots. I much prefer the IRL version btw.

Maeve smiles. God though, if you google me you'll end up seeing all those one-star reviews too.

Four texts then in quick succession. Don't worry, I'll review them back for you.

Ugly profile pic – One Star.

Taste in books – One Star.

Tedious review – One Star.

Maeve laughs. Then another text from Nisha. I've sent you an email.

Her heart trips. (It really does, what is happening?) She

feels like a teenager again. She's just about to open the app when Jamie walks in. She quickly replies. K, chat later.

'Hi, love,' she says to him. It can be risky addressing him first, especially using a term of endearment.

'Why do you type like that?'

'Like what?'

'Like this.' He stoops and, squinting, pokes the air in front of him with his forefinger. 'It's retarded looking.'

'Don't use that word. And how am I supposed to type?'

'With your thumbs. Like normal people.'

Maeve sits back, taps the side of her head. 'A-ha. Now I get it.'

'Get what?'

She puts on an exaggerated midwest American accent. 'Why the Good Lord gave us opposable thumbs.'

He shakes his head. 'That's not funny.'

Once again, Maeve finds herself unable to make sense of this animosity towards her. It's like he's blaming her, but she has no idea for what. As a small child – a time that feels like a heartbeat ago and also in another galaxy, far, far away – he always preferred her to Cillian. *Mommy, read me story, not you, Daddy. Mommy, get me drink. Mommy, wash my hair.* Mommy's knee, Mommy's hand. Mommy's kisses. 'Pretend I've gone out,' she'd say to Cillian, hiding behind the sofa when he yelled from the top of the stairs for Mommy to come tuck him in for the tenth time that night. Once she was so tired she said, 'Tell him Mommy's dead.'

'Have you seen my black hoodie?'

'Which particular black hoodie would this be?'

Sigh. 'The Nike one.'

'Yes, it's washed and on top of the folded washing in the utility.'

He drops his shoulders and sighs heavily again, as though the room is in Outer Mongolia, not about seven steps to his left.

'You're welcome,' she says as he walks away.

'Ugh. Can you just not?' he says without turning back.

'Just not what?'

'The whole martyred mother routine. It's boring.' He disappears through the pocket door, installed to maximise space in the utility room, thus theoretically making time spent in there doing chores a fun experience. You'd swear by the way the designer talked about it that by simply crossing the threshold you'd be transported into Narnia.

She closes her eyes, takes a deep breath and exhales slowly. When he emerges from the room, still slope-shouldered, untransformed by his odyssey in there, she says, 'Shall we go out for ice cream?'

'Ice cream?' He looks baffled. As though it's a word she's made up.

'Yes, that frozen sweet stuff you used to love.'

Now he looks at her as though she's mad. She wonders how she exists in Jamie's head. Some amorphous blob, a featureless shadow in the periphery of his universe? Or worse, an actual impediment to his happiness?

When he's gone, Maeve walks over to the blackboard. Before the renovation this strip of wall was where they marked the boys' height. They took such delight in each centimetre. Excited, they'd try to guess beforehand. 'I bet I've grown ten centimetres!' Luke, ever the optimist, would say. Jamie, more circumspect, anxious to get it right, 'I think I will have grown one point five centimetres.' Maeve didn't pay enough attention to the fact that all the time they were shooting upwards, they were also growing away from her.

She thinks of them as babies and her heart feels sore. She can physically feel the weight of them in her arms, and also the unbearable absence of them. She thinks of Lily coming to stay with them in Harold's Cross for a few weeks to lend a hand after Luke was born. Maeve came down to the kitchen one morning holding Jamie to find her mother crying, the paper laid out in front of her. 'What's wrong?' she asked, shocked at the sight. Her mother never cried. Lily wiped her eyes then, stood up and said, 'Nothing, I'm grand. Now, give that child to me and I'll get him ready for a walk. You get yourself some breakfast.' Once she left the room, Maeve looked down at the open page of the newspaper. She'd been reading the death notices. Her eyes scanned the print and stopped then at one name – *Joseph Griffin, Ballinasloe* – and she knew suddenly it was her mother's father. She read the full notice and then realised with a kind of horror that Lily's name hadn't been included amongst his children. They'd written her out of his life. And her own.

She picks up the chalk and scrawls *Maeve was 'ere*. Then she lets it drop, grabs the eraser and aggressively wipes off her own name.

JULIET

It's the morning after being in Erica's house and she's driving Ruby and Denise to visit her father's grave. Juliet hasn't slept well. Kept seeing that dawning expression on Erica's face. Feeling that she's ruined something again. A notion strikes her and she pulls in abruptly at a petrol station.

'Flowers.'

'Okay,' Denise says, side-eyeing her. Juliet had been surprised that her mother wanted to come with them. She doesn't think she'd be able to visit a graveyard with death feeling like more than a hypothetical.

Juliet takes three bunches from the buckets by the front door. They're a little bedraggled, a couple of the blooms wilting. She places them, dripping, up on the counter and says to the woman there, 'Any chance of a discount on these? They've seen better days.'

'Haven't we all,' the woman says, not even bothering to look up, which Juliet admires. The friendliness of New Zealand shop assistants can be terrifying. Well, other shop assistants who are not Juliet. She hasn't checked her emails in a couple of days, possibly she no longer has that job anyway. 'But sure look, God loves a tryer, I'll knock a third off for you.' She glances up then and her expression changes into a smile. 'Juliet Quinn. I don't believe it.'

Juliet looks at the middle-aged face in front of her. For a moment she thinks it must be one of her mother's friends and then she realises it's a girl she went to school with. She keeps getting shocks like this. When she's away people and places exist in her imagination as fixed, immutable portraits, in a sort of back-to-front Dorian Gray scenario. It's always a jolt to see the reality.

'Oh my God, Sandra Blake. You haven't changed a bit,' she lies.

In school, they were the two top art students. But Juliet's work regressed that final year. 'Inaccessible, Juliet, the viewer feels excluded. What's going on?' her teacher Miss Doyle would say. She couldn't explain to her how she wasn't capable of accessing it herself anymore. Felt alienated from that part of her, which was the only good part, the part that might make something of her life. And the one she felt undeserving of. In her exam, Juliet read the first question, which mentioned Gauguin and the post-impressionists, wrote underneath 'Gauguin was a fucking paedo' then stood up and walked out. Sandra was the one who got a place in NCAD.

'Ah go 'way,' Sandra laughs. 'Don't be annoying me. Every

time I look in the mirror I wonder how Mam, who's been in her grave for ten years, managed to sneak in.'

'So, how's it going?'

Sandra gestures around the shop. 'Well, Juliet, as you can see, I'm living the dream here.'

Juliet gives a grim laugh.

'And you? Over in Australia, I hear.'

'New Zealand, actually. Also in retail. But not even anything useful like this. Selling candles that'll never be lit to bored housewives. So you know, same shit, different place.'

Sandra rolls her eyes. 'Ah yeah, tell me about it.'

She doesn't mean it, of course. No-one really cares. Occasionally she makes things up to amuse herself. Like *Oh, in New Zealand the moon isn't visible because we're so far south* or *If you're fat in New Zealand you're not allowed to wear polyester.* But their eyes glaze over just the same. The thing is, she thinks about Ireland all the time, is acutely aware of its environment, as though there are two clocks and two calendars running concurrently in her head. And she knows that to everyone here she is immaterial, a sort of abstraction. Her own mother still hasn't grasped the concept of the time difference, or opposing seasons. Juliet doesn't blame people for this. After all, she's not aware of, say, the current climactic conditions in the Congo or what hour of the day it is in Azerbaijan at any given moment. Still, it can all feel a little one-sided at times.

After they chat for a while, she pays and turns to go, and then, as if compelled by some masochistic urge, hears herself ask, 'Do you still draw, Sandra?'

'I do. Just some portraits as a bit of a side hustle. It'll never make me rich, of course. Hence this place. I have a website with my stuff. Here.' She takes an old receipt and writes down a domain name and passes it to Juliet. 'How about you?'

'Nah, haven't in years.'

'But you were so good! Miles better than me.'

Juliet shrugs as though it doesn't matter but it's so true it's painful.

On her way out the door, Juliet looks around. Sandra has her back turned and is organising chocolate bars behind the counter. Juliet picks up a packet of crackers from the nearest shelf and slips it into her bag. Outside she throws the receipt from Sandra in the nearest bin.

'Are you okay, Mum?' Ruby asks, studying her, when she gets back in the car.

She's so full of potential, this girl. How did it feel to be on the brink of everything? Ruby's life must seem to stretch in front of her, a languid slow-moving body of water. She wants to impress upon her the fleeting nature of it, the urgency. *It's all whitewater rapids and waterfalls and riptides, Ruby!* But it's impossible. You can only understand it when you've been spit out the other end and by then it's too late.

'Yes, fine,' she says. 'Cracker, anyone?'

At the graveyard they stand in front of her father's headstone. A majestic silvery-black crow lands on it, eyes them before cawing hoarsely and flying away.

Denise shivers. 'I hate crows.'

'They're clever,' says Ruby. 'One of the few animals who are more intelligent than required for their own survival.'

'Like people, then,' says Denise. 'Too much knowing for their own good.'

'I miss them,' says Juliet. 'There's none in New Zealand.'

'What?' says Denise in disbelief. 'What kind of a place is it at all?'

'If you'd come visit it, Nana, you'd find out,' Ruby says, putting her arm around her.

Denise waves her hand. 'Ach, it's too far.'

They stand in silence for a few moments before Denise says, 'Will you promise me you'll have me cremated? Johnny won't even let me talk about it, so I'm depending on yous two. I can't stand the thought of lying there cold for all eternity. No-one to talk to me except ugly old crows.'

'Don't you want to be beside Daddy?' asks Juliet.

Denise looks at her then in a way that flays her. 'You move on, Juliet. Otherwise, you may as well throw yourself in after them.'

'Sati,' says Ruby. When Denise and Juliet look at her blankly, she says, 'It was a Hindu ritual where widows were pressured to sacrifice themselves on the pyre. Anyway, you're not going to die, Nana.'

'We all die, Ruby,' says Juliet. 'All of us. And much sooner than you think.'

'Jesus, Mum!'

'I don't mean Nana, specifically. I mean everyone, that's all. I'm going to take a walk around.'

It's a fine day and the graveyard looks pretty, set on a small hill, hugged by a gently sloping golden explosion of rapeseed meadow on one side and a thicket of ash trees on the other.

She finds Dan's grave, unwraps the plastic from one of the bunches of flowers and sets it down. They look even more withered now, as though being here, in this place, has accelerated the decay. Maeve told her how she likes to imagine Dan in some alternative reality. She tries to conjure up her own alternative reality. How would it have been when the radiographer in Liverpool – you couldn't get the scan in Ireland if they knew why you needed it – discreetly turned the silent screen away from her so that only he could see it, and pressed the cold probe into her belly, her full bladder feeling like it might burst, so that he could accurately date it. Fifteen weeks, he said, instead of the twelve Juliet had presumed. 'It might make the procedure more complicated,' he said. 'General anaesthetic.' He patted her hand tenderly then, misunderstanding the confused look on her face. 'It'll be fine, dear.' But she wasn't thinking about procedures. She was trying to count backwards, her mind muddled, trying to make sense of it.

Fifteen weeks? So not Rory's baby. What an empty surprise. She'd naively assumed that it couldn't have happened her first time. It seemed logical that there might be more barriers to get through.

The thing is, before her appointment for the scan, in the taxi from the B&B, she started to doubt her decision to go ahead with the abortion. They were driving through an industrialised area, near the docks, the place looked utilitarian, ugly. She could see the driver's baggy and bloodshot eyes in the rear-view mirror, suspended there, like a dopey cartoon dog. 'Over 'ere for a bit of shopping, like?' She was sure he knew; she wouldn't have been the first banished Irish girl he'd had in his car. She turned away, pretended she couldn't hear. Everything felt wrong. This wasn't how she'd imagined her first overseas trip, Santa Ponsa and sex on the beach cocktails by the pool. She shut her eyes to block it all out.

And then . . . 'Thunder Road' on the radio. The taxi driver turned it up and Juliet took it as a sign. Leaned her head back against the seat and as the song built to its giddy crescendo she began to feel a swell of excitement. Two smalltown kids against the odds. Against the world!

Then, sitting in the radiographer's waiting room, which was gaudy with Christmas decorations, surrounded by women with obvious bumps and attentive partners, 'Fairytale of New York' played and it was like the universe was trying to tell her something, screaming at her in fact. The couple in the song volatile, scarred, depraved even, but meant for each other nonetheless. She would have the scan, have a picture to show him (*Look what we made, Rory!*), go back to the B&B run by the kind woman Sharon (so many kind English people over those few days, thank God for them), tell her thanks for everything but that she saw things differently now. She would fly back home, tell him. Deep down she believed that if she'd told him, he'd have tried to talk her out of it. He did love her, he just needed a reason to choose her. He would break up with Erica, no hard feelings. And then no matter what happened they would be tied forever through their love child (what a perfect description!). As the cold jelly was spread across her belly, she imagined the two of them, like those couples in the waiting room, Rory like the bare-chested hunk in the Athena poster cradling a newborn. For those few minutes she had Rory. She had it all.

And then. Fifteen weeks? Trying to make sense of what the radiographer was saying as he wiped the gel from the gentle curve of her stomach. She felt cold and empty inside then, the excitement wiped away too. And despite the radiographer telling her it would be more complicated, to Juliet it was never more simple. She could have lied. And, shamefully, it did cross her mind. But in the end, she couldn't do that to Rory. Maybe if she loved him a bit less. It was the only time in her life she didn't feel herself to be monstrously selfish.

Anyway, what-ifs are pointless, she doesn't understand Maeve's compulsion to discuss them. You could drive yourself mad thinking about what might have been. She walks back along the path and turns left at the end of the row towards the graves furthest from the entrance. She's surprised to see that Rory's plot with its simple cross isn't the most recent. It's all so relentless. She lays the flowers down, then notices the little card stapled to the cellophane. She fishes in her bag for a pen, although of course she knows there is none. When has she ever carried a pen? There's an ancient red lip gloss, though, and with the doe foot of it she draws a thick kiss. It smudges and looks like it was drawn in blood. She is about to rip the card off but thinks of Erica pressing the painful photograph into her hand and decides to leave it. 'For posterity,' she says aloud.

MAEVE

At first, Maeve, woken from that initial tranche of deep sleep, thinks it's her mother's cry coming through the baby monitor. As she comes to, she realises it's the doorbell.

When she opens the front door, Juliet is standing there. Maeve's heart still hops a little at the sight of her. Juliet's hands are behind her back. Maeve almost expects her to hold them up to reveal a bottle of vodka and a packet of Silk Cut Purple. *Hey, Maeve, wanna get locked?*

'Jesus, what's up? It's almost midnight.'

'That money you gave me. For my abortion. Where did you get it?'

'What the hell? It was over thirty years ago. How do you expect me to remember that when I can't even remember why I've entered a room most days?'

Juliet doesn't say anything, just looks at her sceptically.

'God, I don't know. Ehm . . . my credit union account, I suppose. Why are you asking anyway?' Maeve wonders if this is a dream, some strange evocation of her youth where she will be asked to account for her actions.

'Did Rory give it to you? Did he know all along I was pregnant?'

That old look is on Juliet's face now, the one she wore around Rory. Precocious but pleading. Her weakness for him both infuriated Maeve and made her tender. It was the same way she used to feel about the women in the refuge where her mother was a volunteer years ago. Never understanding how they could be so weak. Her mother told her those women weren't weak at all. The men were just expert manipulators but Maeve, young and ignorant and so utterly sure of herself, was unmoved. She sighs. 'Okay, you'd better come in.'

In the kitchen she goes to the kettle and flicks it on. 'Tea? I've a feeling it'll be one of those chats.'

Juliet nods.

'Sit down,' Maeve says, gesturing to a chair.

'Well?' Juliet says impatiently, taking a seat.

'Just let me get this first.' They are silent as Maeve makes a pot. As she does, she thinks of Rory, calling to her door all those years ago, businesslike, the sly humour gone from his mouth. She sets the tea down and pours for them both.

'So?' Juliet's face is tense.

'Yes, he knew. And he knew because I told him. I didn't think it was right that you were facing it alone. I thought that at the very least he'd travel over with you once he was aware. Anyway, within a couple of hours of me telling him he came back with a wad of sterling. Told me I should encourage you to *get the boat over* as he termed it and never let you know where I got the money. God, I hated him in that moment. For the money, for that stupid euphemism. You know, I held a torch for him when we were kids – he was so good-looking it was hard not to. But the coldness of him then. It made him ugly. He didn't want anything ruining what he had with Erica. She was the respectability he craved, I suppose. And I thought, she's welcome to him. I think I even felt a bit sorry for her. I mean, I don't think he was a bad person, Rory. Just consumed with shame. It shrouded everything. Juliet, I think you were lucky to escape him. I think that abortion may have saved your life.'

Juliet is shaking her head. 'But why didn't you tell me? You were my best friend.'

'I knew how much you loved him. And you were so fragile. After your dad and after poor Dan. That summer of death as you called it. I couldn't do it to you. I remember walking with you down to the bus stop the day you were going to the airport. I felt horribly guilty that you were going on your own, I wished I'd tried to get the money to go with you. I watched you climb the steps, being swallowed by the doors, your skinny legs in those ten-hole Doc Marten boots you used to wear, that green duffel bag over your shoulder. And then you sat in the window seat and leaned your head against the glass. Your eyes were closed. You looked exhausted, and I wondered if you'd even wake up in time. I didn't want to cause you any more hurt. I really thought I was doing the right thing.' She takes a sip of her tea. 'How did you find out anyway?'

Juliet waves her hand. 'An email . . . oh, it doesn't matter. Deception, really. I deserved to hear it. As Denise says, eavesdroppers never hear good of themselves.'

Maeve reaches over and touches her arm. 'It was all so long ago, Juliet. We were only kids. Just babies who did things then that we'd do differently now. God knows, I'd do so much differently. And I'm sure Rory would too, you know. I mean, I look at my boys now – around the same age as we were – and think, for all their seeming sophistication, they're still so useless. They wouldn't have any idea how to handle something as big as that. But you! The way you arranged everything, went over to Liverpool by yourself. I was in awe of you.'

'But you see, the thing is. . . I don't think I would have done it differently. It's been the only hopeful part of the whole thing for me.'

'What do you mean, the whole thing?'

'I always thought I could have had him if I wanted. That if he knew I was pregnant, we would be together. That it was my own choice. That deep down he loved me but that I let him stay with Erica. But also, it was a hopeful part of *me*. I thought it was one of the only noble things I'd ever done.'

'Oh, Juliet, I'm so sorry.' Maeve stands up then and puts her arms around her. 'You were still in love with him.' She says it as a statement, doesn't need an answer. Her friend's convulsing sobs are answer enough.

—

The last few days of those summer holidays Maeve saw no-one. They hadn't hung out since Juliet's performance down by the river. Rory was off with Erica all the time, Dan claimed to be busy with rehearsals. Juliet was never home when she rang. Maeve sat, dejected, like those first days when she'd moved to the area, watching out the window of the front room, a book in her hand that may as well have been written in a foreign language for all she was absorbing from it, hoping to catch a glimpse of one of them.

To make matters worse, Lily was driving her crazy. They'd sit at the dinner table in the evening, and she would carry on monologues about some political or social issue while Maeve would sit unresponsive, mechanically shovelling food into her mouth so that she could get away as quickly as possible. As Lily droned on, Maeve became more attached to the idea of being orphaned. She imagined her mother dying of something like consumption, which killed a lot of people in the books she loved, and which seemed a fitting end for a woman who ate up all the air around her. She would tune out from these lectures and fantasise that she was some self-determined *foundling*, the plucky hero of her own life, a kind of David Copperfield/Anne of Green Gables/Jane Eyre hybrid forced to thrive alone. She'd be pitiable, maybe, but ultimately noble.

The Friday before school started back again Lily told her that she was going to spend the night in the women's refuge. She did that occasionally. The refuge had been set up – and was still staffed by – a group of women volunteers from the town. They would take it in turns to provide extra security at night-time for the residents. It wasn't unusual to have irate husbands banging on the doors at all hours of the morning demanding the return of their wives or children, as though they were no more than items of property. Her mother claimed to be unfazed by this. She used to say the most dangerous partners weren't the ones who screamed in public. Those guys were just insecure thugs, so impetuous that it was easy to outwit them. The true devils would appear reasonable and articulate, so tightly controlled on the surface that you knew a manipulative narcissist lurked underneath. They were the ones who always lured the women back in the end. The ones who'd sooner kill them than lose.

Her mother left for the refuge after another dinner of one-sided conversation and as Maeve was washing the dishes the doorbell rang. She opened it to see Juliet standing there. Even though she'd been angry with her friend, now she softened at the sight of her. She looked lovely that night too. It had stopped raining finally and she was leaning against the porch wall, softly backlit from the lowering sun behind her. There was always something so compelling about Juliet; your mind could resist her but not your body. As she stood there, a beguiling smile on her face, Maeve remembered a dream she'd had about her the night before. They were on a train together, interrailing through Europe, a long-held plan of theirs. Juliet's head was resting on Maeve's shoulder and as the train rocked gently she turned her face upwards and Maeve kissed her softly. She felt a hot swell of shame as she remembered it.

'Oh, not today, thanks,' Maeve said, pretending to shut the door. 'We're all Armageddoned out in this house.' They were plagued by groups of doorstep-preaching Jehovah's Witnesses on that stretch of road.

Juliet wedged her foot in the door. 'Hahaha, hilarious.'

'Well, I haven't seen anyone for ages.'

'I've been here.'

'Doing what?'

Juliet shrugged. 'Just hanging around. With Dan mostly. Down at the river.'

'How marvellous for you both.'

She let out a sigh. 'I'm a bit sick of him, to be honest. He gets so stoned he falls asleep most of the time.' She reached her hand out and placed it on Maeve's arm. 'I miss you, but you've been in a kind of shitty mood lately.'

'Maybe that's because I have shitty friends.'

She rolled her eyes. 'Look, are you going to ask me in or what?'

Maeve stood back and Juliet stepped inside. 'Where's Lily?'

'Spending the night in the refuge being all Sarah Connor.'

Her eyes lit up. 'Free gaff? Most outstanding. Time to party on, dudes!' Juliet said doing her best *Bill and Ted* impression. 'I'll gather the troops. One last piss-up before back to prison.'

'Absolutely not, Juliet.'

—

A few hours later the four of them were sprawled around Maeve's front room drinking the Pernod that Juliet had stolen from Denise's drinks cabinet. 'Have some leg opener,' Juliet said, pouring it into their glasses. 'You don't need any help in that regard,' Maeve said sullenly, but Juliet laughed. They were mixing the alcohol with some ancient Ribena Maeve had pulled out from the back of the fridge, making a sort of poor man's Pernod and black. Rory had brought a supply of cigarettes and Dan the hash, Rizla papers and a pouch of tobacco. Maeve normally didn't like to smoke it as it made her paranoid, but she felt like getting messed up that night.

'Sweet Lucifer, I cannot believe we are back in that armpit of an institution on Monday.' Dan inhaled sharply on his joint, held it in and then exhaled slowly. 'Honestly, I want to expire just thinking about it.' His voice was thick and slurred. He'd seemed stoned before he even smoked anything. Maeve held out her hand and he fumbled the joint over to her. She hadn't bothered to open a window. She hoped her mother would smell the weed the next day. ('Maeve, have you been doing drugs in here?' 'Yes, Lily,' she'd say. 'Pray tell what is it to you?') Maeve took a deep toke and held it for as long as she could even though it burned her lungs.

'Go handy on that, Maeve,' said Dan. 'That stuff's not for amateurs. It's end-of-summer-holidays-let's-get-royally-fucked-up chonk.' He was using all these strange new 'townie' terms lately. Maybe it was those musical society kids. Although they all seemed too dorky to get high.

'Our last year, though. How mad is that? Imagine us all out in the world. Going to college, then maybe getting married, having kids,' Maeve said.

'Ugh, that sounds worse than school,' said Juliet. 'No thank you. After college, I'm just going to travel forever. I'll be like your one in the song, you know, the slutty one?' She started to sing the Charlene song 'I've Never Been to Me' and they all joined in to sing their own version, where the poor heroine had tragically never made it to County Meath.

When they stopped laughing, Dan said, 'That is the ultimate nervous-breakdown song. My mother adores it. She sits in the kitchen crying along. I think it's a way of punishing herself even more for marrying Herr Flynn.'

'Denise loves that "Vincent" one by Don McLean. *But no-one appreciated him, so they didn't.* I told her it's a corny crock of shit. That van Gogh's lack of success was overstated and romanticised. He was actually achieving recognition when he died.'

'It's probably just The Change,' said Maeve. 'Women go a bit mental.'

'Luckily all our mothers are that way already,' Juliet said and then glanced sheepishly at Rory, who didn't react. She rolled on her side then, looked at Maeve with lips stained a deep red from the Ribena. 'I can't wait for next year, the two of us interrailing, staying in youth hostels and shifting ridey French and Italian lads.'

Seeing Juliet's mouth and thinking again about her dream, Maeve grew hot. 'I'll probably just work next summer, save up some money for college. That's when my real life begins. You know, with my cool new friends hanging out in cool Dublin bars.'

'Oh, *bars* is it now?' said Rory. 'I can just see you now, Maeve, you and the rest of those pseudo-intellectual Trinners heads, drinking in The Stag's Head and talking shite, thinking you're all that. You'll be right at home.'

'Well, speaking of pretentious people, how's Erica?'

'Miaow,' said Dan.

'And where is she tonight, by the way? You've never introduced her. Is she too good for us plebs?'

'You know, Maeve, she's actually a nice, kind person, if you took the time to get to know her.'

It was so typical of Rory to deflect blame like that, it made Maeve furious. 'How the fuck can I get to know her if you won't let us meet her?'

'That chonk is having the wrong effect and making you sour, Maeve,' said Dan. He held out his hand to get the joint back. She swallowed another deep toke before giving it to him.

'Doesn't worry me what any of you think anyway,' said Rory.

'Have you shagged yet?' said Juliet.

Rory frowned. 'That's none of your business, Jules.'

'Which means you haven't. It's so obvious.'

'We're taking it slowly, if you must know.'

'Bullshit. You just can't get past the chastity belt Daddy's put on her.'

'It's my decision, actually. I want it to be really meaningful when it does happen. She's a classy girl. Worth the wait.'

'Oh whatever, you're so full of it, Rory. And what's going to happen next year? A girl like her is going to go to college and you don't plan to. She won't be happy staying in a shithole like Ballyboyne.'

'Love will find a way,' said Rory, and Juliet snorted derisively.

Rory yawned then to signal he was bored of her, reached over and grabbed the bottle of Pernod and took a swig. Then he rolled on his back, put his hands behind his head and closed his eyes as though he was lying in a meadow sunning himself. Maeve half expected him to start whistling. It was designed to look like a casual gesture, but Maeve felt it to be utterly calculated. He was precisely aware of what he did, of the effect he had on Juliet, and Maeve thought of those dangerous controlled husbands her mother had told her about. She took another drag of the joint and when she drew the smoke down into her chest it seemed to hit her heart directly and caused it to palpitate. Juliet stayed looking at Rory, who remained still, his eyes softly shut, lids fluttering as though he was surreptitiously peeking out. Maeve didn't know who annoyed her more in that moment. She glanced between both and her thoughts started to spiral. They became interchangeable and indistinguishable from each other, two dark shapes, Juliet a bottomless pit of need, Rory a cold, black void. Neither of them capable of accommodating or filling the other.

She squeezed her eyes shut to try to rid herself of the images but behind her eyes was no better. It was like her vision originated in her mind and she could see her own eyeballs, a messy trail of illuminated nerve endings, like radioactive tree roots. It felt painful to even look at them.

She didn't know how long her eyes were shut for. A second,

an hour. But when she opened them, it had started raining. Or maybe it had never stopped. She scanned the room.

'Where's Dan?' she asked, panicked.

'Here, you dope,' said Dan, coming into focus. And it was true, he was sitting right there, where he'd been all night. Everyone laughed and Maeve felt outside of their happy buzz. They were all too cheerful, their faces too bright. Everyone grinning and relaxed as though they were in on a private joke.

She stared out the window. Everything looked thick and sludgy. She turned away. Dan was burning and crumbling hash into another joint. He rolled it deftly and sealed it. Maeve sat hypnotised by his expert movements which seemed to be both lightning quick and painfully laborious. 'Gimme,' she said as he lit it. The burning tip of the spliff grew and seemed to consume his whole face so that when he spoke it was like looking at a giant charcoal ember.

Dan wagged his finger at her. 'No more for you, young lady.'

Maeve wanted to distract herself from the anxiety that was lodged in her chest. She had a crushing sense of aloneness. She looked around at her friends and wondered what it would be like to sit behind their eyes, exist in their bodies. Then she tried to extrapolate it out to all the other people in the world. Instead of feeling this great connection, a union of consciousness, the idea of her own sentience and experience being entirely unique and separate to the other five billion people on the planet felt too difficult and isolating. Other people's humanity felt too enormous. She was overwhelmed.

She was also, she suspected, shitfaced. Why couldn't she even be stoned properly?

'This is so boring,' she said, struggling to her feet. 'Let's do something.'

Dan leaned back against the couch and closed his eyes. 'Settle, Maeve. Just enjoy. In a couple of days, we're going to be tortured with incessant chatter about The Leaving. God, do you know, on my very first day in my very first class last year, the teacher came in, not one word of greeting to us, simply wrote *15,480 hours till D-Day* on the blackboard. Sadist.'

The Leaving Cert! Maeve's feeling of dread doubled. 'No, come on. What about spin the bottle?'

Everyone groaned. 'Cop on, Maeve.'

'Strip poker,' Juliet said.

Maeve was immediately anxious. Had an image flash before her of their bodies being compared side by side. Juliet, the Venus de Milo, beside herself, a garden gnome.

'No,' she said. 'Truth or dare.'

'What are we, twelve?' Rory said.

'You're just afraid of what you'll have to admit, Rory,' Juliet said.

He shrugged. 'Nothing to hide here.'

'Okay.' Maeve plonked herself down and crossed her legs. 'Form a circle.' She picked up the empty Ribena bottle and put it in the middle. 'You can only pick the same thing twice in a row. The person who does the truth or dare gets to spin and ask the next person. No physically hurting yourself or someone else. No law-breaking.'

'Too late for that,' Dan said, holding up his joint as he sat down on the floor.

Rory spun the bottle first, which landed on Juliet.

'Dare,' she said immediately.

'Go out into the front garden and howl at the moon for a full minute.'

Juliet laughed. 'Too easy.' She stood up and, on her way out, turned off the light.

They sat looking at her out the window. She didn't even look slightly mortified, almost as though she was enjoying it, in fact. It should have been comic. That's why Rory had asked her to do it, after all. Yet nobody laughed. Maeve thought there was something serious about the scene, sensual even, her eyes closed, face tilted upwards, ecstatic yelps escaping her and her small breasts outlined distinctly through her now wet, translucent tank top.

'That mad yoke will go all night if we let her,' said Dan. He went over and rapped on the window. Juliet turned and gave a little bow, then came back inside.

It was her turn to spin, and it landed on Rory. 'Truth.'

'If you had to have sex with someone in this room right now, who would it be?'

Rory rolled his eyes. 'Jules, honestly. You're getting so boring.'

'Come on. Answer.' She was smiling at him, still hopeful. It was pathetic.

'Honestly? Dan.' He had a smirk on his face. Maeve knew he was winding Juliet up. Still, would it kill him to say Maeve?

Was she that grotesque that he'd pick a boy over her when he wasn't even gay?

Dan looked startled, confused and then he flushed. 'Wow, I'm flattered.' God, it struck Maeve that everyone in that room fancied Rory. Of course they did. He was a deep dark beautiful sinkhole sucking all the love and light down into him. Even Dan wasn't immune. She'd always imagined him too strong and content in himself to fall for the unattainable boy. They were all such clichés.

The bottle landed on Dan next, who asked for a dare.

'Neck the rest of the Pernod. Straight,' Rory said.

'Too easy.'

'No, don't do it, Dan,' Maeve said. 'You'll be paralytic.'

But Dan was already unscrewing the lid. 'Farewell, it's been a pleasure,' and he raised the bottle to his lips. They all slapped their hands on the ground and chanted 'Chug' as he downed it.

Dan put the empty bottle down and burped loudly. Rory went to high-five him, but Dan's hand missed by several inches. His face was collapsed, like he'd had a stroke. 'My turn,' he slurred.

It landed on Maeve. 'Truth.'

'Hmm,' said Dan. 'Let me see.' He tapped his fingers cartoonishly against his mouth. 'Who do you fancy more, Rory or Juliet?'

Maeve was stunned. Thought again of her erotic dream about Juliet. Did he know? Could he see into her subconscious? She thought of their conversation down at the tennis courts where she hadn't been fully able to voice her feelings, but of course Dan knew what she meant. And was he using it against her now, just for laughs? She felt betrayed.

'That's a stupid question. Neither of them, obviously.'

'Come on, Maeve, you little ambisextrous minx. Don't be a chickenshit. We're all friends here.' His words ran together in a slurred heap.

Maeve felt violated. She hated Dan in that moment for exposing this raw, private part of herself. She held up her hands, said sarcastically, 'Okay. Busted. Juliet.' Hoped no-one would take it seriously.

'Woah, Maeve,' said Juliet, laughing. 'I mean, I love you but *yuck*.'

'Knew it,' said Dan, and winked at her.

Maeve could feel her entire body cringe. She had a sudden urge to make Dan suffer. To make them all suffer.

She picked up the Ribena bottle and nudged it slightly so that it pointed at Dan.

'Hey, that wasn't a proper spin.'

'Shut up, Rory,' Maeve said. 'Truth or dare, Dan?'

'Dare.'

'Kiss Rory.'

'Cop on, Maeve,' Rory said, laughing.

'It's within the rules. It's not dangerous or illegal.'

'Well, technically it is,' Dan said. 'It's Ireland, after all.'

'Now who's the chickenshit, Dan?'

'Alright.' Dan shrugged and staggered to his feet. Rory sat motionless with a smirk on his face as though he was sure Dan would pull out at the last minute. But Dan, serious-looking now, got down on his knees in front of him and put his hands on his shoulders. As Dan's face moved closer to his own, Rory's expression darkened and turned into one of disgust.

'Fuck off, you dirty shirtlifter,' he said, swiping Dan's hands off him, and Maeve's stomach lurched in horror as she remembered Dr Flynn using that same term. Then Rory placed his hand on the top of Dan's head and pushed him away. It wasn't a hard shove, but Dan, limp from booze, toppled easily and collapsed into a heap on the ground.

No-one said anything for what seemed like an age. The room felt charged. Dan lay unmoving for a few moments. Rory stood, stepped over him and went to sit down on the couch. Maeve couldn't even bring herself to look in Dan's direction. She couldn't speak, it was like there was a hand clasped around her throat. What had she done?

'Are you okay, Dan?' Juliet said eventually.

Dan pushed himself up on his arm. He seemed more sober than he'd been a few minutes before. He got to his feet then and made a performance of brushing imaginary fluff off his clothes. It was such a vulnerable gesture that Maeve thought her heart might crack open.

'I think I need to go,' he said.

The three of them sat, unmoving, while he walked out the door, Rory still on the couch with his back to the window. Maeve watched Dan weave down the driveway, pitching from side to side, his shoulders hunched the way they did whenever his father was around.

Juliet turned to Rory then, a furious expression on her face. 'You prick,' she said. 'You fucking worthless piece of shit.' Rory looked down at the floor, put his head in his hands. Juliet stood and ran out the door. Maeve knew she should go too but she felt paralysed by a creeping guilt that had started in her stomach and was now lodged in her chest, making it difficult to breathe. She'd done this. Her own fucking pathetic shame had done this.

Eventually Rory said, 'I think I should leave.' Maeve could only nod.

JULIET

Sometimes she thinks she understood exactly what would happen that night but was too frightened to confront it. Because none of them were certain it was an accident, even if that was the official verdict after the investigation. 'I don't think he slipped,' Maeve would whisper into the dark on sleepovers, to herself it seemed, and Juliet would turn and face the wall, pretend to be asleep. The banks were treacherous, his system overloaded with drugs and drink, he must have toppled, everyone said, heads shaken sorrowfully. What a waste, they said. Forever young. And God only takes the good ones and there but for the grace of God and life is short and tomorrow is guaranteed to no-one . . .

She'd shadowed him silently on the back road down towards the river. He knew she was there, kept yelling back at her to go away, he was fine.

'I vant to be alone,' he said, doing his best Greta Garbo. She told herself he must be okay, he was still making jokes. At

3 a.m. when her eyes fly open after a nightmare, her heart a flapping rag in her chest, she tries to cling to that last line from him as though it was some sort of exoneration. It was raining heavily, drains overflowing and water gushing down the end of the back road where it curved past O'Malley's and joined with the main road. That's where she stopped, taking cover under a tree, watching as he crossed over towards the old bridge and disappeared down the slope of the track that led to the riverbank and the shelter of the arches. The leaves overhead were dropping water on her like tears. She was cold, in nothing but her tank top. She wasn't thinking about her friend at all then but of that old look of shame on Rory's face. That familiar shadow. She'd seen it and recognised it and wanted to go back and comfort him, say she was sorry, he wasn't worthless. As though she was to blame. As though his hateful words to Dan didn't matter. So she turned back. She abandoned Dan, who was in greater peril. Dan, who would never hurt her. That's the truth. She sacrificed him for Rory. Another thing she's sacrificed for Rory.

She went back up the road and saw Rory sitting on the wall outside Maeve's house. She held out her hand and he took it and jumped down and they walked a little way in silence. He stopped suddenly, looked at her. 'I shouldn't have said that to him. I don't even know where it came from. Honestly. I think I just panicked. I didn't mean it. I didn't.'

They were outside the little tumble-down shed on the edge of the field. 'I know. I know you didn't,' she said and hugged him. 'He'll be grand. You can fix it with him tomorrow. You know how easy-going he is.'

He looked at her gratefully.

'You're soaked,' he said then and rubbed his hand gently along her bare arm and she shivered but it wasn't from the cold. And then he looked at her very intently and she knew they would kiss. An involuntary sound like a whimper escaped her. His lips were just as she imagined them to be, soft but also sure of themselves. And it was better than anything she'd ever dreamed of, better than anything that had ever happened to her, in fact, or could ever happen again. She pressed herself into him and felt his erection against her hip and it was the most crushing, gratifying sensation she'd ever felt.

After a time, he drew back, dipped his head and rested his forehead against hers. 'But I'm not a good person,' he said, hoarse, his breathing ragged. That catch of desire in his throat tugged deeply and pleasurably at her.

'You are. I think you're wonderful.'

'You know I love you, Jules. I act like a dick sometimes but I do.'

'I know. And I love you too, Rory.' She smiled at him and then gestured at the shed. 'Come in here with me and I'll show you how much.'

'But, Erica—'

'Shh. Erica doesn't have to know. No-one ever has to know.'

MAEVE

Jamie is raging around the kitchen. 'Oh my God, who unplugged my phone? Now it's only at nine per cent and what am I meant to do all day? I hate this house. Fuck.' He kicks the counter.

'Wow, and there was me a second ago listening to the news and feeling sorry for the Ukrainians,' Cillian says. 'Here's a radical solution. Leave it behind.'

Jamie makes a performance of allowing his jaw to go slack as though Cillian has suggested going to school naked.

'You shouldn't be charging it overnight, Jamie, I've told you. It's a fire hazard,' Maeve shouts over the roar of the Nutribullet. She's glad of the noise, it gives her an excuse to yell. She's trying to make a smoothie that her mother won't find offensive. This basically means frozen banana and milk. If she tries to slip anything else in to boost the nutrition, even a single oat, her mother won't drink it. Like a toddler, she has become the gustatory equivalent of the princess and the pea.

Jamie looks at her accusingly. 'I knew it was you. You ruin everything.' He grabs his phone and stalks out.

'Have a great day, son,' Cillian says light-heartedly to the closed door.

Maeve looks sadly at the pale liquid in the blender and craves again the milky sweetness of the baby years. 'You know when they were small and having a meltdown and some eejit used to say, *Oh this is the easy part, wait till they're teenagers.* And you wanted to stab that person in the eye? Well, I'm that person now. I really feel like it's my duty to warn people. Tell them to cherish their adoring toddlers because one day even the way you breathe will infuriate them.'

'No-one would believe you. You didn't. I'm off to the gym.' He pecks her cheek in a perfunctory way. There's a perfunctory air to everything they do these days.

Maeve looks after him mournfully. She wouldn't have believed it either if she was told walking up the aisle that one day everything her husband did would infuriate her.

She brings the smoothie to her mother's bedroom. Lily is sitting in her armchair, staring into space. Maeve hands her the glass. She takes a sip and shivers.

'Cold,' she says.

'Will I warm it a bit?'

'You're very kind. I know you, don't I?'

'Yes. I'm your daughter.'

'Oh no, I don't have any daughters. Do you?'

'No.'

'It's sad, isn't it?' She says it matter-of-factly, as though it's the least sad thing in the world.

'It is,' Maeve agrees. She'd have loved a daughter, Cillian too, though it seems wrong to admit that with two sons.

They talked about trying for another baby when the boys were in school. But Maeve was forty-one and starting to feel as though her career was really beginning. Her second book was a bestseller, film rights were sold, prizes won, but she sensed she had such a tenuous grip on it all, that if anything were to distract her – and a baby is life's ultimate distraction because you are certain then that nothing else matters – it would all dissolve away into the air like the insubstantial material it was. And having that success made things more stressful in a way, though her unpublished self would never have believed that. The goalposts kept shifting. The only way now was down, unless she worked harder, wrote quicker, wrote better, sold more copies, sold more international rights, won more prizes. 'And you know, Cillian, if we try for a baby with the express purpose of having a girl, we'll probably end up conceiving twin boys,' she said to him, with a mixture of the kind of relief you get from having arrived at a decision and the tinge of unease that you suspect might be a foreshadowing of later regret. Cillian was disappointed but resigned. He said it must be her choice ultimately. Which, as usual, was an oppressively considerate thing for him to do.

Maeve goes back to the kitchen to put the smoothie in the microwave for a few seconds and stares at it as it spins. Next she'll be making Lily bottles and testing the temperature on her wrist. And her life is this inexorable thing turning on itself, the ouroboros eating its own tail. She wants to reach back and hold her babies to her again but, as though the universe is playing a giant practical joke on her, she's been given her own mother to cradle instead.

'Boys break your heart,' Lily says when Maeve goes back into the bedroom, as though picking up a thread of thought midway through. Conversations have become precarious. Maeve is never quite sure how to proceed, although caution is always advised. Like they're playing a game of Jenga.

She sits down. 'They do, Mam, they do.'

'They're more vulnerable, you know. Like that poor lad. That friend of yours who died.'

'Rory O'Sullivan, yes. So sad.'

Her mother squints as though trying to wring her brain out. 'No, that's not it. What's this his name is? Everything feels so peachy.'

Maeve thinks she means fuzzy. 'His name was Rory, Mam.'

'No. Dan. That's it.'

'You remember Dan Flynn?'

Her mother is indignant. 'Of course I remember Dan Flynn. Why wouldn't I remember him? Wasn't he one of my students? In 4A2.'

'Oh, of course, I forgot. Sorry. Was he good at English?'

'Well, I'll be honest, he was the type we call easily distracted.' Her mother taps the side of her nose and chuckles, then looks serious again. 'But I never wrote that on his reports. Because of that awful man, Dr Flynn. You can't give him more ammunition. You have to look out for those boys sometimes. They're vulnerable, you know.'

'Oh, Mam.' Maeve stands and kisses the top of her head with its wispy, defeated hair and wonders what's left for you if your past memories are more real than the present. Maybe that's it, you're done. 'You are a good person.'

'I'm a good girl,' she says.

And Maeve thinks of her moral, vicious family who wouldn't even name her in her own father's death notice.

'You are, Lily. You're such a good girl. Now drink up your smoothie.'

Later, in her snug, she opens her laptop and checks Instagram. She removed the app from her phone so as to limit herself to looking at it sporadically. Not that she finds that difficult. She's conflicted about it generally, the underlying narcissism of it. Even the self-deprecating posts have an air of showing off about them. Too vain to boast. Look at me, they seem to say, my life is so good, I am so loved, that I am secure enough to take the piss out of myself. Promoting herself on it feels uncomfortable, as though she's involved in something dishonest, but it's an expectation now.

She's surprised to see a host of new notifications and messages, as she hasn't posted anything in a few days.

A kind of unease niggles at her then. It's the same way she used to feel after posting an inadvisable drunken tweet, Twitter being like the abusive but seductive ex you text at 2 a.m. She had to close her account a couple of years ago after one such incident involving three glasses of Pinot Grigio, a glowing broadsheet review of a celebrated male author and what she believed to be a throwaway comment on how literary novels written by men about families are called 'state of the nation' whereas a similar book written by a woman is, well, simply a woman writing a nice little book about . . . a family. And probably her own family. Responses ranged from agreement, to accusations of sour grapes ('your jealous coz your nothing but a hack'), to threats of violence ('I no where u live bitch'). In truth she was relieved to leave the platform. Every tweet she ever made sober was accompanied by sweaty armpits and an out-of-control pulse. And was usually deleted moments later anyway.

Instagram is nicer, usually, apart from the odd crank, like the couple of trolls she's had lately. She clicks on the messages through narrowed eyes. It's how she reads reviews too, gets a general impression first, before deciding whether she should let the whole thing in. The messages seem to be from accounts she follows, all writing-related: other authors, Bookstagrammers, bookshops, a literary awards page.

Weird, she thinks. Her stomach feels loose.

She opens the first one, which is a message from another crime fiction author, a woman she likes and respects. Hi Maeve, not sure if your comment was supposed to be funny? I'm giving you the benefit of the doubt, but I found it a bit hurtful, to be honest. I thought we always had each other's backs. It's what makes the crime-writing community so special.

With a racing heart, she goes to the author's page and clicks on her latest post which is a photo of the week's bestsellers where this author has circled her position with the caption 3 weeks in a row in the Top 10! Thanks everyone.

Maeve scans the comments. There it is. Screaming, in black and white @maevegwriter has written: YAWN NO ONE LIKES A SHOWOFF.

Maeve's heart pauses momentarily, before taking off again. It clatters against her then like the slightly malign drumming toy clown Jamie used to own. She opens the next message. It's from a popular Bookstagrammer. I can only assume you're still angry about the review I gave your rather mediocre book. Please go and bully someone else.

She looks up the account. Under the latest post, a review of a newly published debut, @maevegwriter has written: WHO GIVES A FUCK WHAT YOU THINK WHO DO YOU THINK YOU ARE THE BOOK POLICE??

The next is a message from the administrator of a literary awards page: Maeve, this is most unpleasant. Is it because you weren't nominated this year?

He has attached a screenshot of @maevegwriter's comment. Under a post with the list of this year's nominations for best crime fiction she has written: WOULDN'T WIPE MY ARSE WITH THIS SHITE.

She doesn't open any more. Her hands are shaking so much she can't lift the glass of water on her desk to her mouth. She has been forgetful lately, a sort of fog surrounding her. Is she going mad? Does she have dementia too? And has her bitter, ugly subconscious surfaced and made these comments? Because, if she's honest, sometimes these thoughts do cross her mind. Maybe it's that same underlying brutality that her mother has always possessed. And the dementia has made Lily into a sort of distilled version of herself. She has accused them all of heinous acts, trying to poison her, trying to steal her money, abusing her. Sometimes Maeve has wondered if these are things her mother has always believed, delivered now under a subterfuge of insanity.

Maybe Maeve is no different. The real Maeve is the one who hides her resentment underneath a veneer of middle-aged decency and social conformity. She has not evolved from the seventeen-year-old girl who manipulated a game with the purpose of humiliating her friend, simply because she was afraid of her own confused feelings. A game that caused a beautiful boy and incompetent swimmer to enter a swollen river fully clothed. She may as well have put stones in his pockets.

She rings Cillian. He answers straight away, short of breath. She imagines him, sweaty and red, that familiar triangular patch underneath his sternum. She would like to lay her cheek against its vinegary damp.

'Please come home, Cillian. I really need you.'

She notices then that her profile picture has been changed. She moves closer, trying to make sense of it. The black and white professional portrait of her leaning moodily against a brick wall is gone. In its place, a photo of herself grinning inanely and wearing a red MAGA baseball cap.

She feels all strength leach from her bones and lays her head down in despair on the desk.

—

A few hours later she is sitting on the couch beside Cillian, a glass of brandy in her hand. Messages have been sent, amends made, posts uploaded explaining how her account had been hacked.

'You're like the Harvey Keitel character in *Pulp Fiction*. You know, the fixer guy,' Maeve says.

'You mean The Wolf?'

'Yeah, that's it. Like, everything he gets Jules and Vincent to do is totally basic, but they're so flustered they can't think of it themselves.'

It used to be their favourite film. They could quote whole tranches of dialogue to each other. Back when they lived to amuse one another.

Cillian grins. 'Ah yes. I like that analogy. I'm not wearing a tux though,' he says, pulling at his T-shirt, the sweat patches dried now. 'I really need to shower.'

'Thanks, Cillian. I really couldn't think straight. I honestly thought I was going crazy. That I had written all those things. Like it was some perimenopausal episode. Or the onset of dementia.' She squeezes his hand, takes another sip of brandy. 'You said you could get a friend to figure out who's done it?'

'Yes, about that. I was going to wait till tomorrow to broach it. I don't think that will be necessary.'

'What do you mean?'

'The profile photo. Don't you remember it?'

Maeve shakes her head. 'No, I thought it was just a Photoshopped one.'

'Remember when you were in Washington a couple of years ago on a book tour and you sent it as a joke to all of us?'

'Shit. Did I? I can't remember that. So someone has hacked our messages too? Ugh, it's so creepy.'

Cillian shakes his head.

'What? What are you saying?'

'I'm sorry, Maeve, I think it was Jamie. I think Jamie's hacked your account. And probably been the one trolling you lately too.'

'No.' Her hand flies to her chest as though it can protect her heart. 'No,' she says again.

But even as she says it, she knows it's true. And rather than being shocked, she feels a kind of inevitability to it. She's reaping what she sowed.

JULIET

She's sitting at the bar in O'Malley's, listening to Charlie play a Dylan song, 'Simple Twist of Fate'. *That's us*, she wrote to Rory in one of her messages. *The universe always interfering to keep as apart.* Fate, such a pleasingly amorphous concept. You could blame it for everything.

He'd taken his time responding to that too. Sometimes it felt like shouting into a dark cave, or maybe whimpering is a better way to describe it. She'd reread her messages, obsess over them, wish she could edit them, click on the information icon, work out how long after it was delivered that he'd read it, do a little equation whereby the amount he desired her was inversely proportional to the length of time he took to open it. She had no aptitude for maths but even she could figure out the irrefutable answer, the correct solution, which always equalled Not Enough. At times it felt as though nothing was returned except her own pitiful, neurotic echo. *Hello?* she'd type if she saw that tantalising 'online'. *Hello Hello Hello . . .*

Charlie's music, which is Rory's music, in fact, grabs at her. Like his fingers are reaching into that tender spot under her collarbone and plucking her heartstrings. She doesn't turn from the bar, keeps her eyes fixed ahead.

When Charlie stops singing, Liam asks, 'You okay?' His face is concerned and his kindness towards her is hard to bear.

'I think so.'

'Good, isn't he?'

Juliet nods.

'They used to play together the odd time.'

'Himself and Rory?'

'Yeah.'

'Did they go all Cat Stevens?'

Liam grins. 'Yeah, all the angsty father and son stuff. "Cat's in the Cradle", you know yourself.' He looks serious then. 'Poor kid, though, he worshipped him. He's been through a lot. It's tough losing your father at that age. As you well know.'

'You weren't much older yourself.'

'True.' He leans down on the bar. 'It's strange. Since last year, once I passed the age the old man was when he died, I've been dwelling on it so much more. Like this feeling of wrongness. I'm now older than my own father. I can't get my head around it.' He sighs, straightens.

She can't fathom it either, the age she is, the age they are.

A group approaches the other side of the bar and Liam goes over to serve them. She turns around to see Charlie packing up. She beckons to him and he comes over and sits up beside her. Liam sets another glass of wine and a Coke down in front of them. 'On the house,' he says.

'Thanks, Liam,' Juliet says.

'No bother. Got to look after the talent.' He winks at her and goes out the back.

'That was really great,' Juliet says to Charlie.

'Thanks. Some of Dad's favourites.'

'I remember.'

He takes a drink. 'So, I've been thinking about a trip next year, making plans.'

'Oh yeah?'

'Thought I'd stop in the States for a while, probably San Francisco, then Sydney, then on to you in Auckland. If that's still okay?'

As he says this, she feels uneasy, looks away from him towards the optics and catches sight of their reflections in the mirror behind, and she is struck by the image. She thinks of Giorgione's painting of the old woman, degraded by time, 'col tempo', that seems to make a mockery of all vanity. She thinks of the faded and spotted photo stuffed into the hawthorn hedge. She looks to him again.

'Charlie, I might have to rescind that invite. I'm so sorry. It's just that it's a small apartment and I'm not entirely sure what Ruby will be doing. Whether she'll live at home when she's studying. So it might be best not to rely on me.'

'Oh, okay.' He looks down at his hands.

She reaches out and squeezes his arm. 'But look. I have friends who could put you up if you need it. Would that work?'

'Sure.' He looks up and smiles at her and a feeling of relief washes over her. 'Thanks.'

'And it's a good itinerary. I was in San Francisco a couple of months ago. It's so cool. Have you been before?'

'Nah. Dad's been there a bit though for work. He was there earlier this year too.'

She can't help herself. 'Did he have a good time?'

'Probably had a great old time.' His tone is sarcastic. She's never heard him speak like that before. She looks at him in surprise. There's a pall over his features.

'What's wrong?'

'Mum was struggling a bit with him gone.' He's looking down again, playing with a beer mat. 'What were your parents like together?'

'Wow. That's a question and a half. Opposites attract, maybe? Although that's too neat. I don't know, they never made sense to me.'

He nods. 'Mine either. Marry someone. Be faithful. Seems straightforward to me.'

She feels uneasy again. His face looks hard. He would hate her if he knew, and she couldn't bear that. She asks almost reluctantly, 'Was someone not faithful?'

He puffs out his cheeks. 'Huh. You could put it like that. I found out when Dad was in San Fran that they had an open marriage. Well, for him it was anyway. Mum sanctioned his having sex with other people. Encouraged it, actually. Can you believe that? She called it *outsourcing*. How twisted is that? It disgusted me.'

'Outsourcing?' Her voice sounds strange to herself, like she's suddenly underwater.

'Yeah. They didn't have sex anymore. Not for years. So they had this agreement. It was Mum's idea, apparently.'

'How did you . . . find out?'

'She told me. She was drunk one night while he was away. She started telling me all this shit I didn't want to hear. I said I was going to ring Dad and she said not to disturb him, he was probably mid-fuck over there with an escort or whatever. And she never swears. I thought it was just drunken raving. Anyway, I rang Dad to see if it was true. I couldn't believe it. I hated them both for it. So ugly.'

'But he came home? After you rang him?'

'Yup. He came home. Had the big sit-down serious chat with me. "Son, you're almost a man now, you're old enough to hear this stuff." How I'd understand when I was married. How long marriages are difficult and they were just doing whatever they could to make it work. Blah, blah. Bullshit.'

'And did he promise you then that he'd stop doing it?' See, that's why he'd been distant. Fate again. Being faithful for his son's sake.

Charlie smirks. It looks wrong on him. 'Of course. But it was another lie.'

'How do you know? Maybe he was really trying.'

'He was still at it. I looked through his texts. Found hundreds of messages between him and some woman in Dublin. Sick shit too. You wouldn't believe the stuff they said to each other. Like, seriously pornographic. You'd think old people would be past all that. And the hypocrite had put all sorts of parental controls on my computer and phone too. He was going up there a couple of times a week to see her as well.'

She can't speak, a strangled sound comes out. He looks at her, concerned.

'Sorry. I'm sure it's awkward to hear all this. I mean, he was your friend too. I haven't told any of my own friends. I was too embarrassed by it.' He takes a drink. Then in a fake bright voice says, 'And that's the deal with San Francisco!'

'What's the deal with San Francisco?'

They turn. Erica is standing behind them, car keys looped around her fingers. She looks exhausted, hollows like dug graves under her eyes.

'Oh, hi, Mum. Just telling Juliet my travel plans. How I plan to stop in San Fran. Juliet was there on holiday earlier this year.'

'Oh. When?'

'March,' Juliet says. Even as she says it, she's regretting it. It's like she's outside herself, looking down, watching as she fucks up, yet again.

'March?' And something in Erica's expression changes, something so subtle you might miss it. But it's enough to make Juliet want to drop to her knees suddenly with the weight of it.

'Yes, the travel restrictions just—'

But Erica cuts her off. 'Charlie, grab your gear, will you, and bring it to the car.'

'I've only just got this drink.'

'Now, Charlie.' Her tone is severe.

'Wow, okay. Chill. Thanks, Juliet. I'll see you later.'

After he's gone, Erica checks over her shoulder to make sure he's out of earshot, then says quietly, 'I want you to stay away from my son. Tell him he can't come to you in New Zealand. Let him down gently.'

'I've done that already.'

'Good.' Erica turns to go, then, as though something occurs to her, turns back again.

'We renewed our vows, you know. After he came back from San Francisco. He'd lost his wedding ring over there so we thought buying another one might be the perfect excuse to have a little ceremony.'

'Did he . . . tell you how he lost it?'

'Yes, he took it off and left it on the bathroom sink in the hotel. He thinks the maid might have stolen it. He said she had a desperate, shifty look about her. You know the type. Though, actually, he said maid but probably he meant one of the little fucking whores he had over there.'

Erica's voice is shaking, and as Juliet looks at her she sees through the obscenity that sounds wrong in her mouth and directly into the grief and the fear and the loneliness pouring out of her.

She thinks of Marco's, a cute Italian restaurant on Union Square. They sat opposite each other, their thighs touching under the small table with its checked cloth and the candle necked in a bottle decorated with rivulets of wax. They ordered a carafe of wine that Juliet drank most of. There was a couple next to them who didn't exchange a single word. 'Why would you bother?' Juliet whispered, nodding at them. Rory shrugged and she said, 'Do you still love her, Rory?' She was drunk and reckless. He didn't answer. 'Leave her.' It was the first time she uttered it aloud. 'Leave her and we can have this all the time. It's this or . . .' she nodded in the direction of the mute couple '. . . that. You have to choose. It's time to choose now.' She didn't think she really meant it. It was that old urge to push and push. But he ran his fingers through his hair. 'No, I won't do that.' Of course he wouldn't do that, wouldn't choose. Why would he when they let him have it all?

'If you don't tell Erica, Rory, I will.' Provocative then, testing the boundaries. Seeing what she could get away with.

And he had a look on his face, that small smile playing at the corner of his mouth, that at the time she mistook for amusement, or incredulity. But that's not what it was at all. It was just that it didn't matter if she told Erica, who already knew. And it didn't matter because there were others anyway.

She didn't matter now, just as she didn't matter over thirty years ago.

Erica is talking again. 'It's funny how things work out, though. Rory got a new tattoo for me while he was over there. A Dylan quote. About believing the woman he loves is his twin. Do you know it? Anyway, the next line is about him losing the ring. So afterwards he went and got that line tattooed as well. It was a little joke between us.'

And with that she turns and leaves.

Juliet hears the swing of the door behind her. She puts her head in her hands and then feels a firm touch on her arm. A familiar male voice says, 'Christ, Juliet, what's the matter? What happened? Juliet?'

MAEVE

It's late. She and Cillian are sitting in the kitchen, talking and drinking tea and trying to digest it all, after Jamie's gone upstairs, minus his phone and laptop.

He denied it at first, when they confronted him. Cillian took the lead because Maeve felt so betrayed she couldn't speak. And Cillian was rational and gentle as is his way and Maeve was grateful for that, but when Jamie broke down it was Maeve who held him because it's impossible to watch your child sob and not. Even as she had him in her arms, she could sense him stiff and unyielding against her, like she was some foreign object his body was rejecting. And she squeezed her eyes shut and thought back to when she was first pregnant and how sick she'd been and how sometimes she felt as though her body was trying to expel the foetus growing inside her, and she felt guilty then for all the negative thoughts she ever had about motherhood, which was a lot. More than she thinks a good mother should have.

His words came out in an angry, anguished torrent. He said he'd read the emails between her and some Nisha person, said he felt sick because they were full of references to sex and porn and some night when they'd hooked up in an airport hotel. She never tried to hide those emails either, left the app open on her laptop, never deleted them so it's as though she was proud of it. She and Cillian were fighting all the time and suddenly it made sense to him. She was a lesbian and having an affair. As he was saying all this, Maeve stole fearful glances at Cillian and tried to discern his reaction, but her husband kept his eyes fixed calmly on his son, gave no hint of what he was thinking. And she was so grateful for his composure. His ability to be curious without judgement or emotion.

And Jamie went on to say how he checked her search history and found she visited all these lesbian porn sites. And the way she referenced her pronouns on her social media accounts and superimposed rainbows on her profile pictures was weird and embarrassing. And she was pushing him to admit he was gay because she probably would prefer it if he was. That she'd love him more if he was gay or trans and would show off then online about what a great parent she was. He'd heard about same-sex couples wanting their own kids to be gay too so they try to persuade them that way. And how he felt so attracted to these online forums he joined, the chatrooms, the podcasts. It was like a community. These other young men he interacted with or the guys he listened to who all just *got* his life. He felt like he belonged.

'You know, I used to go through all these scenarios in my head,' Maeve says now to Cillian. 'When he'd say things about refugees or whatever. Like, things I would rather him be than some kind of right-wing bigot. I actually thought I would rather he was a criminal or even hurt in an accident. Have you ever heard anything so deranged? And now to realise it's me, it's my fault. I've pushed him even further this way.'

'Don't be so hard on yourself, Maeve. These anti-progressive websites he's been looking at are particularly pernicious. Those knowing, confident groomers bombard teenage boys with their misogyny. They prey on them and their insecurities. It's hideous.'

'Yes, but we've let it happen, haven't we? We're the ones who invented this world for them. We've let them grow up online. You know, I see all these videos. Our generation, bragging about our idyllic pre-internet childhoods. Like, how fucked-up is that? Making videos to post online about how brilliant our lives were before we were all online.'

'I think we're good parents, Maeve. Not perfect, but we do our best.'

'I'm not so sure about myself. I'm a terrible mother.'

'You're not.' He reaches out and squeezes her hand. 'And you were more in tune to him than I was. I think I was in denial about it. You know that old saying about psychiatrists' kids being the most messed up? But Maeve, I'll tell you something else: if someone came to me and said they had no regrets or second thoughts about the way they parent, massive alarm bells would go off.'

She puts her head in her hands.

'Look, it's far from hopeless. There are things we can do. I know a therapist who could help him. She has lots of experience with social media and all those influences. I'll ring her first thing tomorrow and see if she can fit him in. He's just a confused little kid at heart. I know that his core self is good. You know that too, Maeve.'

She looks up at him now, her flesh-and-blood husband, standing in front of her, the realness of him, of them, of this situation. Her life. With Nisha it felt almost surreal, just words on a screen. Like the stupid stories she makes up.

'Do you think we might need to see someone too?' Her tone is light, but she can barely breathe saying it.

'Some talk therapy mightn't be the worst idea in the world, Maeve. There's so much resentment simmering away in this house. And resentment is allergic to open communication.' He looks sheepish. 'Sorry, I sounded like a therapist there.'

He looks serious again then, takes a sharp inhale, and she knows what he is going to ask and she is suddenly terrified. And just as she is aware of the realness of him, she is acutely aware of her own corporeality now, the tightness in her chest, the tense muscles.

'Do you want to tell me what's going on with Nisha?'

'I'm not having an affair. I mean, nothing physical has happened between us. It's true I met her at the airport hotel. I checked myself in there because I was so exhausted with everything. I just wanted to sleep. We got talking in the bar and got drunk, but that's as far as it went. We've been communicating since then by email. The lesbian porn Jamie was talking about was book research.'

He looks at her over the top of his glasses and raises his eyebrows. 'I see. As I recall, that's what you said too about those websites that give advice on accelerating the decomposition of your spouse's body.'

She gives him a grim smile.

'But . . . did you . . . do you . . . want something to happen?' He rubs at the tabletop as he speaks. It seems to her such a vulnerable gesture.

Maeve stands and walks over to the sink, refills her water glass. Her mouth is so dry and her head throbs as though she's been the one sobbing and not Jamie. She thinks about beautiful, seductive Juliet and Nisha's red mouth and her emails that made her feel alive again. She thinks about her dreams and the kiss at the hotel door which might have been a dream too. She thinks about Dan and how frightened she was at being exposed. And she wants to be truthful now, finally, for her old friend. She takes a long drink, then turns to face him.

'I don't think I'd ever have acted on it. But . . . God . . . she did make me feel admired and needed again. Like she cared about what I thought. And yes, I flirted with her. I think I was grasping for one last bit of sexual excitement. Like, even the possibility of being desired again. I feel so old, Cillian, past my sell-by date. Like I don't even belong in this body. I suppose I was just being a sad middle-aged cliché.'

'Maeve, I still desire you.'

'Really?'

'Of course. But you haven't let me near you in months. God, why do you think I was suggesting role-play and all that?' He takes off his glasses then, folds them and places them carefully on the table. 'Is it that you think you prefer women?' He says this looking down.

Her heart beats wildly now. She takes a breath. 'No . . . not *prefer* I don't think. But I did find her attractive. I think it's a part of me I've always been afraid of.'

He nods, like it's no big deal, and there's something so reassuring in this small gesture, in him. 'Well, these things aren't so binary. And it's normal to find other people sexually attractive. I mean, it'd be unnatural if we didn't.'

'Oh, right. So, who do you find attractive, then?'

'Oh boy. Is this a trap?'

'Absolutely.'

He smiles. 'Okay, the woman who does the weather, with the cute gap in her teeth.'

'I mean, like, a real person.'

'She's very real.'

'You know what I mean. Someone we know. You probably fancy Juliet. Like every other human.'

'What? No way, she's not my type. Too . . . *overt*.'

'So, someone more reserved, like Erica, then?'

'Worse! She's like a Stepford wife.'

'Who, then?'

He runs his hand through his hair. 'Eh, okay, the woman who works in the coffee shop with the sleeve tattoo.'

'Seriously? With the wonky nose?'

'Does she? I never noticed. But full disclosure, it wasn't her nose I was thinking about.'

Maeve gives a laugh then that somehow turns into a kind of hiccoughing sob. He stands up and wraps his arms around her and at first she resists and then she allows herself to meld into him. And it is at once familiar and strange, and it occurs to her that they haven't held each other like this in forever. She has never been one for hugging and now she wonders why. It feels so truthful and kind. She lays her head against his chest; he's always been the exact right height. He doesn't say anything while she cries, just combs his fingers gently through her hair.

When she eventually stops, he kisses her on the mouth and says, 'Is it inappropriate that I'd like to take you upstairs?'

She is aware of him then, hard against her, and she pulls back in mock disbelief. 'Jesus, *God*, Cillian. Do you have an actual erection right now?'

He shrugs. 'What can I say? At the end of the day, I'm a lowly unevolved man driven by base primal urges. In essence, a brainstem attached to a penis.'

She smiles. 'You know, you're the opposite, Cillian. And I'm so glad of it.' She puts her hand in his. 'Well, okay, sure. I'll go upstairs with you. On one condition.'

'Anything, my love.'

'You're not thinking about your one with the nose.'

—

Maybe the problem with actual real-life sex for Maeve is that it is much messier, wobblier, clumsier than she'd expected from all the books she read or the films she saw. That type always appears so ecstatic and smooth. But there's great consolation in it now. Here they are as one, Jamie's parents. And the sex surprises her too, with its purposeful vigour, or maybe it's Cillian's purposeful vigour that surprises her. She wonders if abstinence is the key, their hunger feeding off each other. Or maybe it's just all those burpees. When he's above her, his arms taut on either side of her head, she runs her hands appreciatively along the new bulge of his triceps and senses his gratitude for this small gesture. Maybe she's always complicated things, maybe it's not so hard to be married.

Afterwards, she's on her side, while he spoons her, gently snoring. It's the first time in a long time they've done this. They used to lie naked and entwined every night. Then the babies came. Jamie was a regular in their bed for the first two years so she's still unsure how they even managed to conceive Luke. Jamie was such a hungry baby. At times she thought he might eat her to death. They'd find her dry, brittle skeleton, sitting up in the bed, like that poor man in the news a few weeks ago. Sometimes she would fall asleep breastfeeding him and then wake up in a sweaty dread to find him gone from her chest. She'd search under the duvet, panicking, sure she'd smothered him somehow, and then look over to see that Cillian had lifted him, or perhaps she'd done it herself, and put him to sleep in the crib beside their bed. She would peer, fearful, over the edge of the basket and he would just be lying there, staring up at the lace frill on the edge of the hood, perfectly content. 'Hi,' she'd whisper, and his big eyes would find hers, and then as though a spell had been broken his expression would invert and he would start to screech. 'Why does he hate me, Cillian?' she'd ask and Cillian would laugh and say, 'No. It's the opposite, he's crying because he wants you to hold him.'

The thing is, her memories of Jamie's babyhood are so sharp she worries sometimes that the consequence is an edge has insinuated itself into their interactions. With Luke the memories are more mellow, or maybe dulled is a better word, because by that stage she was exhausted and bewildered, inured a little to the shock of it. She can't remember the pain of his birth, the torture of the sleeplessness, the anxiety of the seemingly endless winter viruses. But with Jamie, everything was raw, strange, acute. He transformed her into a parent. First stretching her, hollowing her out, then carving her up and chipping away at her till she resembled something like a mother. They talk about mothers shaping their children but it's only half the story. The reverse is also true.

She hears a bang from down the hall, extricates herself from Cillian's arms – who turns on his other side and continues to snore – and races into her mother's bedroom to find her standing by the bed, agitated, staring down at the lamp that is now on the floor.

'Mam, are you okay? What happened?'

Her mother places her hands over her eyes. 'You've no clothes on.'

Maybe this is also why she doesn't sleep naked anymore. She grabs a blanket off the chair and wraps it around herself like a bath towel.

'You can look now.'

Her mother takes her hands down. 'It's too dark. There's someone under the bed.'

'No-one's under the bed, Mam. I promise.'

Maeve picks up the lamp, winds the lead around the base and leaves it by the door, to be put away later with the hazardous rug and the traumatising mirror and the gouging picture frames and the fragile bottles of perfume. Like her mother's memory, this room is being stripped bare. What remains has been modified: a plastic jug and cup beside the bed, special slippers with grip soles underneath, chest of drawers fastened to the wall. Even the cord for the blind is coiled tightly around a cleat to stop her from accidentally hanging herself. (Or not so accidentally maybe.) Her mother, once so intelligent and ferocious, is now confounded by the figure-eight pattern of it.

Maeve shows her mother the empty space under the bed, then helps her up into it. She goes to her own bedroom, takes a key from the drawer there, then into the bathroom where she opens the cabinet (*Locked! Maeve has key!*) and comes back with half a lorazepam that she places on her mother's tongue. She holds the cup to her mouth and her mother swallows dutifully. She tucks the bed sheet in around her and sits down to wait for the drug to work its magic.

'Thank you, Mammy,' her mother says as Maeve strokes her hand. 'Sorry for being such a nuisance.'

A stinging starts behind her nose and down her throat and she can't speak, so instead pats her mother's hand and lifts her eyes to the window. A sliver of streetlight is visible through the gap in the curtain. The night after Dan's body was found, Maeve, tormented by harrowing images, got out of her bed and turned the light in their hallway on. There was a small bit of reassurance in that scrap wedged under her bedroom door. She was afraid her mother, normally so militant about *not wasting electricity!*, would turn it off. But she never did. Not once. That hall light stayed on every single night until Maeve left home.

JULIET

She disengages from him, swings her leg around and manoeuvres over to the passenger seat, banging her head off the rear-view mirror as she does. She wonders if he was looking at his reflection while they fucked. Most men like to do that, watch themselves; she read somewhere that it's because they're visual creatures, but Juliet thinks it's plain old narcissism. She likes to watch herself too but it's only so she can pretend to be someone else.

She pulls her underwear – currently lassoed around one ankle – back up, smearing the semen that is already coagulating on the inside of her thigh, as though her body wants to expel him as quickly as possible. If the act has been some sort of exorcism to finally rid herself of Rory, then this viscous blob is like some leftover ectoplasm.

'You're full of surprises, do you know that, Juliet?'

'Why's that?' She says it in a bored way. Her own behaviour is depressingly predictable to herself. There's a box of tissues in the centre console, probably kept there for such situations as these. She takes one out, wipes it across her leg, pulls her knickers to the side and swipes her pubic hair and is about to stuff it in the door pocket when she thinks of his children so throws it out the window instead. She's glad Ruby can't see her and not just because of the sex. Once when Ruby was twelve and they were driving on a winding coast road on the Coromandel peninsula, Juliet lobbed a banana peel out the window and Ruby became hysterical. 'It will biodegrade!' Juliet shouted over the screaming. 'Not for two years and it might lure an animal onto the road!' Ruby wailed. Juliet ended up turning her car around and trying to find the skin in the roadside gravel, almost getting killed by passing cars in the process. But by then she welcomed death, which seemed preferable to her daughter's tantrum.

He stuffs himself back in and zips up his fly and she thinks it's maybe the least sensual gesture in the world. Probably on a par with her wiping his spunk off her leg, so, you know, they're even.

'I thought you'd be the type of lady to go full Brazilian. Don't get me wrong. I'm not complaining or anything. Just saying, I was surprised, that's all.'

'And funnily enough it doesn't surprise me that you'd prefer the prepubescent girl look. Anyway, I like a full bush. It gives the artists a bit of texture to work with. Oh, and a word of advice. Don't use the word *lady*. If you ever want to have sex with a *woman* again, that is.'

'Right, so I shouldn't say lady if I want to get laid-y.'

'Somebody fucking shoot me,' she mutters.

'Did you come, anyway?'

She pats his leg. 'Have you any understanding of a woman's anatomy? God, you men just love to thrust. Our clits aren't fastened on the end of our cervix, you know. It requires more than a couple of frantic lunges for a woman to orgasm.'

'My wife used to.'

'The wife that left you for another woman? Trust me, she didn't. She just wanted the whole ordeal over and done with.'

'Christ, you can be an awful bitch sometimes, Juliet.'

She laughs then. 'I do love this tender pillow talk, Colum, don't you?'

He sighs and shakes his head, reaches over, opens the glove box and takes out a packet of cigarettes and a lighter. 'Smoke?'

'Tissues, cigarettes. Quite the little love nest you've got going on. I'm surprised there's no candles or massage oil.' She takes the cigarette and bends towards him so that he can light it.

'While you're down there, love,' he says.

'Oh my God, Colum. Are you twelve?'

He clears his throat. 'So . . . as we're discussing blow jobs—'

'We were not discussing blow jobs. You, me, blow jobs. Those three things don't belong in a sentence together. Never going to happen. So get it out of your head.'

'No! I was just going to say sorry about the wedding and all that. The whole thing with you and Maeve.'

'Forget it. I'd have found some other way to fuck things up, don't worry.'

She takes a drag of the cigarette and swallows it deep. It's been a long time, and the sensation is heightened. It's almost as though she can feel the smoke molecules moving down her throat, along her windpipe and her bronchial tubes and then into her lungs and out through the alveoli to her bloodstream. She wonders if this is how it feels to drown.

They are tucked in beside a gate up a lane on the far side of the old bridge. Juliet could see their childhood swimming spot over the top of Colum's thinning grey hair as she straddled him. It felt odd, a sensation of being very young and very old at the same time.

A man with a dog rounds the bend and is walking towards them. It's dark now but the shape of him looks familiar. As he gets nearer, Juliet realises with horror that it's Liam. 'Oh no, don't let—'

But it's too late. Colum is doing a big gormless wave out the window. Liam slows and stops and, leaning down, looks first at Colum, then past him. He looks very squarely into Juliet's eyes. Something in his expression makes her feel exposed. She looks down to check she has covered herself with her skirt.

'Liamo!' Colum honks.

'Colum.' His voice is flat. 'Everything okay, Juliet? You left the pub in an awful hurry.'

'Yeah, grand. Colum's just dropping me home.'

'Right.' Their eyes meet again, and Juliet feels herself redden. 'Does he realise he's going the wrong direction?'

Colum makes a braying sound and Juliet sighs. She has to look away.

'Well, I'll be seeing you, I suppose.' Liam straightens, raps briskly on the roof, in that secret language of men, and carries on. Juliet watches him in the wing mirror, his reflection getting smaller and smaller, till he disappears again.

'What's eating him, I wonder?' Colum says.

'Just drop me home, please.'

As they drive back, Juliet turns the radio on to discourage conversation. In the news bulletin there's a report about a missing child. Juliet thinks of that boy, she thinks of him often, who went missing in Dublin years ago on his way back to school after lunch. It's always affected her, maybe because he was the same age as her. Nothing was ever found apart from his school bag, one of those canvas satchels that looked like her own. They all had them. The guards listed the contents of it, the pencil case, the textbooks, and every student recognised them, every parent too. It was the ordinariness that got you. His poor mother, leaving the hall light on, night after night, just in case he arrived home. The hope of it. The desperate, unrelenting hope you'd have to cling to. It would be exhausting to carry it all this time. They turn at O'Malley's and drive up the back road and she is haunted by all the missing boys, the dead boys, the same sad stories. This old place that changes but doesn't really.

Colum pulls up into her driveway. 'I meant to say, you smell good. What's that perfume you're wearing?'

'It's aftershave,' she says. 'Armani. Discontinued, though, in case you were going to douse yourself in it when you masturbate as a reminder.'

He rolls his eyes. 'Whatever.'

'Don't whatever me, Colum. I know all of this is being added to that depraved wank bank of yours.' She taps the side of his head as she says this and then undoes her seatbelt.

'When is it you go back?'

'Couple of days.'

'Right, well, if you felt like doing this again, I could make the time, I suppose.' He says it in a wry way and she thinks he has some self-awareness at least. It makes her laugh.

'Thanks, Colum, I'll bear that in mind.'

He surprises her then by reaching over and taking her hand. 'Look, Juliet. I bet you haven't eaten tonight. You could come back to mine. I could whip up a decent carbonara in a few minutes. And I've a big comfy bed. Clean sheets even.' His eyebrows are raised hopefully.

He has nice navy-blue eyes – she's never noticed before. And there's a sadness in them she's never noticed before either. They're all just doing their best, aren't they? Trying to stay afloat. She squeezes his hand. 'Thanks, Colum, but I really can't.'

He winks at her. 'Yeah, no problem. I thought as much.'

―

Ruby is sitting curled in an armchair reading a book and looks up when Juliet walks in. Her long dark hair is hanging damp around her face. She's caught some sun today. Literally, Juliet thinks, captured it so that it has soaked into her skin and is refracted out, illuminating the air around her. There are a few new freckles across her nose. Juliet wonders is there anything as hopeful as a seventeen-year-old girl. The sight of her makes Juliet feel spent and tawdry. She hopes she knows her own beauty. That she never needs to bang men in cars to feel it or look in mirrors while she does to recognise it. That she never defines how worthy she is by how wanted she is. That her desire is its own authentic thing, not borne from some craving to *be* desired. There's so much she needs to warn her about but she may as well try to reach back through time and explain it to her own seventeen-year-old self. Neither would listen. So instead, she touches her daughter's hair, coils a thick strand around her finger.

'My little Bee,' she says.

'Why are you looking at me like that?'

'Like what?'

'All sloppy.'

'No reason.'

'Are you drunk?'

Juliet sighs. 'You're a tough audience sometimes, Ruby.' She lets the strand of hair fall. 'Our flights are booked for the day after tomorrow.'

'I really want to stay. Just till Christmas.'

She looks at her. She's been so afraid of being alone over there. That old predictable selfishness. She is so tired of herself. 'I know. I think it's a great idea. It'll be lovely for Nana.'

'Thanks, Mumma.'

Juliet kisses the top of her head.

'You'll remember to water the plants, though?'

Juliet smiles. 'Maybe just send me a reminder every few days.'

She leaves the sitting room and climbs the stairs, stopping at the window on the landing that looks out over her mother's garden. The low yellow moon is casting a strange glow that gives everything an abstract texture, like some kind of art installation, so that she feels oddly detached from it. The single hawthorn, or May bush as Johnny calls it, is in full white-flowered bloom. Summer's almost here. When she was young, May felt like a month when anything was possible. Now, it means it's time to go, migrate south to winter against the natural order, like some kind of damaged bird.

> Erica,
>
> You asked for my name but you know, it doesn't really matter what my name is. Because I was meaningless to him, as it turns out. I told myself he loved me. I justified everything he did, interpreted everything he did, so that it would fit this false narrative. And even though on some level I was aware that I was doing this, still I carried on. Because, I have to admit, this obsession has sustained me. For years, I've defined myself by him. His presence, his absence. Because who am I without him? I told you in my last email about feeling grateful as a woman. Well, he made me feel so grateful for any crumb he threw me. And those crumbs were so unpredictable that I've been in this constant state of vigilance and insecurity. Turns out I've been involved in a game where I didn't know the rules.

Anyway, I'm exhausted from it now. Defeated.

But he did love you, Erica. I asked him once. He refused to answer, which of course told me everything. And I'm sorry but I also asked him to leave you. Asked him to choose. And you were the answer. He chose you. He always chose you. That's the simple truth of it.

ERICA

She's in the shower and her head and chest are throbbing. She will wash the previous night off, start fresh. She looks down, watches the cloudy liquid pooling around her feet, imagines the water, which she has made almost unbearably hot, dissolving her, the debris leaching away down the drain.

She set an early alarm to spend time with him before school. She resolves to do this from now on. Make him pancakes, which are his favourite. Make him sandwiches for lunch, drive him in. It's time to step up. Take over where Rory left off.

She dresses in a clean white shirt and jeans, puts on subtle make-up, then heads downstairs, passing his bedroom as she does. The door is open, bed made, curtains pulled. There's so much of Rory in him and this thought makes her tender towards them both. She worries then he's left early for some before-school commitment she's forgotten about. She sifts through her dusty brain but finds nothing.

It's a bright morning, the sun tearing optimistically through the circular skylight above the island, creating a halo on the marble. The kitchen is tidy. No sign of dinner. She must have cleaned up last night. She congratulates herself. No breakfast remnants on the counter, he mustn't have eaten yet. She feels pleased about this too. His phone is being charged on the island so he's still here. She hasn't yet fucked up this day.

There's a cool, pleasant breeze and she notices then that the bifolds are pushed back slightly. She thinks of that morning, finding Rory, but slams the image shut. She goes to the door, looks out; he's not in the garden. She's about to go and check the downstairs bathroom when she hears the clink of glass coming from outside. The sound makes her stomach contract, but she forces herself to walk around to the side of the house and he's there, at the bins, his back to her.

'Oh hey, what are you doing?'

He turns and she sees then that he's holding an empty wine bottle. 'I was cleaning up. From last night.'

His voice is flat. And her heart collapses because, yes, there's so much of Rory in him. And he's the one taking over where Rory left off.

'There's no need, I—'

He interrupts her. 'When I was coming out I spotted this too. Stuck in the hedge.' He reaches into the glass bin, pulls out the empty bottle of whiskey from Rory's study.

'Charlie—'

'Did you know he was saving this for my twenty-first? He said it was very special, needed a special occasion to be opened.'

She can't speak. Or move. An airless feeling that is both heavy and empty at the same time settles inside her and above her. His expression is so cold and impassive, she's crushed by it, imagines the relief of crawling into the rubbish.

He averts his eyes from hers, then lets the bin lid drop. 'I'm going to school.'

'But what about breakfast? I can drive you in.' Her voice comes out very small.

He doesn't answer, just brushes past her and goes back inside.

She remains there, unmoving. After a few moments, she hears the sound of the front door and her legs give way and she folds herself into the gap between the bins.

Later, she goes upstairs, takes the box from under her bed and lifts out the yellowing pages. She needs to destroy it in case Charlie was ever to come across it. He knows too much already, he doesn't need to know about that. She may have detached herself, but there's no benefit for Charlie in doing the same. She decides to read it in full now before she destroys it, because there's nothing to fear anymore. The worst has already happened. It's freeing. A feeling like relief washes over her and she doesn't feel scared.

Sweetheart,
I'm so sorry but I just can't do it anymore. I need to go now before I make a mess of another life. I know you'll be

sad at first but honestly, Erica, in the long run you and our son will be better off. I'm like Midas in reverse, everything I touch turns to shit, although the Midas guy came to hate himself too. He'll grow up to be a better person without me on the scene, tainting him. Trust me, I know. When my mother died I was relieved, which sounds ugly. But I think you'll come to understand that feeling.

I woke up today with such an extra-heavy dead feeling. It's Dan's birthday. He would have been thirty-two. That's almost fifteen years of living now that he's missed out on. Think what a person could do in that time. A good person, that is. And today I can feel every single second of those years bearing down. He would have had an amazing life, I know it. He was an amazing person, small but with the biggest heart.

I went to his grave and I met Maeve there. I could see she still blames me, hates me, and she's right. Do you remember how a woman walking her dog found him? He was face down, his clothes caught on an overhanging branch at the river's edge near the old bridge. I never told you but I became obsessed with that woman, thought about her all the time, much more than I thought about Dan, if I'm honest. Maybe it was easier. I kept picturing the scene. The horror of it. It played out like a film. You've always said I have a cinematic brain and, trust me, sometimes it can be vicious. Was she oblivious until her dog noticed a strange shape and started to bark? He was dressed all in black that night; did she think it was a refuse sack at first? Did she try to pull him out? Or just run to alert someone, knowing he was beyond help? She lived nearby, still does, in the big white house that stands on the laneway overlooking the far bank of the river. You can see it from our old swimming spot. Afterwards, did she think about moving? Did she have nightmares? Because I did. For months I was afraid to sleep. One morning, a few weeks after he died, I walked across the bridge and along the lane until I reached the gate of the big house. I'd no idea what I was going to say to this woman but I think I was looking for a kind of absolution, some clue she could give me, anything. I pictured her as being the same age as my mother but plump with soft eyes, and a large bosom into which she would pull me and tell me everything was fine, I was blameless. How I craved that. I was about to go up the driveway when I saw a tall, thin, austere-looking woman come out the front door with a yappy little terrier on a lead.

Dan was still dead. Dogs still needed to be walked. Life goes on.

I turned around and went home. I'm not sure why I'm telling you this story, except I think that's the moment I stopped looking for forgiveness. It was a childish and pointless thing to seek. And anyway, I'd never be able to forgive myself. After that, I sensed myself becoming so cut-off from everything. Like, you know, in that old Superman film, with the villains encased in shards of glass, spinning in infinity. That was me.

But Erica, I still remember with a beautiful and pure clarity, can feel the moment like I'm right back in it, the first time I ever saw you. Do you remember? Me and Dan were playing a game of tennis and you came on to the next court with this little kid. You were showing him how to grip his racket, which was almost bigger than him, and play a forehand stroke. You were so sweet and patient with him and this little kid was looking up at you like he adored you and I knew exactly how he felt. I found it so hard to carry on with the game then; Dan was getting really annoyed with me but I couldn't look away from you. You caught me staring and smiled shyly at me. I saw the future in that moment. I saw a future for me where I could be a normal, good person.

That scene is etched on my mind, a focus for all the later regret, because it appears like the first and last perfect moment in my whole life, a moment when anything was still possible.

I don't have any words of wisdom to leave for our boy. How can I tell him how to live his life when I've made a mess of my own? But please play 'Forever Young' to him. Bob Dylan wrote it as a lullaby for his first-born son. Every line in that song is a lesson in how a life should be lived. If only I'd been able to teach it to myself.

Love always, Rory x

'Oh, Rory,' she says aloud. Then she kisses the letter before ripping it to shreds and putting it in the bin.

JULIET

Denise and Johnny are driving her to the airport. She knows her mother will insist on coming into the terminal. There's no use telling her how excruciating she finds the drawn-out goodbye – it's why she wouldn't let Ruby come. She'd much rather have a hurried embrace by the boot of the car in the drop-off zone, ushering Denise back in so that they don't hold up the people behind. Instead now, she'll have to endure the slow line towards check-in, her mother's presence made more painful because it's only temporary.

She'll spot others like herself, lone travellers, eyes fixed on their phones, caught somewhere between sadness and relief. Before digital tickets, they used to give you a paper one, printed in triplicate, examined at the desk and handed back, the top layer torn off. And you understood that feeling. Of being divided. Then, after check-in, the lonely walk towards security, knowing that if she looks back just before she turns the corner and disappears out of view, she'll see Denise, wiping a tear away and trying to hide it behind a final jaunty wave. And that dystopian no-man's-land of the departure area. Strung out, she'll shop pointlessly, fingering the merchandise that would look tacky as soon as it was presented. Who would she give it to now anyway? And she will drink a last pint of Guinness in the bar, like a ceremony. One last imbibing of the ubiquitous accent too – that always clangs against her eardrums when she first lands but mellows then to a background hum – because at the stopover in Dubai hearing one would make your head turn.

'You're very quiet. Are you alright?' Denise asks, turning to look at her.

'Yeah, it's this jittery feeling I always get going to the airport. Twenty years and I've never gotten used to it.'

'You could always stay, you know,' says Johnny. 'We'd like that.'

Juliet looks out the window, rivulets of rainwater disfiguring the view. There's a Sinn Féin billboard erected at the turn-off they're taking from the M3 towards the airport. People are saying they'll be the largest party after the next election. Sometimes Juliet feels she doesn't understand anything anymore about her native country. Just as there's big holes in her knowledge of New Zealand. She exists somewhere in the chasm between.

She spent last night in O'Malley's. When last orders were called, Liam asked her to wait behind for a drink. He made no mention of seeing her with Colum and she was grateful and felt unworthy yet again. 'With Ruby staying, what exactly are you going back for?' he asked, leaning on the bar with his hands clasped, his face close to hers. His eyes were dark and quiet. There was a streak of silver in the bottom of his beard, fuller now than the goatee he wore when he was younger, and there was something generous and full at the heart of him too.

'My life is there now,' she said, which is the thing she's been saying for years and is a lie. More of her life is here and that's why she needs to go. She couldn't explain how the spectre of Rory is still everywhere here for her. Better to have nothing of him than teasing fragments. Maybe she's learned this too late.

By the time they reach the airport, the rain is coming down at a sharp slant. It always seems to rain when she goes, as though the gods are doing her a favour, telling her she's made the right choice.

'You can drop me here,' she says, certain they won't listen.

Denise turns around. 'Okay, I'm feeling a bit tired to come in, to be honest.' Juliet notices how depleted she looks.

Johnny lifts her bag out of the boot while she hugs her mother. She is so much thinner, and for the first time in her life Juliet feels bigger than her. A shiver of dread runs through her. 'I'll miss you.'

'Sure lookit, you'll be back at Christmas. You'll hardly have time to miss me.'

'Mind Ruby for me.'

'I will. Thanks for letting me borrow her. It was nearly worth having children, so it was, to get her.'

Juliet smiles. 'One word of advice to stay on her good side.'

'What's that?'

'Whatever you do, don't forget to rinse your cartons before you put them in the recycling.'

'Sure what kind of an animal wouldn't do that, Juliet?'

Juliet laughs and hugs her again. As she walks towards the terminal, her mother calls after her. She turns. Johnny and Denise are standing with their arms around each other, and she has a strong sense, a premonition almost, that this image will be one she folds and tucks away and then conjures up again and again.

'Yes?'

'She'll come back to you, so she will. Daughters always do. She just needs to go first.'

Juliet pats her heart. 'Thank you,' she mouths, then turns and walks away, feels herself gulped by the doors.

In the long queue for check-in she takes out her phone, opens her emails. There's a new one from Erica.

> Hello you,
> You sounded so broken that I wanted to reach out. I probably sounded very angry in the last email I sent you. Sorry, mine and Rory's failings are not your doing. I just want to let you know I understand. I see your pain. I've always reined myself in, and it seems I've alienated myself from everyone in my life now so it appears you're the only one I have to talk to! How bizarre is that? It's the kind of thing Rory would probably find funny. Here's the thing . . . I even held in my despair about my mother dying last year because I didn't want to upset Rory. Can you believe that? But you

see, I'd already made him feel shame over his ambivalent reaction to his own mother's death and so I didn't want to do that again by betraying the depths of my grief, which has been a very precise, shocking kind of pain. In some ways even more dislocating than losing Rory. I feel the shadow of her absence behind everything. Every thought, every action, every object, every person. Our mothers are the great thread through our existence, I suppose. And if we're lucky, our great unadulterated love story. You mentioned your mother in a previous email so I presume she's alive. Go easy on her. Though we often fail, we try so hard to get it right.

You sound so sad about Rory not loving you. My feeling is he did, in his own selfish way. But the fact is, he could never love anyone enough. You see, what I've come to understand is that Rory's hatred for himself eclipsed any love he could feel for somebody else. Even his own son, who he loved immensely. Rory's hatred for himself was in fact the greatest, truest love of *his* life, the thing he clung to, held most fiercely. That is the unglamorous, pitiful truth of it. And of course my anger towards him, that metastasised from my grief over my miscarriages, was profound, validated this self-hatred. So I am also culpable.

The way Rory was, well, it's sad for us who loved him, but sad mostly for Rory. And you could say it was because of my anger, or the death of a childhood friend that he felt guilt over, or because of his mother and his father and probably their mothers and fathers and maybe even his friend's mother and father, and so on and on and on . . .

Back to the great twisted darkness of the Famine, possibly . . . or even before then because, you know, it seems to me that, unlike happiness, sadness can travel over great distances. I studied psychology in college and I don't remember a huge amount except there was always supposed to be a reason for why people are the way they are. (Usually it was the mother. You know, as I recall, they even used to think cold mothers caused autism. The Refrigerator Mom, they called it. See what I mean about going easy on yours?)

Sorry, I digress . . .

But above all of that, above me, or you, or the mothers or fathers, or lost friends, or the Famine, or Adam and Eve (if you're that way inclined), there was an innate and shadowy presence lurking inside Rory that would have been there anyway.

So you see, it's not me. Or you.

It's him.

Erica x

Juliet reads it through twice. A message comes through then from Ruby. *Mumma, attached Spotify playlist for you. Stop with the Boomer music! Xxx.*

She smiles, lifts her head and looks around. There's a woman in front of her with a little girl of around three sitting on her jutting hip. Their heads are resting against each other so that they appear as one figure. A small sob catches in her throat at the tenderness of it. She makes a phone call.

'Mam, do you think you could tell Johnny to turn the car around? I think I'd like to come home.'

ERICA

Gently, she pushes the door. It's dark, but she can make out his shape under the covers. She feels her way to the edge of the bed, sits down. His breathing is shallow, and she knows he's still awake but he doesn't acknowledge her presence. The lower half of his right leg sticks out from beneath the duvet. He has always slept like this, with one rebellious limb. She rests her hand on his shin. She can sense him flinch and then his breath pauses, as though he's holding it. They have both been holding their breaths for so long.

'I just wanted to let you know, I'm going to get help,' she says. 'I promise.'

She hears him exhale. Then she stands up and leaves the room.

AUGUST

JULIET

That day at the airport, Denise was much closer to the end than anyone, except perhaps herself, had known. She has insisted on being discharged from the hospital so that she can die at home and wants to be downstairs, 'amongst all the action', as she put it. Johnny replaced the old couch in the sitting room with a sofa bed and it's pushed up now under the window so that she can sit up in it during the day to receive visitors, of which there are many. Juliet imagines she likes to look out, feel a connection to life there, which seems to carry on regardless. Juliet keeps the window open so that Denise can listen to the song of the bluetits that gather at the nut feeder Johnny hung from the front porch.

The final weeks pass in a flurry of friends calling and medication-measuring and community and hospice nurses ministering. There's no telling Denise she should be taking it easy. 'Sure, what's the point now?' she likes to say from dry lips painted defiantly in a face that has started to turn in on itself.

Josh comes home from London too with his young family and the house, even on the precipice of death, has never been more bursting with life. Ruby and her cousins talk loudly and unselfconsciously and sprawl on the sofa bed and drop crisp crumbs on the duvet and delight Denise with their lack of respect for death. Juliet looks at her mother – sitting up and holding court, still the beating heart of the home, defying all predictions to make it to the end of summer – and thinks of course she's not ready to leave with all the attention and love that's around her.

But the nights are hard. Juliet refused a night nurse and she lies listening to her mother's splintered breathing – the cancer now attacking the fluid around her lungs – from her position on the mattress set up on the floor. Denise's sleep is fitful and Juliet's own is punctuated with her disembodied voice floating over from the sofa bed. And years from now – when she struggles to remember her mother's face properly, the nuances and expression, can only conjure up a lifeless image like a photograph, can remember her features, the slant of an eyebrow, the angle of her jaw, but not put them together in a coherent whole, and struggles even more to remember the timbre of her voice – snatches of these conversations will come back to her, whispered across the years, and it will feel like a gift.

―

'Juliet? Are you awake?'
    'Yes, Mam?'
    'Do you believe in heaven?'
    'Totally.'

'Don't lie to your mother.'

'Okay, honestly, I'm not sure. But you know, when I stood under the statue of David, I was certain that God or maybe even heaven existed. Because how else could you explain such beauty. Do you?'

'I never used to. But I think I've changed my mind. Is that allowed? Will God mind?'

'I doubt God will mind one bit.'

———

'Juliet?'

'Yes, Mam?'

'At the funeral, will you play that song, you know the one, with the blind fella and whatshername, was married to the musicals fella. God, why can't I remember anything?'

'I know the one you mean, Mam. "Time to Say Goodbye". Subtle.'

'That's it! What was her name again?'

'Sarah Brightman.'

'Sarah Brightman! People used tell me I looked like her. It must have been my hair. I had lovely hair, so I did.'

'You had gorgeous hair, Mam.'

———

'Juliet?'

'Yes, Mam?'

'I know about your abortion.'

'How?'

'I found a card in the pocket of your coat one time. A clinic in Liverpool. I put two and two together.'

'Oh.'

'I wish you'd have told me. I would have helped. Come with you.'

'I know, Mam. But I was fine. It all worked out fine.'

'I did often wonder if you regretted it.'

'Not at all. It was one of my better decisions. Do you regret having Josh so young?'

'Not at all. I mean, I had my doubts at first, but it all worked out well in the end.'

'You see, I think it's the same for me.'

'Who was the father? Was it that Rory O'Sullivan lad?'

'No. It was Dan.'

'Dan Flynn? Well, now. I always thought he was gay.'

'He was. Mostly.'

———

'Juliet?'

'Mam?'

'The thing no-one tells you about being a mother is that you'll always love your children more than they love you. It's just a fact, so it is. And it's the way it's meant to be. Otherwise, life would be unbearable for everyone.'

'Oh, Mam.'

'Don't cry, love.'

———

Denise dies on a late summer's morning to the soundtrack of Johnny and Josh's quiet sobbing, with Juliet and Ruby holding a dry hand each. Denise's face is turned to the window as though trying to absorb a last bit of light before an eternity of nothingness.

'It's so unfair,' Johnny says. 'I had to wait so long to find her.'

And Juliet says, 'I know,' but is thinking of herself really. She kisses the slack skin on her cheek that once was so plump, deflated now, so that her nose and chin protrude, like one of those Punch and Judy puppets that terrified her as a child. She marvels at the complete absence of her.

Later, when the undertakers take her away with a red and pink dress to lay her out in that she had chosen herself, Juliet pulls the duvet and sheet off the sofa and Ruby comes then and together they curl up in the cooling hollow of the mattress that Denise's body has left behind.

—

It was early August and raining heavily. She and Dan were sheltering under the old bridge smoking hash. The drug was working its magic on her. She felt very at one with him, with her surroundings, like her consciousness was part of all humanity and her body was part of the earth, and the sound of the rain and the river and the traffic was being echoed inside herself in the rushing of her blood. She thought if only she could cling on to this state forever, life would be bearable.

'How was rehearsal today?'

He shrugged. 'Average to poor.'

'I thought you loved it.'

'Yes. Normally I do.' He sighed. 'But there's this boy. I thought we had something. But today he made a comment that made me wonder if I misinterpreted the situation. It made me question my own instincts.'

They were sitting opposite each other, and she reached and touched the side of his face. 'I sure know how that feels. I'm sorry, Dan.'

'I'll survive. I've experienced worse. Anyway, more importantly, how are you, my wretched little fatherless friend?'

She felt beautifully stoned then, felt she had a lot of perfect, lucid thoughts in her head if only she could express them. 'You know what they don't tell you about grief? That it's boring. Waking up every morning with the same blank feeling in your soul is monotonous as hell. You imagine it as melodramatic but it's not like that at all. I feel . . . I feel like there's something between me and everything. More than numbness, though, or . . . or like it's wrapped around me. Like a . . . a prophylactic.'

Dan nodded, took a long thoughtful toke, held it, then blew a smooth stream of smoke towards her. 'So, Juliet, just to be clear, what you're saying is that you feel like a condom-sheathed penis.'

'That pretty much nails it, Danny boy.'

She could feel a giggle start in her toes and engulf her and then suddenly they were both hysterical. When they finished laughing, she felt spent and heavy again. As though he could sense this, he patted his lap and she lay her head back on it, took his hand and clasped it to the side of her face. There was such reassuring solidness to it. With his other hand he held the joint to her lips for her while she took a toke.

She looked up at him. He was so beautiful and kind and *good*. His eyes, so warm and dark that often it was hard to differentiate pupil from iris, were shining and radiant, so she imagined she could see herself in them. And her reflection there did not make her want to turn away.

'Please help me feel things again, Dan.'

He took a drag on the joint, bent down then, placed his lips gently on hers and blew into her mouth. Along with the hash, she had a sense of his goodness coursing through her own body.

'Did you feel that?' he said, smiling at her.

And she nodded and pulled him down towards her again.

And it was fumbly at first but so intensely sweet with it. 'Are you okay? Is this okay?' he asked as he moved tentatively inside her, and she laughed and said it was perfect. Because it was. Because for those moments she felt outside of sadness and remembering. She was only flesh and blood and sensation and his lightness inside her. Afterwards, as they lay with their arms around each other, she said, 'How do you feel, Dan?'

He thought for a moment and then said gravely, 'No offence but I feel I'm still *mostly* gay.'

And they laughed so much again her sides ached and the pain was good.

ERICA

Hello you,

I know we haven't been in touch in a while but I was thinking about you today and I suppose I just wanted to check in and see that you're okay. I'm doing a tiny bit better myself. I got a job. It's just in the local florist's. (I know, how menopausal of me!) I spend my day in the back room arranging bouquets and I love it. And . . . perhaps even more radically . . . I got myself a tattoo. I still can't quite believe it. I keep touching it to make sure I'm not imagining it. It feels hot and tender and alive. I can see why people become addicted to getting them. Can I tell you something embarrassing about it, though, that might give you a bit of a laugh? I decided to get a Bob Dylan quote as a way of honouring Rory. Or, if I'm being honest, maybe it was also a bit defiant too . . . he never did like tattoos on women. I googled *Dylan lyrics on love*, because I really don't know much about his music and I found one I thought was perfect. *Though Lovers Be Lost, Love Shall Not.* Anyway, I showed the tattoo to Charlie when I got home, who said he was pretty certain that wasn't a Bob Dylan lyric. So we googled it again. Turns out it's *Dylan Thomas*. Anyway, we laughed a lot about that. I think it's the first real laugh I've had since Rory died. I think he would have found it funny too. He'd probably call it karma. It's still a great line, and, to be honest, poetry is probably more me than a rock 'n' roll lyric anyway. I've never been very rock 'n' roll . . .

Charlie and I went away for a few days last week. I was keen to go back to Greece and a neglected pomegranate tree that I had seen there one time. You know, when I got home from that holiday with Rory, I thought of that tree a lot and did some reading about it. Apparently, it's a paradoxical sort of plant, representing life and fertility but also barrenness and death. I liked the idea of that, the duality of it. I found it comforting, that we're not just one thing or another. Anyway, Charlie didn't want to go anywhere we would have to fly because he was thinking about carbon emissions. I think he was anticipating his round-the-world trip next year and trying to atone. I think young people are so much better than my generation in many ways. I look at Charlie and see how he contains the best parts of Rory and me that have somehow combined into something transcendent. The whole being greater than the sum of its parts, and all that. In the end he did some research, and we went to a little eco-friendly guesthouse in the heart of the Burren with solar panels and wind-generated electricity and its own sustaining vegetable plot. We had a slow, gentle time. I think that's what we both needed. I've got a lot of atoning to do myself when it comes to Charlie. He's had to bear witness to our unhappiness for years and it's been so unfair. Anyway, every day we walked to the local pub for lunch, past barren-looking slabs of limestone with colourful wildflowers poking through, and we would linger to take in the strange lunar wonder of the landscape and I would remind myself that, despite the fissures and deep painful brokenness, life is insistent and unexpectedly beautiful. I looked at my son then whose face is his father's face but also completely, perfectly his own and I experienced a pause, or a settling maybe, that felt like peace, for the first time in a long time. It's simply the great trade-off, isn't it, of the exquisite, wrenching experience of being alive. Grief and loss are a result of loving and being loved. You don't get one without the other. Those flowers need the cracks to grow.

Anyway, this is just to say, thanks for listening. Take care of yourself.

Love, E x

MAEVE

They're in O'Malley's. The place is thronged and awash with bright colours – *No Black Allowed!* printed on the funeral notice at Denise's insistence. (Juliet added *So it's not!* underneath.) Ruby, who works here now, has made a shrine up on the bar out of a glass of Chardonnay and the photograph of Denise winning the Sally O'Brien lookalike competition. Maeve and Juliet are sitting together in front of it.

'So, what's the plan with the house now?'

'Denise had it all organised. Bossy to the last. We're not going to sell it yet. Johnny will stay there for as long as he lives, or wants. It'll be nice for us all to have a base here too. I'm getting an advance on my inheritance but only under the strict condition that I use the money to go to uni and get my fine-arts degree.'

'Ah, that's brilliant, Juliet. I'm so delighted. Where will you do it?'

'In Auckland. Ruby will be studying there too, so it makes sense.'

'I'll miss you.' She really means it.

'Don't worry. We'll be here till January. And then I'll be back all the time with those lovely long holidays students get. And once I have the degree, who knows, I may be back here for good.'

'I hope so.' Maeve squeezes her hand. She looks around. 'You know, I didn't see Erica today at the church. Still keeping herself apart from everything.'

'Ah, Erica's alright,' says Juliet.

'Ladies!' comes a voice like an asthmatic frog from behind. 'Can I get you a drink?'

'Only you, Colum, being as tight as a fish's arsehole, would offer to buy a drink at a free bar,' says Juliet.

'Free bar? You're joking. Then why did Liam charge me for the last round?'

Juliet shrugs. 'Search me.'

'Okay, folks,' Maeve says as she hops down off the stool, 'I better get back to the funny farm.'

'How's it all going there?' says Juliet.

'Oh, you know. We're not exactly *The Waltons* yet but . . . we're trying to mend ourselves.' She pats Colum on the arm and then kisses Juliet's cheek. 'Goodnight you,' she says to her.

Juliet stands up and hugs her. 'Thanks for everything, Maeve. I couldn't have got through today without you.'

Back at the house it's the weekly family movie night, as suggested by the therapist. They are also, at her suggestion, trying technology-light Tuesdays and phone-free Fridays. She had recommended a game called the feelings walk – like musical chairs minus the prizes. And the fun. Jamie said it was the dumbest thing he'd ever heard and if they made him play he would 'literally abscond'. The therapist said, 'Let's park that idea for now then, will we?' Maeve was quietly relieved.

It's Maeve's turn to choose tonight so she picks *E.T.* and is nervous for their reaction. Last time she chose *Big*, which she remembered as being charming but which the boys declared to be *deeply weird* and *paedo-ish* and honestly, watching it again, Maeve could see their point. Some things just age badly. But the Spielberg film is as tender-hearted as ever and she can see that they are as moved by it as she is. She's relieved, if she's honest, when she sees Jamie's face contort as though struggling not to cry. There'd been 3 a.m. moments when she worried she'd raised some kind of sociopath. But as she looks at him now, she still recognises the little boy who would slide a leaf under a flailing bee on the ground to carry it to the safety of a nearby dandelion and then hunker sturdily beside it, willing it to fly away. She and Cillian are book-ending the boys on the couch, her mother asleep in the armchair. At a particularly poignant moment, the couch vibrates, and she looks over her children at her husband. His glasses are perched on his head, and he is pressing a cushion to his face. He too has aged well. Looking at him gives her hope for her sons.

Her phone beeps. 'Um, hypocrite,' says Jamie. 'You said no phones during movie night.'

She holds up her hands in defeat. 'You're right. I'll put it away. I'll make tea while I'm at it.'

In the kitchen she reads the text, which is from Nisha thanking her because she has received positive feedback on her manuscript. It's the first message since Maeve told her about the drama with Jamie and they agreed to stop communicating. She still thinks about her but mostly keeps her tucked away like old love letters in that secret space in her heart. She's about to reply with the thumbs-up emoji, decides this is too cold, so chooses instead the clinking glasses one before putting the phone in a drawer. Maeve has negotiated some time off with her editors, abandoned her own *Sylvia* manuscript, and is writing a collection of personal essays instead that she may or may not seek to have published. It doesn't feel important. For the first time in her life, she's proud of her work. She thinks these essays might be the only honest things she's ever written.

She can feel summer has slipped away; already the mornings are cooler and she experiences that familiar ache this time of year brings. It's Dan's anniversary today. She stopped at his graveside earlier and left a flower, and it occurred to her then that she should stay here in Ballyboyne, stay near him and the place where it happened. She owes him that. Thirty-two years since he died. It hardly seems possible, like some glitch has occurred in the universe and here she is, catapulted unwillingly to almost fifty. Fifty! She thinks of Rory, his conspicuous kind of beauty but also his hands shoved deep in his pockets, who didn't quite make it to half a century. She thinks of the fact of her mother's death, of her own, of Cillian's and – unbearably – of her children's too. Jesus, *God*, let her be decades in the grave before that happens.

As the kettle boils, she lifts her gaze above the sink to the window, which is more a mirror now in the dark, so that a ghostly version of herself looks back. She and Cillian have talked of going back to Dublin once Lily has moved into the nursing home after Christmas. And Maeve's reflection now is like a glimpse of the future, a prophetic portrait contained there in the glass. She is not going anywhere.

Lily has deteriorated rapidly in the last few months, more agitated, grappling to make sense of the house and the people in it. Her doctor explained how this half-state, this half-belonging in the real world, is perhaps the most distressing stage. Once she fully crosses over into the realm of dementia, is free of her own haunting shadow, she'll be happier. Maeve imagines her mother like Alice, passing through the looking glass.

Once the tea is made, she carries the tray from the kitchen and pauses outside the closed sitting-room door. She can hear Luke's sweet voice, that will soon crack and break, followed by Jamie's deep one, that still makes her startle, as though there's an intruder in the house. Her mother must have woken because she hears her voice then, weaker, a frayed echo of itself. They say you don't know what you've got till it's gone but she's not sure this is true. She's already mourning everything that's in the process of being lost. It feels like trying to hold water in your hands. She wants to drop the tray, go lie on her bed and weep for it.

After her mother speaks, there's silence from the room for a beat or two and then an eruption of laughter from her boys. She hears her mother laugh then too. She hopes that this surrender is a small upside for Lily.

It's imperfect and messy, this life of hers, but expecting more is, she realises, a greedy and childish impulse. She surrenders now too. This is it, she belongs here, she fits. Careful to keep the load balanced, she uses her elbow to nudge down the door handle.

JULIET

The mood is tilting to sombre now, and Juliet, fearful that any minute someone will resurrect a painful dirge, slips out the door to get some air. Standing with her back to the pub, looking out across the carpark and up the back road, the crowd still feels too close, so she crosses over to the old bridge and leans on the parapet. She stares at the restless churn of black water below, imagines something furtive and cold lurking there. Water has always soothed her but tonight it upends her. She thinks about Denise and her father and Dan and Rory and how eventually, everything that she attaches meaning to will be swept away. Water under the bridge, as they say. She gives a surprised little laugh then because she's never thought about this expression before and she wonders how she can live her life this way, without ever thinking about what things actually mean. The damp of the stone seeps through the sleeves of her dress, making her shiver. It's quiet, little traffic at this hour, so that a hum from the pub faintly reaches her. She imagines the crowd in there, a tipsy, swaying homogenous mass, as she stands here, alone, with nothing but the relentless water and her elusive ghosts. A louder burst of conversation escapes as the door swings open. Her phone vibrates with a message and, for a moment, a current of hope courses through her. Her body betrays her still. It won't be told. Where are you gone?

She turns her head and sees the shape of him, lit by the pub's exterior lanterns. She types her reply – Not far – and then puts her phone back in her pocket. She watches as he checks right, left, then right again, cautious, despite it being late and the road deserted. She knows by the hesitant way he walks what he's likely to say. She has a sense that she will always know. And she tells herself that this is a good and admirable thing. There'd always been such an unpredictability to Rory. You could love opposite things about people equally, though, couldn't you? She walks towards him.

The night after the funeral, Ruby comes into the kitchen, where Juliet is washing the dinner pots. 'There's a woman at the door for you. She says she won't come in.'

Juliet wipes her hands on a tea towel, goes to the door expecting to see a friend of Denise's, but it's Erica. She's facing away, as though engrossed in something on the opposite side of the road. It's the way Rory used to stand on this doorstep too. Then he'd turn, as though surprised she was there, as though he just happened to be standing in this place, her front porch, anyway. And it occurs to Juliet then, looking at Erica, that it was because he didn't want her to feel he'd gone to any special effort to see her.

'I brought a pie,' Erica says, offering up a dish.

Juliet takes it from her. It's still warm. 'That's so kind of you.'

'Your daughter is very beautiful.'

'She is.'

'I just wanted to say I'm sorry. About your mother. It's hard.'

'Yes. Thank you. I feel like the world has gone a little askew. Shifted off its axis.'

Erica nods, then, 'Quinn. As I read the death notice, seeing your name there in black and white, I . . . well, I've been somewhat dim. Not connecting you to the emails.'

'Oh.' Something urgent and penitent rises in Juliet. 'I'm so sorry, Erica, I—'

But Erica cuts her off by holding up her hand. 'No,' she says. 'Please.' She turns to go and then, remembering something, faces her again. 'That dish. It's not a good one. So you don't have to worry about returning it.'

'I'd like to, though. If that's okay?'

Erica shrugs. 'As you wish. We're moving in two weeks, fresh start and all that, so you'd need to come before then.'

'Oh, okay. Where to?'

'Just a bit further out the country. An old place I plan to renovate.'

'Good for you. I always imagined that house was more him than you.'

And they share a small, knowing smile, before Erica nods once and then turns again. Away she goes, straight-backed, contained, down the drive. Even though it's dark, her blonde hair gleams so she appears almost holy. Like a figure in one of those religious paintings, a Renaissance Madonna, surrounded by a sacred, white light. Juliet's eyes follow her until she turns at the pillar and disappears behind the hedge that encloses the garden. For a moment she has an urge to run after her, but remains standing on the porch, the dish warm against her belly, transfixed by the crescent moon above the trees, a bright sliver revealed, the rest in shadow.

ACKNOWLEDGEMENTS

Huge thanks to my editors Ciara Doorley, Kate Stephenson and Sherise Hobbs for knocking my messy first draft into shape. It's a pleasure and a privilege to get to work with you.

Thanks to Emma Dunne for both the insightful line edit and proofread. You've made the book so much better.

Thanks to Aonghus Meaney and Joanna Smyth for the intensive copyediting which makes me realise that even though I call myself a writer, I am, in fact, barely literate.

Thanks so much Ami Smithson for the lush cover design.

Writing the words is only the start of the work required to get a book out into the world so massive thanks to everyone involved – from the editing and design processes right through to sales, marketing and publicity – at Moa Press, Hachette Ireland and Headline UK: Elaine Egan, Tania Mackenzie-Cooke, Stephen Riordan, Cyanne Alwanger, Sacha Beguely, Mel Winder, Breda Purdue, Ruth Shern, Nic Faisander, Claudia Fletcher, Sharon Galey, Suzy Maddox, to name but a few.

Thanks to all my friends and family in Aotearoa New Zealand and Ireland. I'm so lucky to call two beautiful countries home.

And special thanks as always to Matt, Molly, Oscar and Jack for putting up with me.